Spider Light

Also by Sarah Rayne

Roots of Evil
A Dark Dividing
Tower of Silence

Spider Light

Sarah Rayne

SIMON & SCHUSTER

LONDON • NEW YORK • SYDNEY • TORONTO

First published in Great Britain by Simon & Schuster UK Ltd, 2006
A CBS Company

1 3 5 7 9 10 8 6 4 2

Simon & Schuster UK Ltd
Africa House
64–78 Kingsway
London WC2B 6AH

www.simonsays.co.uk

Simon & Schuster Australia
Sydney

A CIP catalogue record for this book is available
from the British Library

ISBN 0-7432-5732-4
EAN 9780743257329

Typeset by Palimpsest Book Production Limited,
Polmont, Stirlingshire
Printed and bound in Great Britain by
CPI Bath

AUTHOR'S ACKNOWLEDGEMENT

My grateful thanks are due to Craig Ferguson and his National Trust colleagues at Nether Alderley Mill in Cheshire, who were so very helpful when I was researching this book.

The time I spent at the beautifully maintained Mill was immensely valuable in the writing of *Spider Light*, and Craig and his team gave generously and enthusiastically of their time and knowledge.

The layout and atmosphere of Twygrist are unashamedly based on Nether Alderley Mill, but there the similarity ends. Nether Alderley has almost certainly never been the setting for the strange and often macabre events that take place within the walls of Twygrist.

Sarah Rayne
2005

Quire House
Scraptoft
Charity Cottage
Amberwood Village
St Michael's Church
Post Box
The Rectory
0

louse

Latchkill

Lane

Twygrist Mill

ken
e

Reservoir

River Amber

To
Amberwood
Magna

1/2 mile

MC

CHAPTER ONE

After five years away from the world, the first thing to strike Antonia Weston about her return to it was the noise. She had forgotten how loudly and how energetically people talked, and how shops and eating-places were filled with intrusive music. It was, it seemed, dangerously easy to believe you had kept up-to-date, but when it came to it, you might as well have been living on the moon.

Even something as simple as entering the restaurant where she had arranged to meet Jonathan Saxon was a culture shock. Antonia managed not to flinch from what felt like a wall of sound, and to avoid staring at the people at other tables. But just as she had forgotten how loud the world was, she had also forgotten how fashions could change for ordinary people. Not startlingly, not drastically – not in the way of celebrities or TV stars – but more subtly. Had these sleek svelte girls, who were having their lunch and who probably worked in management consultancy or PR or in the still bewildering world of the internet, always dressed in dark, almost masculine suits, and worn their hair quite so casually?

One thing she had not forgotten, though, was Jonathan's habit of opening a door with an impatient rush, so that people looked up from whatever they were doing or saying to see who had come in. It was a trick Antonia remembered him using at meetings, deliberately arriving late and then switching on a beam of crude masculine energy at the exact right moment. It had always annoyed Antonia and it annoyed her now, especially since at least six people in the restaurant were responding exactly as if somebody had tugged an invisible string. (All right, so it was an *effective* trick. That did not make it any less irritating.)

'I'm sorry about the tumult in here,' said Jonathan, sitting down and studying Antonia intently. 'I expect it's a bit shrill for you. But I wasn't expecting you until next week, and I couldn't think of anywhere else that was easy to get to.'

'Change of date at the last minute,' said Antonia offhandedly. She studied the menu and, with sudden anger, said, 'I don't know what to order.'

'Poached salmon?'

'Oh God, fresh salmon. I'd forgotten there was such a thing in the world. Yes, please.'

'And a glass of wine with it? Chablis?'

'I – no, I'd better not.'

'You used to like wine,' said Jonathan, raising an eyebrow. 'Or are you frightened of the consequences?'

'I'm frightened of sliding under the table. You try not having a drink for the best part of five years and see how strong your head is.'

'Fair enough,' he said equably, and ordered mineral water for her and a carafe of wine for himself.

When the food came he ate with swift economy. This was something Antonia had forgotten about him. For all his tricks and deliberately created effects, his movements were always oddly pleasing. Feline. No, make that wolfish. This was the man who was rumoured to have systematically slept his way through medical school and to have continued the process when he became head of psychiatric medicine at the big teaching hospital where he and Antonia had first met.

'I thought,' he said, 'that you'd want to get right away for a while. That's why I wrote to you. And someone at the hospital mentioned a cottage that's available for a few months – it's somewhere in Cheshire.'

It would be one of his women who had mentioned it. Saxon's string puppets, someone had once called them: he pulls the strings and they dance to his music.

'It's apparently a very quiet place,' the man who pulled the strings was saying. 'And the rent's quite reasonable.' He passed over a folded sheet of paper. 'That's the address and the letting agent's phone number. It might give you a breathing space until you decide what to do next.'

'I haven't the least idea what I'm going to do next,' said Antonia, and before he could weigh in with some kind of sympathy offer, she said, 'I do know you can't re-employ me. That the hospital can't, I mean.'

'Yes, I'm sorry about that. We all are. But it would be a great shame to waste all your training. You could consider teaching or writing.'

'Both presumably being available to a struck-off doctor of psychiatric medicine.' This did not just come out angrily, it came out savagely.

'Writing's one of the great levellers,' said Jonathan, not missing a beat. 'Nobody gives a tuppenny damn about the private life of a writer. But if you're that sensitive, change your name.' He refilled his glass, and Antonia forked up another mouthful of the beautifully fresh salmon which now tasted like sawdust.

'I don't suppose you've got much money to fling around, have you?' he said suddenly.

Antonia had long since gone beyond the stage of being embarrassed about money. 'Not much,' she said. 'What there is will probably last about six months, but after that I'll have to find a way of earning my living.'

'Then why don't you rent this cottage while you look for it? Whatever you end up doing, you've got to live somewhere.'

'It's just – I'm not used to making decisions any longer.' This sounded so disgustingly wimpish that Antonia said firmly, 'You're quite right. It is a good idea. Thank you. And can I change my mind about that wine?'

'Yes, of course. If you slide under the table I promise to pick you up.'

'As I recall,' said Antonia drily, 'you were always ready to pick up anyone who was available.'

Appearance did not really matter, but one might as well turn up at a new place looking halfway decent.

Antonia spent two more days in London having her hair restyled into something approximating a modern look and buying a few clothes. The cost of everything was daunting, but what was most daunting was the occasional impulse to retreat to the small Bayswater hotel where she was staying and hide in the darkest, safest corner. This was a reaction she had not envisaged or bargained for, even though it was easily explained as the result of having lived in an enclosed community for so long and a direct outcome of being what was usually called institutionalized. Still, it was ridiculous to keep experiencing this longing for her familiar room, and the predictable routine of meals, work sessions, recreation times.

'I expect you like to simply wash your hair and blast-dry it, do you?' said the friendly hairdresser while Antonia was silently fighting a compulsion to scuttle out of the salon and dive back to the hotel room. 'So much easier, isn't it, especially with a good conditioner?'

Antonia said yes, wasn't it, and did not add that for five years she had been used to queuing for the communal showers each morning, and hoarding a bottle of shampoo as jealously as if it was the elixir of eternal life.

Clothes were more easily dealt with. She bought two pairs of jeans, a couple of sweaters, and some trainers, at a big chainstore in Oxford Street. Then a cup of coffee and a sandwich at the crowded self-service restaurant – yes, you *can* cope with being out for another hour, Antonia! After this modest repast she hesitated over a trouser and jacket outfit the colour of autumn leaves. Useful for unexpected invitations, and an absolutely gorgeous colour. Oh sure, and when would you wear it? Or are you expecting the locals at this tiny Cheshire village to sweep you into a dizzy social whirl the minute you arrive? In any case, you can't possibly afford clothes like that, said a bossy voice in her head, this is the boutique section, and look at the price tag for pity's sake! This remark tipped the balance irrevocably. Antonia came out of the shop with the autumn-brown outfit lovingly folded into its own designer-label bag.

The cottage suggested by Jonathan's contact or newest bed partner or whatever she was, apparently stood in the grounds of an eighteenth-century manor. It was called Quire House and it had been converted into a small museum – Charity Cottage was apparently a former tied cottage in its grounds. Antonia thought the name smacked of paternalism and gentrified ladies visiting the poor with baskets of calf's-foot jelly, and thought she would probably hate it.

But by this time she was committed. She had sent a cheque for two months' rent which she certainly could not afford to forfeit, and had received by return of post a standard short-term lease agreement. This granted her full and free enjoyment of the messuage and curtilage, whatever those might be, permitted various rights of way depicted in red on a smudgily photocopied plan which presumably allowed her to get in and out of the place, and wound up by forbidding the playing of loud music after eleven at night, the plying of any trade, profession or business whatsoever, and the entertaining of any rowdy, inebriated or otherwise disruptive guests.

Charity Cottage, Amberwood. It sounded like a cross between Trollope and the *Archers*. I won't be able to stand it for longer than a week, thought Antonia, rescuing her car which had been standing in an ex-colleague's garage for the past five years, and which the ex-colleague had generously kept serviced for her. It'll either be impossibly twee or tediously refined, and Quire House will be one of those earnest folksy places – afternoon classes in tapestry weaving, and displays of bits of Roman roads dug up by students. Or it'll be a sixties-style commune, with people trading soup recipes or swapping lovers. If they find out I'm a doctor they'll consult me about bunions or haemorrhoids, and if they find out I'm a psychiatrist they'll describe their dreams.

But I certainly won't get within hailing distance of any rowdy guests. Nor will I be plying a profession.

It felt odd to have a latchkey again; the agents had sent it by recorded delivery, and Antonia had had to phone them to confirm its arrival. This was somehow rather comforting; it was a reminder that there was still a world where people cared about privacy and where they took trouble to safeguard property. Perhaps it might be all right after all, thought Antonia. Perhaps I'll find I've made a good decision.

There was more traffic on the roads than she remembered, and it was much faster and more aggressive, but she thought she was doing quite well. She did not much like launching out into the stream of cars on the big roundabouts, but she managed. So far so good, thought Antonia. All I've really got to worry about is finding the way.

Richard had always teased her about her appalling sense of direction; he had usually made some comment about the Bermuda triangle, or quoted the old Chesterton poem about the night we went to Birmingham by way of Beachy Head. But then he would reach for the map and study it with the intensity that was so much part of him, after which he would patiently and clearly point out the right route and send Antonia the sideways smile that made his eyes look like a faun's. It had been five years since Antonia sat in a car with Richard, and it was something she would never do again.

She stopped mid-journey to top up with petrol and have a cup of tea – it was annoying to find it took ten minutes to talk herself into leaving the safety of the car to enter the big motorway service station. I'll master this wretched thing, said Antonia silently, I *will*, I'll turn on the car radio for the rest of the journey or put on some music – yes, that's a good idea.

Before starting off again she rummaged in the glove compartment for a tape. There was a bad moment when she realized that some of Richard's favourite tapes were still here, but she pushed them determinedly to the back and sorted through the others to find something sane and soothing. There was some old pop stuff, which would be lively but might remind her too much of the past. Was it Noël Coward who said, 'Strange how potent cheap music is?' Ah, here was Beethoven's *Pastoral Symphony*. Exactly right. Hay-making and merry peasants and whatnot.

Beethoven had just reached the 'Shepherd Song' and Antonia thought she was about forty miles short of her destination, when a vague suspicion began to tap against her mind and send a faint trickle of fear down her spine.

She was being followed.

At first she dismissed the idea; there were enough cars on the road to mistake one for another, and there were dozens of dark blue hatchbacks of that particular make.

She watched the car carefully in the driving mirror, and saw that it stayed with her, not overtaking or quite catching up, but persistently there. I'm seeing demons, thought Antonia. There's nothing in the least sinister about this, just two people going in the same direction.

Without realizing she had planned it, she swung off the motorway at the next exit, indicating at the last possible moment, and then took several turnings at random. They took her deep into the heart of completely unknown countryside and into a bewilderment of lanes, out of which she would probably never find her way, so it really would be Beachy Head by way of Birmingham. But getting lost would be worth it if it proved to her stupid neurotic imagination that no one was following her.

It would prove it, of course. The man who had once driven a dark blue car – the man who had ruined her life – could not possibly be tailing her along these quiet roads. He was dead, and had been dead for more than five years. There could not possibly be any mistake about it. And she did not believe in ghosts – at least, she did not believe in ghosts who took to the road in blue hatchbacks, and whizzed along England's motorways in pursuit of their prey.

She glanced in the driving mirror again, fully prepared to see a clear stretch of road behind her, and panic gripped her. The car was still there – still keeping well back, but definitely there. Was it the same car? Yes, she thought it was. She briefly considered pulling onto the grass verge and seeing what happened. Would the driver go straight past? (Giving some kind of sinister, you-are-marked-for-death signal as he went . . . ? Oh, don't be ridiculous!)

Still, if he did drive past she could try to see his face. Yes, but what if there wasn't a face at all? What if there was only something out of a late-night, slash-and-gore film? A grinning skull, a corpse-face?

It had not been a corpse-face that first night in the tiny recovery room off A&E. It had been an attractive, although rather weak face, young and desperately unhappy. Antonia could still remember how the unhappiness had filled the small room, and how the young man in the bed had shrugged away from the doctors in the classic but always heart-breaking gesture of repudiation. Face turned to the wall in the silent signal that said, I don't want to be part of this painful world any longer. At first he had turned away from Antonia, who had been the on-call psychiatrist that night. She had been dozing in the duty room on the first floor when her pager went, and she had paused long enough to dash cold water onto her face, slip into her shoes and pull on a sweater before going quickly through the corridors of the hospital.

Straightforward overdose, they said resignedly. Stuffed himself chockful of sleeping pills – something prescribed by a GP – then downed the best part of a bottle of vodka. Poor boy. Or stupid sod, depending on your point of view. Whichever he was, he had been found near the riverbank, and an early-morning dog-walker had realized he was a bit more than just drunk, and had called the paramedics. Oh yes, he had been pumped clean, although he was still a bit drowsy and still very withdrawn. Yes, they had a name – Robards. Don Robards. They were giving him fifteen-minute obs and someone was trying to find out about family – there had not been any identification on him. But in the meantime he was stable, pretty much over the worst, and Dr Weston was welcome to him from here on.

The boy in the bed looked impossibly young. He had thick fair hair that would normally fall in a glossy thatch over his forehead; at the moment it was damp and matted from the sickness.

'Hi,' Antonia had said softly, sitting on the edge of the bed. 'I'm Doctor Weston – Antonia Weston. I'm the on-call psychiatrist, and your doctors thought we might have a talk to see if I can help you.'

'You can't help me,' said the boy. 'I've found out something absolutely appalling, and I don't want to be in a world where things like that can happen.'

He had turned to look at her then. His eyes were a very vivid blue; the pupils were still pinpoints from the sleeping pills, but they were perfectly sensible. He had reached in a questing, uncoordinated way for Antonia's hand and without thinking much about it, she had taken his hand and held it hard.

Setting the nightmare in motion.

The blue car turned along a narrow lane winding off to the left, and was swallowed up by the trees and farmlands. Antonia discovered that she was shaking so violently she could barely grip the steering wheel. Half a mile on she came to a small village pub with a placard advertising bar food, and remembered that she could quite openly walk inside and order food and sit at a table to eat it. Parking as close to the door as she could manage, she locked the car and went thankfully into the dim cool interior.

One of the things that had improved in the almost forgotten world was pub food. Antonia was directed to a small table near an inglenook, and served hot soup with a twist of fresh warm bread, a plateful of delicious home-cured ham with a crisp salad, and a large cup of fragrant coffee.

Three quarters of an hour later, feeling able to face all the demons in hell's legions, she got back in her car, consulted the map carefully, and drove on to Amberwood and Charity Cottage.

CHAPTER TWO

Over the last five years Antonia had visualized doing quite a lot of things out in the world – some of them had been quite possible and sensible, and some of them had been so bizarre as to be wild daydream stuff – but none of them had included renting a former almshouse tucked into a remote sliver of the Cheshire countryside. As she drove away from the little pub the sky was overcast, and there was a feeling that even at three o'clock in the afternoon night was poised to sweep in. She managed to find her way back to the motorway and, although she kept glancing in the driving mirror, there was no sign of any dark blue hatchback tailing her.

Amberwood, when she finally reached it, was much nicer than she had expected. It was a small market town that looked as if it had not progressed much beyond the early years of the twentieth century. It did not appear to have reached the twenty-first century at all. Antonia found this rather endearing.

Driving along, the agent's sketch map propped up on the dashboard, she passed what looked like an old watermill. It was low roofed and ancient-looking, and Antonia slowed down to take a better look. Yes, it was an old mill, built up against a reservoir. It was clearly disused but by no means derelict, and there was what appeared to be some kind of memorial clock set into one of the gable-end walls.

She pulled on the handbrake and sat in the car for a moment considering the mill, wondering if it was a remnant of Victorian paternalism, or whether it might have been one of the dark satanic mills of Milton and Blake's visions. No, it was too small for that, and probably in the wrong county as well. This was clearly a local affair, used to grind corn for the farmers and, despite its look of extreme age, it might only be eighty or so years since it had stopped working.

How must it have been to live in those days? Never travelling far but belonging to a close-knit group of people who knew one another's histories and who stuck loyally by each other and shared the good and the bad equally: celebrations of births and weddings; mingled tears when there was death or sickness or hardship. It sounded very attractive. Oh sure, thought Antonia cynically, and I suppose the child-mortality rate sounds attractive as well, does it, and being carted off to the workhouse if you couldn't pay your way, or the barbarism of surgery without anaesthetic . . . ?

She drove on. The main street was pleasing: shops and tiny coffee places, and a small hotel at one end. There was a square with a war memorial – Amberwood had sent its share of young men to both world wars it seemed – and a number of the buildings had the unmistakably wavy look of extreme age and the straight chimneys beloved by the Tudors. Either the place came under the aegis of town planners with an unusual vein of municipal aestheticism, or the residents of Amberwood were militant about preserving their history, because there were no converted plate-glass-fronted monstrosities blurring Elizabethan or Queen Anne façades, and everywhere was immaculate. There was certainly a small supermarket, but it was tucked discreetly away in a side street, politely self-effacing amidst a couple of picture galleries, and craft shops of the dried-flowers and raffia-mat type.

I'll still hate being here, thought Antonia but I can't really hate any of this. I'll come into the high street for shopping, and look at the paintings, (I'll manage to stay out for long enough to collect shopping and have a cup of coffee, surely to goodness!), and it'll all become familiar and ordinary.

Quire House was efficiently signposted. It turned out to be a couple of miles outside the town centre, which was further than Antonia had been expecting. It was annoying to experience a fresh stab of panic at leaving the friendly cluster of streets and embark on a stretch of open road. She flipped the radio on, and voices instantly filled the car – a trailer for an afternoon play and a preview for a gardening programme.

Quire House itself was not visible from the road. There were double gates with stone pillars on each side and a neat sign pointed along a wide curving carriageway, proclaiming this was Amberwood's 'Museum and Craft Centre', and that it was, 'Open from 11.00 a.m. to 4.00 p.m. each day.' Antonia glanced at the agent's directions: once inside the gates she should turn immediately right and fifty yards on she would see an old brick wall, at which point she should turn sharp left and she would be there.

She turned right obediently, refusing to feel grateful for the high yew hedges which closed comfortingly around the narrow roadway. Here was the old brick wall; it looked as if it might once have had vines growing up it. Nice. In summer the bricks would be warm, and you could sit and read and dream. It occurred to her that there was all the time in the world for that now. Reading and music and dreams. Perhaps she would finally get round to reading things like Pepys' *Diaries* and listening to all Mahler's symphonies – Richard used to say her musical tastes were hopelessly unadventurous. She was aware of a sudden stab of longing to hear Richard calling her unadventurous again – in fact, to hear Richard calling her anything at all.

She swung the car to the left, and, just as the directions had said, she was there.

It was the ugliest house she had ever seen and if, as its name suggested, it had once been somebody's idea of charity for the indigent, Antonia was glad she had not been the recipient because it looked as if it had been a very bleak charity indeed.

It was built of dirty-looking stone, which might have been attractive if the stones had weathered or mellowed, but they had not and the cottage was all hard angles – an oblong box with a no-frills roof slapped firmly onto its walls. Antonia, who had subconsciously been expecting rose-red brick, latticed windows and a garden with lupins and hollyhocks, took note of the fact that the place was sturdy and weatherproof, even down to the uncompromisingly modern windows someone had thought it suitable to install: square white frames in heavy-duty plastic. The front door, which was on the left-hand side of the house, was of the same white plastic, with an unpleasant steel letterbox like a rat-trap mouth.

But you did not live on the outside of a house, so it didn't really matter what the place looked like. Antonia produced the key, and discovered a particular pleasure in inserting it in the lock and pushing the door open with a proprietorial air. No matter what it's like, she thought, for the next two months it's mine. Providing I don't play loud music at one a.m. or hold orgies of the bacchanalian kind, no one can boot me out or come crashing in to disturb me.

There was a moment when she felt the past brush her mind, exactly as it had done while looking at the ancient watermill. Like stepping up to the windows of an old house to peer through its cobwebby panes and seeing a blurred flicker of movement from within.

But the moment passed, and she went inside, aware only of curiosity as the scents and atmosphere of this as yet unknown place folded round her. The main door opened straight into a fair-sized sitting room, and it was at once apparent that the inside of Charity Cottage was far nicer than the outside. The sitting room had a brick fireplace enclosing an electric fire, and the furniture was better than she had hoped: a sofa, a couple of easy chairs, a low coffee table and some nice framed sketches on the walls.

The windows, one on each side of the door, overlooked grassy parkland.

As well as being nicer, the cottage was deeper than it had looked. A door opened off the sitting room onto a large inner room with stairs winding up to the first floor. This had been utilized as a small dining room. There was a gateleg table with four bentwood chairs, and an oak dresser with blue and white plates. Antonia, glancing towards the stairs, thought the bedrooms could wait, and went through to the back of the cottage. This would be the kitchen, and hopefully there would be the promised crockery and cutlery, and a workable hot-water system. She pushed open the door which was of the old-fashioned kind with a high iron latch.

A bolt of such strong emotion hit her it was as if she had received a hard blow across her face. The room spun sickeningly, and Antonia reached blindly for the solid old door to prevent herself falling. For several nightmare moments she clung to it, fighting for breath, struggling to get free of the waves of fear. Stop hyperventilating, you idiot, take deep, slow breaths – you know how it goes. In for a count of five, out for a count of five. She concentrated and, after a moment, was able to let go of the door frame and shakily straighten up.

It was, indeed, an entirely ordinary kitchen: sink, draining board, some cupboards and worktops – not up-to-the-minute, state-of-the-art stuff, but not so very old. There was even a grocery box on one of the worktops, which struck a friendly note. Antonia investigated this, and found a compliments slip tucked inside.

> From Quire House, with good wishes for your stay. Perishables in fridge. We hope to meet you ere long – do come over to the house for a drink or a cup of tea. PS: Spare key in teapot.

There was a scrawled signature – Godfrey Toy, and the legend at the top said:

Quire House Trust. Museum and Craft Centre. Incorporating Rare and Out of Print Booksearch Service. Curators: Dr Godfrey Toy and Professor Oliver Remus.

And if you were going to tumble without warning into a bottomless black well of panic, at least the climb back to normality was more pleasant if there was a box of groceries and a friendly note waiting for you at the top. Antonia liked the idea of someone who stored keys in teapots like Lewis Carroll's dormouse.

Closer investigation revealed that the unknown Dr Toy's tastes ran classily to a hefty portion of Brie, some beautifully fresh French bread, an earthenware dish of pâté, a dozen free-range eggs, some pre-packaged strips of smoked salmon, a bag of apples and one of plums, and four neat half bottles of wine – two red and two white. With the tinned food and cartons of milk she had bought with her, this added up to quite a well-stocked larder. I'll learn to be a householder all over again, thought Antonia, carefully distributing everything on shelves and in cupboards. I'll have a milk delivery and newspapers.

The rest of the cottage was fairly predictable. There were three bedrooms upstairs and a bathroom which had clearly been fashioned from an old box room. Clean sheets waited in an airing cupboard, and there was a modern immersion heater for hot water – she switched this on at once, and then lugged her suitcases up the stairs. After some food, and one of Dr Toy's half bottles of wine, she would feel in tune with the world again. In fact, she might make that two half bottles of wine.

She had not brought very much with her, aside from clothes and food, except for a small CD player, along with her CDs, and a carton of books. After she had cooked a meal from tins and Dr Toy's hospitality, she sorted through the CDs.

Once she would automatically have reached for Mozart, but tonight she needed something stronger, something that reflected her mood and knew how it felt to fall fathoms deep into the heart of black bitter agony, but something that also demonstrated how the agony could be torn out and ripped to shreds before it was exultantly discarded. Schumann's Fourth? She did not know very much about the lives and motivations of the great composers – what she did know she had picked up from Richard – but she knew Schumann had created that symphony on emerging from a period of intense depression, and that it depicted the trapped, tortured spirit finally breaking free of dark savage unhappiness and soaring joyfully into the light.

After that flight of rhetoric it would have to be Schumann. Antonia thought she would pour a glass of Godfrey Toy's wine, and then curl into the deep armchair by the window and listen to the symphony. The rain pattered lightly against the glass and a little gusting wind stirred the thin curtains, but inside the cottage it was warm and safe.

Warm and safe. Except for that well of clutching terror that might still lie waiting for her in that perfectly ordinary kitchen . . . Except for that blue hatchback that seemed to have followed her for three quarters of the journey here . . .

Dr Godfrey Toy looked out of his window on Quire House's first floor, and was pleased to see lights in the windows of Charity Cottage.

It was very nice to think of someone being in the cottage for the winter; Godfrey always felt much safer when people were around him. Stupid, of course, but ever since – well, ever since what he privately called the tragedy – he had always been a touch uneasy about being in a house by himself. Just a touch. Particularly at night, and particularly in a house the size of Quire – all those empty rooms below him, all those stored-up memories.

But he loved living at Quire; he loved his flat with the high-ceilinged rooms and the big windows. This summer he had had the men in to spruce it up. He had chuckled quietly to himself over this, because it sounded exactly like a twittery maiden lady furtively recounting something slightly risqué. I'm having men in, my dear.

Anyway, they had done a good job – nothing grand, just a coat of emulsion everywhere, well, and one or two rolls of wallpaper if you were keeping tally. And, if you wanted to be really pedantic, a few licks of varnish to banisters and picture rails. But nothing so very much, and it had cost the merest of meres, despite the professor's caustic comments about extravagance. Anyway, Godfrey considered it money well spent.

His flat had a view over Quire's grounds. They were nothing elaborate, they were not in the Capability Brown or Gertrude Jekyll league, but Godfrey enjoyed them. The Trust kept everywhere in immaculate order, and visitors to the museum were very good about observing the 'Do Not Leave Litter' signs, although you still got the odd sprinkling of picnic wrappings, and occasionally there were other kinds of detritus which Godfrey preferred not to put a name to. (He could never understand people choosing somewhere so *public* for that kind of carrying-on.)

The letting agent had told him that a single lady had taken Charity Cottage. No, they said, in response to Godfrey's anxious questioning, they did not know anything about her. They did not need to know anything, they added, except that she had paid two months' rent in advance and the cheque had been cleared. She was a Miss Weston, and had given a London address. All entirely in order and Quire Trust might think itself fortunate to have a tenant for the place during November and December. And so Godfrey, who did think the Trust fortunate to have a tenant in the cottage for November and December, and who was pleased at the thought of a possible new friend, had put together what he thought of as a welcome-to-Quire box, and had felt guiltily relieved that Professor Remus was away because he would have been a bit scathing about it. An unnecessary gesture, he would have said, in the tone he always used when Godfrey gave way to an impulse. If he had seen the contents of the box he would have said, with sarcasm, 'Good God, foie gras and smoked salmon, how very luxurious!'

So it was better that Oliver was currently away on a book-buying expedition – there had been the promise of a very nice early copy of Marlowe's *Jew of Malta* in an old house where someone had lately died, and a rumour of some warmly romantic letters from Bernard Shaw to Mrs Patrick Campbell which one of the theatrical museums might like. Godfrey was hopeful that both possibilities would materialize. He would enjoy seeing the professor's discoveries.

He was glad he had taken the little gift to the cottage. The unknown Miss Weston might find it bleak coming to a strange place on her own, and the first night in a new place was always lonely. Godfrey had said as much that afternoon to the young work-experience boy they had at Quire, and the boy had stared at him with what Godfrey felt to be quite unwarranted scorn. But that was youth for you. They had no romance in their souls. They stared at you with that curled-lip contempt, and sometimes they said things like, 'What is your problem?' or, 'What part of "I won't do that" didn't you understand?', which Godfrey never knew how to answer.

He closed the curtains, hoping Charity Cottage's new tenant had liked his little gift, and hoping she was able to sleep on her first night there.

CHAPTER THREE

Either the memory of that well of terror in the cottage's kitchen, or the recurring image of the dark blue car, or possibly a combination of the two had prevented Antonia from sleeping.

At half past midnight she gave up the struggle, and went downstairs to make a cup of tea. The kitchen was shadowy and cool, but if the clutching fear still lurked, it lurked very quietly. Good.

She paused to look out of the window for a moment, remembering how, not so long ago, she had been deeply afraid to look out of her own window in the middle of the night. But nothing stirred, and the parkland was a smooth stretch of unbroken sward, the trees bland and unthreatening. A large, dark-furred cat appeared from their shadows, considered the night landscape with the unhurried arrogance of its kind, and then padded gracefully across the park, vanishing into the night on some ploy of its own. The kettle boiled, and Antonia made her cup of tea and took it back upstairs.

It was probably madness to unlock the small suitcase, and take the five- and six-year-old sheaf of curling newspaper cuttings from their envelope, but there were times when you needed to confront your own madness. Sometimes you could even pretend to relive the past and sidestep the mistakes.

She spread the cuttings out on the bed and looked at them for a long time. The wretched gutter-press had dug up a remarkable variety of photographs to illustrate their articles. It was anybody's guess how they had got hold of them but the sub-editors, predictably, had chosen the worst and the best.

Seen in smudgy newsprint, the boy called Don Robards who had stared up at Antonia from a hospital bed – the boy who had discovered something so appalling within his world that he had not wanted to live in that world any longer – looked impossibly young. Antonia's own image, next to it, appeared sharp and predatory by contrast. Did I really look like that in those days? Do I look like it now? Might anyone here recognize me?

She thought this unlikely. She had not deliberately tried to change her appearance, but the years had pared the flesh right down, and the once-long, once-sleek leaf-brown hair was now cut short and worn casually. People might remember Don though; he had been very good-looking.

Some of the sub-editors had slyly positioned Richard's photograph on the other side of Antonia's, so she was shown between the two of them. The message was unpleasantly clear: here's a woman with two younger men in her toils, and look what happened to them both. One of the tabloids had called Antonia a Messalina, and it was probably the first time in recorded history that a tabloid had used an early Roman empress to score a point.

Richard, too, looked soft and defenceless in the photo – it was a shot that had been taken at the piano, head and shoulders only, but it was well-lit, emphasizing his fragile-looking bone structure and luminous eyes. It was a false image, of course; beneath the translucent skin and the Keats-like air of starving in a garret, Richard had been as tough as old boots, and had a gourmet's delight in good food and wine. It had been one of his quirkier pieces of luck that the calories were burned up by his amazing energy and that he remained thin.

Antonia traced the outlines of the frozen black-and-grey images with a fingertip. I miss you so much, she said to Richard's photo. I still can't believe I'll never see you again.

Beyond the crowding memories, she was aware that it was raining heavily. She could hear it lashing against the windows and wondered vaguely if the large black cat had found shelter. But she only accorded the rain a small part of her attention. Her thoughts went deeper and deeper into the past; a ribbon of road unwound in front of her, and she was pulled helplessly along it. It was a road that was five years long, and it echoed with the clang of a heavy door being locked at precisely the same time each night. It was a road deeply shadowed by bars of moonlight that fell on exactly the same place on a bare floor every night. Between midnight and two a. m. had been the worst hours. They still were. She glanced at the time. Quarter past one.

She stood up and pushed the envelope of cuttings back into her suitcase, locking it with the tiny padlock. Stupid to take such needless precautions, but she was not yet used to taking her privacy for granted.

It occurred to her that so far from her original concern that the residents of Amberwood might seek her out to tell her their dreams and cure their phobias, if they discovered she was a convicted murderess who had served five years of an eight-year sentence, they were more likely to lynch her or revive the medieval custom of ducking her for a witch in the village pond.

Godfrey Toy was charmed to meet the new tenant of Charity Cottage on the very morning after she had moved in, and delighted to invite her into his little office. It was a good thing he had had a new visitor's chair delivered only that week. (A really good soft leather it was as well, in a rich dark brown. It had cost just a tad more than perhaps he should have spent, but there had been no need for Professor Remus to use words like squander or wastrel.)

Godfrey had been hoping Miss Weston would turn out to be a pleasantly gossipy lady with whom he might form a friendship. He did not often travel outside Amberwood, but he liked meeting people and hearing about their lives and work and families.

Sometimes he imagined himself with a family: a distant cousin had just had a baby and Godfrey was going to be its godfather. He had already chosen a silver porringer as a christening present – late eighteenth century it was, and he had had it engraved since you should not stint on these things – and he was visualizing being called Uncle Godfrey, and planning trips to wherever children liked to go these days. Quire's work-experience boy, Greg Foster, had said, when Godfrey asked, that kids mostly liked computer games and burger bars and boy-band concerts, which had rather disconcerted Godfrey who had been thinking more of the pantomime at Christmas and the zoo in the summer.

But although Miss Weston was perfectly polite, thanking him for the box of groceries and saying how friendly it had been to find them at the cottage on her arrival, she was very reserved. So Godfrey, who would not have pried if his soul's salvation depended on it, talked about Quire House and the Quire Trust for whom he and Professor Remus worked, and how they both lived over the shop, so to speak.

'I have the first-floor apartment, and the professor has the second. He's younger than I am and more active, so he doesn't mind the extra flight of stairs. We've been here for five years now.'

He thought there was a reaction from Miss Weston at the mention of five years, and he instantly regretted his words. But surely she was unlikely to know what had happened here five years ago. He had vowed not to fall into that way of thinking: 'Ah, that was something that happened before the tragedy,' or, 'That came the year afterwards,' as if the thing itself was an unpleasant milestone.

So Godfrey went on talking, saying Miss Weston must please have a look round Quire; it was such an interesting place. Here were some leaflets they had had printed – nothing very grand, of course; the Trust had not the largest of budgets, but they had done what they could.

'Thank you very much.'

And, said Godfrey, when Miss Weston had settled in, perhaps she could come to the flat for a proper visit. Out of museum hours. A glass of sherry one evening, or afternoon tea one Sunday.

Antonia, who had not drunk sherry or anything approximating it for five years, and who had become used to the barely digestible tea brewed in the vast urn by whichever prisoners were on kitchen duty, said, gravely, that that would be very nice.

It was ironic to think that once she would have accepted Dr Toy's modest invitation with pleasure. She and Richard had enjoyed meeting new people, and Richard, with his enquiring mind and his lively sense of humour, would have loved Godfrey Toy's cherubic donnishness. He would have loved Quire House as well, and he would have enjoyed the little legend that its first owner, the precentor of the nearby cathedral, had called it Choir House, but some Victorian postal official had spelt it wrongly in the records so it had metamorphosed to Quire.

Trying not to think about Richard, Antonia put the leaflets in her pocket, and wandered through the rooms, which were light and spacious, polish-scented and attractively arranged. Some of the furniture looked as if it was quite valuable, and there were several displays of really beautiful old glass and chinoiserie. It's that narrow world from another era, thought Antonia, but I find it alluring. If I came across a time machine now, what would I do? Set the dial to the 1890s, and press Start without thinking twice about it? Travel back to that narrow undemanding life? She frowned and moved on, looking at the other displays.

The old watermill she had noticed on the way here had been treated to a display all by itself. It was called Twygrist, and there was a neat little account of how farmers had brought their grain to be ground by the miller. The Miller of Twygrist. It had a faintly sinister ring, although Antonia supposed it was only on account of the grisly ogre's chant about grinding men's bones to make bread. Literature had not always been kind to millers, of course, depicting them as apt to sell their daughters into that peculiar servitude where the spinning of straw into gold was obligatory.

Someone had drawn a careful diagram of how the Amberwood mill had worked, and rather endearingly studded it with tiny men and women in what looked like the working garb of the Victorian era.

There was no mention of Twygrist's age, but Antonia thought it could be anywhere between the compiling of the Domesday Book and the Regency craze for fake-Gothic. However old it was, it had the appearance of having grown up by itself out of the ground when no one was looking.

But to balance that, there was a pleasing little story of how a memorial clock had been put onto Twygrist's north wall in the opening years of the 1900s, to commemorate a Miss Thomasina Forrester, and how a tiny trust fund existed to pay for the winding and maintenance of the clock. 'And even today,' ran the careful lettering beneath the photographs, 'the Forrester Clock of Twygrist is faithfully wound every Wednesday morning, and the post of Clock-Winder still exists, and is in the gift of the local council, although very much regarded as a family appointment and frequently passed from father to son.'

There again was the touch of Middle England or even Middle Earth. Clock-winders and a lady whose name might have come straight out of Beatrix Potter.

Quire House itself was documented in an orderly fashion. The precentor who had built it in the eighteenth century had, it seemed, needed a large house for his eleven children. Luxurious tastes and uxorious habits, thought Antonia. That's another entry on the debit side of those days. No convenient birth pill or condoms on supermarket shelves, least of all for churchmen and their spouses.

She moved through to the back of the house, to a music room overlooking the gardens. As she went in, a large black cat with a white front like an evening shirt appeared from nowhere and jumped onto a spinet at the far end, regarding her with lordly indifference. 'I suppose it was you I saw from the cottage window last night,' said Antonia softly, and put out a tentative hand. 'You looked like a ghost in the moonlight. There's nothing ghostly about you today, though.'

The cat twitched an ear, leapt down from the spinet, good-manneredly accepted a caress, and vanished through the half-open French windows, leaving Antonia to walk round the room on her own.

There was a framed charcoal portrait on the wall near the spinet, with a neatly printed card underneath explaining that this was Thomasina Forrester in whose memory Twygrist's clock had been installed (see the display in the drawing room and please ask for help if you need it). There was a photograph of the clock which Antonia thought very ugly, but she studied the sketch of Thomasina with interest. She was firm featured, dark browed and quite large boned. But there's something slightly unpleasant about the eyes, thought Antonia. A squint? Almost a leer? She certainly wasn't a lady you would have cared to cross. But probably the artist was an amateur, and the eyes hadn't quite worked out or had been smudged.

She turned back to examine the spinet, and glanced at the music on the stand. The quiet room and the gentle scents of Quire House whirled crazily into a sick distortion and Antonia thought for a moment she was going to faint. She managed to reach a low window ledge and sit down, feeling deeply grateful that no one else was looking round Quire this afternoon, because if she was going to pass out with such dramatic suddenness, she would prefer to do so without witnesses.

The music on the spinet was a piece Antonia knew very well indeed. It was one of Paganini's *Caprice Suites*: the series of twenty-four complex violin solos composed in the early 1800s, and adapted and transcribed for the piano since then by more than one eminent composer.

It was the music Richard had been playing on the night he died – the night that Don Robards had finally tipped over the edge of sanity. The sight of it plunged Antonia straight back into the five-year-old nightmare.

* * *

If she had arrived home at her normal time on that never-to-be-forgotten evening, she might have been able to save Richard, but she had stayed late at the hospital to help Jonathan Saxon with some reports for a budget meeting, and he had suggested a drink at the nearby wine bar afterwards.

'If you feel like giving Richard some excuse, we could even have dinner at my flat. I'm a very good cook. I'd impress you.'

'You do impress me,' said Antonia. 'But not in the way you want. And no, I don't feel like giving Richard some excuse and having dinner at your flat. But a drink on the way home will be very nice.'

And so they had the drink, and when Antonia left the wine bar she had been light-hearted from the wine. Jonathan might flirt extravagantly, but it was never offensive or sexist, and he was very good company.

It had been a few minutes after nine when she got home, and discovered that the glass in the front door had been smashed and the lock broken.

Richard was lying on the floor of the big sitting room in a muddle of overturned furniture, his bloodied fingerprints all over the piano keyboard where he had tried to clutch onto it. The sheet music of the *Caprice* suite – which had occupied most of his concentration for the past fortnight – had lain on the piano. It was unreadable because Richard had been stabbed several times and the final thrust had gone into the caratoid artery so that blood had sprayed everywhere.

He had bled to death while Antonia was drinking wine and laughing with Jonathan, and Antonia had hated Paganini's music ever since.

CHAPTER FOUR

Thomasina Forrester did not much care for music. A lot of time-wasting and flummery. But the thing was that Maud liked music. In fact music played quite a big part in Maud's life – piano lessons and practise, to say nothing of unutterably tedious musical evenings at Maud's house when guests had perforce to listen to recitals and solos – and so it looked as if music would have to play a big part in Thomasina's life as well. But she would accept that and cope with it. She would accept and cope with anything if it meant getting Maud in her bed.

It was remarkable that after all these years of love 'em and leave 'em Thomasina should find herself bowled over, knocked for a loop by a pretty face and a sweet smile, but so it was. Maud Lincoln. Utter perfection. Quantities of fair fluffy hair, a china-doll complexion and a bed-post waist. And just seventeen. A delightful age for a girl, seventeen. Fresh, unspoiled. *Ripe* . . . The smile that very few people saw curved Thomasina's lips as she considered Maud Lincoln's unspoiled freshness. Rather a pity about the name, however. Gardens and black-bat nights, and a green sound to the surname. With a face like that she should be called something more lyrical: Imogen or Daphnis or Heloise. Still, what was in a name? And once the bedroom lights were out and you were in bed together with your clothes off, who cared? More importantly, how should she go about this latest seduction?

Gentlemen, when engaged in the pursuit of a lady, often plied the object of their desire with wine. In fact Thomasina's cousin Simon had once told her that there was nothing like a judicious drop of wine to get rid of inhibitions. Thomasina had merely smiled and not commented, but she had thought to herself: I must remember that one, and had indeed remembered it to very good purpose on more than one occasion.

But she did not think Maud Lincoln was one who could be coaxed or tricked into bed by the use of alcohol. Maud would have to be seduced very gradually, almost without her realizing what was happening. That could mean a vastly frustrating few weeks for Thomasina, but if it went on for too long she could always make one of her discreet trips to London. There was that cat-faced child in Seven Dials, all of fifteen years old, who did not appear to differentiate overmuch between getting into the beds of gentlemen or ladies, and whose fingers and tongue were quite amazingly adept . . .

After some thought Thomasina decided to invite Maud to Sunday lunch at Quire House. When they had eaten she would ask Maud to play some music for her – there was a piano in Quire's music room – and surely she could get through an hour or so of listening to some stuffy sonata.

The invitation would not be very remarkable, in fact it would be entirely in keeping with the Forrester tradition. Josiah Forrester had believed in showing consideration towards the people who worked for him, and he had taught his daughter to have the same sense of responsibility. Paternalism they called it nowadays, he had said, but it was still plain old-fashioned consideration for dependants. Thomasina smiled as she remembered her father had always been especially considerate to George Lincoln who had run the mill profitably and efficiently for so many years. The Miller of Twygrist, he used to say. Good faithful George. Pulled himself up by his bootstraps, of course, married money and learned how to be a gentleman as he went along but none the worse for that.

After lunch on Sunday, Thomasina would take the miller's daughter for a walk in Quire's park, and then accompany Maud to her home. It would all be entirely chaste and perfectly respectable, although there would be a secret pleasure in walking close to Maud along the dark lanes, and slipping an arm around her waist to make sure she did not turn her ankle on an uneven piece of ground.

It was unfortunate that the lane leading to the Lincolns' house lay alongside Latchkill – she frowned briefly over that – but they could hurry past the gates.

When Maud was small, her mamma used to take her for walks along the lanes around their house, and the walks nearly always took them past Latchkill. You could not actually see Latchkill over the high walls surrounding it, but you could see the little lodge at the side of the big iron gates. If you looked through the bars of the gates you could see along the carriageway to where Latchkill itself stood, squat and dark and frowning on its upward-sloping ground. Maud was always frightened that one day the gates would be open and mamma would go inside and Maud would have to go inside as well. It would be the most frightening thing in the world to hear the iron gates clanging shut behind you, shutting you in.

One afternoon, as they went past Latchkill, mamma said in a voice that made Maud feel cold and fearful, 'It's almost spider-light, isn't it? So we'd better walk straight past Latchkill today. You must never be caught near Latchkill when it's spider light time. That's when the bad things can happen.'

'Spider light?' said Maud nervously.

'Spider light's the in-between time. It's the light that spiders like best of all – the time when it isn't quite day or night: early morning, when the day hasn't quite started; or evening, when the daylight's beginning to fade.' She paused, and then in a faraway voice, said, 'All those grey winter mornings when you go down-stairs from your bed in the dark and open the curtains to find a huge black spider crouching in the half-light. It's been there all night, that huge black spider – perhaps it's been watching you and waiting for you, only you didn't know it was there . . .

'That's the dangerous thing about spider light, Maud: it hides things – things you never knew existed in the world. But once you have seen those things, you can never afterwards forget them.'

Maud had never forgotten about spider light, and even when she was grown up, if she had to walk past Latchkill she always did so quickly, determinedly not glancing in through the gates. There were bad things inside Latchkill: there was spider light, and there were huge heavy doors that shut in things you had not known existed . . . When she was small, Maud used to dream about the black iron doors that would be inside Latchkill – doors that would be there to shut something terrible away from the world and must never be opened. Sometimes she had woken up crying because of the nightmare. Father always came into her bedroom if she cried, and he seemed to understand about the nightmare. He told her everyone had nightmares, and he would always keep her safe.

After lunch at Quire House, Maud and Miss Thomasina had walked past Latchkill. It had been nice of Miss Thomasina to invite her to lunch, Maud thought, although parts of the afternoon had been a little strange. Miss Thomasina had kissed her very warmly on her arrival which Maud had not expected, and said she had a present for Maud; she loved giving people presents.

The present, laid out on Thomasina's own bed, was a set of underwear: a chemise, an under-bodice, little silk drawers and stockings to match. At first Maud did not know where to look for embarrassment; underwear was not something you were supposed to discuss, never mind spreading it out on a bed.

'There was a rose pink set as well,' Thomasina was saying. 'But I thought blue matched your eyes. I hope I got the size right. Perhaps we ought to make sure it all fits. Let's try them on you. I'll help you out of your things. How slender you are – an eighteen-inch waist, I expect? Yes, I thought so.'

Of course, it was perfectly all right to be undressing like this in Miss Forrester's bedroom. It was not as if there was a man watching. Even so, Maud felt awkward and a bit shivery, and she felt even more awkward and even more shivery when the chemise was dropped deftly over her head. It probably did not matter that her breasts were touched in the process. Thomasina did not seem to think it mattered; she said Maud had pretty breasts, and dear goodness, there was no need to be blushing so rosily! She had intended a compliment. Had Maud a beau, at all? She was so pretty, there was surely a gentleman interested in her.

Maud said at once that there was not. Once or twice she had been invited to take a drive with a gentleman, but she usually made a polite excuse. She was not, said Maud in a rush of confidence, very comfortable with gentlemen. They were so coarse, weren't they?

'Perhaps you prefer the company of ladies?' said Thomasina, and Maud said, gratefully, that she did. Ladies were somehow less threatening. Gentler.

'You don't want to be married some day? Most girls of your age do.'

But the thought of marriage, of getting into a bed with a man and doing whatever it was married people did in a bed was so utterly repugnant that Maud felt quite sick even to think about it. A man's hands – a man's body- She shuddered and said, Oh no, she thought marriage would be horrid, and then hoped she had not said anything wrong, or offended her generous hostess.

But Thomasina did not seem to be offended. She said Maud was very sensible, and hugged her again. This time her hands seemed to slide inside the chemise, but Maud did not like to object. It was not like letting a man touch her.

'Oh no,' said Thomasina when Maud rather hesitantly said this. Her voice suddenly sounded different. Husky, as if she had a sore throat, but sort of whispery as well. 'Oh no, my dear, this is nothing like letting a man touch you.'

* * *

George Lincoln was delighted to receive a visit from Miss Thomasina. He knew her well, of course – he had always called her Miss Thomasina, ever since she used to visit Twygrist with her cousin, Mr Simon Forrester.

He was very gratified indeed by the suggestion that Maud might spend a few weeks at Quire House. It would be a wonderful opportunity for the child. It was like Miss Thomasina to think of such a thing: she had always been so kind to the young ladies of the neighbourhood, taking them out and about, inviting them to Quire House, taking a real interest in them. So George was very pleased to accept for Maud, after which he made haste to offer Miss Thomasina a glass of sherry. His wife used to say it was a drink for a lady, sherry, and it was one of the things George had always been careful to remember.

But it seemed Miss Thomasina had an appointment and could not stay. She had a great many calls on her time, of course, George knew that. She still concerned herself with the families of people who had worked for her father in the old days. Only last week she had moved that ruffian Cormac Sullivan into the little almshouse recently built on Quire's land. A very nice cottage it was, and far better than Sullivan deserved.

After Miss Thomasina had gone, striding briskly down the drive, George thought he would miss Maud while she was at Quire, and that his house would seem sadly empty. But at Quire Maud would meet all kinds of people, which pleased George who worried where a husband might be found for the child. There was a real shortage of young men in Amberwood – why, even Miss Thomasina herself, with all her opportunities and her money was not married. A lot of people said she ought to have married her cousin Simon, but neither of them had ever seemed to care for the idea.

Best of all, the visit would take Maud further away from Latchkill. It was far better – far safer – for the child to be kept as far from there as possible.

*   *   *

Latchkill Asylum for the Insane
Day Book: Sunday 5th September
Report by Nurse Bryony Sullivan.

Midday.
Several patients uneasy due to thunderstorm mid-morning. Reaper Wing particularly troublesome – situation not helped by two patients remembering old story about thunderstorms being caused by wrath of the gods, and relating this to rest of wing.

4.00 p.m.
Reverend Skandry persuaded to enter Reaper Wing, where he held a prayer service with the intention (in his words), of 'Restoring calm and order to the poor unfortunates.'

4.30 p.m.
Prayer service ended in some disarray, when four Reaper Wing occupants began throwing things at Reverend Skandry, who retired in panic and stated that he is not to be asked to minister to that section of Latchkill again.

6.00 p.m.
Dr Glass called out to Reaper Wing (Matron Prout's orders), and administered bromide all round.

Memorandum to Bursar
Tea given to Dr Glass in Matron's room. Please to ensure this is shown on daily costings, since it was from Matron's personal store.

Also deduct cost of breakages (two cups and one plate) from Dora Scullion's wages this week.

Signed *F. Prout* (Matron)

Bryony had always wished she could write more details in the day-book reports; she especially wished she could record some of her suspicions of Matron Prout.

'I daren't do it, though,' she said to her father. 'She'd have the pages torn out before you could turn round. But she's milking Latchkill for all she's worth. I'll swear that half the poor souls in there are being fleeced of every farthing they own.'

'Chancery lunatics,' said Bryony's father. 'I wouldn't put it past the old trout.'

Bryony asked what a Chancery lunatic might be.

'Remember your Dickens, my girl,' said Cormac. '*Bleak House*. Jarndyce versus Jarndyce. The diverting of inheritances and the snaffling of land by greedy families – God Almighty, have you never heard of it, Bryony? It stems from an old English law – twelfth or thirteenth century – wouldn't you know the English would still be using rules from the Dark Ages. It gave the Crown custody of the lands of natural fools and guardianship of the property of the insane. If your Prout isn't up to that little game or one very like it, I'll take a vow of chastity and enter a monastery.'

'There isn't a monastery in the world that would have you,' said Bryony at once, and he grinned and said, 'Nor there is, thanks be to God. Are we having supper soon?'

'Yes. Why? Are you going out later?'

'I am.'

It would be better not to ask where he was going, so Bryony did not. It might be poaching or it might be a lady. He was about as trustworthy as a sleeping wolf, Cormac Sullivan but Bryony did not really mind. She loved him better than anyone in the entire world, and what was even better, she *liked* him. The two things did not necessarily go together.

So she just said, 'Don't get caught, will you?' and he smiled his guileless smile and said he would not.

CHAPTER FIVE

There was no cut and dried textbook treatment for coping with ghosts, even if you believed in them, which Antonia did not.

Richard was dead; Don Robards had certainly died more than five years ago, and the presence of Paganini's music in Quire House had been merely a coincidence. Yes, but there had been that car – the same as the car Don used to drive – that followed her yesterday. Had that just been another coincidence? Antonia supposed it was possible.

What about that dark pocket of fear inside Charity Cottage itself? It was still there, like a bruise you avoided touching, but how much of it was due to Antonia's own state of mind? Could it conceivably be connected to the cottage's past? Sensitivity to an atmosphere was not an unknown phenomenom. It was something a surprising number of psychiatrists would cautiously admit existed. Antonia was not quite admitting it now, but she was open to persuasion. She thought she was no more and no less receptive than anyone else, but a number of times, trying to reach deeply disturbed patients, she had been able to feel very distinctly the muddy tangle of their confusion and unhappiness. Like poking a stick into a stagnant pool and feeling the silt stir before you actually saw it reach the surface.

So did the silt sometimes stir in Charity Cottage? Had something violent and tragic once happened here and left a lasting imprint?

On balance, ghosts and the imprints of old emotions might be easier to cope with than delusions. Routing ghosts was not a question of reciting some Macbeth-like incantation or waving garlic and crucifixes around. The solution, quite simply, was to systematically crowd the wretched creatures out. To immerse your mind so thoroughly in something else that there was no room left for spooks and no energy to spare for noticing their presence.

A project. A programme of work, a quest, a venture.

There were a few possibilities for this, but it was Amberwood and Twygrist that came strongly into her mind. Amberwood and the people who had lived and worked here. The Twygrist miller, whoever he had been, and Thomasina Forrester with that off-centre stare and uncompromising jaw, and the quirky little post of Clock-Winder of Amberwood. And this cottage.

She retrieved the leaflets about Quire House, and spread them out on the table. It looked as if Godfrey Toy might have had a hand in their compiling; they were neatly written, with little potted histories of some of the people who had lived in the house.

Thomasina Forrester appeared to have been something of a personality in Amberwood. She had administered the Quire estate and been involved in various charitable activities. Antonia supposed these would have been ladies' committees for fund-raising events or sick-visiting, and turned over a page to see what Thomasina had got up to.

It had not been organizing charity concerts or sick-visiting at all. Thomasina Forrester had been a trustee of something called the Forrester Benevolent Trust – Antonia thought there was a disagreeable air of patronage about the name – whose purpose appeared to be the providing of comforts to inmates of the local lunatic asylum. The asylum itself had been called Latchkill and, according to the leaflet, it had been a dark byword for miles around.

Latchkill. It was a harsh, ugly word. Latchkill – the place where all the locks had been killed. Was that what the name was meant to imply? Do not risk coming here: this is the place where doors cannot be opened because there are no keys. Once you are in here, it is very difficult indeed to get out again.

The words scraped against Antonia's mind, taking her back to another place where latches had been killed. A place where some of the females preferred their own sex and practised their own initiation rituals when the wardens were not around.

But she had survived it. She had even survived the night she was beaten up in the showers, when four of the women subjected her to rape. She had known, of course, that women could and did rape other women – she had had two girls as patients who had been the victims of female rape. But listening to a distraught patient describing the act was no preparation for the experience itself – for the glitter in the attackers' eyes, or the smell of cheap soap in the shower stalls and the body scents of the women bending over her, or the feeling of their hands . . .

Afterwards she had pushed the memory down to the very deepest level of her mind, and it had stayed there until the word *Latchkill* touched a raw nerve, and a pair of skewed eyes looking out of a framed drawing brought back the fear and humiliation of that night. You never entirely erased any memory, but it was odd that the sketch of the long-dead Thomasina Forrester should have dredged up that particular one.

Godfrey had been inclined to discount Miss Weston as a possible new friend, so it was a nice surprise when she turned up just after eleven o'clock next morning, and asked if he knew of any sources she could explore to find out more about the Forrester family. She did not know exactly what she was looking for, she said, just general things: background, how they had made their money, why they had come to Quire House, what descendants there might still be in the area, Twygrist and its place in the scheme of things – it seemed to be bound up with the Forresters, what with the memorial clock and so on. No, there was no especial reason for her interest, she said, but the leaflets Dr Toy had given her had been interesting, and she would like to read up about local history and local personalities while she was here. Nothing very scholarly, only a bit of relaxation.

This was meat and drink to Godfrey, although he always flinched inwardly if anyone asked about Twygrist. But he had become quite adept at dealing with this by now, and so he said Miss Weston was welcome to any information that would help. They had disinterred a few things for the leaflets and the displays, but there was still oceans of stuff in Quire's cellars which they had hardly looked at. There might be something about the Forrester family down there, although the term *family* was stretching it a good deal, because only old Josiah and his daughter had lived here.

'Their bit of Quire's history only spanned sixty or seventy years and when the daughter – Thomasina – died, the family died with her. So there won't be a great deal of Forrester stuff.'

Antonia said that anything there was would be fine, and Godfrey said it was a pity that Professor Remus was away at the moment, because he would know what material they had on Thomasina, although it had to be said that when Oliver did return his mind might still be attuned to first-folio Elizabethan plays or autographed verses from the Romantic period. It might take a day or two for him to adjust to Amberwood again, although when you did have his attention, you had it two hundred per cent, if Miss Weston knew what he meant.

Miss Weston said she knew exactly what he meant, and there was no particular rush and she could come back another day, but Godfrey would not hear of this. He looked out the keys to the cellars, and summoned the sulky Greg Foster to help carry things up the stairs.

'I don't mind carrying boxes,' said Antonia, but this did not suit Godfrey's idea of what was right, and he swept the unwilling Greg down to the cellars with them, issuing worried warnings to Antonia about the stairs being narrow and rickety, and the lighting a bit dim.

As she went down the steps, Antonia said, 'There was a reference to an old asylum in the leaflets as well. Would you have anything on that, d'you think?'

'Latchkill,' said Godfrey, nodding. 'Yes, there might be a few fragments. Sad old place, from all accounts, but those places usually were, weren't they?'

'What happened to it?'

'It was demolished in the 1960s or early 1970s,' said Godfrey. 'I think there was some attempt to get it registered as a listed building, but in the end they said it was beyond restoring, and it went.'

'How sad,' said Antonia, trying not to feel disappointed.

The large black and white cat appeared from somewhere and elected to accompany them into the cellars, seating itself on a ledge and preparing to watch their exploits with an air of indulgent curiosity. Godfrey said they had better shoo him out in case he got shut in down here, and before doing so introduced him to Antonia as Raffles.

'Raffles?' Antonia's mind went to the famous hotel, but Godfrey said, 'He's a very gentlemanly cat-burglar. He's always perfectly polite about his crimes, but if you let him into the cottage, never leave out food.'

'Oh, I see.'

Raffles took his unhurried leave, and Godfrey burrowed, white-rabbit-like into the packing cases, tea chests and boxes. In a surprisingly short space of time he identified a small carton marked 'Forrester', which contained four or five large but very battered manilla envelopes.

'Newspaper cuttings, a few letters and financial statements. It looks as if there's some stuff from Latchkill, as well. But there isn't very much, I'm afraid. Would it be enough to give you a start?'

He looked so anxiously hopeful that Antonia, eyeing the envelopes hungrily, said it would give her more than a start.

'But everything looks terrifyingly fragile. Would it be better if I had photocopies to work from? I'll happily pay—'

But Godfrey would not dream of making a charge, and said that copies could be made right away. He would have thought of that himself if he had not been so woolly-minded about machines and technology. Professor Remus was urging him to learn how to operate a computer, which he was trying to avoid, although he supposed it would make the cataloguing a lot easier.

To her horror, Antonia heard herself say, 'I've got a laptop. And I've done a bit of cataloguing work. I'm here for a couple of months, so if you wanted any help—' At this point she managed to shut up in case she let it out that the cataloguing experience had been acquired by re-vamping the prison library, a project which had gone some way to saving her sanity in gaol.

But Godfrey was entranced at the offer, and said he would certainly take her up on it. How extremely kind of her. He had a party of visitors due after lunch, which would take up most of today, but perhaps Miss Weston could come back tomorrow and they could discuss it? Should they say half past three? Quire closed at four, so there were unlikely to be many visitors still around.

The laptop had been a gift from Jonathan. 'Call it a coming-out present,' he'd said, giving it to her after their lunch in London, and speaking in the offhand tone of a man who would be torn into pieces by wild horses galloping in different directions rather than admit to a generous action or an emotional response. Antonia had tried to accept the laptop in the spirit in which it had been given. She could not imagine what had prompted her to offer it and her own services to Godfrey Toy this morning.

It was already surprisingly comforting to see the squat, ugly cottage standing on the edge of the parkland. Antonia approached it buoyantly, because it already represented a degree of safety even with that patch of dark fear in the kitchen. But let's not think about that. Let's enjoy unlocking the front door and coming into the sitting room, turning up the heating against the damp autumnal day and seeing the glow of the electric fire reflected on the windowpanes. Recognizing the house's scents – old timbers and the occasional drift of woodsmoke from the fireplace.

It was just on one o'clock. She would have some lunch, and while she ate she would read the letters and newspaper cuttings about Thomasina and Latchkill, making notes as she went along. I want to know about you, she said to Thomasina's ghost. And I want to know about that patch of extreme fear in this cottage. I don't know if you were anything to do with that – whether you suffered the fear or whether you caused it – but you're a starting point. A link.

She went into the kitchen, still thinking about Thomasina, rather than about what might be invisibly in wait for her, and stopped dead in the doorway.

Raffles was composedly seated on the table, and between his paws were the remains of Godfrey Toy's smoked salmon.

The clawing fear leapt out of the room all over again, and it was several moments before Antonia could think or reason.

Let's take this calmly. There's a cat on the table, and it's eating the salmon. Nothing so very sinister about that. Dr Toy said Raffles was a well-mannered burglar, and any cat will trade its virtue and barter its soul for fish. But how did he get in?

The likeliest explanation was that Antonia must have left a door or window open, and Raffles, in the manner of his kind, had come to investigate. He was, as Godfrey Toy had said, being perfectly polite about it.

Keeping a firm hold of this probability, she checked the back door which was locked, and then systematically went round the rest of the cottage, determined not to give way to panic.

Every window was closed. Nowhere was the smallest chink through which even the most accomplished feline thief could have got in. But there must be a chink somewhere.

Although how had he opened the fridge door, removed the salmon from the foil wrapping and then closed the fridge door behind him?

CHAPTER SIX

Forrester Benevolent Trust
Friday 17th September
In attendance: Miss Thomasina Forrester, Matron Freda Prout, Reverend Skandry, Dr Daniel Glass.

Nurse Bryony Sullivan taking notes of proceedings.

Matron Prout proposed the closure of Reaper Wing, on the grounds that it was costly to maintain, and a large proportion of the nurses did not like dealing with the inhabitants. There was a certain biblical superstition.

Dr Glass strongly opposed this. Said the inhabitants of Reaper Wing had, in the main, been cast off by squeamish or snobbish families, and must not be cast off by people dedicated to helping the sick. Added that there was nothing in the least biblical about Reaper Wing patients, and offered to talk to the nurses in question.

Reverend Skandry was of the opinion that we should be charitable to those less fortunate than ourselves. When Dr Glass said that this remark did not further the meeting's purpose, Rev Skandry said he would pray for the poor souls in Reaper Wing.

Matron Prout then proposed that funds be diverted from the Forrester Benevolent Trust to help with treatment of Reaper Wing patients, who often had to be sedated. By way of support for this proposal, she passed round bills, pointing out that items such as sulphate of quinine (frequently given as an infusion in carbonate of ammonia), were becoming very costly.

Miss Forrester asked if any of the patients in Reaper Wing could be regarded as men or women of quality, which is a particular requirement of money from the Trust being paid out. Matron Prout said, they were people of quality, and appealed to Dr Glass to confirm this.

Dr Glass said he could not confirm it because he had never noticed and he did not care anyway. He expressed himself as being opposed to using the Trust in the way Matron was requesting. If Reaper Wing – in fact if any patients at all – were so severely disturbed that regular sedation was needed, the cost of treating them should be borne by public monies such as the Poor Law funds, and not have to come from charitable bequests with obscure terms of reference, set up by well-meaning but misguided philanthropists thirty years earlier.

Reverend Skandry suggested that Dr Glass should apologize to Miss Forrester for appearing to cast a slur on her father, to which Dr Glass replied that in a properly run world all sick people would be given the same treatment irrespective of financial or social standing, and he would like it recorded that he will treat all patients in Latchkill regardless of whether he is paid for his services or not. (So recorded.)

Reverend Skandry seconded the proposal that the Forrester Benevolent Trust be drawn on for ministering to Reaper Wing.

Dr Glass put a counter-proposal that if Trust funds were to be used for basic medicines, they might as well also be used to provide better food for all patients.

Objection made by Matron Prout, who said if the Trust permitted this, the next step would be that the patients would expect all manner of luxuries, even down to wine with their dinner, and chicken and game for their supper. Dr Glass said he did not see why patients should not be given chicken and game – stewed venison very nourishing. Pointed out that partridge presently in season, and poachers as likely to supply Latchkill with birds as anywhere else. Said that for himself he had no objection to eating misappropriated partridge and did not suppose Latchkill's patients would mind either, and that a particularly good way to cook it was *au choux*. Added that if it was Matron's intention to administer prison diet to the patients, then Dora Scullion might as well bring on the bread-and-skilly now and have done.

Original proposal carried. Dr Glass's counter-proposal not seconded.

Today had been the first time Byrony had taken the notes for a Benevolent Trust meeting and it had been quite an experience. The Reverend Arthur Skandry had spent most of his time staring at Bryony's ankles, and Thomasina Forrester had spent her time staring at her bosom. Neither of these things were entirely a surprise, although Bryony would have preferred not to have Thomasina eyeing her in quite that manner.

Dr Glass had not eyed Bryony at all; there was nothing in the least bit ogle-some about Dr Glass. The Prout sometimes wondered audibly about his private life, asking whether there was not something a little *strange* about a gentleman of thirty-five or thirty-eight who was not married, but most of Latchkill's nurses considered this to be pure pique. There had been a story a year or two back that Prout had tried to inveigle Dr Glass into a romantic liaison with her, only to be rejected. This surprised nobody.

Bryony had no idea if the story was true, but it was certainly true that most of the nurses were halfway in love with Dr Glass.

Byrony was not even a quarter of the way in love with him, although she would not have minded if he had stared at any part of her during today's meeting. But he was far too much of a gentleman to do any such thing.

Maud could not imagine how Thomasina could bring herself to go to Latchkill – to go through those gates and walk along the gloomy tree-fringed drive, and step across Latchkill's threshhold – but Thomasina said it was something that had to be done. Her father had set up a trust to help some of the poor souls in the place, and the mantle of that had fallen on Thomasina's shoulders, so to speak. Noblesse oblige and all that.

Maud had said, 'Oh. Oh, yes, I see,' but had to repress a shudder at the thought of Latchkill with the spider light inside its rooms, and the deep badness at its heart.

There had been quite a lot of shudders to repress since coming to live at Quire House not connected with Latchkill but with what Maud thought of as 'It'.

'It' had happened about a week after she had gone to Quire. She had been enjoying her stay, and she had liked the bedroom Thomasina had given her and everything had been very nice indeed. And then, one night after Maud had retired, Thomasina came into the bedroom and sat down to watch Maud get undressed. This was disconcerting, but Maud was still a bit overawed by Quire and by Thomasina's friendship. Thomasina had already given Maud several beautiful silk and velvet gowns and had talked about how they would go into Chester one day soon to buy brushes and painting materials so Maud could set up a proper artist's studio while she was here.

So Maud did not want to seem ungrateful, and it was silly to feel embarrassed about taking one's clothes off – it was not like undressing in front of a man. So she undressed, trying not to shiver as she did so – it was September, but the night was warm, and she could not possibly be feeling cold – and put on the delicate lawn nightgown laid out on the pillow for her. This, it seemed, was another of Thomasina's presents, and so Maud said how pretty it was.

'White,' said Thomasina. 'Wear it tonight, will you?'

It was a bit worrying to see Thomasina watching her so intensely. Maud had never before noticed what red, wet-looking lips Thomasina had, but probably that was only the glow from the gas jets. Once in bed with the sheets pulled up to her chin, Maud felt better. Safer. Less vulnerable.

She did not feel less vulnerable for long because Thomasina then undressed. It was embarrassing to see this important lady taking off her clothes, and noticing that her thighs were lean and a bit stringy-looking, and that she had a lot of coarse hair between her legs – much more than Maud had. Maud shut her eyes and pretended to be asleep, but Thomasina climbed into the big soft bed, and turned down the gas so the room was dark. The wet red lips began to kiss Maud so intensely and so probingly that she could scarcely breathe. She began to feel frightened; it had not previously occurred to her that ladies got into bed together or kissed one another with such fierceness. When Thomasina's hands began to explore her body in the most surprising fashion, she had to fight not to push them away.

She did not do so because of not wanting to offend Thomasina, and also in case this was something people did when they were grown up. Thomasina murmured how Maud was the dearest, sweetest, most beautiful person in the world, which was not something anyone had ever said to her before. Perhaps it was not so unpleasant to be stroked and kissed in this way. Maud was aware of a sudden surge of power when, some little time later, Thomasina's usually stern face twisted and she cried out with joy.

The prodding and stroking seemed to be over, and Maud was able to lie back on the pillows. She had not really understood why Thomasina had cried out and suddenly seemed so weak, but as she drifted into sleep, she thought that if having done this – maybe even having to do it again – meant she could stay in this beautiful house and be given silk gowns and a real studio, then perhaps she could manage it. Father was always complaining about how much things cost nowadays, and saying, 'Oh my goodness, just look at the household books this month', or wondering how he could afford to get the roof of Toft House repaired, and Maud thought she would enjoy not having to hear about that.

But as she finally tumbled over into sleep, she was guiltily aware of hoping that this was not something Thomasina would expect to happen very often.

But Thomasina expected 'It' to happen a great many times – practically every night and sometimes during the night as well. There were even some mornings when 'It' happened straight after they woke up. Maud hated the early-morning times most of all; she always felt crumpled and stale when she woke up, and thought that if she had to be prodded by Thomasina's hands and fingers and be made to prod Thomasina back, she would have much preferred to get out of bed and wash, clean her teeth and brush her hair first.

But there were compensations. Three days after that night they had driven into the nearby town to talk to someone about artists' materials, and had returned to Quire House with the forward seat of the carriage piled with packages containing silky paintbrushes, sticks of charcoal, blocks of satiny paper and – best of all – a real easel which was to be set up in the music room.

'That will be your very own room,' said Thomasina watching Maud unpack her parcels and smiling indulgently. 'And next week we'll see about a new piano.'

So really, being prodded and licked a few times each night (and some mornings), was quite a modest price to pay for such bounty. Maud thought that surely to goodness she could learn to put up with it.

Apart from the inevitability of 'It', Maud's days at Quire were filled with good things. Sketching in the park where you could make the trees appear to have faces – 'How very macabre,'

Thomasina said when she saw them – and mastering new piano pieces. She was trying to move away from the delicate filigree sounds of Chopin and Debussy, to more ambitious works: Mozart, Beethoven, Paganini.

'That's a bit gloomy,' said Thomasina, listening to Maud playing Schumann's piano arrangement of one of Paganini's *Caprices*. 'What's it supposed to represent?'

Maud had already realized that Thomasina, so kind and generous, had absolutely no glimmering of the intriguing darknesses you could find inside music, or the way it had a voice that told you things you had not known. But she tried to explain about Paganini, who had composed beautiful eerie music, and had been such a virtuoso on the violin that at one time he had even been suspected of being in league with the devil.

'I'm not surprised after hearing that,' said Thomasina caustically.

And then, on the very evening of Thomasina's meeting at Latchkill, while they were having dinner, came the bolt from the blue.

Thomasina said she wanted Maud to have a child.

At first Maud stared at Thomasina in bewilderment, because although she had only the sketchiest idea of how babies were born, she did know that a man had to be involved.

But Thomasina said what a lovely thing it would be – a little baby of their very own to look after and bring up. It would mean that Thomasina would have an heir (or heiress) for Quire House and the farms and cottages. This was not the main reason of course, but it was something to consider.

Maud listened to all this, and then nervously broached the question of the man, to which Thomasina replied quite casually that there would have to be a man, of course, but that was nothing to worry about. These things could be very easily arranged; she would see to it all, and would tell Maud what had to be done.

CHAPTER SEVEN

Thomasina Forrester was not much given to introspection – life was too busy for that – but during these last few weeks she had several times paused to wonder how it was that something could slyly trickle into your mind and end in almost taking possession of you.

A child. That was the idea that had come from nowhere and had gradually come to occupy her mind so overwhelmingly. A child who could be brought up in all Quire's traditions, and who would one day inherit the place and carry those traditions forward into the twentieth century. People said it was wrong to become too attached to buildings and old customs, that these things did not matter, but they mattered to Thomasina because she had been brought up believing in them. She loved Quire with a fierce possessiveness. She would like to think of it going on and on, lived in by people who appreciated and cared for it, and she would like to think of herself going on and on as well: a local institution, about whom people smiled and said, 'Ah, Miss Forrester. She represents Quire and everything it stands for. She *is* Quire.'

Thomasina found this image very satisfactory. It was her forthcoming birthday – her fortieth, such a watershed for a female – that had set her thinking about Quire's future, and what would happen to it when she died. She was prepared to give death a good run for its money, but even so . . .

In the early days of her infatuation with Maud she had wondered about leaving the place to her, but she could see now that she must have been besotted to the point of madness even to consider it, because Maud would never cope. She could never control reprobates like Cormac Sullivan, or keep that furtive old lecher, Reverend Skandry in check, or play a useful part in the administering of the Forrester Benevolent Trust, or fight against the impractical idealism of Daniel Glass. Maud would not, in fact, be able to cope with any of the things Thomasina coped with as a matter of course.

And there was something else Thomasina was becoming increasingly aware of. Maud seemed to have what Thomasina thought of as pockets of darkness within her mind. Only last week she had found a sketch at the back of Maud's wardrobe – purely by accident, of course, she was not one to pry – but really a rather dreadful drawing of a fearsome-looking woman with sly eyes. Thomasina had found the sketch macabre, although it had been difficult to say exactly why. Something about the mouth, was it? Yes, there was something very unsettling about the mouth: it had a greedy, wet look to it. Very unpleasant. In the end, she had replaced the sketch carefully so Maud would not know she had found it, but had resolved to search Maud's things regularly.

There was no reason for Maud to succumb to these dark moods, and what she had to be macabre about, Thomasina did not know. The child wanted for nothing: she had a beautiful house to live in and a devoted lover and friend to share her bed. The pity was that innocent unworldly Maud did not know just how adroit and practised a lover she did have. Thomasina could have named half a dozen females who would not have been a quarter as skilful as she was with Maud!

But as is so often the way with these matters, Maud's very prudishness made her even more alluring. That reluctance, that air of not really liking being made love to, of having to be seduced every time was irresistible. A challenge. Thomasina had the feeling that if Maud were suddenly to become eager, she might lose all interest. But for the moment . . . for the moment it drove her wild, and she could hardly keep her hands off the child.

But how far could Maud be considered as the key to Quire's future?

As things stood, if Thomasina died Quire would pass to her cousin Simon, always providing he had not drunk himself into an early grave or a debtors' gaol, either of which were possible. The thought of Quire in Simon's reckless hands was a bad one, in fact Thomasina would almost rather see someone like that reprobate Cormac Sullivan have the place. There would not be a pheasant left in the woods, of course, and goodness knew the kind of ladies who might be imported into the bedrooms, but Cormac would keep up all the old traditions because he understood about houses and land and would be a far better trustee than Simon.

The only other solution was for Thomasina to marry and have a child of her own. This was out of the question. Not only was the thought of being in bed with a man utterly repulsive, the knowledge that she would have to yield to a man's authority was repulsive as well. No, marriage was not to be thought of, even with the prospect of a son of her own.

But the idea of a child – a son – would not go away. Was there any way a child could be acquired without Thomasina marrying? How could it be contrived? Who could its father be? For a wild moment the image of the cat-faced child in Seven Dials rose up before her eyes, and she could almost see the son the girl would have: strong and tough and rebellious. The girl would probably do it as well if Thomasina paid her enough, and she could find her easily enough: she had her address on a half sheet of paper, which she kept discreetly at the back of her bureau.

But if there was to be a child it had better be Maud's, although Maud would have to be coaxed to take part in the conception, never mind endure the birth. Still, there were ways of breaking down the resistance of a shrinking prudish virgin. Not violence, of course, nothing so crude, but perhaps something discreetly stirred in Maud's food that would make her drowsy? Nothing harmful. There was laudanum which was easy enough to obtain, or even opium which was smoked in certain London clubs. Simon might know how to get hold of opium, or there was the ramshackle house in Seven Dials. A smile lifted the corners of Thomasina's lips at the thought. The occupants of that house would certainly be able to get opium, although the cat-faced girl would charge at least triple for it. There would be some reason for needing the money – the girl always had a good reason: a sister who was sick was a favourite one.

And then Simon wrote to say he was utterly destitute again and his creditors were chasing him all over London. If there was any possibility of his dearest Thomasina helping him out – for old times' sake and all that – he would be eternally her slave, and would do anything she asked of him.

Anything she asked.

The plan slid as sleekly and as smoothly as a serpent into Thomasina's mind.

Latchkill Asylum for the Insane
Day Book: Sunday 26th September
Report by Nurse Bryony Sullivan

Reaper Wing residents allowed in recreation yard last night in accordance with Dr Glass's instructions. (6.45 p.m. to 7.30 p.m.) However, tonight several displayed reluctance to return to wing afterwards, and two were downright defiant and had to be sedated, although nets did not have to be used this time, which is one mercy.

Matron Prout called in Dr Glass, and asked for his approval in putting a stop to this recreation hour. However, Dr Glass says very firmly that it must continue, since it's the only fresh air (and degree of normality) Reaper Wing residents are likely to get. Pointed out that isolated outbreak of childish tantrums hardly on level with French Revolution.

Memorandum to Kitchens
Please to ensure that patients in Reaper Wing are only served with plain bread and water for the next two days – a light diet is very beneficial in calming agitated patients.

There is no need for Dr Glass to be informed of this small and unimportant alteration in their routine.
Signed *F. Prout (Matron)*

Latchkill Asylum for the Insane
Day Book: Tuesday 28th September

7.00 p.m.
Matron caught Dora Scullion and Nurse Bryony Sullivan smuggling supper tray into Reaper Wing. (Vegetable broth and slice of cold roast lamb from midday dinner.)

Both reprimanded by Matron.

Memorandum to Bursar
Please ensure that the week's wages for Dora Scullion (skivvy) and Bryony Sullivan (nurse) are docked by three shillings and five shillings respectively.

Signed *F. Prout (Matron)*

* * *

Antonia did not feel like eating, but she heated some tinned soup for herself, and fed the remains of the smoked salmon to Raffles. There would be a perfectly innocent explanation as to how he had got in – perhaps Godfrey Toy had a key to the cottage and had let the cat in by mistake. This did not explain how Raffles had got the salmon out of the fridge, but it was either that or back to the ghosts or Antonia's own madness. No contest, then. Sorry, Godfrey, for the moment you'll have to be first suspect.

After the soup, she carried a cup of tea back to her favourite part of the cottage, the dining area by the stairs, and flipped on the laptop. The wall light directly over the table cast a pool of soft light, and the heater near the stairs gave out a pleasant warmth. Raffles padded across the floor to inspect the laptop, and apparently satisfied that it did not provide either a threat or an amusement, curled himself up at the foot of the stairs with the tolerant air of one prepared to keep the humans company until something more alluring turned up. It was rather comforting to have him there; Antonia had forgotten how companionable cats could be. She had forgotten quite a lot about companionship during the past five years.

After the rape in the showers, and after her attackers had gone swaggering back to the block, she had been violently sick. She had managed to turn on the shower taps and crouch shivering beneath the jets of water, trying to wash away the smell and the feel and the taste of what had happened.

She did not intend to report the attack. It did not take much logic to know that to do so would only cause further trouble, but her head and mouth had been knocked against the edge of the shower cubicle, and a small scalp wound was bleeding quite badly. It was noticed of course, and she was taken to the prison's infirmary. When she came out, she was moved to what was termed the high-risk wing.

In a curious way, this had been much easier. There she was with the real killers and the child beaters, all of them herded together in one section for protection from the rest of the prisoners – it had seemed that the stories about ordinary thieves and drug dealers hating child molesters were perfectly true – but because of her training she found these women much easier to deal with. A great many of them had suffered abuse in their own childhoods, and some of them displayed unmistakable signs of mental illness, but a number of them were intelligent and articulate, diligently attending classes for creative writing or art or taking Open University degree courses. After a while Antonia even formed one or two wary friendships and managed to forget, sometimes for quite long stretches, that these were women who had committed vicious murders or were guilty of violence against children.

Donna Robards knew all about Antonia's life in prison because she had made it her business to find out.

She had not been drawn into any of the publicity surrounding the trial, and the police had not called her to give evidence. They had interviewed her, of course, and she had told them that her brother's death and the way he had died would be her life's tragedy. Disagreements or rows between them? No, not at all. She and her brother hardly ever disagreed, and they certainly never had rows. But although the newspapers had ferreted around to find out about his family, Donna thought they had been looking for something a bit more sensational than an unremarkable sister, and most of them had preferred the angle of Don being alone and defenceless. The tabloids had gone all out for the image of a manipulative, sex-hungry older woman exploiting a younger man's infatuation. Donna did not think she had been mentioned by any of them.

At the time she had been bitterly resentful at being ignored – she wanted people to know her as Don's dearly-loved sister – but as the months went along, and as her plan began to take firmer shape, she saw how it would work to her advantage. If people did not know about her – especially the people at Antonia's hospital – she would be able to work quietly and anonymously against the bitch. In any case, by the time her plan was ready to put into action, anyone who had known that Don had a sister, would have forgotten.

After the first few months they had given Weston a cell to herself, and assigned her to work in the prison library. A very easy imprisonment for the bitch who had killed Donna's beloved brother, and a very short one, as well! Eight years, that was all they had given her. It was an insult to Don's memory. On Antonia's first night in prison, Donna had known that since the stupid courts and the feeble justice system had not been prepared to deal properly with this creature, this seducer of young men, then she would have to do it herself. The hows and the whens of the punishment would need to be carefully thought out, but she had eight years to do that. As for the *where* . . .

Donna smiled the secret smile – the smile she had once kept for Don, and that no one else would ever see now. There was only one place where punishment could be properly administered to this murdering bitch, and that was the place of Donna's own childhood – the place where her parents had taken her and Don every summer.

The tiny market town of Amberwood in Cheshire. Charity Cottage in the grounds of Quire House: the cottage Donna's parents had liked so much and had rented for a month every summer. A place of great atmosphere, Donna's mother used to say. So restful.

And on Amberwood's outskirts was the old mill. Twygrist. Twygrist was not restful. When Donna thought about it – when she thought of what had happened inside it – the smile curved her lips again, and the embryo plan to destroy Antonia Weston took a darker turn. *Twygrist.*

Could Weston somehow be got to Amberwood when she was released? Once there, could she be lured out to Twygrist?

CHAPTER EIGHT

Maud's birthday present to Thomasina was a framed charcoal drawing she had made of Thomasina standing in the main doorway of Quire House. She had had it properly framed, and had wrapped it in gold-spangled paper. Thomasina was very pleased; she said they would choose a well-lit place to hang it so people could properly admire it. Perhaps the music room would be a good idea.

Maud was glad Thomasina was so pleased, and relieved Thomasina had not seen her first attempt at the sketch. Halfway through she had suddenly seen that she had drawn Thomasina as immensely tall, with dreadful greedy eyes and large teeth, like the ogresses in the stories, whose appetites were inclined towards human children, and who plotted to steal them away. How dreadful of her, after all Thomasina's kindness.

During breakfast, opening her letters, Thomasina said, in what Maud thought was a slightly too casual voice, that she had invited her cousin Simon to stay at Quire for a week or so.

'And he's written to say he'll be here this afternoon. He's in financial difficulties again of course – that's a common occurrence with Simon – but he's the nearest thing I've got to a brother. He spent a lot of his school holidays at Quire; my father always thought him a bit weak and too much of a drifter to ever do any good, but he's a charming drifter and an entertaining companion so I shan't mind having him around. If he gets bored he can go rough shooting with Cormac Sullivan.'

Maud thought it was nice that Thomasina's cousin would be there for her birthday dinner, and Thomasina said they would have a very good evening. After dinner Maud could play some music, providing it was not one of those gloomy pieces by that man who had been refused Christian burial or something, so that his coffin had languished in a cellar for months. Paganini, was it? Well, whatever he had been called, they did not want him tonight.

Thomasina seemed quite excited about Simon's arrival; Maud even began to wonder if there could be something romantic between them, although that was not very likely. Thomasina had no time for men and she looked on Simon as a brother, she had said so.

But there was a hectic colour in her face which was unusual because she was normally sallow-skinned, and her eyes had a glittery look. Maud hoped it did not mean Thomasina wanted 'It' to happen that night. For the last few nights she had pretended to fall asleep as soon as she got into bed, and it was nearly a week since 'It' had happened. So Thomasina might consider it was time for a particularly strenuous session, and since it was her birthday Maud supposed it would be ungenerous to refuse. But the prospect was daunting. There were nights when the stroking and poking seemed to last for hours, and Maud's hands sometimes ached the next day from doing the things that Thomasina liked her to do.

('Dear me, rheumatism at your age,' Maud's father had said when she had visited him, seeing her unconsciously massaging her fingers, and Maud had had to laugh and say that of course it was not rheumatism; she had been practising a particularly difficult piece on the piano. It was unthinkable that her father should so much as suspect what she and Thomasina did together.)

* * *

At dinner Simon was very attentive to Maud, passing dishes to her and pouring wine into her glass. Maud tried not to drink too much of the wine because she was developing a headache, but Simon said a glass of good wine worked wonders for headaches, in fact it worked wonders for all areas of the body. Thomasina said, rather sharply, that that remained to be seen, and she would prefer Simon to moderate his drinking tonight, but Simon only grinned.

'Worried about vintner's droop? I've never been known to fail yet, old girl.'

Thomasina said very sharply that the dinner table was not the place for masculine coarseness, and Simon was not to call her old girl. Maud looked from one to the other in bewilderment.

'We shan't need anything else,' said Thomasina to Mrs Minching when the coffee was brought in. She said this dismissively – she could be quite brusque with the servants – and Maud thought Mrs Minching looked cross as she went out.

Thomasina did not seem to notice or if she did, she did not care. She looked directly at Maud and smiled. Maud felt a nervous tremor at the pit of her stomach. This was the smile she had glimpsed on Thomasina's face several times recently: the smile that had somehow got into that first shameful sketch; the smile that seemed to come up from Thomasina's very marrow, and said, I'm going to enjoy you . . .

Maud drank her coffee, wishing it was not always so very strong at Quire House, but Thomasina could not bear it wishy-washy. Tonight, though, it tasted quite bitter.

Thomasina got up from her chair and moved round the table to Maud. She was saying something about it being time to tell Maud the plan she had made with Simon. But Maud's headache was getting worse and there was a dull roaring in her ears. Thomasina's words seemed to be coming from down a long, wind-swept tunnel. Simon had got up from his chair as well, and came towards her. He had the same smile as Thomasina and his face was flushed with excitement or maybe from the wine he had drunk – he had drunk quite a lot, in spite of what Thomasina had said.

From a long way away she heard Thomasina say, 'I hope you haven't given her too much?' and Simon replied, 'A few drops in her wine and then in the coffee, that's all.'

Thomasina's voice came again, a bit sharper this time, saying she hoped Simon knew what he was doing.

'Of course I do,' said Simon, and bent over Maud's chair, taking her arms and pulling her to her feet. Maud discovered she was quite dizzy and it was difficult to stand up. Simon seemed to understand this and put an arm around her waist to support her.

At first she thought they were going to carry her upstairs and leave her to sleep, and she was deeply grateful. The thought of falling fathoms down into a sleep where there would be no headache and no queer distortion of sounds was wonderful. It must have been her headache that had made her see the glinting-eyed smiles and the greedy, wet-looking teeth earlier on.

There was a draught of cold air as they went out into the main hall, and it cleared Maud's head slightly. It had been suffocatingly hot in the dining room tonight. Perhaps all she needed was a little fresh air.

It was not suffocatingly hot in her bedroom; it was pleasantly warm from the fire burning brightly in the hearth. She began to thank Simon and Thomasina for bringing her upstairs, saying she would get undressed and get into bed. Surely Thomasina would not be expecting to do 'It' tonight? Surely she would sleep in the adjoining room, as she had done a couple of weeks ago when she had a cold and could not stop sneezing?

But Thomasina bent over Maud, unfastened her gown and peeled it down, and then removed her underthings. She stroked Maud's legs and her breasts and Maud felt a stab of anger because, birthday or not, it was thoughtless of Thomasina to do this when she must see how unwell she was. The room began to spin, and the light from the fire became a vaguely sinister crimson blur like blood seeping out into the walls and soaking its way up to the ceiling . . . like a fire behind thick clanging iron doors . . .

Thomasina stood up, and through her dizzy confusion, Maud saw she was undressing very quickly, flinging her things onto the floor. So she did mean to get into bed. The thought of Thomasina's stringy body pressing against her, and Thomasina's hard-boned fingers jabbing inside her was almost more than Maud could bear. Thomasina seldom bothered to trim her fingernails properly so rough hangnails scraped the inside of Maud's thighs.

The hangnails scraped her thighs now as Thomasina thrust her hands between Maud's legs in the urgent way she did if she had drunk more wine than usual at dinner. Maud tried not to shudder or look over Thomasina's shoulder to where the clock ticked away the minutes until she could relax and go to sleep. Fifteen minutes would it take? Sometimes it was a lot longer, but perhaps tonight it would be quick. Where was Simon, though? He must have gone out of the room without her hearing, but when? She had not heard the door open or close. She half turned her head to see the rest of the room, trying not to mind about Thomasina's probing hands.

It was all right; the room held only herself and Thomasina. Maud looked back at the clock, thinking that surely when the minute hand reached the half hour this would be over. She saw a movement from the deep wing chair by the fire – the comfortable old chair in whose depths she had often curled up with a book before going to bed.

The chair had been turned away from the fire, so it faced the bed. Somebody was seated in it, and whoever it was had red eyes from the firelight, and a sly grin. Maud frowned and struggled to make sense of all this. She tried to push Thomasina away, because there was somebody here in the room with them – there was somebody *watching* them!

A log broke apart in the hearth, sending cascades of sparks shooting out, and Maud saw that it was Simon sitting in the chair. Simon Forrester was seated silently in the bedroom, watching the two of them naked on the bed, seeing how Thomasina's fingers were thrusting up between Maud's legs, seeing how she had pulled one of Maud's hands down between her own thighs, so Maud could do the prodding and finger-stroking that made Thomasina gasp and shudder.

Simon was looking straight at them and, as she met his eyes, Maud felt as if she had been flung, neck-deep into boiling water. Fierce shame at being seen like this by a man engulfed her. She struggled free of Thomasina's hands, and clawed blindly at the sheets trying to drag them over her, but it was already too late, Simon had seen, he had *seen* . . .

She cried out to Thomasina to look across the room, but Thomasina was shuddering and jerking and pulling Maud's unwilling hand deeper, and she did not seem to hear, even when Simon got up out of the chair and came towards the bed. His eyes were still shining redly from the glow of the fire and his mouth was slack and wet – it looked ugly, Maud hated it. He had pulled off his tie, and as he crossed the room he was tearing at the buttons of his shirt. Maud saw that his chest was sprinkled with coarse dark hair.

Thomasina moved her hands away from Maud at last, and turned to look up at Simon. Something seemed to pass between them – some kind of acknowledgement, Maud thought it was. Thomasina said, 'Ready, Simon?' and Simon said, in a queer thick throaty voice, 'Never readier, my dear.' He paused, and then said, 'By God, Thomasina, I shall have a good tale to tell in the clubs.'

'You do and I'll make sure half of London believes you're an impotent imbecile,' said Thomasina in the most vicious voice Maud had ever heard her use.

But Simon only smiled. 'Imbecile, perhaps. Impotent, never. Didn't you know that it's every man's wildest fantasy to watch two females in bed together?'

To Maud's horror, he threw off his shoes, and unbuttoned his trousers and took them off. Then he lay down on the bed next to her.

She thought at first that between the pulsing headache and the burning humiliation she might faint; she would indeed have been very glad to tumble down into a black pit of unknowing. But something – perhaps it was even the embarrassment itself – kept her from fainting. Even when Simon lay right on top of her, scraping her breasts with his coarse black chest hair, and crushing her ribs so that it was difficult to breathe, she stayed awake and aware.

There was a kind of fumbling between her legs – at first she thought it was Thomasina's hands again, but then she realized they were masculine hands: larger-boned and with rougher-feeling skin. Oh God, oh God, this could not be happening. But it was. He pushed her legs very wide apart and wriggled his body between them. She felt the skin of his thighs, and a hard insistent thrusting that seemed to be coming from his body and even though his weight was making it difficult to breathe, Maud drew in a gasping breath to cry out. But Thomasina clamped a hand over her mouth and whispered to her to stay quiet, asking if she wanted the servants to hear and come running? This was all part of the plan, hissed Thomasina, it was necessary if they were to have what they both wanted.

The threat of servants almost silenced Maud, but she managed to fight free for long enough to gasp out a question, 'What plan? I don't understand—'

'For pity's sake, the baby,' said Thomasina, sounding exasperated. 'I thought you knew that. I thought you understood.'

But Maud had not known and had not understood. She did not really understand now. All she knew was that she was being half suffocated by a man whose breath smelt of sour wine, and whose body smelt alien and sweaty, and who was doing something to her that was starting to hurt very much indeed.

'I know it's horrid, my love,' Thomasina was saying, and the exasperation had gone from her tone now. 'But it'll soon be done, and then it'll be worth it. You know that. It will be our child, really, yours and mine.' Incredibly, her free hand came up to stroke Maud's hair and then moved down to caress her breast.

But Maud could not spare any attention for Thomasina, her whole being was focused on Simon, on trying to get free and on fighting the pain. Whatever Simon was doing, and however he was doing it, it hurt. Something was slamming hard into her, setting up the same kind of pain she had every month – the pain you must never talk about, only to a doctor. But it had never been as severe as this.

'Almost there,' said Thomasina's voice in her ear. Maud wanted to shout at Thomasina to shut up, because it was not Thomasina lying here, being crushed and with this rhythmic banging going on and on inside her, bruising and tearing . . .

She began to sob and hit out at Simon's face, but Thomasina caught her hands at once and imprisoned them. 'Little cat,' she said lovingly. Maud heard, with a fresh wave of panic, that Thomasina's voice had taken on a familiar thick throatiness. She's finding this exciting, thought Maud, and this was almost the worst thing yet, because Thomasina ought not to find this brutishness exciting.

Simon's face was only inches from Maud's and his breathing was beginning to sound like the pumping of a rusty engine. Thomasina was telling him to go on, go *on*, *Simon*, and saying something about the bloody wine, told you not to drink so much, if you lose it now I'll kill you . . .

She thought Simon gasped something about being nowhere near losing it – 'Hard as the devil's forehead, trust me for that, you bitch.' The pain slammed deeper, tearing her to shreds, and then the rhythmic pumping suddenly became very fast and the pain scaled impossible heights, and Maud began to sob and tried to fight him off, but he was too strong for her. She half fell into a black spinning cavern where there was only the pain and the crushing heaviness of his body.

Simon let out a groan and slumped down, his face buried in Maud's neck so that she could feel his bristly chin. She really must be bleeding, because there was a thick wetness between her legs, and if it *was* blood it would be all over the sheets, and that would serve Thomasina right because she would have to explain it to the servants . . . She wondered if she would bleed to death. Then she wondered whether she cared, because the world had shrunk to this firelit room and the smell of sweat and stale wine, and to the cramping pain at the base of her stomach.

Simon rolled off her, still gasping hoarsely. His eyes closed and he dropped into a dreadful snoring sleep. His mouth fell open and the stale wine on his breath gusted into Maud's face. Even so Maud drew in a shuddering breath of relief, because whatever this had been, it seemed to be over.

After a space of time that might have been two minutes or two hours, she was roused by Simon stumbling back to his own bed. He paused at the door, and smiled across at Maud: it was a fuzzy drunken smile but his eyes still had that horrid, knowing, gloating look. He said, 'Sleep well, Maud,' and went out. Thomasina stood at the side of the bed for a moment, looking down at Maud, smiling the same terrible smile. Then she followed Simon out of the room.

CHAPTER NINE

Maud lay absolutely still, hardly noticing the ache between her legs. There was no room in her mind for the pain of her body or the bloodied state of her nightgown; her entire being was filled with terror in case the cousins came back.

She stared into the darkness, seeing Simon's greedy gloating smile, seeing Thomasina's face red and ugly with excitement, and hearing her voice urging Simon to go on . . .

Thomasina had gone into the nearby bathroom; Maud could hear the clanking of the plumbing as Thomasina washed and brushed her teeth as she always did before going to bed. Was Thomasina going to come to bed as if this was an ordinary night? If she so much as touched Maud, Maud thought she would scream.

But when Thomasina came back she got quietly into bed and lay without speaking. Maud did not move; she was reliving the feel of Simon's body, and the deep spiking pain. What if Thomasina and Simon intended to do this to her every night? She could not bear it. She would do anything other than endure it.

With the thought, the germ of a plan slid into her mind. At first she thought she would not dare follow it, but when she considered a bit more, she knew it was worth taking any risk if it meant she would get away.

She waited for about ten minutes and then got out of bed, not particularly troubling to be quiet, and went across to the big walk-in cupboard. Almost at once there was a movement from the bed, and Thomasina's voice, a bit blurry from all the wine she had drunk earlier, said, 'Maud? Where are you going?'

Maud's heart leapt up into her throat and the palms of her hands turned clammy with nervous sweat, but she said, 'Bathroom. To wash and get a clean nightgown. I'm in a bit of a mess.' She waited, willing Thomasina to open her eyes and see the blood.

Thomasina did open her eyes. She looked at Maud and said, 'Oh. Oh yes, I see. It's on the sheet as well. We'd better tell the servants that it's your monthly bleeding, not that it's anything to do with them. It's stopped though, hasn't it?'

'I think so.'

'Poor little virgin bird,' said Thomasina, and closed her eyes again.

Poor little virgin bird. The words ought not to have stung – virginity was something to be prized, it was what every good girl saved for marriage – but there had been a patronizing pity in Thomasina's voice that Maud hated. She clenched her fists and thought that one day she would make Thomasina pay.

She took her dressing gown from its hook on the back of the cupboard door, and made a play of putting it on. In fact she put on her dark woollen cloak, wrapping it firmly around her, then draping the dressing gown on top of it. If Thomasina was watching in the unlit bedroom it was not very likely she would realize what Maud had done. Even so, Maud was careful to keep the cupboard door wide open to screen her from the bed. Under cover of pretending to look for her slippers, she took the day-gown she had worn that morning, and crammed it under her dressing gown. Underthings were in a small drawer; she grabbed several garments more or less at random, and thrust them into the dressing-gown pockets along with stockings. Shoes? She remembered she had rubber boots in the little room near the sculleries; she could slip those on downstairs.

Her heart was hammering as she left the bedroom. Supposing Thomasina came after her? But there was no movement from the bed, and Maud reached the bathroom safely, shut and locked the door.

The bathroom had been very modern in Thomasina's father's day, but it was not modern now. The plumbing clanked embarrassingly loudly so that everyone in the house knew when you visited the lavatory which Maud normally hated, but tonight it would hide the sounds of her escape. First, though, she threw off the bloodied nightgown and sponged the blood from her legs. She supposed she ought to be frightened by it, but she was beyond being frightened and Thomasina had seemed to think it was all right. There were gluey smears of something that did not seem to be blood on Maud's legs as well; she had no idea what they might be, but she washed them off.

Then she pulled on her underthings and the day-dress, flung the cloak around her shoulders, and pulled the cistern chain. Under cover of the pipes banging and the water whooshing, Maud tiptoed down the stairs and through the darkened house. Her rubber boots were where they usually were, and she stepped into them, and slid back the bolt on the scullery door.

She ran across the parkland. A thin dispirited rain was falling, but she did not care. She did not care, either, that it was a fairly long way to Toft House: she would have walked all night to get there. As she went along, she thought up a story to tell her father. Once inside dear familiar Toft House, she need never go out again. Her mother had gone out less and less over the years – Maud could remember that very clearly indeed. She could remember how frightened her mamma had become of the world. 'Not safe,' she used to say, cowering in her room with the curtains closed. 'Nowhere is safe.'

Maud understood now how her mamma must have felt. Tonight she was frightened of the world, frightened that no matter where she went, Simon and Thomasina Forrester would be waiting for her.

As she went down Quire's wide tree-lined carriageway, she heard a soft laugh from somewhere, and her heart jumped with fear before she realized it was her own laughter. This was quite worrying because only people who were not wholly normal laughed out loud to themselves. What if I am a little bit mad, thought Maud defiantly. I think I might be allowed to be a bit mad after what's just happened.

She went on towards the gates, wondering if she would have to climb over them; the gardeners usually locked them when they went home. The night was filled with little stirrings and rustlings. Twice Maud froze thinking there was a soft footfall behind her, but when she whipped round, nothing stirred. Just to be sure, she stepped off the drive and walked on the soft grass that fringed it. Ah, that was better.

But the sound came again, and this time it was nearer and more definite. Maud stopped in the deep shadow of one of the old trees, and listened. Surely it was only the rain dripping from the trees? Or was it someone creeping along after her? Thomasina? No, Thomasina would come stomping loudly and angrily through the night, shouting for Maud, like the ogres in fairy stories did when they put on seven-league boots and strode across the landscape after the humans.

Simon would not stomp through the night shouting. Simon would slink slyly and silently, smiling his dreadful smile, his hands opening and closing as if they were savouring the thought of Maud's body again. Could it be Simon who was coming after her? Whoever it was, he – or she – was a lot nearer. Maud cast a frightened glance around her. Could she run down the drive and hope to outrun her pursuer, and get to the gates first? But if she had to climb over them – they were very high and she was encumbered with her long skirts and cloak – Simon, if it was Simon, would be on her before she was halfway over.

She would have to hide. Quire's park was quite big and there were lots of trees and shrubberies, but Simon and Thomasina knew every inch of the parkland because they had grown up and played their games here. Maud shuddered away from the thought of what kind of horrid games those two might have played as children.

Then she saw the little path that turned off the carriageway and wound into the trees and beyond the copse, and she remembered the cottage Thomasina's father had built to house workers on the estate, and Thomasina nowadays rented to that poacher – the man everyone said was a scandal and a disgrace. Sullivan, that was his name. Irish. He was a poacher and probably a thief. He had a daughter a few years older than Maud; Maud did not know her, but she thought she had a peculiar name. Something to do with hedgerows or meadows or something.

She stepped back into the deeper shadows, pulling her cloak more firmly around her, so that no glimmer of paleness would show from her gown. Yes, there went the footsteps again. Somebody was definitely creeping through the darkness behind her.

Maud bit down a gasp of fear, and began to run down the narrow path. The soles of her boots skidded in the soft wet ground several times and low branches caught at her hair like snatching goblin fingers, but she was beyond caring. She had no idea if Mr Sullivan or his daughter would hide her, and she could not think how she would tell them what had happened, but surely they would not turn her away.

Here was the cottage, directly ahead of her. She had a pain in her side from running, but she was almost there and she was almost safe.

The cottage was in darkness. Maud supposed she should have expected this, but somehow the sight of the curtained windows brought her to an abrupt halt, and doubt rushed into her mind. Could she really hammer on a stranger's door at this hour – it must be well past midnight by now – and say she was being pursued by two mad creatures who did terrible things to her body?

She glanced back nervously; there was no one in sight, but she could hear her pursuer coming along the path. Maud darted around the side of the cottage, keeping well in the shadows, and there, at the back of the building, was a little huddle of outbuildings jutting out from the main part of the cottage. Wash-house and privy, most likely. Would they be locked?

The first one was locked, and Maud, gasping with terror, hearing her pursuer coming along the path, moved to the other one. Wash-house, was it? Coal shed? It did not matter because its lock was a brittle flimsy affair, and it snapped when she pushed against it. The door swung in and Maud tumbled thankfully inside, closing the door and leaning back against it.

It was the cottage's wash-house. It had a stone floor and brick walls, and on one side of the door was a big mangle with a huge copper boiler on the other side, nastily crusted with green where the pipe came out of it. Other than this there was only a deep sink under the little window; the window itself was a bit grimy and cobwebby so the outside looked blurred as if there was thick fog everywhere.

She was shaking so badly she was almost afraid her ribs would break, and there was a pain in her chest from running along the path. But she kept her eyes on the door. Doors could be dangerous things; you never knew what might lie behind them.

After a moment she managed to stop gasping for breath, and listened for the sound of her pursuer. Had he gone? No, here he came, walking quietly, but betrayed by the wet ground – she could hear his feet squelching in the mud. Her heart began to hammer against her ribs all over again. He would surely look in here, and he could not fail to see her.

He was trying the other door – there was the impatient clicking of its latch, and then a soft creak as he pushed against it. Would he see the broken lock on this door? There was nowhere she could hide, but was there any way she could fool him by wedging the door closed? Maud looked frantically about her. Could she drag the mangle across the door? No, it was much too heavy for her, and even if she could manage it, it would take too long and he would hear her.

There was a scrape of sound outside, and Maud gasped and shrank back against the wall. As she did so there was a movement at the window, and a face appeared in the blurry oblong. It pressed against the pane, the features distorted and terror engulfed Maud so overwhelmingly that for a moment the dank room spun sickeningly around her. She bit down a gasp of fear, because if he heard her, if he realized she was here . . .

But he already knew she was here. Even if he could not see her, he would have sensed her presence in the way predators sensed the presence of their victims.

The latch clicked and the door swung open. The rainy light lay across the floor, and when Maud slowly turned her head she saw the figure outlined in the doorway – an impossibly tall figure it seemed to be, wrapped in a long dark cloak, the hem swishing around booted feet.

The figure stepped inside and spoke. It was not Simon after all, it was Thomasina.

In a perfectly ordinary voice, Thomasina said, 'My dear child, what on earth are you doing here? Let me take you home.'

Thomasina spoke as if nothing very unusual had happened, and for a moment Maud stared at her and wondered if she had dreamt that firelit bedroom and Simon's body suffocating her.

Then she said, 'You pretended to be asleep, but you weren't. You've been following me.'

'Of course I followed you. You were not very subtle, Maud. Scrabbling in the wardrobe for your clothes, and getting dressed in the bathroom. Did you think I didn't know what you were doing?'

'I won't go back to Quire House,' said Maud, and was pleased to hear her voice sounded quite brave. 'If you try to make me go back, I'll scream for help.'

'Scream away. There's no one to hear you. Cormac Sullivan's not very likely to be in his own bed at this hour of the night, and his daughter will be at Latchkill – she's a nurse and she's on night duty. So scream until your throat bursts: no one will hear you.'

Maud had no idea if any of this was true, or if Thomasina was just saying it to keep her quiet.

'And,' said Thomasina, not giving Maud time to reply, 'even if you did scream, and even if anyone did hear you, I have only to say you're a young relative and your mind is a little disturbed; that I'm caring for you.'

'No one would believe that,' said Maud, but she knew people would believe it, because of who Thomasina was. Miss Forrester of Quire House. Important and rich and with that indefinable authority that everyone recognized and respected. Yes, people would believe Thomasina over Maud.

As if she had heard this last thought, Thomasina said, 'My poor child, of course people would believe you were disturbed. I would only have to tell them how I found you huddled in a dank wash-house, when all the time there's a warm comfortable room for you at Quire House, and people there who love you and want you back. You're not displaying much sanity at the moment, are you, Maud?' She paused, and then said, in a soft, pitying voice, 'You do know what happens to people who aren't sane, don't you?'

Latchkill . . . The place of locked doors and barred windows . . . The place you must always avoid when it's spider light . . .

Maud said, 'Yes, I do know. But I'm not mad.'

'Of course not. But perhaps confused. And so you'd better come back with me and be properly looked after,' said Thomasina. Incredibly there was a note of affection in her voice. She held Maud's arm very firmly, and took her outside, pushing the door closed with her foot as she did so. Maud tried to resist but Thomasina's hands were too strong. As they went back across the park Thomasina talked soothingly – something about soon being home and how no one needed to know about this absurd flight through the darkness.

Maud, by this time sobbing with despair, scarcely heard her, but when Thomasina said, 'Where on earth were you going anyway?' she replied, 'I was escaping from you. And Simon. I was running away because of what he did to me.'

'Then you're definitely a little mad,' said Thomasina lightly. 'Half the girls in the county would like my cousin to make love to them. He's greatly admired. In fact he's considered quite a matrimonial catch. I was even thinking we might arrange for the two of you to be married. Wouldn't you like that? Simon would, I know. Oh do stop crying, Maud, and don't shudder like that. It would be a wonderful marriage; your father would be delighted. But we'll talk about it properly in the morning.'

As they went inside Quire House, Thomasina said, 'Don't try shouting to the servants, will you? We don't want them knowing you're a little disturbed. In a small place like this people do love to gossip, and gossip is never particularly kind anywhere. Within twenty-four hours the whole of Amberwood would be convinced you were a raving lunatic.'

Maud thought: that's quite true, but the real truth is that she's afraid of people knowing what she and Simon did to me. She glanced at Thomasina; in the dim light of the passageway off the main hall, Thomasina's eyes were wild, and she was frowning, as if she was making plans in her head. Her grip loosened slightly and Maud wondered if she dared attempt to get away. She could run back along the hall and out through the garden door again. But when she tried to remember if Thomasina had locked or bolted the door when they came in, she could not. And even if she ran as fast as she could, Thomasina would stride across the park again, as she had done earlier, and catch her.

She thought Thomasina would take her back to the big bedroom overlooking the park, but when they reached the first floor, Thomasina hesitated.

'The real worry now, Maud, is that for the moment I don't think I can trust you not to run away again. And I don't want you to do that, my dear. So not this room, I don't think. It's too near the main part of the house and there's no lock on the door. So I'm afraid – yes, I really am afraid it will have to be the next floor.' She glanced at the narrower stairs leading to the second floor. 'But you'll be perfectly comfortable up there.' Again the smile. 'I wouldn't let you be uncomfortable,' said Thomasina. 'I think too much of you.'

'Do you?' said Maud, staring at her.

'My dear girl,' said Thomasina, 'don't you know I'm absolutely devoted to you?'

CHAPTER TEN

Donna and Don Robards had been absolutely devoted to each other. They had been all in all to one another and had not needed anyone else. Donna and Don, a single entity against the world. It had always pleased Donna to think of them in that way, and it pleased her now, even with Don dead.

Within the family they had been Domina and Don. 'So pretty,' their half-Spanish mother had said when they were small. 'The old names for lord and lady.'

Their father, with his permanent round of meetings and reports and too much to do, had liked the names as well. He said they were echoes of almost defunct academic terms for a fellow of Oxford or Cambridge. Not that Domina and Don would need university careers; there would always be more than sufficient money for them to live comfortably without having to work at all. Trust funds were being set up, investments made . . . Domina and Don, fortune's darlings.

'And Domina is so *good* with her little brother,' their mother told everyone, delighted with the timing of her children's birth, perhaps even slightly smug at having managed a three-year gap between them. It was exactly right: it was wide enough for Domina to look after Don while they were small, but narrow enough for it to dwindle to nothing when they were grown up; to allow them to be friends.

To the nearly four-year-old Donna, Don's arrival in her world had been the most wonderful thing she had ever known. He was perfect, this small brother. She spent hours staring into his cot or his pram, sometimes stroking his face. From the very start she had fought his battles and flown into a rage if anyone criticized him. 'Sweet,' said their mother indulgently. 'Domina is so protective of Don.'

When Don reached his teens, people said he was spoilt and a bit selfish and lazy, but that often happened to the children of wealthy parents. Donna knew this to be untrue and mostly due to sheer jealousy. Don was not spoilt and he was not really selfish or lazy. You might perhaps say that different rules applied to him, and you might also add that you did not apply the rules for a carthorse to a thoroughbred.

The simile of a thoroughbred pleased her – Don was sleek and aristocrat-looking, he was exactly like a thoroughbred. His hair was fair and silken, and he was slender and supple. In the summer holidays he lay in the garden of their house, just wearing cotton shorts. Donna usually joined him, pretending to read, but secretly watching him, and seeing how his skin gleamed with health. Once or twice he had asked her to rub sun-tan lotion over his back – he could never reach it all himself and he liked his tan to be even. His skin felt satiny and warm under Donna's hands, and the scent of the lotion and the sun's warmth and the masculine scent of his body blurred together in her mind. She spent a long time rubbing the lotion into his back, and when it was done she waited for him to say he would turn on his back so she could rub the lotion on his front, but he did not.

Lack of money was not something Donna ever thought she would have to cope with, but when she was eighteen and Don was fifteen, their parents died and they had to cope with it very abruptly indeed.

Donna was never sure, afterwards, how they got through that

time. She had been grief-stricken, of course she had, but Don had been in pieces. He cried for hours over their parents' death, flinging himself on his bed, not bothering to hide the sound of his sobbing. He pushed Donna away when she tried to put her arms round him, thinking this was the one time they should cling to one another.

But Don had not wanted Donna's arms. Leave him alone, he'd said. His life was in tatters, and he would never get over this, not if he lived to be a hundred. He wanted to die in this bed, now, tonight; he knew he would never be happy again. Dramatic. Even melodramatic if you wanted to be truthful. He had always been like that and he always got over it, but it had torn Donna apart to hear his grief.

And then within days – *days*! – of the double funeral, they had been dealt a second blow. Their father, it seemed, had been teetering towards bankruptcy, and his business – outwardly so prosperous – had been on the verge of collapse for months.

Donna listened to the solicitors who came to the house to talk to them, and had at first simply stared in blank incomprehension. No money? But that was utter nonsense; of course there was money, there was a great deal of money. Their father had been extremely wealthy – everyone knew that, said Donna. They had this house, cars, ritzy holidays. Her mother bought expensive clothes and jewellery – it was a joke within the family that even mundane things like tights or face flannels went on the Harvey Nichols account. Donna and her brother had both been to costly boarding schools; Don, only fifteen, was still at his school, of course. There were trust funds, investments, fat share portfolios, many of them intended to safeguard her and Don's future. It could not be right that there was no money.

But apparently it was right. As well as there being no money, there were a number of debts and business obligations to be met. There were salaries due to the people in her father's company which had to be paid, said the solicitors solemnly. This house would have to be sold, and the cars and most of the furniture would probably have to go as well – there were some quite valuable pieces and one or two good paintings. There would have to be a proper valuation, of course; they would see to that as soon as possible. Unfortunately the house was heavily mortgaged and the bank would probably call in the debt fairly soon, but something might be salvaged.

Well no, Donna and Don would not be thrown homeless into the world – of course they would not, said the solicitors, shocked at such an idea. A little money would have to be squeezed from somewhere, and a suitable place found for them to live. Unless there was anyone in the family who might take them in? Ah, there was not. No relatives? Oh dear, that was a pity. Well yes, they did appreciate that Donna was eighteen, and therefore an adult . . . Oh yes, she would almost certainly be regarded as Don's legal guardian. And a modest house, or perhaps a little flat would somehow be managed for the two of them.

Donna did not want these stupid smug men squeezing out money to buy a modest house or a flat for them to live in, and she did not want them computing income and selling things or knowing all the details of her father's financial ineptitude. But she did not let them see this, and somehow she managed to control the cold furious rage that welled up inside her. She asked if her mother had been aware of the situation, and the solicitors hemmed and hawed and avoided her eye, and said, Well, possibly she might have, but they were not here to judge.

It was instantly obvious to Donna that her mother had known all along. She had known all about the mounting debts and the tangled finances, and Donna, realizing this, hated her mother very fiercely indeed for continuing to expect expensive holidays and first-class travel and lavish entertaining. She hated her father as well, for continuing to provide all those things, and for not giving so much as a hint to Donna or Don. When Donna thought about her father's deceit and her mother's selfish extravagances she knew she would never forgive either of them, and she was very glad they were dead.

She had politely told the solicitors that she and her brother would be perfectly all right. No, they did not need anyone's help, thank you so much. They would manage. They did not want anyone finding somewhere for them to live; they would find their own place. Donna had already left school and would look after Don, who must, of course, finish his education. Two more years that would be.

To herself she thought that even though they were financially out in the cold, at least she and Don still had each other.

There had been the tag-end of a single-premium insurance policy to cover the rest of Don's school fees, and even if Donna had been agreeable to cashing this in for living on, the terms of the policy would not have allowed it. So Don, protesting angrily, had to go back to school.

There was just enough money for the renting and furnishing of a tiny flat for the two of them to live together. Just about enough. The unfairness of it all was a permanent ache in Donna's throat, but once having found the flat she had taken a job, because it was necessary to have money. She had, in fact, taken several jobs, mostly of the Mayfair receptionist/dinner-parties-in-your-home kind, drifting from one to another, hating almost all of them. But her school French was quite good, and she was fluent in Spanish learnt from her mother, which was occasionally useful.

One or two former friends of her mother helped out with introductions and recommendations. 'Dear Domina, so brave and really quite clever, she'd be so useful to your little business . . . Well no, no actual *qualifications*, but we knew the family – such a tragedy it was, so do employ her if you can.'

It was humiliating to have to depend on people's charity in this way, but Donna put up with it because of Don and because it was necessary to have money. And if nothing else, the jobs filled in the time until Don left school and they could be together, properly and for always. Then something better would turn up. Donna and Don, golden girl and boy.

The flat felt horridly poky after their lovely house, but Donna made it as attractive as she could for when Don came home for the school holidays. She emulsioned walls and painted skirting boards and searched junk shops for nice old pieces of furniture. She furnished Don's bedroom lovingly, putting the very best furniture in this room – a beautiful little Victorian bureau for him to store his things, and a cherrywood table to stand by the window.

She placed the bed so its head would catch the early sun, imagining Don lying in it, warm and safe and cherished, his hair on the pillow looking like spilled honey in the morning sunshine . . .

Exactly as it had looked in the bed at Charity Cottage on that summer's afternoon . . .

Renting Charity Cottage for a month each summer had been a quirk of Donna's mother. Rustic and rural, she had said delightedly when she first discovered the place, somewhere where they could live simply and plainly. She said this every year. 'And usually,' observed Don, 'she says it just before she starts ordering food supplies from Harrods.'

'And just after buying new outfits from Harvey Nichols,' added Donna.

But they quite liked going to Charity Cottage, partly because it was so different from the places they normally went, and because they liked exploring the surrounding countryside. Donna had passed her driving test that summer, which meant she and Don might take the car and go off on their own sometimes. Their mother had a different project each year. So far there had been water-colour painting, a study of old churches and horse riding. One disastrous year it had been tracking down local witchcraft customs.

This year's project was local buildings; she was going to scour the area for really interesting landmarks, and compile a proper, scholarly notebook about their histories. She would illustrate her notebook, of course – she had already asked in Harrods about the right kind of camera, because if you were going to do something you wanted to do it as well as possible.

'Four hundred pounds for a camera and goodness knows how much else for new clothes,' said their father, half-exasperated, half-indulgent. 'Maria, you'll ruin us.' But he smiled as he said this, and Donna, looking back at this memory from the other side of that disastrous summer, thought no one could have told from his voice or his expression how very close to the truth his words must have been.

It had not seemed anything like ruin at the time, nor had it felt like the onset of tragedy. Charity Cottage, that last summer, was exactly as it always was: a bit shabby with its slightly battered furniture, and a bit basic with its old-fashioned kitchen and bathroom. Their parents always had the big bedroom at the front, overlooking the park round Quire House, and Donna and Don had a bedroom each at the back. They went for walks and drives, and cooked the evening meal on the old-fashioned cooker, after which their father usually retired to the bedroom to study reports sent by his assistant. So boring, said their mother gaily, they were supposed to be on holiday, for goodness' sake.

But there was not, actually, a great deal to do at Charity Cottage. Donna and Don played music on the portable CD-player they had brought with them, and their father complained and said music was not what it had been in the sixties. Burt Bacharach and the Beatles and all the great musicals. *Fiddler on the Roof* and *Hair* – goodness, do you remember how shocked everyone was by *Hair*, Maria?

Don thought it was gross to even mention things like that, and Donna thought it embarrassing to have your parents singing 'All You Need is Love' all round the cottage, and trying to remember the sequence of the verses in 'American Pie'.

But after the first week their father discovered all over again how much his children's constant presence interrupted his study of the quarterly business review, and their mother discovered afresh how tedious it was to have to cook every night, and demanded to be taken out to dinner at the local pub, or at the very least into the nearest big town to buy good-quality prepared food. One forgot how extremely tiresome it was to peel potatoes and cut up meat, she said, while as for washing-up after every meal . . .

The only thing that had really been different at that stage of the holiday, had been Maria's project about historic landmarks, and a sudden out-of-the-blue question from her as to whether it might be possible to buy Quire House. It was a bit dilapidated, but it would scrub up very nicely and it would be splendid for summer entertaining and weekend parties, what did anyone think?

What Donna thought – what she later said to Don – was that their mother had spotted a new toy, and was visualizing herself playing lady of the manor. Donna did not much like Quire House which seemed to her a rather sad place, and which Don, who was going through a slightly effete stage, said was an ugly specimen of an ugly architectural period. But they walked dutifully round the house one afternoon, peering in through windows and disturbing jackdaws' nests. Their father was forced into agreeing to try to track down the owner, although the owner would probably be some inaccessible property company and there would be preservation orders and listed-building prohibitions on every square inch of brick so you could not even change a light bulb without permission. That being so, he said, Maria was not to build up any hopes.

Maria Robards promised not to do so, and switched temporarily back to her scavenging expeditions for historic buildings. She went off most afternoons armed with camera and loose-leaved notebook, dressed in co-ordinating trousers and tweed jackets because she refused to be seen in public, or even in private, wearing denim (shudder) or trainers (God forbid).

These well-dressed expeditions, inevitably, took her to Twygrist.

CHAPTER ELEVEN

Twygrist. Even years afterwards, the name conjured up a smothering darkness for Donna.

Twygrist was the old watermill just outside Amberwood's little market town. It was no longer working, but it was a bit of a landmark; local people said, 'Turn left just past Twygrist,' or, 'He lives about a mile along from Twygrist.'

Twygrist might have been any age at all, but it had an air of extreme antiquity as if it had crouched there malevolently all through the Dark Ages. Even the clock set into one wall in memory of somebody or other, looked a bit like a face, so that from some angles you could imagine it was watching you as you went along the road.

Donna's mother was fascinated by Twygrist. She scoured the local library and the offices of the local newspaper to find out about its history, which she related to her family. ('Ad nauseam,' said Don, who thought watermills nearly as gross as spending summer holidays with parents.)

Twygrist, said Maria undaunted by Don, had once stood on the edge of a vast estate owned by the local baronial lords, but a fire had destroyed almost the entire estate in the middle 1800s. After this, somewhere around 1860, the mill had been bought and put into working order by a certain Josiah Forrester, who had clearly been one of those canny Victorian gentlemen with an eye to a profit. 'Your father would have had a lot in common with him, dears.'

Maria was trying to find a photograph of Josiah, although that was proving difficult, with photography having been in its infancy at the time. Still, there might be a painting somewhere – one of those municipal portraits in a library or something. Dundreary whiskers and a large stomach, like Edward VII, most likely.

She was also on the track of a man called George Lincoln, whom Josiah had employed as his miller towards the end of the nineteenth century. George, it seemed, had been a man of some substance. One had not known that millers were so highly regarded, but there were records of him having owned quite a big house with servants, so there you were, you could never tell who might be prosperous from one century to the next. She was going to spend the day at the nearby archive office, to see what she could find out about George and his family.

'Your father's going to drive me straight there after breakfast, aren't you, Jim? It'll be quite a long day, so we'll have lunch out somewhere and get home around mid-afternoon. Are you two sure you won't come with us?'

'Quite sure,' said Don, who had bought several new CDs in Chester the previous day, and was planning to lie on his bed and listen to them.

Maria thought this very antisocial of him, and would have started an argument, but their father interrupted, saying, 'Oh leave the boy alone, my dear, he's probably got girl problems, I know I had them at his age.' Maria retorted that she did not see how having girl problems gave Don an excuse for sulks and moods. This, as Donna could have told them, had the effect of sending Don flouncing from the breakfast table, stumping crossly up the stairs to his bedroom and slamming the door so hard that the crockery on the dresser jiggled.

'Typical teenager,' said Donna's father resignedly, and her

mother suggested they leave Don to his romantic sulks, and that Donna came with them.

But Donna did not feel like chasing millers across half of Cheshire, and her mother would expect her to act as assistant and make masses of tedious notes. So she said she would stay at the cottage, and perhaps walk down to Amberwood later. She could look round the little art gallery – they'd some quite good jewellery last summer. She was into chunky modern jewellery at the moment, said Donna. Don might come with her if he could be torn away from his CDs, but she did not care if he did not. Whatever they did they would be perfectly all right. Yes, they would prepare a meal for tonight.

After her parents left, Donna wandered around the cottage, trying to summon up the energy to walk down to Amberwood. Girl problems, their father had said. *Girl* problems . . . Donna had not known about any girl in Don's life. Who was she, this unknown girl, who might be the cause of his flouncing tantrums? Probably she did not exist. But if she did, how old was she? Don's age? Younger – fourteen or so? That was not too young for sexual adventures these days – Donna knew that perfectly well. Had Don been to bed with this girl?

The thumping of a CD was filling the little house, and it seemed to insinuate itself inside Donna's head. It was a hard, rhythmic pounding, and the longer it went on, the more it drummed up all kinds of images . . .

One of those images was of Don lying on his bed upstairs, his hair tousled against the pillows so that it looked like polished tow . . . He wore his hair a bit longer than was currently fashionable, but Donna rather liked that. It gave him a romantic soulful look. Like a poet. You could not imagine Byron or Keats having a convict-type haircut.

Had he stripped off his shirt to listen to his music? It was high summer and it got quite hot under the roof. Was he lying on the bed wearing only cotton jeans or shorts? His hair and his skin glowed from the sun, and his body was lean and supple from playing games at school. He was good at games, although at the moment he was pretending to find them too exhausting for words.

Girl problems. It was inevitable there would be girls in Don's life: he was so charming, so good-looking. There would be the sisters of schoolfriends, and girls he would meet in the holidays . . .

The pounding music was no longer inside Donna's mind, it was scudding and throbbing through her whole body. Like the scudding and throbbing you felt with a boy when you were in bed with him. There had not been many boys with whom Donna had been to bed but there had been a couple; you could not reach eighteen these days without having explored your sexual prowess. It was necessary to conform, to go with the crowd, to take part in slightly hysterical giggling sessions with girlfriends, relating how far you had gone and whether it had been any good, and whether he had been any good. Sometimes shrieking and saying things like, 'Oh God, you didn't do it with *him*, did you, how utterly *gross* . . .'

The trouble was that none of the boys Donna had met matched up to Don. She had sometimes thought she might be a bit cold. But this was not something that could be admitted so she had dutifully yielded her virginity, since not to do so meant being regarded by your contemporaries as a freak, a sad old vestal. Imagine being eighteen and still a virgin, said Donna's friends pityingly, and Donna had agreed and laughed at the very idea.

But imagine being eighteen, and standing in the kitchen of a battered old cottage, trying to beat down a pulsating lust for your own brother.

Of course Donna was not going to do anything – well – anything wrong with Don. This was the last quarter of the twentieth century, and they were living in a civilized society. It was only in the Dark Ages, in tiny rural backwaters with no means of travelling anywhere or seeing people beyond your own family, that brothers and sisters ended up in bed together. There was a sick old joke, wasn't there, that incest almost died out when the railways came?

Incest. It was an ugly, sly word. Donna thrust it away, and

went to the foot of the stairs to shout up to Don that she would walk down to the village to pick up some food for tonight. She pulled on her trainers, slammed the cottage door, and went out into the warm sunshine before anything could make her change her mind.

But as she walked into Amberwood, and as she looked at the hand-crafted jewellery in the gallery, her mind was full of images of Don. She bought a pair of jade earrings, and picked up some cooked ham and chicken from the nearby delicatessen, together with ingredients for a salad. By midday she was walking back to the cottage. The sun was high overhead; if you looked straight at it, you got sunspots in front of your eyes.

When she reached the cottage she put the food in the fridge, and unlaced her trainers. The sunspots were still dancing across her vision, but the cottage was cool and dim, and the old oak floors were smooth and friendly under her bare feet. She went up the narrow creaking stairs, intending to go into her bedroom to put the earrings away.

Don's bedroom was on the half-landing, where the stairs turned sharply to the right. Donna hesitated, and put out a hand to touch the door. Was he in there now? Had he heard her come in? She tapped, and called out his name, and heard a movement from within. The sunspots whirled across her eyes again, like showers of gold flecks. She was aware of the scent of the deodorant she had put on that morning diluting the sweat forming under her arms.

After a moment, she pushed open the door and went in.

It was like stepping into the image she had had earlier. Don had stripped off his shirt, and was lying on his back on the bed staring up at the ceiling. The CDs had apparently come to an end or he had not bothered to replay them, and the room was very quiet. What had he been thinking?

There was a scent of old timbers, as there was in most of the rooms of Charity Cottage, but there was the faint scent of masculine sweat as well, which was exciting, because it was Don's sweat. Donna found the silence exciting as well. The feeling that she was entering her own fantasy deepened. If either of them spoke, or if any sound at all disturbed the utter quiet, the fantasy would shatter, and she would simply go back downstairs and wash the lettuce and radishes for tonight's supper, and the moment would pass into ordinariness.

But Don did not speak, there were no sounds from outside and the moment did not pass into ordinariness. The silence went on and on, and the sunspots, the heat of the day and the room's scents began to blur in Donna's mind. Don had not moved; he was watching her from the bed, and his eyes had a slanting, beckoning look. Was this how he looked at those girls – those unknown, possibly nonexistent girls? Donna suddenly hated all the girls Don might know or who he would come to know in the future. She could not bear the thought of those girls eyeing him with giggling teenage lust, wanting to touch him, perhaps being touched by him . . . Telling one another about it afterwards – 'I did it with Don Robards last night, and he was terrific . . .'

She was not aware of having crossed the room, or of having sat down on the edge of the bed, but she discovered she had done so. She was close enough to see the faint sheen of perspiration on his skin, and the slight flush across his cheekbones. Beautiful. Oh God, he's so beautiful. And just as she had not meant to walk across to the bed, nor had she meant to actually touch him. But they were inside the fantasy together, of course, so it was all right. Her hands reached out to him, tracing the line of his chest, feeling the warm firmness of his skin against her palms. Like a cushion of satin.

His reaction to her touch was instant; it sizzled between them, Donna could feel it – it was like an arcing light, like watching fireworks ignite on a dark river. Donna and Don, moving together towards the deepest, most intense intimacy there could ever be . . .

He was nervous – Donna could sense that, but she could also sense that he was trembling with fear and passion. When she pulled off her shirt he seemed to flinch. Donna laughed, understanding that he was fearful of what they were about to do, pulling him against her for a moment to reassure him, and then reaching down to unfasten his jeans, pulling them open and sliding her hand inside. There was no mistaking his response now. As her fingers closed around him, he hardened instantly, and made an involuntary thrusting movement. Donna unfastened her own jeans with her other hand and kicked them off.

The feel of Don's beloved body against her bare thighs was so fiercely exciting she thought for a moment she might actually faint. When she pulled his hand down between her legs the throbbing excitement was almost more than she could bear.

She thought he flinched again when she began to guide him into her, but then there was the helpless thrusting once more. There was nothing in the world except this hot bedroom and the two of them, nothing except the feel of Don's body, the brush of his hair where his head was buried in her bare shoulder and his frenzied excitement. Utter perfection. Body and mind blending and fusing. Was he feeling the same? Oh, but of course he was.

Too soon – far, far too soon – he gave a gasping shudder, and fell heavily onto her. Donna lay still, not caring that he was crushing her ribs, only caring that after this he was hers, utterly and irrevocably. It no longer mattered if the entire female population of the world set out to screw him, because this afternoon she had printed Don with her own stamp and no other girl would ever be able to measure up to this.

The sun poured in through the half curtained windows and the bed, although a bit old, was soft and comfortable. There was no need to get up yet; the bedside clock was only pointing to half past one, and their parents would not be home for ages. Don was still lying half across her, but he was no longer squashing her and he had fallen into a half sleep. The room was warm and drowsy; Donna's own eyelids grew heavy and she, too, slept.

She was woken by the sound of footsteps – two sets of footsteps – on the stairs, and by her mother's voice laughing and calling to know where the children were. Were they in bed asleep at this hour, the pair of lazybones they were! They had had such a good day, there was masses to tell, and lots of research to discuss . . .

The bedroom door opened.

Donna would never forget the sight of her mother's face as she took in the sight of her children lying in bed, their bodies still tangled together, the sheets pushed aside. She would never forget the sight of her father standing behind her mother, his face white with shock and anger, his eyes suddenly hard and cold. Donna was suddenly aware that there was a patch of wet stickiness under her thighs, and that the stain was probably visible. She was conscious of her own uncovered body, and of Don's. She sat up and pulled the sheet over her.

There would be a dreadful row, but they would talk their way out of it, just as they always did. Don would be with her – he would help her through it. He would not let her down.

CHAPTER TWELVE

Don did not really let her down. Not really. He stammered and flushed, was sulky and truculent and tearful by turns. It was important to remember he was only fifteen, and had not the experience of life to help him deal with such a situation. Donna had not really the experience of life to deal with it either, but she would bluff her way through.

But when it came to the crunch, there was no bluff that could change her parents' decision and there was nothing that could dilute their horror. Disgusting, said their mother, who had rushed from the bedroom to be sick in the bathroom. Perverted and disgusting and just plain wrong. How on earth were they to deal with such a situation? That was what she wanted to know.

Donna thought it a bit over the top of her mother to keep shuddering and sipping brandy, and to keep pressing a handkerchief to her lips as if she might be sick again at any minute. She glanced at Don, but he was watching their mother cry and ply the handkerchief, clutching at their father's hands. When their father spoke, Don listened without interrupting. Donna always had a shock when her father spoke in that stern authoritative voice, although presumably it was the way he sometimes spoke to people at the office.

Standing in the sitting room of Charity Cottage, Jim Robards said in an unshakeable and severe voice this was how it was going to be, and neither Donna nor Don need argue with him: they would be separated at once. He ignored Donna's gasp of dismay and said Don would go back to school, of course – there was only another couple of weeks of the holidays in any case – and Donna would go somewhere out of England. Perhaps to one of those places in Switzerland that had once been called finishing schools. She could study languages or cooking or train to be a model or any damn thing she liked, but she would not live in England for at least two years, was that quite clear?

'Oh, perfectly,' murmured Donna. 'But you can't absolutely make me do any of that, can you? I'm eighteen – I can do whatever I want. I can live where I want.'

'With no money? No job?'

'I'd manage.' Donna did not say she would scrub floors for a living because that would sound immature and adolescent which were the last things she wanted to sound. Also, she did not think she actually would scrub floors if it came to it. So she said, 'I could get some kind of job. In a shop or an hotel – something like that. And a flat. I could get a flat of my own.' And Don could be with me . . . She did not need to look at Don to know he would be thinking the same thing.

'You won't do any such thing,' said Donna's father, still in the same cold hard voice. 'You and your brother will live apart for as long as I can manage it.'

Live apart? Donna and Don to live apart? There are times in life when the power of a desire can be extraordinarily – almost frighteningly – strong. Donna, lying sleepless in her bed that night, knew absolutely and utterly, that she and Don would not be separated and that they were not going to live apart. Something would happen to prevent it. She did not yet know what it would be, but something would happen.

The last few days of the holiday were a nightmare.

They could not return home at once which was what their father wanted to do, because their mother had arranged for their house to be redecorated during the holiday and for the main bathroom to be refitted. There would be decorators and plumbers crawling all over the rooms, and the water would be turned off, she said. She was not going to camp out among ladders and dust sheets, even if her children had broken every law known to man and God.

So they stayed on at Charity Cottage. There were a couple of squalid conversations between Donna and her mother who tried to find out with ridiculous roundabout phrases if they might have to deal with any consequences of what had happened. '*You* know what I mean, Donna,' she said, and Donna, who by that time would not have put out a hand to save her mother from drowning or being burned alive, had pretended not to know at all.

'Well, might you be – I mean, did it— Did he manage to—'

'Did he withdraw in time or did he come inside me?' said Donna in a hard cold voice and was rewarded by her mother's flush of embarrassment. Serve you right! 'Or were you simply wondering if I'm on the pill or anything like that?'

'Well, yes. Yes, that is what I meant.'

'You'll have to wait and see,' said Donna, and went furiously out of the room. Let her mother stew over that one for the next two or three weeks! In fact she was not on the pill, and Don, poor inexperienced boy, had been much too far gone to think about the old-fashioned method of withdrawal. Donna thought they would be the unluckiest pair of lovers ever if that one encounter resulted in pregnancy.

For the last few days of their stay, their parents dragged them to various places in order to fill up the time and to avoid having to talk to each other more than absolutely necessary. They trekked out to stupid tourist centres, boring craft displays and to dull-as-ditchwater museums. It was all more tedious than Donna had imagined anything could ever be. If one of them moved more than five yards, either their mother or father followed. It was ridiculous and unnecessary, and it showed a complete lack of understanding of the deep passion Donna and Don had shared. Probably by the laws of the land – absurd man-made laws – what they had done together was wrong. Donna could accept that.

But she could not accept that she and Don were to be split up.

Two days before they were due to leave Charity Cottage, shortly after five Don came into the kitchen, and said, 'Where are the jackboots? They haven't finally gone out somewhere and left us on our own, have they?'

'No idea.' Donna had been sitting at the kitchen table, drinking tea and staring out at the rain that had just started to fall. 'D'you want some of this tea?'

'Thanks.' Don had been lying in the garden reading for most of the day, but the sudden rainstorm had driven him indoors a quarter of an hour ago. He took the cup and slumped moodily at other end of the kitchen table. He did not say anything else and he did not look at her. Donna felt a fresh wave of hatred against their parents who had created this painful restraint.

She said, offhandedly, that perhaps the jackboots had gone into the village, to get an evening paper. 'They haven't taken the car – it's parked outside.'

'Both of them out together, though? Leaving us alone for as long as an entire fifteen minutes?'

'I don't know,' said Donna impatiently. 'I've been lying down with a headache all afternoon.'

'Perhaps they left a note. Have you looked?'

'No, I couldn't be bothered.'

But by six o'clock they were both sufficiently bothered to look for a note. When they failed to find one in any of the ordinary places – tacked to the fridge, or propped up on the dining table – they went into their parents' room to see if things like jackets or wallets or handbags were gone.

'Dad's brown jacket's not here,' said Don. 'Nor is his wallet – he always leaves it on the dressing table.'

'No. And Ma's handbag isn't here either, or that blue linen thing she had on yesterday.'

'Dad's mobile phone's here though.'

'That doesn't mean anything. He's always forgetting it or letting it run out of charge.' Donna sat down on the edge of the big double bed to think. 'It doesn't look as if they just went for a stroll along the lane, does it? It looks as if they went somewhere where they'd need money and keys and things.'

'But wherever they are, they've walked,' said Don. 'Because the car's still here. That means they didn't intend to go very far.'

This was unarguable. Maria Robards had brought four pairs of expensive leather walking shoes with her, but she had never had any real intention of actually walking anywhere in them. The little post-office-cum-shop on Amberwood's outskirts was her absolute limit, and even then she complained about blisters when she got back and wanted to plug in the foot spa she had brought with her.

'I expect they're just sheltering from the rain,' said Donna at last. 'It's coming down in torrents.'

'Ought we to do anything? Go out and look for them?'

'Yes, we'd better. Let's walk along the lane. We'll go as far as that little shop that sells newspapers – that's the likeliest place they went to anyway.'

'OK.'

They put on waterproofs and hoods, and tramped along the road. The little shop was closed at this hour, but they walked all round it. There was nothing to be seen, and there was only the dismal wet splatter of the rain everywhere.

They got back to the cottage just after seven. Donna heated some tinned soup, and Don made ham rolls and coffee to go with it. They ate at the kitchen table, trying not to look at the clock on the old-fashioned mantel ticking the minutes away. It was not getting dark yet, but shadows were certainly starting to creep across the garden and the parkland that surrounded Quire

House. Twice Don said that there was most likely some perfectly ordinary explanation – a sprained ankle or something, and they must be out of reach of a phone box.

'If so, he's probably cursing like fury. Is there any more soup? I daresay it's heartless of me, but I'm starving.'

They finished the soup and washed-up, and by this time it was quarter to nine. They looked at one another.

'Police?' said Don at last.

'Yes, we'll have to.'

'Where's the nearest station? We haven't got to go all the way into Stockport or Chester, have we?'

'No, there's a little station in Amberwood. One man and a phone, probably, but they'll know what to do.'

'They'll say we're being neurotic and not to worry,' said Don.

But the officer at the little police station did not say this at all. He took the details, and said they would make a few checks. Well, no, they would not actually mount a search – not for two adults, at least not yet – but they would get in touch with the local hospitals and so forth. You never knew. Oh yes, people did vanish for several hours and then turn up unharmed. They fell into ditches and knocked themselves out, or they broke their ankles clambering across stiles, and were stranded. Neither Donna nor Don said that their parents were not the kind of people who walked in ditches or clambered across stiles.

Donna drove back to the cottage in silence. Don leaned forward eagerly when they swung off the main road and turned along the narrow track leading to the cottage, and she realized he was hoping to see lights blazing from the windows, indicating that their parents were safely back. But Charity Cottage was still in darkness, except for the table lamp they had left burning in the little sitting room and the rather dim light over the front door.

Neither of them went to bed that night. Don fell asleep on the settee but Donna stayed awake, lying in one of the armchairs, trying not to listen to the rain that was still pattering ceaselessly down on the roof. It would be a dreadful night to be lying injured somewhere. Half of her – more than half of her – wanted to join Don on the settee, but she did not.

The police came at nine the next morning to see if the absentees had turned up. Ah, they had not. Oh dear. They had drawn a blank with their own inquiries, they said, and so the next thing was to draw up a bit of a timetable, in order to establish who had been where at what time.

This was simple enough. The morning had been spent at the cottage. Don had taken a book and his unfinished holiday homework into the garden after breakfast, along with his Walkman. He had stayed there until lunchtime, half-heartedly writing the essay he was supposed to be working on, and listening to CDs.

All morning, was that?

Yes, and most of the afternoon. Oh, wait though, he had come in about eleven to get a drink of orange juice. Everyone had been here then.

'I sort of mooched around doing nothing most of the morning,' said Donna. 'I had a bit of a headache as a matter of fact. I walked down to the little shop shortly before lunch to get some air. I got back just after twelve, I think.'

How about lunch? Had they all had lunch together?

'No. My mother made some sandwiches about half past twelve,' said Donna. 'I took some out to Don in the garden.'

'I brought the plate back in at quarter past one or thereabouts,' said Don. 'And got some more orange juice from the fridge. They were here then.'

'We're narrowing it down,' said the sergeant, making notes. 'And then?'

'My headache was still quite bad,' said Donna, frowning in an effort to report the precise details. 'So I took a couple of paracetamol and went upstairs to lie down. That was probably about half past one. My mother said she'd bring up a cup of tea later on. But I fell asleep and when I woke up it was four o'clock and that's when I realized they weren't here.'

'And neither of you heard your parents go out?'

'No. I told you, I was asleep for most of the afternoon.'

'And I was listening to the Walkman. I was at the far end of the garden anyway,' said Don. 'They might have called out to say they were going somewhere, but I don't think I'd have heard them.'

'No. Loud things, those Walkmans,' said the sergeant, rather feelingly. 'So seemingly, they went out somewhere between half past one – say, quarter to two – and four o'clock, when you came downstairs, Miss Robards?'

'Well, I can't absolutely swear to the minute, but it's near enough. And Don came in from the garden when the rain started. Half past four or quarter to five.'

'Neither of you thought it especially odd that your parents might have gone out without telling you, or leaving a note?'

'No,' they said together. Donna felt the same thought form in both their minds: after what happened our parents would never have gone out and left us alone. But this could not be said. Not now and not ever.

'Could they have been mugged or anything like that?' asked Don, suddenly sounding rather endearingly young and uncertain. 'Or even kidnapped?'

But it appeared there were not many cases of mugging in Amberwood, and as for kidnapping . . .

'Are they wealthy enough?' asked the sergeant. 'Not meaning to pry but—'

'I shouldn't think so,' said Donna. 'My father's quite successful, but we're not in the millionaire bracket. I don't think he's high-profile enough for a kidnapper: he's not a politician or a celebrity. He just imports and exports stuff.'

She saw the words, *arms dealer*, form in the sergeant's mind, and to dispel ideas of Iraqi terrorists or IRA gunmen, said, 'Mostly porcelain and good-quality pottery. Delft and Wedgwood and so on. He deals with Holland and the Low Countries in the main.'

'Oh, I see. Then,' said the sergeant, glancing at the young

police constable who was with him, 'I think what we'll do next is to take a look around the cottage, if that's all right. Oh, and we'll arrange for someone to go to your house. Just as a routine check, you know.'

He said this rather offhandedly, but Donna saw he was thinking there might have been some sort of family row, and that their parents had gone home in a fury.

'But after that,' said the sergeant carefully, 'I think we'd better start searching the immediate vicinity. I'll call Area and get a few extra men.'

Once the Robards' home had been checked and found entirely innocent of any leads, the nightmare that Donna was living in ratcheted up several notches. Over the next twenty-four hours the police asked questions in shops and houses, showing hastily copied photographs taken from the snaps Don had in his wallet. Have you seen this man or woman recently? Some of the restaurant owners remembered Maria and Jim Robards, who had been in for lunch once or twice, and some of the shops remembered them buying provisions. Holiday people they were, staying up at Quire. Pleasant enough. But no one had seen them in the last day or so.

It was a nightmare that teemed with police officers tramping across fields and copses, peering for wisps of clothing or shoelaces, looking for signs of disturbance or for footprints, although as Don said, footprints after all the rain seemed wildly optimistic. Donna wanted to go with the searchers, but the police said best not. Best stay at the cottage with your brother, my dear, then we'll have a base, so to speak. A checkpoint. And who's to say that your parents mightn't turn up at the cottage when we're least expecting it?

A policewoman stayed at the cottage with them, offering to make cups of tea every ten minutes, trotting out little reassuring stories about people who had turned up after being lost for days on end. They wouldn't believe the odd things that happened in life. Amnesia and so on. And how about a bit of lunch? They had to keep their strength up, didn't they?

On the third day, the police brought in dogs, and Donna was asked to provide items of recently worn clothing that would be imbued with their parents' scent. She found a pair of her father's socks and some of her mother's underwear which the inspector said was exactly what they wanted.

Donna thought you heard a good deal about the agonies families went through when people vanished, but nobody ever mentioned that you had to burrow sordidly in linen baskets to find unwashed knickers to wave in front of police tracker dogs.

CHAPTER THIRTEEN

Inevitably, the police search for Maria and Jim Robards included Twygrist. Donna had told them about their mother's interest in the place; there had been no reason not to tell them. Her parents liked local history, she said, determinedly speaking in the present tense; they often had a project like this when they were on holiday. They had stayed at Charity Cottage for several summers, so they were sufficiently at home to enjoy delving around in the area's past.

The police had searched the inside of the mill, as well as combing the surrounding hillsides. They did not tell Miss Robards or her brother that they were now hesitating worriedly over the reservoir, created over two hundred years ago to power the mill's unwieldy mechanism. They had not yet reached the stage of dragging it, and they were hoping not to do so – dragging any expanse of water was a messy, long-winded procedure never mind being unreliable, and it was more than seventy years since Twygrist's sluice gates had been raised. The mechanism was likely to be rusted beyond use.

On the morning of the fourth day, the inspector who had been called in to head the search decided to go back inside Twygrist with more powerful lights and with the dogs. It was such a labyrinth when you actually got inside, he said, it was possible they had missed something.

Donna went with them. She could not bear it any longer, she said to the inspector. Please let her come along, if only for a couple of hours. She would feel so much better knowing she was joining in the search and in any case, they could hardly prevent her from driving out there herself, even if they would not actually let her into Twygrist. The inspector was not very keen but eventually agreed, stipulating that she was not to get in the way or try to climb into any of the inaccessible parts of the mill. It had been derelict for years and parts of it were probably dangerous. She was to regard herself as under police orders, was that clear?

'Perfectly clear,' said Donna politely.

Whoever had built Twygrist, had taken advantage of the natural slope of the land, and it was set into the hillside with a good part of it below the ground. Donna did not know if this was because the mill had sunk over the centuries, or if it had been built like that in the first place so as to get the full weight of the water from the reservoir directly behind the mill, a little way up the hillside. The roof was a long steep structure, its eaves so low that at the front they were only a few feet from the ground. Tiny slatted windows were set into the roof, but most of the slats had rotted away so the windows resembled empty eye sockets.

On the side was the over-elaborate clock her mother had said was to commemorate someone. There was some sort of local fund to pay for the regular winding and cleaning of it – the office of Clock-Winder was passed down in one of the local families, father to son or nephew, apparently. Maria was hoping to discover the identity of the family, and talk to them. It was very rustic, wasn't it? She thought it perfectly charming.

Donna had not thought it perfectly charming at all, and she thought the clock itself was very ugly. It had a bulbous surface, so that from some angles it looked like a swollen face poking through the wall. It was rather unnerving to approach Twygrist and look up to see those empty windows and that swollen-faced clock.

The roof overhung the doorway so much that the policemen had to duck their heads to go through, and Donna, who was fairly tall, had to do so as well. The door itself was black with age and half hanging off its hinges, but one of the men propped it open to allow daylight in. But even with that amount of light, entering Twygrist was like stepping into a dank black cavern. It was like walking beneath an old, old lake, with the uncomfortable knowledge that directly over your head was a huge volume of dark stagnant water. Donna wondered how long it was since the old sluice gates had been raised, and the water had poured out of the reservoir, down through the tunnels and culverts, to gush into the mill and power the two massive millwheels. She had a sudden unpleasant suspicion that it would not take much to set the rusting mechanism in motion again: that if she leaned on something unwisely, or trod incautiously on a particular part of the floor, she might feel a shudder go through the old timbers, and the massive waterwheels would slowly begin to rotate once more. Sheer nerves, nothing more.

The police searched this floor first, sweeping their powerful torches over the long-disused mechanism, and brushing aside festoons of grey-white cobwebs in order to check all the corners and tucked-away little recesses. Almost all of Twygrist was decayed and rotted beyond repair, and there was a smell of sour dirt and extreme age. Donna stayed by the door, wanting to keep a low profile in case they decided to order her out, but watching where the searchers' torches went, trying to see if there were any clues that were being missed.

But there was nothing to be seen anywhere, and after a while the search was moved to the upper level. Donna watched the police go warily up the rickety staircase. She thought the upper level was where the workers had shovelled corn into a chute so it could be fed down to the millstones for the actual grinding. Josiah Forrester had employed local women and girls for that – it was one of the things Maria Robards had discovered and talked about. They had all sat in the upper rooms, she said, picking over the corn before it was fed into the chute, and there had been a legend that some of them were witches. That was because they had worked in near-darkness on account of it being dangerous to have lit candles or rushlights inside Twygrist, and because they had usually worn black cotton gowns and hats to protect their hair from the corn dust.

There was the chute overhead, a little to her left, and directly beneath it were the two millstones that had worked together to crush the corn to flour. She walked across to them. They were both badly cracked – one was almost in two completely separate pieces – and their surfaces were deeply pitted. Donna glanced round and then reached down to the nearer stone. By leaning over she could brush it with her fingertips. It felt cold and hard and she stepped back at once, repelled. As she did so, the floor-joists around the millstones creaked protestingly, almost as if the voice of the mill was wheezing and grating its way back to life again . . .

I am not really past my work, my dear, so be wary of me . . . I can still grind and I can still crush and mill. Once songs were sung about me and once children's rhymes were chanted about how I could grind men's bones to make bread – and women's bones as well, my dear. I was never particular whether it was a man or a woman who fell into my hands . . .

Donna looked around, scanning the shadows, but although she could still hear the police moving overhead, nothing stirred at this level. She realized she had been holding her breath, and let it out with annoyance. This was sheer nervous reaction: she was short on sleep and long on worry – it had been four days since her mother and father had disappeared. But no matter how sinister Twygrist might be, she was not going to start having the kind of whimsical imagination that ascribed malevolent personalities to old buildings.

The police had taken the torches and lights with them but there was enough light from the propped-open door to see the outlines of the immense oblong tanks enclosing the two great waterwheels and the complexity of axles, shafts and cogs that linked them. Above the larger wheel was what remained of the culvert where once the water had come rushing in. Donna studied it for a moment. Would the police search inside that? Surely no one could have got up there and become trapped inside the culvert – no one would want to go up there in the first place?

Her nerves were becoming stretched almost to snapping point by Twygrist, and she realized she was glancing over her shoulder every few minutes, as if expecting to see someone watching her from the shadows. Ridiculous. There was nothing—

Or was there? Wasn't there something here that the police inspector and his searchers had still to find . . .

And what is that, Donna? What is it you can feel – or you think they will find? Bones, ground up to make bread? Because I have had my victims over the years, you know . . . You're really quite afraid, aren't you, Donna, AREN'T YOU?

Donna turned her back on the crouching mechanism and walked determinedly to the doorway. She sat down. The floor was disgustingly dusty, but she was beyond caring. She leant back against the door frame, looking out at the warm sunshine. The sun was high; it must be about midday. Normally she would be thinking about lunch, but she felt as if she would never be hungry or thirsty again.

Below the mill was the road that led to Quire House and then wound its way on to Amberwood. Cars were speeding along, and a fat little country bus chugged to or from a local school. It was all normal and unremarkable, and it was a reminder that the ordinary world was still going on out there. But for the moment I'm stuck here, thought Donna, and I've got to stay here because I've got to know if they find anything. I've got to stay here in this dark place, with that clock ticking the minutes and the hours and the years away.

The policemen were coming down from the upper level. They nodded to Donna with an air of awkward apology, and the inspector called out that they had not found anything, but they were going to check the lower levels. Best if she stayed up here while they did so, he said.

'I didn't know you could get to a lower level,' said Donna.

'Neither did I,' said the inspector shortly. 'And neither, it seems, did anyone else. But Dawkins has just told me about it.' He glanced angrily at the unhappy Dawkins.

'Oh, I see.'

It was entirely understandable that the inspector and most of the men, except the presumably local Dawkins, had not known about the steps leading down to Twygrist's bowels. A small doorway was tucked behind the lower waterwheel, and unless you had known it was there you would certainly have missed it. It was, in fact, necessary to squeeze round the wooden tank to get to the opening, and the space was so cramped that the larger of the policemen had a struggle to get to it. Donna, watching, thought how Don would have enjoyed seeing that; he loved it when authority figures were made ridiculous. *Don* . . .

She waited until the men had gone through the door, and then got up and went quickly and quietly after them. Shallow steps led down from the doorway, curving round as they went. The walls had the smoothness of extreme age so there were no hand-holds anywhere – it would be treacherously easy to miss your footing and tumble all the way down to the bottom. You might lie down there in the dark for days, badly injured – dead or dying – with no one knowing where you were. Donna shivered, but went all the way down, thankful there was enough light from the searchers' torches to see her way, trying not to brush against the black stones of the walls which were crusted with the dust and grime of years.

'There's a lot of dirt and debris everywhere,' said the inspector's voice from deeper in the tunnels. 'So it's difficult to be sure about footprints, but I think there are several sets. See them?' The torchlight moved around. 'They look fairly recent, but they might just have been made by local kids on a dare, or a version of "chicken", or something. Dawkins, since you know the place better than the rest of us, you'd better lead the way.'

A dreadful stifling warmth seemed to push downwards, and the drumming of the clock's mechanism was more noticeable down here. *Twy-Grist* . . . *Twy-Grist* . . . That was what it was saying. Twygrist meant twice ground, presumably. Or was the clock saying, *Two-dead* . . . *Two-dead* . . .

Twygrist's bowels were a series of stone and brick-lined cellars, most of them so narrow they were scarcely more than tunnels. Donna counted the rooms as she went. Three, four, five . . . Would they search every one? The inspector had said earlier that Twygrist was a labyrinth, and Donna found herself remembering that all labyrinths have a centre, a heart, a dark core . . .

And there, at Twygrist's dark core—

'What in God's name is that?' said one of the voices, and Donna jumped nervously. She stole forward, hoping to see without being seen.

'Just another cellar, isn't it?' said the inspector.

'No, it's doors,' said someone, shining one of the torches. 'In fact, steel doors, by the look of it.'

'It'll be the old kiln room,' said Dawkins' voice. 'We're most probably directly under the floor where they used to spread the grain to dry it out – the drying floor, they called it. You can't see it from outside any more because they concreted over it years ago, but it's a kind of flat roof near the ground at the back of the mill. It's clay or terracotta or something like that, and it was made with hundreds of tiny holes.' He paused as if waiting to see if anyone interrupted, and when no one did, went on, 'They spread the grain over it, and then lit a fire down here directly underneath so the dry heat rose up and drove the moisture out of the grain. My grandfather used to farm around here, and he remembers it being done.'

'And you reckon this kiln room's on the other side of those doors?'

'Seems logical, sir.'

'So it does,' said the inspector thoughtfully. Donna was keeping well back in the shadows, but she could see the men grouped around the doors.

'We're right at the heart of the building here,' said the inspector. 'So the kiln room is surrounded by all these other rooms. If a fire ever got out of hand, there'd be some protection.'

'And,' said Dawkins, 'The steel doors seal it off.' He paused and the inspector said, 'And if the drying floor is concreted over, it'd be virtually airtight in there.'

The hot bad-smelling darkness seemed to gather its forces and jump out at them, and then in a completely different tone, the inspector said, 'Get those bloody doors open *now*!'

The doors were not locked, and although there were indentations where handles must once have been, they had long since rusted off. The doors were wedged tight together and virtually seamless.

'They open outwards,' said the inspector after a moment. 'But without the handles they're as smooth as eggs – there's nothing we can get hold of to pull them back. What we need here is a set of old-fashioned burglars' tools.'

'The jemmy principle, sir?'

'Exactly. See if you can break off any sections of the old machinery to use as levers – anything that looks strong enough and thin enough.'

The cellars seemed to Donna to be filling up with panic, and the smooth-as-eggs doors began to take on a dreadfully sinister appearance. Airtight. *Airtight* . . . The clock was still beating out its rhythm, but the words of the rhythm had changed. *Airtight* . . . *airtight* . . .

The inspector's voice cut through this horrid tattoo. 'One of you had better go back upstairs and radio Area to ask about the availability of oxyacetylene cutters in case— Oh, wait though, it looks as if you've got some purchase on it at last. Don't let it slip back!'

The door did not slip back. Its old hinges screeched like a thousand souls in torment, and the metal scraped protestingly against the rough and ready levers the men had inserted, but Donna saw it begin to swing outwards. Dry stale air gusted out, and something that had been huddled against the other side of the door fell forward.

'Oh, God,' said Donna, no longer bothering to remain hidden. She clapped both hands over her mouth as if to force back a scream or a sob. 'Oh, *God* . . .'

They were both there. They must have been there all along – all the time. Four days. And the room had been airtight . . .

Maria Robards had fallen onto her back, and the glare of the torches showed up her terrible face. The skin she had taken such care of – beauty treatments at expensive salons, her insistence on buying the best make-up obtainable – was suffused with purple where the veins had swollen in her frenzied efforts to escape and the panic-filled struggle for air. Her eyes were wide open – bulging from their sockets – and the whites were stained crimson where the tiny capillaries had haemorrhaged.

She had taken care of her hands as well. Scented hand lotions, manicures, always wearing costly rings. The rings were still there, but the once-perfect nails were broken and the finger-tips were crusted with blood where she had clawed at the heavy steel doors.

Donna's father was not by the door; he was lying near the brick chimney. His face was turned away from the torchlight, but it was possible to see that his hands were also bruised and bloodied. Perhaps he had been trying to find a chink in Twygrist's structure: a tiny tear in the fabric which could be widened to let in air. Perhaps he had not known where he was, though, and had been beating uselessly against the bricks, in the mad, dying belief that they were doors that could be forced open.

In a high strained voice, Donna said, 'They're both dead, aren't they?' and in the small enclosed space, her voice seemed to bounce back at her, mingling with the steady beating of the old clock.

There was the sound of the inspector's voice, kindly and concerned. 'Yes, my dear. I'm afraid they're both dead.'

Both-dead . . . *Both-dead* . . . The clock snatched at that. *Tick-tick, both-dead, tick-tick, twice-dead* . . .

Twygrist's darkness reared up and wrapped itself round Donna in a dizzy, sick-making vortex. She pitched forward into this swirling dizziness and the inspector caught her as she fell.

CHAPTER FOURTEEN

It hurt Thomasina very much to put Maud in the room on Quire's second floor, but if she was to get a child – a boy who would be a worthier heir for Quire than Simon – there was no alternative. And after all, the room was not some grim stone-floored, iron-barred cell like something in Newgate; in the precentor's time it had been a nursery – inside it an inner door opened onto a night-nursery. Admittedly there were bars at all the windows – they had been put there to stop the precentor's sons from toppling out while fighting one another – but they were quite thin bars and there were only a couple of them across each window. As well as that, the two rooms were conveniently far away from the main part of the house, and there was a lock on the outer door.

A story would have to be thought up for the servants, of course. Thomasina might say Maud had succumbed to some infectious disease – no, that would bring Daniel Glass to Quire. She would simply say that Maud had influenza, and she wanted to nurse the child herself. In a few days' time Maud might be more biddable and Thomasina and Simon could decide on their next move.

Thomasina had found the threesome love-making rather piquantly exciting, but that had mostly been because she liked knowing she was controlling Simon and forcing him on. Other than that, Simon's part in the business had turned out to be as gruntishly repellant as Thomasina had always suspected and rather messy at the end. If that was the famous act that had inspired all those miles of lyrical poetry and acres of ballads, and for which people toppled thrones and waged wars, well, as far as Thomasina was concerned, they could keep it and welcome. She would stay with her velvet-skinned, silken-haired girls.

It was a pity Maud had reacted so violently. Running away and hiding in that wash-house – there had been no need for such melodramatic behaviour, but Thomasina was not going to abandon her wonderful scheme because of an hysterical tantrum. The idea of a child – a son – whom she would adopt and who would be almost her own had taken firm hold of her mind.

Maud and Simon would have to be married, of course. Maud's boy – who would really be Thomasina's boy in all other respects – must not bear the stigma of bastardy, and it ought to be easy enough to put round the story of a whirlwind romance. Maud's father was certainly not likely to object to his daughter's marriage into the wealthy Forrester family: Thomasina was well aware of George Lincoln's pretensions and she knew he would welcome Simon as a son-in-law with open arms and no questions asked. He would be delighted to think Maud's boy – George's own grandson – would be heir to Quire Park. As for Simon himself, if he wanted his debts paying and the £3,000 Thomasina had promised him, he would have to do a bit more than tup Maud a few times until she conceived. Tup. The hoary old rural expression pleased her. There was no reason why Simon should not see the thing through to its proper conclusion and, to make sure, Thomasina was going to withhold part of the £3,000 until after the marriage ceremony.

The child, when it was born, should be named Josiah for her father. She could see him quite clearly in her mind this small Josiah, and the longer she looked at his image, the more real he became. She could see him at all the stages of his life . . . toddling around Quire's park, loved by all the local people and the tenants. Young Master, they would call him in the villages, knowing he was Miss Thomasina's nephew by Mr Simon, and Quire's heir. The women would cluck indulgently over him and marvel at how strong and straight he was growing. And even though he would go away to school, there would be the holidays and he would be at Quire for those.

Maud would have to be allowed a hand in Josiah's growing-up, of course, and so, presumably, would Simon. But Maud could be manipulated and Simon could be bought, and Thomasina was not very worried about either of them.

She would teach Josiah about Quire and the obligations that owning it brought. When he was older there would be hunting and fishing and all the country things, although she dared say there might be nights when he would sneak off, the young rogue, to go poaching with the likes of Cormac Sullivan. She would turn an indulgent blind eye to that.

Later it might be possible for the family business to be revived, so that Josiah could occupy the place that the first Josiah, had occupied in Amberwood. The more Thomasina thought about this, the better she liked the idea. She might even take a look round Twygrist to see exactly how dilapidated it was, although she would have to steer clear of George Lincoln. For one thing George was too old to resume his work and for another, Thomasina could not risk awkward questions about Maud at this stage of the plan, least of all from Maud's father.

Maud. As she got back into the big double bed, Thomasina wondered how far she could trust Maud's state of mind. Tonight's hysteria would pass, but what about those curious darknesses in Maud's nature: the macabre sketch Thomasina had found, and the obsession with that gloom-filled music? Might such darknesses indicate a genuinely disturbed mind? More importantly, might such a disturbed mind be hereditary? Thomasina did not want an heir who could have inherited some flaw from his mamma. Quire in the hands of a madman would be as bad as

Quire in the hands of a heavy drinking gambler like Simon, in fact it would be worse.

But she did not think there was much risk. Her involvement with the Forrester Benevolent Trust had given her a nodding acquaintance with the care of the insane, and she had never once heard it suggested that madness was hereditary. If Maud's mental condition became troublesome, or if she refused to do what Thomasina wanted, then Thomasina would simply resort to opium again.

She smiled, thinking how shocked most of Amberwood would have been to see the correct respectable Miss Forrester striding through London's sleazier alleys, haggling with the cat-faced child over the purchase of a paper cone of opium. And *how* that impudent creature had haggled!

Thomasina had not really minded though – she had found the girl's defiant bargaining exciting, and the girl had known it. When the opium had finally been bought, she had said, 'Coming home with me now, are you, Thomasina? I got a lady to pleasure at five – she likes me to go to her own house, but we got an hour before that. Cost you double, though.' Thomasina had so hated the thought of the girl going from her narrow bed in Seven Dials to that of some rich soft-living female, that she had offered her not twice, but three times the usual amount not to go. The girl had taken the money, and this time, as well as her lips and her hands, she had used one of the polished leather phalluses on Thomasina, saying three times the payment deserved three times the pleasure. When Thomasina walked down towards St Martin's Lane, where she could get a hansom to take her to Waterloo, she had looked back and seen the girl leave the house, and had known she was going to that other woman anyway.

She turned away from these thoughts, and began to plan how she could make Maud's second-floor prison as comfortable and as pleasant as possible.

However comfortable and pleasant the second-floor rooms might be – however many books and painting things were brought up here – there was still a locked door and there were still bars at the windows: Maud knew she was in a prison.

Every night after dinner Simon and Thomasina came up the stairs and unlocked the door. Maud's world had shrunk to the sound of their step on the stairs and the turning of the key in the lock. And then, once the lock had been turned, came the slow opening of the door, exactly as the black door in her nightmare used to open, and with it came the crowding terror, because there was something dreadful waiting behind that door . . .

Once they were in the room – the key firmly turned again in the lock – Thomasina got undressed and Maud had to get undressed as well. Sometimes Thomasina undressed her and once Simon undressed her, which was dreadful. Then there was the stroking and licking with Thomasina that constituted 'It', and then Simon got undressed and there was the banging and pumping into her body and the wet stickiness that happened at the very end.

Twice Simon was flushed and slurry-speeched, and the pumping did not hurt as much and Maud was grateful. But both times Thomasina flew into a rage and said Simon was drunk and he had better go away and sleep it off. The second time, the colour suddenly drained from Simon's face and he lurched off the bed and stumbled across to the washstand to be sick. Thomasina compressed her lips, and carried the bowl away to empty it in the bathroom, and Simon shambled back to his own bed. The following night they both pretended it had not happened.

A cottage piano arrived at the end of the first week and was carried up to the second-floor room, and until she could escape properly Maud escaped into music. She tried out the Chopin and Debussy pieces her father had enjoyed, and some of Beethoven's compositions, although she had to stop playing the *Pathétique* after the first few bars, because it made her cry to think of Beethoven facing deafness, unable to properly hear this beautiful music.

But the best music of all for escaping was Paganini's *Caprice*

Suite. There was a piano arrangement of this by Schumann, and Maud resolved to master it. Paganini had known about being locked away and accused of madness – there was a story about how he had been accused of murdering his mistress while he was in the grip of insanity. Whether the story was true or not, prison had not killed his spirit: he had turned his mind to honing and polishing his marvellous musical gifts, and he had emerged stronger.

Maud would emerge stronger from all this as well. She would play Paganini's music, and while she did so she would plan how to be revenged on Thomasina and Simon. Some of the plans she thought of shocked her with their brutality, but after a time she stopped being shocked, because such punishments were no more than those two deserved.

Thomasina was enjoying making plans. Since she had always adhered to the robust maxim of, no sooner the word than the deed, she went along to Twygrist the very next afternoon. Even without the dream of that young Josiah, there was no point in letting the place crumble into decay. She took the keys from her desk, and tucked a candle and matches in the pocket of her skirt, because parts of Twygrist were as dark as hell's deepest caverns.

As she walked briskly along the lanes, she thought how pleased people would be if the mill were to come alive after so many years. The farmers would bring their corn again, and Twygrist would hum with life and activity. It would be as it had been when Thomasina and Simon had played their games there as children, and been smiled over and doted on by the workers. Young Mr Simon and little Miss Thomasina, the women had said, beaming, and the men had touched their caps politely. Thomasina had loved it.

She and Simon had made up a song about Twygrist to the tune of the old nursery rhyme, 'The House that Jack Built', which had been Simon's favourite. 'This is the mill that Joe built,' they had sung – 'Joe' had been Thomasina's father, of course.

This is the mill that Joe built
This is the door, that creaks like a crone
That opens the mill that Joe built.

Twygrist's door still creaked, and as Thomasina went inside the remembered atmosphere engulfed her: old timbers, because Twygrist was extremely old itself, the scent of machinery and a faint sourness of stagnant water. This last was not good; it was to be hoped that the sluice gates were not leaking and letting water seep in from the reservoir.

These are the gates that shut off the lake
That turns the wheels
And drives the mill that Joe built.

Simon had added a ruder verse when they were older, dealing with the fate of the maiden all forlorn, who had given the miller's assistant the horn, and been laid in the mill that Joe built. Remembering this as she climbed to the upper floors, Thomasina thought it a shame that Simon had not turned his abilities to something worthier than drinking, gambling and womanizing.

The massive machinery looked reasonably sound, although there were ominous patches of rust in places. The millstones were starting to dry out and crack from disuse. Proper workmen would have to be called in to overhaul all that, but Thomasina did not think any of it was beyond repair. She lit one of the candles and, shielding it with her cupped hand, went down the steps to the kiln room.

Had Twygrist always been filled with the little scufflings and scuttlings she could hear? But then really old buildings were never completely silent. As if in response to this, there was what sounded like footsteps overhead and Thomasina was suddenly aware of Twygrist's lonely situation. She strode back to the foot of the stairs, and called out, 'Is someone there? Who is it?'

'Thomasina? It's me. Simon. I saw you walking along the lane

– I tried to catch you up but you were too quick. What on earth are you doing in here?'

'Taking a look at the fabric. Checking the sluice gates and so on.'

'Oh, I see.' He came down the stone steps and stood at the opening to the tunnels, looking around. 'Lor, do you remember how we used to come down here as children? I used to tell you ghost stories – you never cared much for them, but they always frightened me half to death, and—'

'Why did you follow me here? There's nothing wrong, is there? With Maud?'

'There's nothing in the least wrong with Maud, providing you discount the fact that she's only half a furlong from raving lunacy. You'll have to do something about her eventually, won't you? Still, that's your problem, old girl. My problem is sordid coinage. That's why I followed you. To talk about it.'

'Money? I've already given you—'

'A thousand pounds, with the promise of another two if Maud conceives. Yes, I know that.'

'And I paid your debts,' said Thomasina dryly. 'Very substantial debts they were as well.'

'Oh, a man's known as much by his debts as by his enemies,' said Simon, carelessly. 'I've heard Cormac Sullivan say that many a time. But that thousand wasn't enough, Thomasina. And three thousand isn't really enough either.'

They looked at one another. 'You want more,' said Thomasina at last.

'A lot more.'

'We could say another five hundred, perhaps.'

'I think we'll have to say a lot more than that.' He moved closer, and in the candlelight his face looked sharper.

'I was thinking we'd double the three thousand,' said Simon. And, as Thomasina made a quick gesture of annoyance and refusal, he said, 'And then a yearly payment of five hundred on top of that.'

'It can't be done,' said Thomasina at once. 'I'm sorry, Simon, I simply can't afford it.'

'Then,' said Simon softly, 'you'll have to find a way to afford it. Because, my dear, if you don't I shall make sure the entire county knows what you get up to with your plump little girls. There've been quite a few of them over the years, haven't there?' he said. 'All the seductions of those pretty daughters of the local landed gentry. And all those trips to London to pick up street girls – Oh yes, I know all about that, Thomasina. An old schoolfriend saw you near Seven Dials in the summer – he recognized you from when he used to stay at Quire in the holidays. He was surprised to see you in that part of London. You were striding along with what he described as a very queer look in your eye, and he couldn't imagine what you were doing there. But I can imagine,' said Simon. 'You were after the girls, weren't you? The ones who don't much mind if they do it with a man or a woman, providing there's money to be made.'

'No one would believe any of this,' said Thomasina, but she felt as if she had been punched in the stomach. She thought: how much does Simon really know about me? Supposing this friend of his followed me? Along to the familiar turning off St Martin's Lane, and into the place where the seven streets meet. Seven Dials. And from there into the little yard nearby. Number 17 Paradise Yard, that's the address. I wrote it down, even though I'd never forget where my cat-faced girl lives.

'I'll bet there are a few whispers about you in Amberwood as it is,' Simon was saying. 'Believe me, Thomasina, it wouldn't take much to fan the flames of those whispers, and inside a week you'd be a byword. And on top of that, I could tell them about your latest adventure, and that's first-hand information, isn't it? I can describe it exactly: how you're paying me to make your newest little paramour pregnant. How we're enjoying those cosy threesomes in bed together – except that Maud isn't enjoying them, is she? You've had to lock her up to stop her running away, and I'm having to drink myself into insensitivity every night because oddly enough, Thomasina, I don't much care for doing it to a female who finds it – and me – so repulsive. But I think you've got your way – I've heard her being sick on three mornings in succession.'

There was a moment when Twygrist's whispering darkness swooped around Thomasina's head almost knocking her off balance. Maud was being sick in the mornings – she was being *sick*. After a moment, she was able to say, 'I don't believe you. I empty the commode and the washing bowl – I'd have known.'

'She's sick out of the window,' said Simon exasperatedly.

Thomasina stared at him, and then, because he could not be allowed to get the upper hand, said, 'I don't believe you'd talk about any of this. You wouldn't come out of it so very well yourself, would you? That arrangement we had—'

'My dearest girl, I shouldn't give a tuppenny damn what people in Amberwood said about me, because I shouldn't be around to hear it,' said Simon. 'I'd be back in London, living on your money. But a tale like that wouldn't do me much harm, you know. The women would eye me with that particular kind of nervous fascination they always reserve for libertines. And most of the men would be rather envious – I told you, didn't I, that it's every man's private fantasy to be in bed with two women together? Even if one of the women is you.'

From within the turmoil of Thomasina's mind, two things came uppermost. One was that if Maud really was pregnant, Simon's spiteful greed must not be allowed to taint the future of that small Josiah. Her thoughts flew ahead to the whispers that would hiss round Amberwood. Something odd about young Josiah Forrester's conception, people would say. Something unsavoury. And her lovely boy would find himself shunned and cold-shouldered. That must not be allowed to happen.

But there was a much deeper danger here, and that was Simon's threat to tell people about the visits to Seven Dials. Thomasina did not mind so much if people knew about the sweet innocent young things she had seduced in Amberwood over the years – the daughters of solicitors and businessmen who lived in Amberwood and the surrounding villages. The girls had been flattered and slightly awed at being pampered and petted by Miss Forrester, and they had probably not understood the actual seduction anyway. Thomasina thought she could very easily deal with any sly rumours about that. But she was not sure she could cope with the truth about Seven Dials coming out. How much did Simon actually know about the girl who lived at 17 Paradise Yard? Might this friend of his have followed Thomasina, and seen her enter the ramshackle house with the peeling façade?

Thomasina's first visit there had horrified her. The girl, who seemed to be called the Cat by most people, shared her two disreputable rooms with two other girls who plied a similar trade, and with a thin girl of about fourteen who sat in a corner of the room with a book, never spoke and scarcely looked at Thomasina.

Thomasina had been appalled by the squalor and the poverty, although the Cat had only laughed and demanded a half-sovereign – she set her charges according to her clients' prosperity, she said, and one day she intended to be very rich indeed – and then had gone through to the squalid bedroom that was barely bigger than a cupboard, and flung off her clothes and thrown herself onto the bed.

Listening to Simon's threats, Thomasina knew she would do anything to keep her association with the Cat a secret.

CHAPTER FIFTEEN

For a long moment neither of them spoke, and then, in an ordinary, slightly grudging, voice, Thomasina said, 'It doesn't look as if you're giving me much choice, does it, Simon? I'd better see what I can work out.'

'I think you had,' said Simon. And then, in a slightly more conciliatory tone, 'Sorry to do this to you, old girl, but needs must.'

'Oh yes, I quite see that.' Thomasina did not even care that Simon had called her old girl. 'We'd better go back to Quire,' she said. 'You lead the way up the steps, and I'll bring the candle.'

'Yes, all right. Uh – no hard feelings?'

'None in the world,' said Thomasina and waited for Simon to turn away and go back up the steps. He had reached the third step when she snuffed out the candle, and at once made a little *tsk* of annoyance.

'Oh what a nuisance – I'm sorry about that, Simon; it must be the damp air. I can relight it, though – I've got matches in my pocket.'

'Ever efficient,' said Simon, waiting. 'It's jolly cold down here, isn't it?'

'Yes, it— Here's the candle, and— Oh, no.'

'What?'

'It's the keys. I had them in my pocket with the matches, and now they aren't there. I must have dropped them while I was in the tunnels. I'll have to go back; I must lock the doors when we go.'

'Are you sure you didn't leave them on the upper floor? Or even in the door? If they'd fallen out of your pocket down here, you'd have heard them, surely?'

'They were definitely in my pocket when I lit the candle. But I stumbled against some of the bits of machinery down here – a rusty cog-wheel as a matter of fact – and they probably dropped out then. I don't think I'd have heard them, what with getting tangled up with the cog-wheels.'

She felt, rather than heard, Simon's sigh of exasperation. 'Give me the candle,' he said. 'You wait here and I'll go back to look for the wretched keys. How far along the tunnels did you actually get?'

'Only to about the third cellar. I wanted to see if the roof had caved in anywhere. I'll light another candle for you, shall I? I brought two.'

Simon took the candle and set off. His footsteps echoed in the enclosed space, and the candle flame flickered, sending his shadow leaping grotesquely across the roof and the walls. His voice came back to her, distorted by the enclosed tunnels, saying he could not see the keys.

'Keep looking. It's quite a large bunch, so you won't miss them.'

'I'll go a bit further along. Stay where you are.'

It was no part of Thomasina's hastily conceived plan to stay where she was. She waited until she thought Simon was far enough into the brick-lined cellars not to hear her footsteps, and then snuffed out her own candle and stole after him.

It was very dark, but there was sufficient light from Simon's candle up ahead to see her way well enough not to trip over, or make any sound that might alert him. Although she did not much like what she was about to do, there was no doubt in her mind about doing it. Simon must not be allowed to make good his threats.

Padding stealthily along, Thomasina thought again what people would say if they knew about the Cat. Imagine it, they would say, shocked. Miss Thomasina Forrester and a fifteen-year-old prostitute from Seven Dials. Buying her clothes, sending her food.

The parcels of food and clothing had been because Thomasina had been unable to bear the thought of the girl going hungry, or facing a winter's night in the thin garments she always wore. Once, when she had been looking through the bills for those things, Maud had come into the study, and had said in a pettish voice, 'Dull household books *again*.'

It had been in the early days of Thomasina's infatuation with Maud, but she had been stung to a sharp retort. 'It's for a girl who lives in a poor part of London.' She's exactly your age, Maud, in fact she even resembles you a bit – the same colouring. But over the years she's had to do some dreadful things to avoid starving in the gutter. There's a sick sister – I think she'd do anything in the world for that sister. If it wasn't for the chance of birth, you might be in her shoes and she might be in yours. So I give her a little help from time to time.'

Maud had said, 'Oh, I see,' and wandered disconsolately away.

Thinking back to that conversation, Thomasina wondered if it was possible for anyone to trace those presents back to her. Little treats she had called them. There had been bottles of preserved pears, cheeses carefully wrapped in waxed paper, chicken in aspic, a woollen cloak and some dress lengths. Had the Cat worn the things or had she simply laughed scornfully and sold them? At Christmas Thomasina had even sent a parcel of books for the girl with the translucent skin, although she had not known if the books would be read or sold.

Simon must be nearing the kiln room now; he had already called back twice to say there was no sign of the keys. In a moment he would probably give up the search and come back down the tunnels. Fearing this Thomasina quickened her steps.

Here was the tangled rustiness of machinery that was at the heart of her plan. She bent to pick up a piece of iron, weighing it carefully in her hand. Heavy enough? Yes, surely it was. A shower of rust came away from the iron, marking her hand and speckling the front of her gown; in the dim light it looked exactly like blood. Thomasina kept a firm hold of it, concealing it in a fold of her skirt. No longer bothering to move quietly, she caught Simon up.

He heard her approach and turned round at once, saying he had not yet found the keys. It looked as if they would have to leave Twygrist unlocked for a day or so.

'I suppose we'll have to,' said Thomasina. 'Unless George Lincoln still has keys— Oh, but what's that in that corner?'

'Where?'

'Over there. Isn't it the keys?'

Simon bent down to look, exactly as he was meant to do, and Thomasina raised the iron bar high and brought it heavily down on his head. There was a crunch of bone – sickening! She had not allowed for that! Rust specks flew up against the darkness. Simon gave a sort of 'Ouf' of surprise and slumped to his knees, then crashed to the floor. He lay prone, not moving, a rim of white showing under his eyelids. Thomasina set her teeth and brought the bar down on his head a second time. Simon's eyes flicked open, and stared unseeingly into the darkness.

Thomasina sat down on the ground, heedless of the dirt and scuttling crunchy-backed beetles, furious that she was feeling dizzy, and even more furious to realize she was feeling slightly sick. She put her head down between her knees, and willed herself not to faint: she had never fainted in her life, and she was damned if she was going to do so now.

Ah, but you've never killed a man before, have you? said Twygrist's soft voice inside her mind. *You didn't know what it would feel like, did you?*

Thomasina pushed the whispers away, got briskly to her feet, and held the candle up so she could examine Simon's face. Was he dead? He certainly looked it: that glassy stare, the dead-weight feeling of his whole body. She felt for a heartbeat, and thought there was the faintest flutter in his chest. Or was there? Her hands were shaking so badly she could not be sure. She took several deep breaths, and tried again. No, there was nothing; it must have been her imagination. She kept her hand across the left side of his chest for another minute, but it was absolutely still and silent. He was dead.

And really, she must be more disturbed by the atmosphere than she had thought, because she could still hear the hoarse creaking voice of the mill all around her.

Does it matter if he's dead or not, Thomasina? You know what you're going to do next, so it really doesn't matter if he's dead or alive. You don't need to care.

'I don't care,' said Thomasina angrily to the voices, and standing up she brushed the dust from her skirt. Simon was dead – of course he was, and a very good riddance to him – and she must get on with the next part of the plan.

If she had been able to drag Simon's body as far as the reservoir, or out to the Amber River, she would have tipped his body into the water and trusted to luck that he would not be found. But she did not think she could manage it. Simon was too heavy for her, and there was also the risk of someone seeing them. She was taking no chances about this; Simon's death must look like an accident.

She relit her candle and the one Simon had been carrying which had rolled into a corner and snuffed itself out, and positioned them both on the ground at intervals along the tunnels.

Beacon lamps to light the way to a man's tomb, Thomasina?

No, just to show me where I'm going.

Hooking her hands under Simon's arms, she dragged him towards the kiln room. It took longer than she anticipated, because she had to keep stopping and moving the candles along with her to see her way, but eventually she got him to the steel doors, thankfully released her grip, and straightened up.

The kiln-room doors were shut, of course: when Twygrist was empty they always were shut to contain any fire that might break out from a spark kindling in the brick grate. But they were also kept shut to prevent people wandering into the kiln room and being trapped if the doors closed. George Lincoln had explained this to Thomasina and Simon, and had impressed on them that they must never go down there by themselves. Dangerous, he said solemnly. The doors were constructed so they would swing inwards at the lightest touch, and if that should happen, Thomasina and Simon might be imprisoned and might not be found for a very long time.

Thomasina grasped the handle on the left-hand door and pulled hard. At first the door refused to budge – it was solid steel and there seemed to be some kind of track that sloped down into the room itself, so that opening the door was almost like pulling it uphill. But eventually there was a screech of protesting hinges and she was able to force it all the way back and wedge it against the wall with the iron bar she had used on Simon. Only when she was satisfied that it could not swing shut and trap her, did she drag Simon inside.

Even though it was years since fires had burned down here, the air felt dry and raw and Thomasina found herself disliking the place very much. After a moment's thought she arranged Simon's body just inside the door, half-propped against the right-hand side. When he was eventually found – which might be quite a long time – it would appear that he had accidentally shut himself in and been trying to get out.

And the blows to the head? What if they're noticed, Thomasina?

What if people wonder what Simon was doing inside Twygrist?

It would be easy enough to say that she and Simon had discussed the possibility of reviving Twygrist and the family business, and that Simon had mentioned taking a look at the mill while he was here.

As for the blows to the head, they would probably be thought the result of his falling down while trying to get out, but it did not really matter what conclusion was reached about that, no one was going to suspect Simon's own cousin of killing him.

Thomasina took a final look round, shining the candle into all the corners. There was nothing to indicate she had been down here, and as soon as she got back to Quire she would get rid of the rust-stained gown she was wearing, and wash the smell and the taste of Twygrist away. Her mind dwelt pleasantly for a moment on a lavishly hot bath, scented soap and fluffy towels.

Finally, she bent down to remove the iron bar that had wedged the door. She would not risk leaving it down here. She would throw it into the reservoir on her way back to Quire.

For a moment she thought the door was not going to swing back into place, but then the hinges gave another banshee-shriek, and began to move. Thomasina watched it, gnawing at the knuckles of one hand with nervous anticipation. Supposing she had knocked the tracks out of true when she forced it open, or supposing the door itself had warped with age and would not close? But it was all right. The door scraped grittily over the ground, and then with a muffled clang, locked into place alongside its fellow.

Twygrist's kiln room, with Simon inside it, was sealed.

It was already growing dark outside – Thomasina saw she must have been inside Twygrist for a long time. All to the good, however; it meant she was unlikely to be seen walking back to Quire House.

She threw the iron bar into the reservoir, waited to be sure it sank, and then set off along the lanes. Her mind was already moving ahead, working out what she would say to people – it might be as well to say Simon had left Quire without any word, not even taking his luggage. She could appear puzzled and slightly concerned which would be natural and innocent behaviour.

Her original plan for Maud and Simon would obviously need to be altered. Thomasina considered telling people that Maud and Simon had actually been married, but decided against it. Simon's body would eventually be found, and if Maud was believed to be his widow all kinds of complications might arise.

She needed to give Maud a fictitious husband, an unknown man. The more Thomasina thought about it, the more she could see that the whole thing would work better without Simon. It should be possible to take Maud away for a few weeks, after which they could announce that there had been a private marriage ceremony in London – a long-standing but secret romance, they would say; people liked that kind of thing. Then a tragic honeymoon accident. Everyone would be sympathetic, and there would be no raised eyebrows at the child, no stigma surrounding his birth, because it simply would not occur to anyone in Amberwood that innocent little Maud Lincoln might have misbehaved before marriage.

She and Maud would choose a name for the man – even Maud would understand that she could not have a child outside marriage – and they would think up a few extra details to make it really plausible.

Maud's father would have to be squared, but Thomasina could deal with George Lincoln. He could probably be paid to keep quiet; as well as being a social climber, he was greedy for money. Toft House, he often said proudly, was an expensive old place to maintain.

As she crossed the park, her brain busy with all these details, one other thing kept uncomfortably crossing Thomasina's mind, and it was something she could not quite ignore. That faint fluttering heartbeat she had felt in Simon's chest . . . had she felt it or hadn't she? She relived the moment when she had bent over to examine him the first time. She *had* felt something, but when she tried again, there had been nothing, she was sure about that.

But as she went into the house, she had to make an effort to ignore the thought that Simon had not really been dead when she slammed the steel doors of the kiln room.

* * *

The last person Bryony Sullivan had expected to see loping along Quire's carriageway was the Reverend Skandry, but as she returned from an evening stint of duty at Latchkill there he was, like a thin black spider capering through the twilight. He hailed her almost at once, which meant Bryony could not whisk along the path to the cottage and pretend she had not seen him.

The last time she had met Reverend Skandry had been the previous afternoon at Latchkill. A patient in Forrester Wing, annoyed with the meagre dinner, had prophesied various grisly fates for the Prout, which had included being consumed by swarms of locusts and immersion in burning lakes where chained devils roar. The Prout, recognizing these allusions as biblical, had sent Dora Scullion for Reverend Skandry. Scullion had run all the way to St Michael's Church and back, but as Bryony could have told anyone, Skandry had been of no help at all, and so poor Scullion had then gone pelting along to Bracken House to get Dr Glass.

Walking home, Bryony smiled at the memory of how Dr Glass had called Reverend Skandry a canting old preacher unable to recognize plain hysteria when he saw it. He had unbuckled the restraints from the patient and thrown them into the corridor. After this he said that if ever he found restraints used again in Latchkill he would take the place apart brick by brick to find every buckle and strap, and would then make a bonfire of the whole lot in the town square.

Reverend Skandry had taken his leave, his dignity in tatters, and Bryony had hoped it would be the last she would see of him, but here he was in the park, calling out to her in his thin reedy voice.

'Ah, Miss Sullivan. Late duty at Latchkill, was it? Dear me, there's quite a flurry going on at Quire, I fear.'

Clearly there was to be no escaping the man, so Bryony asked what the flurry might be.

'It's Mr Simon Forrester,' said Reverend Skandry. 'He seems to have vanished from Quire House without a word of explanation. Miss Thomasina is very worried.'

'Vanished?' Bryony did not know Simon Forrester very well,

but he was not someone you would associate with vanishing. 'How peculiar. When did he vanish? I mean – when was he last seen?'

'Not for two days, seemingly, and Miss Thomasina has asked me to make some inquiries – I am going along to the railway station in Chester first thing tomorrow morning. I am very glad to give my help, of course.'

He would be very glad indeed, the two-faced old hypocrite. Anything to ally himself with Quire House. By the end of the week, he would be making it seem as if he and Thomasina Forrester were bosom friends.

Bryony said, 'I daresay he'll turn up. Have you thought of asking at the post office? A telegram might have come for him, and he might have had to leave suddenly.'

Reverend Skandry conceded that this was a possibility, although he did not, it appeared, entirely approve of telegrams. He did not think the Lord had intended messages to be sent whizzing across hundreds of miles by electric power. He had even been in a house recently where there was a telephone which he had thought shockingly intrusive.

'Useful, though,' said Bryony.

'That's as maybe, Miss Sullivan. And I make no doubt Mr Simon will be found safe and sound. Gentlemen do not simply vanish without trace.'

There was a single light burning in one of Quire's windows until very late that night. If Bryony curled up on the windowsill of her bedroom she could see it shining through the trees. Was it Thomasina who was wakeful up there worrying about where her cousin might be? Byrony was not inclined to think so; she did not think Thomasina ever worried about anything very much.

Everyone said Quire was a beautiful house, but it was a bit too symmetrical for Bryony's taste. That was probably because she could remember the sprawling old house on Ireland's west coast, where sunshine poured in through the latticed windows and the gardens were a romantic wilderness of wild primroses and broken stone statues crusted with lichen.

'You're seeing it through rose-tinted spectacles,' Cormac had once said when Bryony was in a nostalgic mood. 'The house was falling down around our ears – there wasn't a whole brick in the place or a sound tile on the roof, and most of the furniture was nearly in matchsticks from woodworm. It's all probably crumbled into nothing by now.'

But they both knew the Irish house would not really have crumbled into nothing, and Bryony thought that children did not really notice or care about crumbling roofs or worm-eaten furniture. When she thought about the house she only remembered how the rooms had been scented with beeswax from when there had still been housemaids to polish the furniture, and how, if you stood on the terrace and looked across to the west, you could see the purple smudge of mountains and the glint of the sea . . .

Her father said that when he was a boy his mother used to walk in the gardens wearing a huge shady hat and cutting sheaves of lilac. 'As unruffled as if she had all the time and money in Christendom and all the leisure in the world,' he said, but then he would add, 'And as if there were no bailiffs permanently camping out in the kitchen, or men arriving with a distraint on the furniture three times a week.'

When he talked like this, Bryony told him he had no romance in his soul, to which he usually replied that their family had kept the noble profession of debt collectors in business for at least two decades. He always sent her his slant-eyed smile when he said this, and Bryony thought they both knew that one day they would find a way to go back to that house.

CHAPTER SIXTEEN

The photo-copied papers Antonia had brought from Quire House did not seem to be in any particular order. The first set appeared to contain financial statements and accounts, mostly relating to maintenance of the fabric: repairs to the roof and gutters, to broken windows and kitchen supplies. Antonia flipped through these rather perfunctorily, pausing over a set of accounts headed Forrester Benevolent Trust, which appeared to be a specially created trust fund for the benefit of patients at Latchkill Insane Asylum who for some reason could not be admitted to the paupers' ward, but who had no money of their own for the private section.

There was an exchange of letters between a local doctor and Latchkill's matron. They did not seem to be in chronological order, which might have been because someone had thrust them carelessly into a box or an envelope twenty or even a hundred years earlier, or it might be down to haphazard photocopying by the sullen Greg Foster. Who cares about the dates on a load of boring old letters, he had probably thought. But it was easy enough to put them in sequence. Some of them were in a small, rather mean-looking hand, and others appeared to have been dashed off by somebody who was either in a hurry or was exasperated with the intended recipient.

The earliest was one of these exasperated in a hurry letters. The date was October 1899 and the address was Bracken House, Amberwood. Antonia wondered if Bracken House still existed. She would make enquiries tomorrow.

She began to read.

Bracken Surgery
Tuesday p.m.

My Dear Matron

I am appalled to learn you have administered apomorphine mixed with hyoscine to two Reaper Wing patients. Please never use this method again – it's a terrible and inhumane treatment.

I also believe that despite my request, you have discontinued the exercise hour for Reaper Wing because of the apparent attempt by two patients to escape. Even if any of them did escape they would not get very far, and in any case they would be too bewildered by the world to inflict any real harm on anyone. So please restore that hour to them at once. It's an important part of their day: they look forward to it and it gives them a semblance of normality, which is vital.

Thank you for the recent invitation to afternoon tea, but I regret I shall not have time to accept. I do not, in fact, normally drink afternoon tea.

Sincerely,
Daniel Glass

Latchkill Asylum
Wednesday a.m.

Dear Dr Glass

In re. your letter of yesterday, the apomorphine/hyoscine was administered as an emergency measure. On this occasion, my nurses were being distracted from seeing to the breakfasts. It is my rule that breakfast is at 7.00 sharp, which means the night staff have to begin preparations around half past five – porridge for sixty people does not prepare itself. The hyoscine draught was intended as a calming method and it proved effective, allowing staff to attend to their other duties.

Reaper Wing's recreation hour has been reinstated as per your instructions, although I am unhappy about it. It seems unnecessarily *public* to actually allow them into the grounds.

I am afraid your little protegée, Dora Scullion, is not turning out very well. I believe her to be quarter-witted, and doubt her suitability for the work here even in the kitchens.

I am sorry to hear you cannot take afternoon tea with us. Perhaps morning coffee another day might be more convenient. Shall we say Monday of next week?

Cordially,

Freda Prout (Matron)

Bracken Surgery
Wednesday p.m.

Dear Matron

I am not surprised your treatment had a calming effect. If you were forced to swallow a violent emetic and spent the next twenty-four hours vomiting, you would end in being very calm indeed. I don't care if these patients try to take Latchkill apart brick by brick, or if you and your staff have to stand guard on them from now until the start of the second millennium, apomorphine and hyoscine are *never* to be given again, not to any patient in your care.

I can't see that it matters how *public* Reaper Wing's recreation hour is. The patients can never be allowed out of Latchkill, of course, and keeping them in their own wing is obviously necessary, but that's no reason not to give them a little normality.

As for Dora Scullion, please leave her to me. She is most certainly not quarter-witted; it is simply that, to quote the words of another, she dances to music other people cannot hear.

Sorry, but I never have time for morning coffee and will be extremely busy on Monday anyway.

Daniel Glass

Latchkill Asylum
Thursday a.m.

Dear Dr Glass

It is most generous of you to take an interest in Scullion. I hope your musical project, whatever it is, turns out well.

I have always considered the hyoscine mix very beneficial and, as you know, I feel that isolation and restraint is often necessary. Perhaps we may try electro-hydrotherapy instead?

Cordially,
Freda Prout (Matron)

Bracken Surgery
Thursday p.m.

Dear Matron

No!

Water and electricity are a potentially lethal combination, and, in the wrong hands, disastrous. Do you want to take Latchkill back to the days of starvation, fetters and flogging, or try rearranging the brain by means of the spinning stool!

I have recently been studying the use of mesmerism at Bart's Hospital in London – or, to give it its modern name, hypnotism – and I am coming to believe that it can be very beneficial in understanding the hidden conflicts and buried memories of the mentally ill. I intend to talk to Latchkill's governing board about the possibility of attempting this procedure on several of the patients.

Daniel Glass

'I'd have liked you,' said Antonia, coming up out of the nineteenth century, and addressing the long-ago Daniel Glass. 'I like the angry compassion you had for the patients, and I like the way you tried to help some poor frightened little kitchenmaid. I wonder if you did try hypnotism on your patients, and if so, how successful it was?'

As she worked through the rest of the papers, making notes as she did so, she wondered how Dr Glass would react to today's methods and treatments, and how he would feel about Antonia reading his letters. She had the feeling he would not have minded at all, and might have been rather amused. You could be one of the ghosts that occasionally wander around in this cottage, Dr Glass, but I don't mind that because I think you're rather a friendly ghost.

The ten-minute walk to Quire House this afternoon ought not to be such a massive ordeal. It was a lovely autumn day – the kind of day Richard had always enjoyed. Antonia wondered if she could think about Richard as she walked, and this struck her as a good idea because if Richard was with her when she went out, she would be fine. It would probably not be too painful, after so long she could blot out that last sight of Richard lying on the floor, with that hellish *Caprice* music spattered with his blood. She could focus on good memories instead: on how his eyes used to narrow when he was amused, and how immensely still he always was when he listened to music. The way they had always laughed at the same things, and how she could never hide it from him if she was upset or angry, no matter how much she tried, because he always sensed what she was feeling. No one but Richard had ever done that; Antonia did not think anyone else ever would.

Godfrey Toy was delighted Miss Weston kept their appointment. He had been a bit worried as to how serious she had been over helping to catalogue the cellar's contents. Halfway through the morning he had begun to wonder if he was being too trusting and whether he ought to ask Miss Weston for a reference of some kind – Oliver would probably think he ought to. But it seemed rather discourteous and even a touch melodramatic. It was not as if there were likely to be any state secrets or incriminating letters in Quire's cellars, and even if there were, Miss Weston would hardly turn out to be a Middle East spy, or a blackmailer of cabinet ministers or royalty. It was true that one or two of the smaller display items had recently vanished – jewellery and a pair of enamelled snuff-boxes – but that was one of the hazards of running this kind of place. Godfrey did not entirely trust Greg Foster, but he was trying to be fair to the boy, so he had not said anything. The thief was just as likely to be one of the visitors.

Still, he hoped the professor would not make one of his snarky comments about gullibility or manipulative females. If he did, Godfrey would just remind him of the other occasions when they had allowed people to do local research at Quire.

In case Miss Weston might be regretting her offer, he had thought out a little speech about forgetting she was here on holiday, and not wanting to impose on her time. But so that she would not think he was being dismissive, he had also rushed down to the town to buy some really nice things for a little afternoon snack which they could have with a cup of tea. Cinnamon toast, which Godfrey loved and which hardly anyone ever bothered with nowadays, and some of the really delicious scones from the bakery. Cherry conserve to go with them. Just as he was preparing to go back to Quire, he spotted some stuffed olives and smoked oysters in the delicatessen, so he put these in his shopping bag as well, in case Miss Weston stayed on for a glass of sherry. You never knew. He added a bottle of Croft's Dry Original, and then a second bottle of an amontillado because you had to cover all contingencies.

But far from regretting her offer, Miss Weston seemed genuinely keen. She said she was working through the photocopied material, and finding it absorbing. She had been particularly intrigued by the material on Latchkill Asylum.

'The actual building's long since gone, of course,' said Godfrey, proferring the cinnamon toast. 'But you could try the county library, or the records office – although that would probably mean going into Chester. But they'd have details about land transfers and so on.'

'Would it be all right if I made notes on anything I find about Latchkill? Because— Oh, this is lovely toast. I haven't had cinnamon toast since I was a child.'

'Of course you can make notes,' said Godfrey.

'It's truly just for my own interest – I'm not writing an exposé on anybody or wanting to solve some ancient mystery or anything like that. It's only a holiday project.'

'You can have the run of the cellars for as long as you like,' said Godfrey. 'In any case, you'll be helping us out by starting the cataloguing. I thought you could work in the little room near the old sculleries – providing you don't mind it having been the butler's pantry. It's not pantry-esque now, in fact we use it when the VAT inspector comes in, or for the auditor's visit every year. The professor usually deals with that, of course; I haven't a very good head for figures.'

Miss Weston said gravely that she did not in the least mind working in a butler's pantry. She could bring her laptop with her or she could just make sheaves of notes and take them back to Charity Cottage to list everything in whatever way they agreed. They could see what worked best.

The curious thing was that Godfrey had been thinking of Miss Weston as rather ordinary – polite and pleasant and she had a nice voice – but nothing very remarkable. She was a good listener.

But when they talked about Latchkill and Amberwood's history, her whole expression altered and she looked quite different. As if a light had flared behind her eyes.

It was silly to feel awkward about introducing the question of payment, but it had to be done and so Godfrey plunged in.

'I don't expect any payment at all, Dr Toy. I approached you, if you recall. And I'm not qualified for this kind of work. I might make all kinds of a hash of it.'

She would not make a hash of it, of course, because she was not the kind of person who would make a hash of anything she undertook. Godfrey found himself thinking that if he had had the necessary confidence (all right and maybe been a few years younger as well), Miss Weston might have been precisely the kind of lady he could have become a bit romantic over. Intelligent. Unusual. Not somebody you would necessarily look at twice, until something caught her interest and then there was that sudden glow that made you want to go on looking at her. He liked and admired ladies, but he had never felt he understood them and he had never dared approach one on any sort of emotional level, certainly not on any physical level. But he found himself hoping that Miss Weston would stay at the cottage for a long time.

If enough material on Latchkill turned up, they might even think about setting up a display on it – it was as much part of Amberwood's history as anywhere else, and the Trust liked the museum to come up with new exhibitions and new angles on the area. If so, Miss Weston might agree to help with that as well. But Godfrey thought he would save that suggestion until they saw how things went. He also thought he had better keep in mind all the stories of foolish old men who became enamoured of much younger ladies. Not that he was so very old, of course – he had a good few years yet before he began collecting his pension!

So he just said that if Miss Weston was absolutely sure about the money . . .?

'I'm quite sure, Dr Toy.'

Then, said Godfrey, they would not mention it again. He passed on to the pleasant suggestion that they abandon the tea cups in favour of a glass of sherry.

Walking back to Charity Cottage, Antonia felt distinctly light-headed, which was probably due to a mixture of cinnamon toast, scones and two large glasses of sherry.

It was not dark yet; it was the in-between time that was neither quite day nor quite night. Antonia always found it a rather eerie time, because the light and the shadows could play tricks on you. She had always disliked going into her own house at this hour, unless she knew Richard would be there. But the sooner she was inside the cottage the sooner she could switch on lights and turn up heating, and perhaps put on the radio or the television. She unlocked the front door and stepped briskly into the sitting room, flipping on the electric fire and the old-fashioned standard lamp near the window, liking the friendly warm glow that instantly flooded the room. She left her jacket on the back of a chair, and opened the inner door. She would not want much supper after all those scones and toast, but there was some salad stuff in the fridge that could be washed and left to drain, and she had bought ham and cooked chicken in Amberwood yesterday; it was still a novelty to be able to walk into a shop and choose whatever she wanted.

As she went across the dining room, there was a faint movement just beyond the kitchen door which she had left half open. She hesitated, and then thought it was probably Raffles who had got in again. Had he? Yes, something had definitely stirred within the kitchen, although it did not seem substantial enough to be a human intruder so there was nothing to feel scared about.

Or was there? Antonia took a cautious step forward, aware of little creakings and rustlings that might only be the cottage's timbers contracting in the cool evening air, but might as easily be the sounds of an intruder, creeping away into hiding. Of all the neurotic ideas to have! But something had moved in the kitchen, and it was still moving – Antonia could see the faint stirring of the shadows.

There was a symmetry to the sounds. Footsteps, was it? No, it was more like something moving backwards and forwards. Something rocking? Yes, that was exactly what it sounded like. She paused by the gateleg table, and glanced over her shoulder towards the friendly, warmly lit sitting room. She had closed the front door when she came in, and dropped the latch, but if there really was someone in the cottage she could be at the door in seconds, and outside.

It would not be an intruder, though. It would be Raffles or the plumbing or something in the central heating; it was certainly not her imagination. Whatever it was, it had to be tracked down and dealt with.

Despite her resolve, she had to take a deep breath before she could push open the kitchen door and step inside. The kitchen was dark and her apprehension increased but she reached for the light switch along the left-hand wall.

Something brushed against her face. Something that was light and dry, and felt for a terrible moment like an old, dead hand reaching out of the shadows to touch her cheek.

Panic grabbed Antonia, constricting her throat, so she could not even scream. The unseen thing touched her face again, a little more definitely this time, and she gave a sort of strangled half-cry, and hit out blindly. But her hands met only air, although there was the impression of some kind of thin movement directly in front of her. She was shaking so much she thought she might fall down, but she finally managed to locate the light switch.

The entire room and what it held sprang into dreadful clarity, and this time she did cry out.

Hanging from one of the rafters was a long thick rope – as thick as Antonia's wrist, almost as thick as a man's neck – and it was this rope that had swung into her face. The end of it had been looped up and knotted to form a shape that was sickeningly familiar from dozens of images. A hangman's noose. The method of punishment used until the middle of the twentieth century on men and women convicted of murder. Antonia stared at it in frozen horror. It was swinging slowly to and fro, pulling gently against the old ceiling joists as it moved and causing them to creak. It was several minutes before she managed to put out a shaky hand to still it, hating the coarse feel of the hemp, but unable to bear the swaying back and forth like a hypnotizing snake.

The rope had been moving because of the kitchen door opening, of course: the movement of air would have disturbed the rope, or the edge of the door might have caught it. Or had it been the soft creaking she had heard when she came in?

Whoever had let Raffles in that day must have come back. That person might even be hiding in the cottage now, watching her.

There was a faint warning creak from the ceiling beam, and the rope stirred slightly, and then began to sway again. Exactly as if someone was holding one end of it, swinging it menacingly.

Come closer, murderer . . . Step nearer so that I can loop this around your neck, and snap your spine, or strangle you in a slow death – it could go either way, you know . . .

Antonia's precarious control snapped. She gasped and ran from the kitchen, slamming the door hard. Somehow she got across the sitting room and wrenched the front door open, tumbling outside.

She leaned against the old stone wall of the cottage, still shuddering, and took several deep breaths of cold night air. And then, since to go back into the cottage, even to find her mobile phone or keys, was unthinkable, she began to run across the park, towards Quire House.

CHAPTER SEVENTEEN

Quire's main front door was closed, but when Antonia turned the handle, it swung open, and she went thankfully into the big shadowy hall and leaned against a carved chest for a moment to get her breath back and regain a degree of calm before seeking out Godfrey Toy. In a moment she would go through to his office at the back of the house, and explain to him that someone was playing some kind of sick joke on her.

Or would she? Could she tell anyone what had just happened without her real identity coming out? Without Richard's and Don's death being dragged into the light once more? But it would have to be done. Whoever had put that rope in Charity Cottage was sick and dangerous. Antonia went determinedly across the hall and through to the back of the house, which was in darkness. Darkness inside a house again . . . that eerie in-between darkness, when anything might be hidden by the shadows . . . Oh, for pity's sake get a grip!

The door to Godfrey's office was closed, but it was not long since Antonia had left him so there was a good chance he was still here. If he was not, she would decide whether to venture upstairs to find his flat. She was just preparing to tap on his door, when a man's voice behind her said, 'I'm afraid this part of the house isn't open to visitors. And the museum closed two hours ago.'

Antonia had not heard anyone approach, and the words made her jump. She spun round at once, hoping she did not look as startled as she felt. Whoever the speaker was, he was brown-haired with rather narrow deepset eyes and in the uncertain light he might almost have been part of the shadows, except for the voice. There was nothing in the least shadowy about the voice: it was distinctly frosty. It was a you-have-no-right-to-be-here voice, and a who-the-hell-are-you voice.

'In fact,' said this cold-voiced man, regarding Antonia with unmistakable hostility, 'the main doors ought to have been locked.'

'Well, the front one certainly wasn't locked,' said Antonia returning his stare, 'so I didn't break in, if that's what you're thinking. I'm staying at Charity Cottage for a few weeks, and I'm going to be doing some cataloguing work for Dr Toy – My name's Antonia Weston.'

'How do you do.' It was said with the slight impatience of someone paying lip-service to the conventions. The tone was still challenging. 'I'm Oliver Remus.'

Godfrey's professor. The half-academic, half-dynamic gentleman who had sounded like the most positive force in Godfrey's gentle life. There had not really been anyone else he could be, and through the still-lingering fear, Antonia registered that he was not in the least as she had pictured him. But by way of establishing her own credentials, she said, 'You're just back from a buying trip, aren't you? Dr Toy mentioned it.'

'Did he?' He took a step nearer. 'I'm sorry if I was sharp just now, Miss – Mrs? – Weston, but there are several quite valuable things in here and one or two have recently vanished, so you'll appreciate that I'm always suspicious of anyone wandering in after hours. We're considering a proper alarm system, but until then—' He did not sound especially annoyed about any of this or particularly apologetic at having spoken sharply to Antonia.

'In that case I'm sorry to come in when the house is closed to the public,' she said, trying to match his formality. 'But there's been a – I think there's been an intruder at Charity Cottage, and I'm not sure what I should do about it, so I thought I'd have a word with Dr Toy—' Infuriatingly her voice wobbled treacherously on this last part of the speech, and she broke off, frowning, because of all things to do – of all people to break down in front of . . .

Oliver Remus did not appear to notice the wobble. He said, quite sharply, 'What kind of intruder? A burglar, d'you mean? In that case you should definitely call the police. I can give you the number of the local station if you don't want to invoke a dramatic 999 response. Not that anyone ever behaves particularly dramatically in Amberwood.'

'It's not an ordinary burglar,' said Antonia, ignoring this last part. 'It's some freak who's getting into the cottage and playing sick jokes on me. I've just encountered the latest example, so I'm a bit off-balance.'

She had his full attention now. 'Did you say, "getting into the cottage"?'

'Yes. Even when it's all locked up.'

'How?'

'If I knew that,' said Antonia angrily, 'I probably wouldn't have run so wildly across the park just now to get help from Dr Toy.' This was the most bizarre discussion to be having in the unlit passageway of Quire House with this unfriendly stranger who was still regarding her with suspicion. She said, 'I don't *know* how he's getting in, but he's certainly been there this afternoon!'

'Is anything missing?'

'I don't think so.'

'Then how d'you know someone's been in?'

'I'll explain it to the police,' said Antonia, feeling awkward and consequently sounding aggressive. 'Did you say you had the number of the local station?'

'It's in my flat. I'll go up and get it for you.'

'Please don't bother. I've got a mobile phone, and I can as easily get it from Inquiries or something.'

Antonia turned to go, but he stopped her.

'You're not going back to the cottage, are you?'

'Yes.' Where else did he think she was going?

'Don't be stupid,' said Oliver Remus impatiently. 'If there's an intruder around you can't go back across the park on your own and you certainly can't go inside the cottage until it's been properly checked.'

'I'll be perfectly all right.'

'Yes, but I won't be perfectly all right if I hear afterwards that you've been mugged or raped, or knocked out and left for dead. You'd better come up to my flat; we'll phone the police from there and then I'll walk back with you.'

Without waiting for her answer, he went through to the main hall, and up the wide curving staircase, clearly assuming she would follow him. Since there did not seem to be anything else to do, Antonia fought down her annoyance and did follow him.

The main stairs wound up to the first floor where Godfrey Toy had his flat, and a narrower flight went up to the second floor. Oliver Remus unlocked a door at the top, and went in ahead of Antonia, switching on lights. The flat was surprisingly large; it apparently took up the entire second floor of Quire, and the rooms were high-ceilinged with an elegant fireplace in the big sitting room and several nice old pieces of furniture. There were a great many books, some on shelves, some spilling onto the floor, and there were brass lamps on side tables, and scatterings of pens and sheaves of notes. In one of the window recesses was a large Victorian desk, with a computer and a fax machine on it. A battered suitcase stood in the centre of the room, with two large boxes of books propped against it.

'Gleanings of the trip,' said Oliver Remus, seeing Antonia glance at the boxes. 'A house that belonged to a former headmaster of a minor public school. I picked up two quite nice first editions and a Rex Whistler book plate. Oh, and a set of Ruskin's books but only what's called the Waverley editions which aren't particularly valuable. Would you like me to phone the police for you? It'd probably carry more weight.'

'Because they know you?'

'That sounds as if you think I'm an old lag, Miss Weston.' It was lightly said, but Antonia's eyes flew upwards to his face. 'You'd better have a glass of brandy first, though. Antidote to shock.'

He poured the brandy, and then checked an address book and made the call, merely saying that there were signs of a break in at Charity Cottage and that the cottage was presently occupied by a lady living on her own. He listened to the voice at the other end for a moment, and then said quite sharply, 'Yes, I do think you should send someone out at once. I don't know if anything's been taken, but Miss Weston's presumably got to sleep in the cottage tonight and if the prowler's still around . . .' There was a pause, and then he handed the phone to Antonia. 'They're sending someone out to take a look round and get statements in about half an hour, but they'd like more details from you first. It's Sergeant Blackburn.'

He left her to it, going into one of the other rooms – presumably his bedroom because he took the suitcase with him – but even though he closed the door Antonia thought he could probably hear what she was saying. Infuriatingly, relayed to the stolid-sounding sergeant, the two incidents sounded like the delusions of a neurotic female: the first ridiculously trivial – the cat got in without my seeing how or where; the second over-dramatic. A hangman's noose tied to a beam in the kitchen, left there for her to find.

Yes, she had said a hangman's noose. Yes, she was sure. No, she had not touched anything, she had simply got out of the cottage as fast as— Well, presumably the thing was still there, unless the person had sneaked back in and removed it in her absence. 'I should think that's perfectly possible, shouldn't you, Sergeant?'

Sergeant Blackburn said cautiously that anything was possible when you were dealing with the workings of a disturbed mind, madam, and passed on to the question that Antonia had known would come at some point.

'You said you were here on holiday, Miss Weston, is that right? In that case, I'll need a note of your permanent address. Oh, and a phone number.'

Antonia gripped the phone tightly, and said, 'I haven't got a permanent address – I've been away for a long time.' But this sounded so absurd and so redolent of nineteenth-century lunatics locked away for years and the truth covered up with euphemisms, that she gave the sergeant the hospital address, and said he should record it as care of Jonathan Saxon, head of psychiatry.

'Psychiatry?' said the voice at the other end with a suspicious edge, and at the same time Antonia was aware of a sudden stillness from the adjoining room.

'My boss,' she said, into the phone, and this time there was an edge of authority in her voice she had not known she could still summon. Either this or Oliver Remus's brandy gave her sufficient confidence to add, 'Thank you, Sergeant Blackburn. I'll see you at Charity Cottage in half an hour,' and to hang up before any more difficult questions could be asked.

As they walked back across the park, Professor Remus had the air of someone who wanted to get a necessary task over so that he could get back to more important things. Antonia found this depressing and annoying in equal portions. But as they turned into the walkway between the old yew hedges, he suddenly said, 'You did tell the police that someone had put a hangman's rope in the kitchen, didn't you? I did hear that right?'

'Yes.'

He half turned his head to look at her. 'How extraordinary.'

'That's one word for it.'

'The front door's open,' he said, as they rounded the curve in the path and the cottage came into view. 'Did you leave it like that?'

'Yes. I ran out of the place as soon as I saw the – the rope. I wasn't thinking about locking up, and anyhow the intruder had already got in so it didn't seem to matter about keys and locks and things.'

'I wasn't criticizing. That looks like the police driving up now. We'd better wait here and let them go in ahead of us, I should think.'

Sergeant Blackburn was very much like his voice: large and a bit ponderous. He introduced a young PC who was with him, and said this sounded like a strange business so they would go inside on their own first, just to see what was what.

'We'll wait here,' said Oliver. 'All right, Miss Weston?'

'Never better.'

The police search took quite a long time. Antonia sat down on the little low wall that surrounded part of the cottage's gardens, and tried not to shiver too noticeably. Lights were switched on inside the cottage, and there were sounds of doors being noisily opened, and of the two policemen calling to one another. When they eventually came out, Antonia's heart skipped a few beats, but she said, 'Well?'

'You did say the rope was in the kitchen, Miss Weston?'

'Yes. You can't miss it. It was hanging down from the ceiling,' said Antonia. 'You'd walk smack into it if you didn't know it was there.'

Sergeant Blackburn exchanged a glance with his constable, and looked at Oliver Remus. 'There's nothing there,' he said. 'The kitchen's perfectly normal – no rope, no signs of one anywhere.'

The constable added, 'And there are no signs of any break in.' He glanced at the sergeant, who studied Antonia for a moment and then said, 'Can you think why anyone would put a hangman's noose in your kitchen, Miss Weston?'

After they had all left, Antonia was angrily aware of her isolation.

What am I doing here, cut off from everyone I've ever known, with a madman attempting to spook me? Hangman's nooses in the kitchen, teleportation of cats and cars driven by dead men – it's classic horror-film material. All I need to complete the picture is for someone to hammer on the door, and say his car's broken down so could he possibly use the phone, oh, and please not to take any notice of the dripping axe he happens to have in his hand, it's just a rather outré accessory he likes to carry . . .

What would Richard have done in this situation? It was impossible to visualize him physically tackling the madman, but it was certainly possible to imagine him working out some kind of subtle trap. For a moment, Richard was with Antonia so vividly that she could almost hear him saying, 'I'll teach the sick bastard to frighten you half to death!' She could see his eyes glowing with fury for the cruel mind that had fashioned the hanging rope and played the other tricks.

Donna was extremely pleased at how well this part of the plan had gone.

It had been quite tricky to set it up – trickier than the cat ploy, which had been a suddenly seen, quickly seized opportunity – and certainly trickier than playing the part of a visitor to Quire last week and unobtrusively placing the *Caprice* sheet music on the spinet in the hope it would stay there long enough for Weston to find it. But she had managed it and it had worked beautifully.

As she drove away from Quire House, she smiled to think how predictable this murderous bitch actually was, and how predictable she had been all along the way. Even renting Charity Cottage – the cottage that Donna had forced on her, like a conjurer forcing a playing card.

CHAPTER EIGHTEEN

The playing card had been prepared a long time ago, of course. Five years ago, to be precise. Quite soon after Antonia's trial, Donna had quietly and unassumingly set about joining several charity organizations attached to the hospital where Antonia had worked. She used a false name, and explained to people that she had not a great deal of money but that she would like to help.

She had been welcomed enthusiastically of course, and after a year or two she became quite well known for her work. Absolutely tireless, people said. A real godsend to the Friends of the Hospital, to the fund-raising committee for the new scanner, to the campaign for more ICU and HDU beds. Always willing to organize flag days, charity discos, sponsored walks or swims. Pure gold. We'll have to invite her to a few official things, by way of a thank you.

The invitations to the few official things snowballed – Donna made sure they did – and she got to know people on the hospital's staff quite well. After a time it was easy to form several convenient friendships with a few of the bitch's former colleagues. Antonia's name was quite often mentioned, especially in the first year or so, when people were still in shock. A dreadful thing, they all said. How on earth would she cope with eight years in gaol?

Donna listened politely to this, and to people saying what a loss to the hospital Antonia was and what a good and committed doctor of psychiatry she had been. Great company as well – those terrific supper parties she and Richard used to give, oh dear, life could be so cruel, couldn't it?

Antonia Weston had not been a good psychiatrist, and Donna did not give a damn if she had been good company or the most boring person in the world. Weston was going to die for what she had done to Don, and she was going to die alone and terrified, as Don had.

Two years later, moving the plan along, Donna took a long lease on Charity Cottage, using the name of Mrs Romero – her grandmother's maiden name. She posed as a widow, modestly affluent, who travelled a good deal, but who wanted a base in England. She would be at the cottage at infrequent intervals, but would keep the place clean and safe between times. The Quire House Trust had only just been formed and was still in its infancy, so the letting of Charity Cottage was dealt with by agents in Chester who did not care if the place was lived in every day or only an hour every year, providing the rent was paid.

Donna paid the rent promptly, sending a cheque every month from a specially created building-society account so her real name never appeared. It was quite a drain on her resources, but she did not mind because she could not risk the cottage being let when Weston was released. She needed to be sure Charity Cottage would be available.

She stayed there at intervals so people would not wonder why it was empty for such long periods, and she made sure she was seen in Amberwood, although she kept her distance from people. During the winter months she set up a time switch for the lights so anyone seeing the place from the road would assume it was occupied. She kept the inside aired and clean and the little fenced-off garden neat.

At the hospital she kept her ear to the ground for mentions of Antonia's release.

It was as well she did this, because one summer came the news that the bitch was being released early. Good behaviour, remission and time served prior to the trial, said people at the hospital. It had all been added up and what it amounted to was that Antonia would be out this coming autumn – the end of October, in fact. Wasn't that marvellous? She would need a few weeks to recuperate of course – somewhere to readjust to the world – but perhaps by Christmas . . . They went about beaming, and Donna hated them for liking Antonia so much. She hated the dumb-witted, insensitive prison authorities who were letting a murderess walk free after only five years.

She almost panicked at the short time this gave her to finalize her plan. Barely two months. Was it long enough? It would have to be.

As September drew to a close, she ended the lease on Charity Cottage. It was not very likely the agents would find anyone to take the place at this time of year. Before handing in the keys, she had two extra sets cut, using one of the big, while you wait key-cutting places in Chester, and paying cash, so she would be able to get back into the cottage whenever she wanted. And she would want.

After this, she began to slide the name of Charity Cottage and Amberwood into conversations within the hospital network, saying offhandedly that a friend had mentioned the area, referring to it as a wonderfully peaceful part of the world, a marvellous place to heal wounds – somewhere to go if you were recovering from an illness or a bereavement or a divorce.

Or a prison sentence.

She was as sure as she could be that these carefully casual references reached people who had known Antonia and who had stayed in touch with her. Some of the clerical staff and the therapists who worked at the psychiatric clinic occasionally wrote to Antonia, and one or two of them had visited her a few times. Dr Saxon, the consultant psychiastrist who had been Antonia's immediate boss, had certainly visited her. Donna thought Jonathan

Saxon had rather fancied Antonia at one time, although if you listened to hospital gossip, you would have to believe that Jonathan Saxon had fancied most of the females in the hospital at various times. Donna did not care if he screwed every female in sight providing he knew about the marvellously peaceful cottage, and providing he mentioned it to Antonia.

Apart from the bitch's earlier than expected release, the plan was proceeding almost exactly as Donna had hoped. The only thing she could not predict with any confidence was whether Weston would take the carefully prepared bait. Donna was not given to praying, but during those weeks there were several times when she almost did. If her plan failed at this stage she would have to start all over again. But it would not fail. It must not.

It did not fail. The timing worked, and Donna's own psychology worked as well. Less than a week after Antonia Weston's release, she heard from one of the therapists that the bitch was renting Charity Cottage for a few weeks.

Antonia had walked straight into the trap Donna had so painstakingly set. Now all she had to do was keep a careful watch, and move the various stages of her plan along.

She kept watch by the simple expedient of parking her car at a big new garden centre about three quarters of a mile away, and walking up to Quire House each day, going openly through the gates in the wake of ordinary visitors. It was easy to step off the main drive and take the footpath that wound through the trees. Quire had not yet entered the world of CCTV cameras, and if anyone had challenged her, Donna would have assumed the mien of a rather thick visitor, apologetic at having missed the 'Private' sign. But no one did.

She watched the cottage from the concealment of the trees, which was tedious, but had to be done. There was a brief alleviation of the tedium quite early on when she was able to let the large inquisitive cat into the cottage and unwrap food from the fridge for him. It only took a few moments and although it was a small incident Donna thought it would unnerve Weston. On the fourth day her patience was rewarded more substantially. Shortly before four o'clock Antonia set off across the park, carrying a large envelope. Donna waited to make sure she was not coming straight back, and then slipped into the cottage, the rope looped around her waist under her anorak.

She was wearing gloves, of course, and she had tied her hair under a scarf and then drawn up the hood of her anorak. You had only to watch a TV crime programme to know how very precise forensic science was nowadays, a single hair could be enough to identify a suspect, and she did not intend to be caught.

It was easy to pull out a kitchen chair, stand on it and tie the rope to one of the old ceiling beams near the door. Fashioning the noose was the best part of all; it looked amazingly real and startlingly sinister. She got down from the chair and dusted the seat, even though she was wearing cheap mass-produced trainers which were unlikely to be traceable. Then she returned the chair to its place. Yes, the rope looked all right, and the time of day was a bonus: it was nicely dark – that oddly macabre dusk-light you got at this time of year. She had closed the curtains so Weston would come into an unlit room.

Donna moved the rope back and forth experimentally. It was tied quite tightly to the beam and the movement pulled on the old ceiling timbers, making them creak softly. It was quite a spooky sound, and it brought a forgotten memory with it: the memory of how the kitchen joists had always creaked in just that way when someone walked across the floor of the bedroom directly overhead, and of how Don, before that last summer, sometimes pretended the cottage was haunted and made up scary stories about ghosts. There was definitely something in the far corner of the kitchen, near the door, he used to say. You had only to go in there to feel it. Occasionally he sounded perfectly serious about this, but Donna knew the cottage was not haunted, of course. Even so, it was still quite eerie to stand down here and hear the ceiling beams creak as the rope swayed gently back and forth . . .

You did not abandon a plan you had spent months putting together and years polishing, but nor did you close your mind against an improvement. Donna gave a final look round the room, checked she had locked the garden door, pocketed the key and went quickly out of the kitchen and up the stairs.

It was a bit of a gamble to hide in the cottage when Weston came in and saw the noose, but Donna did not think it was much of one. She thought Weston would be so frightened when the rope began to move – apparently of its own accord, but really, of course, from the pressure on the joists overhead – that she would not search the cottage by herself.

But if by any chance she did remain there, Donna could get out unseen through the window in the back bedroom. At some stage of its history the cottage had been extended to join the kitchen to the old wash-house and make it one big room; the extension had a flat roof which was directly below the bedroom window, and there was a tough-looking drainpipe which she could climb down.

But it probably would not be necessary to do that and, in the event, it was not. Antonia ran out of the cottage, and Donna gave her a couple of minutes to get clear and than went down the stairs. Her heart pounding, she pulled the chair out again, and reached up to unfasten the knots. The rope slid down into her hands like an obedient snake, and she folded it under her jacket and went out through the garden door, locking it behind her.

Driving towards the motorway link road and the anonymous service station motel where she would spend the night, she was looking forward to the next move. She already knew which of Quire House's occupants would be part of Antonia's destruction.

After Antonia Weston left, Godfrey Toy had asked Greg Foster to look in the cellars for any more papers marked either 'Forrester' or 'Latchkill'. No, it did not matter precisely what, just anything labelled with either of those names. He had not really expected Greg to find anything, and was delighted when he came shambling back an hour later with a bundle of what looked like letters and some kind of ancient account book. Godfrey tucked them tidily into a cardboard folder, and decided to walk across to the cottage tomorrow to give them to Miss Weston.

He was just about to lock up his office when Oliver arrived home a day earlier than expected. Godfrey was pleased because he never felt really comfortable alone in Quire. He was still prone to dreadful nightmares and could not drive past that terrible old mill without first talking himself into doing so.

He pottered up to Oliver's rooms to be told how the buying trip to the ex-headmaster's house had gone. It was disappointing to hear that the hoped for Bernard Shaw letters had not materialized, although Oliver had never expected much of that. A too enthusiastic nephew, he said in the disparaging way that had gradually become natural to him over the last five years, but that Godfrey always found upsetting. The letters had no more been written by Shaw than the morning's note to the milkman, said Oliver, and the Marlowe folio had been a mid-Victorian reprint.

Godfrey had gone back to his own flat, feeling quite glum. He exchanged a word with Raffles who had wandered in, and started to put together his supper. The prospect of walking over to Charity Cottage tomorrow cheered him up, and while the potatoes were cooking he poured himself a glass of Madeira. He liked Madeira, and he sang the fruity old Flanders and Swann song to himself while he drank it – the one about, Have some Madeira, m'dear – and tried to imagine how it might feel to put on a mulberry velvet smoking-jacket and embark on a seduction, although actually he had no idea how you went about seducing someone and mulberry was not his colour anyway.

It was at this point that Oliver knocked on the door to tell him about the extremely peculiar events at Charity Cottage.

Godfrey was so upset to hear about Antonia's distressing experience (she had already ceased to be Miss Weston in his thoughts), he abandoned the Madeira and potatoes in favour of a gin and tonic, and listened to the whole tale. At the end of it, he said he hoped Oliver had been sympathetic, and vanishing rope trick or not, oughtn't they to invite Miss Weston to stay at Quire for tonight?

Oliver said he had been as sympathetic with Miss Weston as the situation had warranted, and that they could not be taking in flaky female holiday-makers who turned up out of the blue and had bizarre hallucinations all over the place. He also added that in future it would be better if Godfrey refrained from making absurdly trusting arrangements with unknown ladies to catalogue the contents of Quire's cellars. Good God, this Antonia Weston might be anyone, said Oliver, and went up to his own flat and banged the door on the world, leaving Godfrey to a disconsolate and solitary supper, which he ended up sharing with Raffles.

He hoped he would not have nightmares when he went to bed.

CHAPTER NINETEEN

For two nights after Thomasina killed Simon, she suffered fearsome nightmares.

In them Simon was trapped and frenzied, clawing at the heavy steel doors of the kiln room, screaming for help . . . Dreadful. Thomasina tossed and turned in the big wide bed that had been so wonderful when Maud had been there with her, and tried to push the nightmares away. But they clawed deep into her mind, causing her to wake in the small hours, gasping and covered in perspiration.

The days were easier, and once she began to spread the story of Simon's puzzling disappearance, starting with that gossipy old Reverend Skandry, she felt better. Probably an official search had better be set in motion quite soon, but if – when – Simon's body was found, nobody would be especially surprised because Thomasina had prepared the ground by saying she and Simon had discussed opening up the mill. Everyone would believe he had gone to take a look at the old place. In the meantime, Thomasina asked Mrs Minching to keep Simon's room cleaned and aired, because no doubt he would turn up sooner or later.

Other than this, Thomasina went about her normal tasks, carrying trays of food up to Maud, visiting neighbours, letting it be known that Maud was on the road to recovery from influenza, although not yet quite up to visitors. She talked to Maud very carefully about her health, although that was difficult because Maud thought it embarrassing to refer to the monthly cycle. Mrs Plumtree, who had explained about these things when Maud was thirteen, had emphasized that it was not a matter to be talked about, except perhaps with a doctor or a nurse if the need arose.

Surely there could only be one reason for Maud being sick in the mornings: Maud had conceived. Quite soon Thomasina would explain her plan for a secret marriage and tragic widowhood. Maud would go along with it; she would understand what a scandal it would be if she did not. She might not actually want to allow Thomasina to adopt the child after its birth, but Thomasina could apply a little firm persuasion when the time came. It occurred to her that Maud was becoming so strange it might be necessary to remove the child from her care anyway.

But if Simon was still alive, the whole thing would start to go very wrong indeed. Supposing the nightmare turned out to be true and he was able to talk? 'My cousin hit me over the head with an iron bar, and shut me in the kiln room and left me to die . . .' Would anyone actually believe that?

But the nightmares and the worries were only nervous reaction. Even if Simon had not been quite dead, he could not survive for very long. Even if he had shouted for help until his throat burst, no one would have heard him, and no one could have got into Twygrist anyway, because Thomasina had the only set of keys.

On the morning of the third day after her attack on Simon, Thomasina, who prided herself on never being ill or feeling out of sorts, went down to breakfast feeling very unwell indeed.

The nightmares had persisted, and last night there had been the hoarse dark whispers she had heard inside Twygrist.

Did you really kill him, Thomasina? said these grating voices. *Are you sure he was dead when you left him down there, are you, ARE YOU?*

She had woken at 3 a.m. with the voices reverberating inside her head, and with fear clenching and unclenching so badly in her stomach she had to run to the bathroom. Back in bed she managed to get to sleep, but an hour later the process repeated itself. It was annoying to find that fear was something that grabbed you not romantically in the heart but sordidly in the gut. It was especially annoying because the use of Quire's bathroom at such a silent hour of the early morning would be heard all over the house.

But it was important to behave as if nothing was out of kilter, and so Thomasina appeared in the morning room as usual. When Mrs Minching brought in kippers she forced herself to eat them and even asked for more toast.

After this she determinedly spent half an hour in Maud's room, while Maud toyed pettishly with her own breakfast, consisting of coddled eggs and thin bread and butter – invalid food.

Questioned as to her day's plans, Maud hunched her shoulders and said there was not very much you could plan for when you were locked away like this. Still, she might practise her music, she thought. Or she might read a little. And again there was that *distant* look, as if Maud's mind was no longer quite with her body. It made Thomasina uneasy. Normally Simon had been with her when she came up here.

As if she had heard this last thought, Maud suddenly said, 'Where's Simon?' and Thomasina felt a warning twist of discomfort in her stomach again.

But following her plan, even with Maud, she said, 'I don't know. He seems to have vanished – I've asked Reverend Skandry to make a few enquiries, but I should think we'll find that he's taken himself back to London without so much as a goodbye.

'Oh, I see. I wondered where he was.' The words were quite ordinary, but there was the furtive sliding away of the eyes again, as if Maud had grabbed Thomasina's words and taken them into a secret corner to pore over them. Thomasina did not like this at all. She gathered Maud's breakfast things onto the tray, and carried it to the door. Then she paused, and glanced back. Maud was still seated in the chair near the window, and she was watching Thomasina from the corners of her eyes. They had a dreadful sly glint; her lips were curved in a smile that seemed to bear no relation to the rest of her face. It was as if she was thinking: I know what you've been up to, Thomasina Forrester . . . I know all about you . . .

But Maud could not possibly know what had happened at Twygrist – she had been locked away up here. Even so, Thomasina was aware of the clenching pain she had felt in the small hours returning, like a hand dragging itself down in your bowels. Oh God, not again . . .

She murmured something to Maud about returning later, pushed the tray hastily onto a table, and got herself out of the room as quickly as she could, before half running down the stairs to the bathroom.

As soon as the colour drained from Thomasina's face, leaving it pinched and sickly grey, the chance to escape suddenly presented itself to Maud. In her haste to get out – presumably to be unwell in decent privacy – Thomasina had forgotten to lock the door.

At first Maud did not believe it. She had not believed what Thomasina said about Simon leaving Quire, either, and she had sat down to play some of her beloved Paganini's music: the eerie *Caprice* suites; the piece called *Le Streghe* which translated as *The Witches*. As she played, she laughed to herself over Thomasina's discomfort. The laughter did not quite seem to belong to her, it seemed to bubble up of its own accord and become mixed up with the music. Maud found this a bit disconcerting, so she played louder and faster to drown the laughter out. When she stopped playing and laughing, she thought about the door.

It might be a trick. Let's allow Maud to escape, Thomasina and Simon might have said. Let's pretend one of us has gone away – we'll pretend you've gone away, Simon, shall we? – and let's leave her door unlocked, and hide on the stairs and watch her think she's free. Then, just as she gets to the door, just as she thinks she's going to walk free in the park, we'll pounce. Yes, Maud could just imagine those two behaving so sneakily, but she was not going to be caught like that, not she! She was going to be too clever for Master Simon and Miss Thomasina!

Presently she heard the clanking plumbing in Quire's bathroom one floor down. Pressing her ear against her door she heard the bathroom door open and close, and footsteps going down the stairs. A few moments later she heard the big main door opening. Was it Thomasina going out? Maud darted to the window. She had to be careful, she would not put it past Thomasina to watch the window from below. Sneaky. Sly.

No, it was all right. There Thomasina went, striding out as she normally did, wearing her woollen cloak with the hood. It was not especially odd for her to be out in the hour before lunch but it was unusual. She had quite an orderly pattern to her days and this time of the morning was generally devoted to correspondence. Dull stuff Maud had always thought it, but Thomasina had been strict about it, and said these things had to be done.

Against the grey morning she looked very formidable indeed. It was like a pen and ink sketch. If Maud had been going to stay in her prison she might have wanted to sketch it and use the Indian inks which Thomasina had bought for her.

But there was no time for that. The door of her prison was unlocked, she must take advantage of Thomasina's being out of the house. Mrs Minching would be in the kitchen preparing lunch, and the two young maids would be with her.

Her heart thudding with excitement, Maud wrapped herself in her own woollen cloak – the very cloak she had worn that other night when Thomasina had found her hiding at Charity Cottage – and pulled on a pair of stout walking shoes.

She opened the door very carefully, and began to creep down the stairs.

* * *

After Thomasina had emerged rather shakily from the bathroom, she made the decision to put this nonsense to rest once and for all. She would go out to Twygrist this very morning, and go down to the kiln room and make sure Simon was dead.

The prospect of definite action steadied her, and her insides were immediately calmer. Once outside in the good bracing fresh air, she felt even better. She walked at a smart pace across the park – Charity Cottage's little garden was looking very nice. Someone – most likely Cormac Sullivan's daughter – had planted a lavender bush near the door.

She went on down the lanes. Twygrist, when she reached it, looked exactly as it always did. Of course it does, thought Thomasina. What did you expect? She glanced about her to make sure no one was around, and then unlocked the door and stepped inside.

It was an eerie repetition of her visit of three days ago. She lit a candle again, and went across the wooden floor to the lower waterwheel and through the narrow door behind it. The creakings and rustlings went with her – Thomasina shut them out because she was no longer worried by Twygrist's macabre echoes; she was concentrating on what might be ahead.

She would not have been surprised to find the steel doors open – by now she would not have been surprised at anything – but the doors were as tightly closed as she had left them. She pressed her ear to the surface, trying to listen for any sound from within, but there was nothing. Or was there? Wasn't that a faint tapping from the other side?

Thomasina stood back, trying to summon the resolve to open the doors. Logic dictated that Simon was dead – that he had been dead when she dragged him in here. Supposing he was not? But it had been three days now and he had been in there without food – more importantly, without water. Surely he could not have survived? She would open the doors and satisfy herself that there was nothing to worry about. Then she would go home and leave somebody else to discover Simon's body.

She set her candle down on the ground and remembered about finding a wedge to hold the door open. It would be the worst of all ironies if she got herself shut in. She wondered if she should have some kind of weapon to hand, but she dismissed this notion as ridiculous and grasping the handle of the left-hand door, began to drag it open. It moved more easily than it had that first time, but the screeching of the old hinges filled the tunnels exactly as it had done before. As the door swung slowly back there was a faint gusting of dry stale air in her face, and then the room was open.

Thomasina pushed the wedge into place, reached for the candle and held the flickering light up. For a moment she thought the room was empty, and she wondered wildly if the events of three days ago had been a grotesque dream or even a delusion. Perhaps Simon had secretly fed her opium as well as Maud.

And then she saw the room was not empty after all. Near the brick chimney, where once Twygrist's fires had burned to dry the grain overhead, was a huddled shape. In the dimness it looked like a bundle of rags. Now she was a little nearer, and now the candle was burning up a little more strongly in the dry air, she could see the tumble of hair and an arm protruding from the bundle, the hand turned palm upwards in a terrible gesture of entreaty, the nails broken and crusted with blood.

Thomasina's knees suddenly felt as if they could not support her, and for a truly appalling moment there was the watery quiver in her bowels she had experienced earlier that morning. She took several deep breaths and after a moment was able to take several steps towards the prone shape. Simon's distinctive hair had fallen forward over his brow – he had always worn his hair slightly longer than most men – and Thomasina had to repress a ridiculous urge to bend down and smooth it back, and whisper how sorry she was that it had come to this. Because after all, Simon had been the closest thing she had to a brother – all those holidays at Quire, all those shared memories.

This is the mill that Joe built
This is the man who blackmailed and drank
Who died in the mill that Joe built.

But Simon's son would live. He would grow up at Quire, and Thomasina would make sure he did not know that his father had been a weak blackmailing drunkard.

This is the boy conceived in the night
Who will inherit the mill that Joe built.

She was just turning to go when the flung-out beseeching hand moved and snaked its fingers around her ankle.

In a thread of a voice, Simon said, 'Help me, you bitch . . .'

Thomasina recoiled, and tried to back away to the door. She was shaking so much the candle was in danger of going out, and she had no idea what to do.

'Help me, you bitch . . .'

It came again, like the dry rustling of old bones scraping together, like the brittle tapping of fleshless fingers against a night windowpane.

'Harder to kill – than you – think – Thomasina . . .'

'I didn't intend to kill you,' said Thomasina, recovering her wits slightly. 'Only to teach you a lesson.'

'Liar . . . It's been too long.'

'No. You're delirious. I miscalculated.' But oh God, what do I do? Do I strike him over the head again? I can't. I *can't*. And he's nearly dead as it is – how did he survive this long?

Playing for time, she said, 'Can you get back upstairs if I support you?'

'No . . . Too weak to walk, old girl. Kept alive by . . . drinking own urine. Cupped hands . . .' And, as Thomasina made a gesture of distaste, the dreadful voice said, 'Soldier's trick – in desert.'

'I'll get you out,' said Thomasina, not moving.

Simon made a feeble movement, and then fell back against the bricks. His voice, when he spoke again, was thin and weak, 'You've found out, haven't you? That's why you've come back.'

'Found out?' Thomasina's mind snapped onto a different course.

'About Maud.' said Simon. 'You know that I – lied . . .'

'What? *What?*'

'Morning sickness – it wasn't true . . . but couldn't stand another night . . .'

Thomasina stared at him, but before she could take this in, a faint sound from within the tunnels made her turn sharply to the door. A stealthy footstep, had it been? No, it was only the old timbers creaking.

She looked back at Simon, and said, 'Now, how do we get you out of here, I wonder?'

She thought Simon started to speak, but the sound came again, and this time it was not Twygrist's timbers. This time it was unmistakably the sound of footsteps running along the tunnels. A cloaked figure appeared in the doorway of the kiln room. Maud! Maud, her eyes wild and unseeing, her hair whipped into disarray. She grasped the edge of the door, and before Thomasina could gather her wits sufficiently to do anything about it, had pushed it inward.

The hinges shrieked with a teeth-wincing sound, and the door slammed shut.

In the gust of air caused by the door's closing, the candle went out.

Maud had not intended to follow Thomasina. What she had intended was to go home to Toft House and tell her father that Thomasina had gone away for a few days.

The prospect of this had buoyed her up all the way across the park, but just as she went through the gates, and set off towards Toft Lane, she saw Thomasina some way ahead of her, walking along very purposefully indeed. Maud went after her keeping well back and hoping not to be seen. It was a surprise when Thomasina turned off the road and went up the slope to Twygrist. She waited to be sure Thomasina was not coming out of the mill and then went after her.

The door was partly open, and the minute she stepped through it Twygrist's dark sourness fell around her like a cloak. When she was small, her father had liked to bring her here to show her off to the women workers. They had all made a fuss of her, saying she was a dear little soul, what pretty hair she had, and how much would she charge for one of her sunny curls? After Maud's mamma died, the women had said sorrowfully that she was a poor motherless lamb and must learn to be a good little housewife and look after her papa. Even so, she had hated Twygrist and she hated it now.

It looked as if Thomasina had gone down to the underground rooms, because the little door behind the waterwheel was propped open. Maud, slipped behind the wheel. There was a faint spill of light from the stairway, so Thomasina must have brought candles or an oil lamp with her. Maud took a deep breath and went down the steps, doing so very softly.

She could hear Thomasina somewhere up ahead – she even heard her muttering to herself, as she sometimes did. Most likely she was tutting at the mess down here; Maud could not hear very clearly. But she did hear the scrape of the kiln-room doors being opened.

This was puzzling. Why should Thomasina be going into the kiln room? But the reason did not matter, because a marvellous plan was shaping itself in Maud's mind. Would it work? Would she dare? She went a bit nearer. Yes, the kiln-room door was open. Now? Yes, *now!*

Her cloak billowed out behind her like dark smoke as Maud darted along the last few feet of the tunnel and grasped the edges of the door. For the space of three heartbeats the moment froze, and she stared into the candlelit room. She saw the brick lining of the walls and the floor, smeary with cobwebs and dirt, and the old oven with the brick shaft rising up behind it.

Thomasina stared at Maud, astonished but not actually frightened. Lying on the floor at her feet was a grey-faced man. Simon! Aha, then Simon had not gone home after all. He had been hiding here all along. But whatever sly plan these two might have had, it was going to be turned against them because Maud was going to punish both of them in one fell swoop!

Before they could realize what she meant to do, Maud pushed the door as hard as she could. It swung inwards and locked, trapping Thomasina and Simon inside.

Coming up into the afternoon sunlight again, huge dazzling lights opened up inside Maud's mind. Marvellous. She had not known how good it would feel to punish those two cruel beings. It would have been better if she could have locked Twygrist's main door, but of course she had no keys.

There was no one around as she began to walk back to Quire, but Maud had not gone many yards when she heard the sound of tapping. She slowed her footsteps and half turned, listening. For a moment there was nothing, then it came again. Light, but insistent. *Tap-tap* . . . Tap-tap. It was probably someone carrying out some sort of work nearby: hammering nails into a roof or chopping wood.

Or a faltering hand knocking feebly on the inside of a door, trying to get out?

That was ridiculous. Even if Thomasina or Simon were tapping on the walls, Maud could not possibly hear them all the way up here. It would be a workman somewhere, and she would soon be out of earshot.

But she was not soon out of earshot. The sounds followed her as she hurried through the lanes towards Quire House. *Tap-tap . . . Tap-tap* . . . As she went through the gates, the sounds changed to *Let-us-out* . . . Maud shivered and went into the house, slipping up to her room unseen.

Tap-tap . . . Let-us-out . . .

The sounds stayed with her while she had her lunch in the

dining room. Mrs Minching was pleased to see her downstairs at last. It was a nasty thing this influenza, wasn't it, and it was to be hoped Miss Maud was properly recovered?

Maud said she was feeling very much better, thank you. No, she had not seen Miss Thomasina that morning, perhaps she had gone out to one of Quire's tenants.

Several times in the hours that followed Maud had to fight not to clap her hands over her ears to shut the tapping out. *Could* it be those two in Twygrist?

Of course it could not. She was hearing her own guilty conscience because of what she had done. Except she did not feel any guilt.

She drowned out the sounds by playing some music.

CHAPTER TWENTY

It had been a bitter blow when, after all Donna's care over furnishing the small flat for the two of them, Don did not want to live at home. He had not got a university place – Donna had not really thought he would, although she could have borne his absence on that account and would have enjoyed it. She had even dared to imagine herself and Don in an Oxford common room, or dancing together at the May Ball, and strolling across one of the famous quadrangles, arm in arm . . .

The reality had been harshly different. Don said the flat had been all right for school holidays – of course it had. But he had arranged to go with a couple of friends (what friends? Donna thought she knew all his friends) on a grape-picking tour of southern France. And then on to Spain, perhaps. There would be enough money for that, wouldn't there? Oh, well, if not, he would manage. They were going to live very simply anyway in pensions, or they might take one of those old farmhouses for a few months. It would be great fun and he did think he was owed a little fun after the last couple of years. His French would improve immensely – he might get all kinds of work at the end of it. Not teaching, which would be too tedious for words, but translating or something like that.

Donna had tried not to think that Don was going to spend the next couple of years drifting around western Europe, using up money they did not have, going aimlessly from one thing to another, not really living any sort of life at all . . . Leaving her on her own in the beautiful flat on which she had lavished so much love and care, never mind money she could not really afford, and where she had spent endless lonely nights counting the days until the next school holiday . . .

But she let him go, of course. She trusted him to come back to her. She smiled and hugged him when he left, and said he was to be sure to write and tell her what he was doing, and to remember that there was always a home for him here. If he was in trouble – if he needed money – he must not hesitate to let her know.

'And you'll come to my rescue, will you?' For a moment there had been a glimmer of the beloved boy who used to smile with come-to-bed eyes, and there had been a stirring of shared memories – of how they had laughed together, and of how they had lain in the tangled bed in Charity Cottage on that enchanted afternoon . . .

Donna had hardly been able to bear it. She said, quite briskly, 'Of course I'd come to your rescue. All the king's horses and all the king's men.'

'I believe you would.'

'I always will,' said Donna, and let him go.

The terrible thing was that when he finally came home for good, it was not as Donna had hoped. He was not the same: he was moody, sometimes sullen, occasionally he was very nearly violent. If she put her arms round him, he hunched his shoulders and shrugged her off, saying, 'Oh for heaven's sake!' or, 'Leave me alone!' Once he said she was not living in the real world at all: she was living in some absurd dream existence.

And then had come the night of the quarrel.

It came out of nowhere, and predictably it was about money.

Don had come back to England because the bank had refused

to cash any more of his cheques. He had no money sense – Donna knew that and she accepted it. He had thought he was going to be well off – they had both thought so – and he could not understand that there was not enough money for him to do the things he wanted to do: go to wine bars and clubs with his friends, travel, go to concerts, have a good time. Why should he not do those things? He was good-looking and charming, and he had masses of friends. Donna understood that, as well.

When he was first home from the French grape-picking jaunt, taking up the threads of his English life again, she thought he would ask her to go with him to the clubs and the parties he attended. She had bought new clothes, wanting to look good for him, planning how his friends would admire her, and how they would give little dinner parties in their flat. People would tell one another how enjoyable it was to be invited to the flat.

Don would be proud of her. 'You outshine all the rest,' he would say when they gave a party or went to one, and the old intimacy would be there between them again, and perhaps one night . . .

But Don did not take her with him and the old intimacy was not there. If she asked where he was going he gave a vague answer. He would be clubbing, he said or there was a bit of an evening at somebody's house. 'No one you know. You wouldn't like it.'

He bought expensive designer clothes and expensive drinks – Donna did not even dare wonder if he was taking drugs. Yes, he would get a job, he said vaguely, when she questioned him. He was only waiting for the right one to come along.

On the night the quarrel blew up, Donna had driven to collect him from a wine bar. She had managed to stop him using her car when he went out – she was struggling financially to keep it taxed, insured and roadworthy as it was – but the result had been massive taxi bills: double fare after midnight, of course; triple if it was the small hours of Sunday morning. And so on this particular night she had resolved to collect him, and she parked near the club's entrance, hearing the throbbing music coming from the doors. It reminded her of that magical afternoon at Charity Cottage. Was Don dancing in the dimly lit underground room, pressed up against some girl, some cheap little tart who wanted his body? If he came out tangled with a girl, Donna would drive away and leave him to find his own way home, and sod the taxi fare. But if he was on his own . . .

He was on his own. He was not walking entirely steadily, but he was not incapable. Donna drove forward, and leaned across to open the passenger door for him. A look of such rage showed on his face that for a moment she thought he was going to ignore her and walk home by himself, but he got in and slumped in the passenger seat. His hair was dishevelled and tumbling over his forehead, and his eyes were brilliant from drink (or drugs). He was so outrageously good-looking that Donna could hardly bear to think of all the girls who must have been watching him, planning to get their claws into him, the over-sexed bitches.

He was furious with her. He was not a child, he said, to be collected at the school gates by an over-anxious parent. Why must she do this all the time?

For a moment Donna could not speak. But she refused to be hurt because this was just one of his tantrums. One of the nerve-storms he had sometimes because his sensitivity was more finely tuned than most people's. So she simply switched on the ignition and released the handbrake, preparatory to driving home.

He snatched the handbrake back on, and leaned over to turn the ignition off. He smelt of stale cigarette smoke and sweat.

'Tell me,' he said, turning in the seat to face her. 'Tell me what the fuck this is all about!' And then, with a sudden change of expression, he said very softly, 'Oh, but of course, that's what it *is* about, isn't it? It's about the fuck.'

Donna stared at him, seeing real cruelty in his eyes. She started to speak, but he cut her off.

'It's that afternoon at the cottage, isn't it?' he said. 'That afternoon when you couldn't get enough of it – when you couldn't get enough of *me* – and they caught us. And now you want it again, don't you? Jesus Christ, you'd wanted it for years before that day, and you've wanted it ever since – all these years.' He grabbed her hand suddenly, and thrust it between his legs. 'You can have it for all I care,' he said, and his voice was jeering. 'Providing I can get it up, of course, because I'm pretty pissed tonight. In fact I'm pissed off, pissed off with life. But if it's really what you want, I daresay I can manage.' He began to unbuckle the belt of his jeans.

Donna snatched her hand away from him as if it had been burned. She said, in a low furious voice, 'How can you! How can you speak about it like that!'

'About "it"? Jesus God, Donna, it was a single bizarre fuck! Nothing more! I was bored out of my mind and you were panting for it, so I thought, "Oh, why not? What's incest, after all? Only a shag kept in the family, isn't it?"'

Donna could hardly believe it was Don's beloved voice. He was drunk of course, and he might be high as well. Let it go, said her mind, but the disappointments of the last years rose up in her throat like acid, and she said furiously, 'Was it just for that – just for a bizarre fuck – that I did what I did that day at Twygrist?'

In the silence that followed she could hear the dull thrum of the traffic on the nearby main road and the throbbing beat of the heavy rock music from within the club. She could no longer look at Don; she stared unseeingly through the windscreen at the unfriendly darkness.

At last he said, in a voice stripped of the hurtful jeering note, 'What did you do? Donna, for God's sake, tell me what you did that day.'

Donna turned to look at him at last. In a cold tight little voice, she said, 'Don't pretend. You know perfectly well what I did.' And saw with sick horror that he had not been pretending at all; he had genuinely not known what she had done that last summer at Amberwood.

* * *

On that last day, Donna had woken up with a headache, just as she had told the police. A queer, clawing headache, it had been.

Unable to bear the confines of the cottage Donna had walked along Quire's main driveway and through the gates. She told the police she walked all the way to the shop on the village's outskirts; in reality she simply sat on the grass verge outside the grounds, fighting the clawing images inside her head.

Very faintly she heard the church clock striking twelve, and although the chimes had come to her fuzzily, as if the clock were under water, the sound seemed to mark something hugely important – the crossing of some kind of line, the giving up of a struggle. With the sound had come the sudden slotting into place of half memories, of things seen and unconsciously stored away: local knowledge absorbed – Amberwood's history and its industry and the workings of Twygrist, and of how they could all be put together. It would work, thought Donna, hugging her bent knees against her chest, her mind seething. Oh God, I believe it would work.

She got up, dusting bits of grass from her skirt, and went back to the cottage. Her headache had vanished, although she felt a bit odd: remote and over-calm, in the way you sometimes felt when you had taken a hefty dose of paracetamol.

Her mother was making sandwiches for lunch in the kitchen. She accorded Donna a brief nod – they were not really speaking to one another at this stage – and Donna poured herself a glass of fruit juice from the fridge, and looked out of the window while she drank it. To say it? To say it *now*?

It seemed, much later, that she was still trying to make up her mind when she heard her own voice saying, quite casually, 'I've just been down to the village shop – I heard something there about Twygrist that might interest you.' Pause there, Donna, remember the value of a pause at what's called the psychological moment.

The name Twygrist acted as a hook, as Donna had known it would. Her mother looked up from slicing ham. 'Yes?'

'That old clock on the side of the mill,' said Donna, sounding disinterested, sounding very nearly bored. 'Apparently it's a memorial clock—'

'Yes, I know it is. They have a clock-winder – it's an appointment that gets handed down—'

'Well, somebody in the shop was telling me that when the clock was put up, a stone tablet was put inside the mill at the same time. Sunk into the floor or the wall or something. It's engraved with the date and the name of the person whose memory it's for, and something about the clock-winder tradition as well.'

She had her mother's full attention now; it was almost as if the ugly scenes of the last few days had not happened. 'What sort of stone tablet? What does the engraving say?'

'I don't know,' said Donna moodily. 'For all I know it's the life and times of the Amberwood miller. Or just one of those Kilroy-was-here things.'

'Oh, I think it would be worth seeing,' said Donna's mother at once. She cut the sandwiches into quarters and heaped them on a plate, not speaking. Donna thought she would give it a count of twenty, and then say, in the same bored voice, that she supposed it might pass an afternoon to go out there and take a look. But it would be better if the idea came from her mother. Start counting, Donna. Twenty, nineteen, eighteen . . . Damn, she's not going to say it. Fifteen, fourteen, thirteen . . .

She had reached eleven when Maria said thoughtfully, 'I wonder if your father would drive us out there after lunch. I don't see why he can't; he's been glooming over sheets of figures for most of the morning, some fresh air will do him good.'

'He likes glooming over sheets of figures,' said Donna. 'Are we having some of that quiche with the sandwiches? I'll take Don's out to him; he's not likely to come in.' She tipped some of the sandwiches onto a smaller plate.

'Well, come straight back—'

'Why? Were you thinking we might have a quick shag on the lawn?'

'Don't use words like that, Donna!'

'Oh, join the modern age,' said Donna, and went out to the garden.

She gave Don his lunch in an offhand way – he was plugged into his music, and barely acknowledged her – and went back to the kitchen, walking slowly as if it was too much effort to do anything else. Her parents were seated at the kitchen table eating the sandwiches, and Maria was talking animatedly about the stone tablet and the memorial clock, saying how interesting it was and that she might as well see if they could find it. She did not suppose any of them would want to come back to Amberwood again, but she had found the old watermill very interesting and would like to have another look inside it before they left.

'You won't mind driving down there, will you, Jim? It isn't as if you had anything else to do.'

Donna's father said something about a quarterly forecast to prepare, but this was swept aside on the grounds that nobody could be expected to prepare forecasts on holiday. It might rain tonight – the television had said it might – so they should do this while the sunshine lasted. They would take torches and the camera; it was only a quarter past one now. They could set off sharp at a quarter to two and have a good couple of hours. 'Donna, you and Don had better come with us.'

'Bor-ing,' said Donna, deliberately drawling out the word.

'Listen, I don't care which of you comes, but one of you must, because—'

'Because you won't leave us on our own in the cottage in case we leap into bed and start screwing like stoats,' said Donna. 'Oh, all right then, but it had better be me. I shouldn't think anything short of an atomic bomb would budge Don from the garden today. He didn't so much as speak when I took his food out.'

'He's finishing a holiday task,' said her father reproachfully. 'A history essay. And Donna, you will not talk to your mother in that way—'

'She has no shame whatsoever,' said Maria at once.

'Oh, let's get going if we've got to,' said Donna. She glanced out of the window. 'Don looks as if he's asleep anyway. We'll be back before he knows we've gone.'

'I'll go upstairs to get ready,' said Maria. 'I'll only be five minutes.'

It was, of course, a lot longer than five minutes before Donna's mother was ready to leave. She had to find the correct shoes – 'No, I want the brown ones, for goodness' sake. Would I wear navy shoes with this jacket, now *would* I? Well, I don't care if it is only a mouldy old watermill, I have my standards, you should know by this time that I have my standards, and one of them is not wearing navy shoes with a brown jacket.'

Donna put on jeans and a clean T-shirt in her own room, found a straw sunhat to wear, and stabbed crossly at her hair with a brush as if she could not be bothered to brush it properly. This was to maintain the image of a sulky intractable teenager, in case either of her parents happened to be slyly watching her through the partly open door. She thought she was giving quite a good performance.

She went on giving a good performance on the short drive to Twygrist, slumped in the back of the car (deliberately slumped very low in case any of the locals happened to see the distinctive people-carrier go by with Donna inside), and replying in monosyllables to any remarks made to her.

But once at Twygrist, she livened up a bit, and even agreed to come into the mill. It would be better than frying inside the car on a hot afternoon like this. No, she didn't know where the memorial tablet about the clock might be. No, she had not thought to ask, because she found the whole thing utterly— Oh wait a minute, though, something had been said about a kiln room. (This was in a slightly more animated tone.) Did you have kiln rooms in mills? Well, anyway, it was somewhere right down below ground – there were some old tunnels that led to the centre, or stone cellars or something.

This had the effect of galvanizing Maria into instant action.

The camera in its leather cover, was slung around her neck, and the small folio case, was tucked under one arm. Jim was to bring the big torch, and Donna could have the smaller one and carry the large notebook and pen so she could make notes from Maria's dictation as they went.

'What'll you do if it's locked?' said Donna's father resignedly, but Maria said it would not be locked. It had not been locked the first time they came, and there was no reason to think it would be any different now.

It was no different at all. The worm-eaten door was still sagging on its frame, and its hinges still shrieked when they pushed it inwards and stepped cautiously inside. The smell was exactly the same as it had been last time as well, and Donna wrinkled her nose fastidiously and said this was a repulsive way to spend an afternoon, she was getting disgusting cobwebs in her hair because she had left her sunhat in the car.

'Give me the car keys, would you, and I'll go back for it,' she said. Mentally she crossed her fingers. If her father refused to give her the keys, or her mother said she would go back for the hat herself, a linchpin of the plan would fall out, and she might have to rethink the whole thing.

But Jim Robards only said, 'You're a nuisance, Donna. But here you are.' He fished in a pocket for the keys. 'Make sure you lock the doors, won't you? And check that the alarm re-sets. It's an absolute magnet for thieves, that car.'

'No, I'll leave all the doors open, with a notice on the windscreen saying, "Please steal me so we can claim a whopping great amount on the insurance and buy a better car." Of course I'll lock it,' said Donna, crossly. 'What d'you take me for? Wait for me here, will you? I don't want to go wandering around this spooky old place looking for you; it's a lot bigger in here than it looks.'

'It's a lot deeper than it looks,' said her mother. 'But we'll have to find how to get to the lower levels before we can start looking for the tablet.'

Donna was only a minute getting the hat which she had deliberately left behind. She locked the car and checked the alarm, because her father would ask if she had done so. She put the keys in the pocket of her jeans – the keys were crucial to the plan – and glanced at her watch. Five past two.

She took a deep breath and went back into Twygrist's ancient darkness.

As the three of them walked across the old floor, little creakings and groanings seemed to come from deep within the old mill. Donna's mother said she had not thought to look for the kiln room when they came before. Presumably there must be stairs leading down. What did they both think?

'What's over there?' said Donna, pointing towards the water-wheel. 'Where's the torch – no, shine it over *there*. No, behind the actual wheel.'

Maria Robards said excitedly, 'It's a door.'

'And it's propped open,' said Donna, moving the torch again. Her heart beat faster. There had been the possibility that the vague village talk she had heard had been wrong or misleading, and that Twygrist did not have any underground levels at all. Or the kiln room might no longer be accessible. But it was all right, and her plan was unfolding with almost mathematical precision. Her heartbeat increased; it was no longer fear but excitement that drove her.

'There are steps leading down,' said Donna's father. 'Shine the torch a bit more to the right. That's better. Maria, if you're definitely going down there, we'll have to be careful. It might be dangerous.'

'Nonsense, if one of us stays at the top of the stairs . . .'

Really, thought Donna, her mother might almost have been reading from the script. She said, 'I'll stay. Going into filthy underground rooms isn't my idea of fun.'

'We'll leave you the smaller torch,' said Maria. 'You'll want some light. And we'll keep calling out so you know we're all right.'

Donna did not care if they recited the entire works of Shakespeare or sang hymns. She did not care if they left her in the pitch dark or with enough light to illuminate the whole of Cheshire. She just wanted them to go down the bloody steps and towards the kiln room. In a don't-care voice, she said, 'OK.'

'Ready, Jim?'

'If we must, we must,' he said. 'I'd better go first, to test the weight of the stairs, though. The wood's probably rotten.'

'They're stone steps,' said Donna's mother. 'Stone doesn't rot.'

'No, but it crumbles.'

Donna sat cross-legged at the head of the stairs, leaning her back against the stone wall, rather unpleasantly aware of the silent waterwheel directly behind and above her and of the chasm beneath it. She flicked the torch's beam beneath the wheel, pointing it straight down, and caught the black glint of water, with patches of grease lying on the surface and amorphous shapes within. Horrid. She brought the torch hurriedly back up.

Now that she was on her own on this floor, she could hear the rhythmic beating of the memorial clock. She glanced round, trying to work out where the clock was. That wall to the left? So the clock was actually quite near. It was somehow very eerie to think of the clock in this lonely darkness, steadily ticking its way through the hours and the months and the years.

It sounded as if her parents had reached the foot of the stone steps. Maria's voice floated up to Donna, calling out that they had reached the bottom without mishap, and there were some brick-lined tunnels in front of them. Imagine not finding all this on those other trips, she said. They were setting off into the tunnels now – was Donna all right?

Donna shouted back that she was all right. Had they expected the ghost of the old miller to come lurching in and smother her with a flour bag?

'Your voices are getting a bit faint, so I'll come part way down the steps, so I can hear you better,' she said.

'Well, be careful. They're very worn at the centre, and there isn't anything to hold on to. Don't slip and break your ankle.'

'I wish you'd stop fussing,' said Donna, and directing the torch onto the ground, she began to descend the steps to Twygrist's subterrenean rooms.

The tunnels were wider than she had expected, in fact they were more like small rooms leading out of one another. She tried to fix the position of the walls in her mind so she would not crash into them or trip over the bits of discarded machinery and alert her parents, then she switched off her torch. At once the darkness reared up, like a solid black wall, but it would have to be coped with. Her mother and father must not suspect she was creeping along the tunnels towards them. After a moment her eyes began to adjust, and she saw that it was not pitch dark; a trickle of light from her mother's torch came back along the tunnels.

Donna hesitated. Am I really going to do this? Don came strongly into her mind, and she knew it had to be done.

She could hear her parents – her mother was saying surely they must be nearly at the kiln room by now. Her sharp heels clacked loudly in the enclosed space, and Donna, who was wearing trainers, thought only her mother would come into a place like this wearing shoes with two-inch heels.

As she went silently forwards, she had the feeling that Twygrist was coming alive all round her, and that its dark and ancient heart was beating in exact synchronization with the unseen clock overhead. She began to time her footsteps to match the ticking so that the sound would be smothered.

The tunnel-rooms were not as labyrinthine as they had seemed, and were exactly as Donna had hoped: a series of stone and brick rooms opening out of one another, protecting the rest of the mill from the kiln-room fires.

She heard her mother's heels halt, and Maria said, 'This must be the kiln room. D'you see, Jim, those are iron doors.'

Another wave of thankfulness engulfed Donna, and she edged nearer.

'Steel,' her father was saying. 'Good God, they're heavy. For goodness' sake stay clear of them – they're pretty antiquated, but the hinges are still in place. They'd swing shut and trap you before you knew what was happening. Stay here – just shine the torch inside.' His tone said, let's see what it is you want to see, and then let's for Christ's sake get out of this dismal place.

'That's the fireplace,' said Donna's mother after a moment, and Donna tensed her muscles. In another two seconds she would move. 'It's quite big, isn't it? And there's the chimney breast going upwards.'

'The drying floor must be directly over that chimney,' said Donna's father, sounding interested despite himself. 'They'd spread the damp grain over it, and the heat of the fire would have dried it before it was milled.'

'I don't remember seeing that.'

'I noticed it last time we were here,' said Donna's father. 'On the side of the mill. It looked as if it had been concreted over, though. That's probably why the air's so stale down here.'

'I don't see the stone Donna talked about, do you? Unless it's set into that wall—'

The unsuitable heels clattered across the floor, and there was a sigh of exasperation from Donna's father – the enclosed rooms picked the sigh up quite clearly and sent it hissing back to where Donna was standing. Was this the moment? She tiptoed a couple of steps further along, hardly daring to breathe, placing her feet down slowly and carefully so that there would be no sound. If either of her parents heard her – if they turned round and saw her there – the plan would fail.

But they did not turn round and they did not hear her. They were examining the walls flanking the ancient kiln, shining the torch with ridiculous solemnity. Donna could have laughed aloud to see how pedantic they were being, trying to find a stupid, non-existent memorial stone.

She waited until they were at the furthest point from the door, and then set her own torch on the ground, making sure it would not roll away. OK, now for it.

Taking a deep breath, she ran forward, grabbed the edges of the thick steel door with both hands and threw her whole weight behind it. For the space of three heartbeats she thought it was not going to budge and panic threatened to engulf her, but then the massive door gave a teeth-scraping moan of protest, and moved away from the wall, gathering momentum as it did so.

The two people inside the room swung round at the sound, the torch fell from Maria Robards' hands and rolled into a corner. Incredibly it did not shatter, and its triangle of brilliance lit up the scene like a stage set. Donna had a final sight of her parents' faces, white with shock, their eyes suddenly huge with horror, their mouths forming round Os of fear. They both cried out, and then the door slammed home, cutting off all sound.

For several minutes Donna shook so badly she could not move. She knew she must get away from this place, but she sank to the floor, hugging her knees, her heart pounding as if she had been running hard.

After a while she managed to shine her torch onto her wrist-watch. She felt as if she had lived through several hours, but incredibly it was only just on half past two. She must drive back to Charity Cottage, hoping not to be seen, and slip up to her bedroom. She had no exact idea how long it would take her mother and father to die, but if the room was airtight they could not last very long. Say two days. That meant she would have to delay the inevitable police search for at least that time. Could she lay false trails by saying they might have driven over to the other side of Amberwood? Yes, she could.

The shaking had stopped, and she stood up and placed the flat of her hands against the steel doors, pressing her ear to the surface. The doors remained immoveable, and there was no sound what-soever from beyond them. I'm not sorry for what I've just done, said Donna silently to the two people imprisoned in the kiln room. You deserved this for trying to separate me from Don.

She picked up the torch and retraced her steps along the under-ground rooms and back up the stone steps. It was still only twenty minutes to three. By three o'clock she was back at the cottage, careful to park the car exactly where it had been parked all morning so it did not look as if it had been driven anywhere. She looked out of the kitchen window, and saw that Don was in the same place, sprawled on the grass, either listening to the Walkman, or asleep. Donna went into her bedroom; the curtains were drawn against the afternoon sunshine. She rumpled the bed so it would look as if she had been lying down with her headache.

At quarter past four she went downstairs, and saw it was clouding over. By half past it was starting to rain, and Don came in from the garden. They had a cup of tea, and by five o'clock they began to wonder what had happened to their parents, and what they had better do about looking for them.

CHAPTER TWENTY-ONE

'Was it just for that – for a bizarre fuck – that I did what I did that day at Twygrist?'

In the enclosed confines of the car parked outside the night club, Donna's angry words lay on the air like acid, and the car seemed to seethe with violent emotions.

'Was it just for a bizarre fuck . . .' 'Don't pretend. You know perfectly well what I did . . . What I did . . . WHAT I DID . . .' The words seemed to burn into the darkness, and the echoes sizzled and spun around Donna's head, along with the knowledge that he had not known, that if only she had not said that . . .

But horrified comprehension flared in Don's eyes, in a voice of such loathing that Donna flinched, he said, 'Oh Christ, Donna, you killed them, didn't you? You shut them into that room. You're a murderess.'

He turned away from her, slumping down in the passenger seat, not looking at anything, and after a moment Donna switched on the car's ignition.

They were almost home when he said, 'You're a monster, Donna.' He half turned in his seat and stared at her. 'What makes you think I won't tell the police?'

'What makes you think they'd believe you?' said Donna at once. 'I covered my tracks very well, Don. No one suspected the truth then, and no one would suspect it now. A tragic accident, that was the verdict.' As he hesitated, she said in a softer voice, 'Our parents were going to separate us – you knew that. And I couldn't bear it. So I killed them. I did it for us. For you.'

'That's the really monstrous part,' said Don. 'That's the part I don't think I can bear,' and although Donna had not taken her eyes off the road she knew he was looking at her. She took one hand off the steering wheel and reached for him, but he brushed her away angrily.

'Get off me. I can't stand you touching me.'

'You're lying.'

'I'm not.'

'What are you going to do?'

'I don't know.'

When they reached the flat he went blindly into his own bedroom, and banged the door against her. Donna heard him flinging open cupboards and drawers.

It was after two a.m. when he left the flat, not speaking to her, simply walking straight through the door and slamming it behind him. Donna flew to the window and watched him walk along the road, his shoulders hunched against the thin drizzling rain that had started to fall, his head down.

She had absolutely no idea where he would go, and although once she would have followed him, tonight she did not dare. She could only hope he would come home in the morning.

He did not come home in the morning. Donna sat helplessly in the flat, jumping every time there was any sound from outside, willing the phone to ring, and staring through the window to the street below, praying that at any minute he would walk down the street.

At four o'clock she left the flat for the pretentious but expensive French bistro where she had managed to work her way up to being restaurant manager. Don would certainly be home when she got back, and the evening stint of duty would help to fill in the hours of waiting.

The bistro was not the glitziest job in the world, but Donna quite liked it. She enjoyed wearing a sharp black suit and white silk shirt, moving around the softly lit restaurant and adjoining wine bar, overseeing people who thought it part of their epicurean experience to be dealt with by a cut-glass accent. The salary Jean-Pierre paid was not immense, but it was not bad because the hours were regarded as antisocial. Donna did not mind the erratic hours, because they could often be adjusted to give her free time when she wanted it.

It was midnight before she got back to the flat. She put her key into the lock eagerly, convinced Don would be there. But the place was empty and silent, and it remained that way for three more nightmare days. It was not until the morning of the fourth day that Don appeared, a bit pale, a bit quieter than usual. Donna tried to ask him where he had been and whether he was all right, but he shrugged her off in the way he had shrugged her off after their parents' death. She supposed he had been staying with one of the friends she did not know – the people he went to clubs and parties with.

A week later a letter addressed to D. Robards arrived. Donna opened it – not prying, just making a mistake – and saw to her horror that it was a hospital appointment card. It set out a list of day clinic sessions arranged for Don at the psychiatric department of the nearby infirmary.

Don was furious. He said she ought to have realized the letter was not for her, snatched it out of her hand and stormed out of the room. But after a time he came back, and when Donna questioned him again he shrugged and said, well yes, all right, she might as well know; there had been a bit of a drama on the night of their row. And if she really wanted the sordid details—

'Yes, I do want them,' said Donna, beating down a mounting fear.

'Very well then,' said Don. 'Before I left the flat that night, I took the bottle of sleeping pills from your bedroom drawer—'

'Why?'

'Oh, so I could sleep somewhere for hours and hours. Somebody's sofa – anywhere – I didn't much care. I just wanted to sleep and not dream of anything—'

But he had walked along by the river, the moonlight had been reflected on the dark surface of the water, and he thought how marvellous it would be to just walk into the water and let it take you along until you merged with the moonlight. Donna would know how it was – you got hold of an idea, an image, and the next thing you knew, it had sort of taken you over.

'No,' said Donna bluntly. 'I don't know at all. What I do know is that you were very drunk that night. What actually happened?'

What had actually happened, said Don, was that as he watched the river and the moonlight, the idea of dying had started to seem immensely alluring – he did not seem to hear Donna's half-stifled cry at this. It was a romantic image, he said. Did Donna not think there was a dark romance about dying young? Elegies and gravestones and always being young in people's memories. He gave Donna his vivid blue stare, and she looked at him helplessly and had absolutely no idea how much to believe of all this stuff about moonlit deaths.

She asked if he had been serious about wanting to die, speaking brusquely because she was afraid of the answer, but Don said, well, no, on reflection, he did not think he had. Not really.

'I'm very pleased to hear it,' said Donna, relaxing a little, but her mind had gone back to that night outside the club, and for the first time she recognized the emotion that had filled up the car: it had been sexual arousal, harsh and raw and unmistakable. Don had hated her that night, but he had also been violently aroused by knowing what she had done. And if he had really been serious about committing suicide – if all that rubbish about rivers and dying young had not just been a smokescreen

– it had not been the discovery that his sister was a double murderer that had triggered it. It had been self-loathing at his own reaction.

Anyway, said Don, in the end he had taken most of the sleeping pills, and washed them down with half a bottle of vodka. Somebody had found him – he did not remember who – and he had been taken to A&E.

The letter Donna had opened – all right, he would believe it had been a genuine mistake – was a note about the follow-up appointments at the psychiatric day clinic. It was nothing heavy, he was not about to be committed to a mental hospital or anything like that; it was just that the doctor had thought it would be a good idea for him to talk to one of the psychiatrists for an hour or so each week. Just to sort things out in his mind.

Sort things out? What kind of things? A new nightmare rose up to confront Donna, but surely whatever else Don might do, he would never betray her. He would never say, 'Well, actually, doctor, my sister and I screwed each other one summer, and our parents tried to separate us, so she murdered them. She murdered them for me, you see, but when I found out, it turned me on . . . and I don't think I can live with any of it.'

Of *course* he would not say anything like that.

But Donna still had no idea if Don had genuinely meant to die that night, or if it had been one of his melodramatic gestures, or even if the whole thing had been staged with the intention of teaching her a lesson. She thought him capable of that. Knowing it, did not affect the strength of her love for him.

Afterwards he seemed oddly happier, as if the suicide attempt – whether it had been serious or not – had provided some kind of catharsis, and as if all the complex self-hatred had drained away. After a time Donna dared to trust this new mood; she began to hope that they might be Donna and Don again, within reach of that enchanted life together she had imagined for them. Don attended the pyschiatric clinic faithfully, although he said it was all a bit of a nuisance; you had to wait around for hours and the chairs were uncomfortable, and there was only the gruesome machine-coffee and tattered magazines to pass the time.

Donna said at once that she would come with him. It would be company, and she could always arrange her hours at Jean-Pierre's to fit. Perhaps the doctors would like to talk to her as well. Had he told them he had a sister?

But Don said he preferred to go by himself, thank you. No, he had not told anyone he had a sister; they had asked about family of course, but he had not wanted a lot of fuss, so he had said he was on his own. Well, he was sorry if Donna found that hurtful, but that was the way he wanted to play it. Take it or leave it, said his tone, briefly returning to the old defiance. And while they were on the subject, would she please stop watching him all the time, as if she thought he was about to fly for the pills or a cut-throat razor. It was unnerving. He was perfectly all right now, mostly thanks to the doctor he was seeing – he was sorry if she found that hurtful as well, but it happened to be the truth. No, it was not a man who was treating him, it was a woman and she was very nice, very helpful. And now could they forget the matter.

After a while he began to go out again in the evenings, always around the same time, sometimes taking the car with or without Donna's permission, sometimes walking. He was not especially late in returning home, and he never seemed to be the worse for drink. He did not say where he had been or who he had been with, but Donna knew it was a girl, and bitterness engulfed her all over again because she knew – positively and definitely – they had been about to regain those magical years when they had been growing up. And now some cheap little tart had ruined everything.

She began to follow him when she could – when her hours at Jean Pierre's could be switched, and when Don did not take the car. This was not prying, it was just making sure he was all right. Because if he really had swallowed sleeping pills and vodka, he had not been just playing with the idea of a romantic death at all; he had been serious.

She was discreet and careful and she was sure he did not know what she was doing, and by dint of being patient she finally found out where he went. He went to the hospital, and he waited for an unknown female who apparently worked there.

From the safety of her car, Donna saw quite clearly the eager adoration on Don's face, and she saw, as well, that the woman he stared at so longingly was not some doe-eyed teenager, or some breathless young girl of whom he would quickly tire. A scalding jealousy filled her entire body.

When she was sure Don was not around to see, she followed the woman a few times on her own account. From there, it was easy enough to make a vague inquiry at the busy hospital reception desk. She needed to put a name to this creature. But when she had the name the entire thing turned itself around 360 degrees, because the woman was the doctor who had treated Don on the night of the suicide bid, and whose out-patients' clinic he had been attending ever since.

Dr Antonia Weston. A qualified pyschiatrist. Successful and clever.

Donna studied Weston as closely as she dared. She was a few years older than Donna herself – perhaps late twenties – and she had unremarkable brown hair, and an ordinary sort of figure. She did not dress very strikingly, and at first Donna could not think what Don could see in her. Don liked people and things to be unusual or rare, or to be beautiful and glossy, and Weston was not even especially good-looking. But then she began to see that the woman had a certain quality – a way of looking at people. Would you call it magnetism? Charisma? Donna did not want to call it either of these things, but she would be fair and admit that there was something indefinable about Antonia that drew you to her.

She made sure Weston did not see her, and she did not stay around to see Weston and Don actually meet or try to find out where they might go, because she could not have borne seeing them together. She supposed they met somewhere discreet – some tucked-away bar or restaurant, because of Don being Dr Weston's patient. But whatever they did and wherever they met, this doctor, this Antonia Weston, had snatched Don away from Donna.

Bitch. *Bitch.* It did not matter if she was all the sex goddesses of the world rolled into one or if she looked like the back end of a bus; she would be a far more formidable foe than some adoring little eighteen-year-old.

So did this bitch return Don's feelings? Or was it the other way around: was she leading him on, secretly amused at the age difference, boasting to her friends that she had a toy boy? Getting a kick out of having an affair with a patient, seeing herself as a femme fatale . . .

Fatale. It was a good word. Things always sounded more dramatic in French. And it was a fatale situation all right, in fact it might be very bloody fatale indeed for Antonia Weston if she did not take her claws out of Donna's beautiful boy.

Donna began to consider what to do about Dr Antonia Weston.

CHAPTER TWENTY-TWO

By the fourth session with Don Robards, Antonia was starting to feel very uneasy.

She could not immediately pinpoint the reason for this uneasiness, but it was a little to do with the straight blue stare he gave her when they talked, and a great deal to do with the growing conviction that there was something very dark and very complex beneath the too facile charm. It was, of course, absurd to feel this nervous apprehension, because she was very used to the strange and often twisted things that lay deeply buried in people's minds.

On the surface Don was a model patient. He attended all the appointments made for him, and talked with apparent openness about his childhood. It had been normal and unremarkable, he said, although the death of his parents had been a dreadful blow. But he had got over it – well, as much as you did get over that kind of thing. No, there was no other family, he said – absolutely none at all. But friends had helped out; he had good friends.

No, he had not got a girlfriend at present, although there had been girlfriends over the years, of course. He had only just returned from three or four years living in France, so he was still picking up the threads of his English life.

Antonia, listening carefully for clues as to what lay beneath this apparent normality, wondered if he might be gay, and if that might be his problem. But she thought not, although you could never be entirely sure.

Don stuck to his story about finding the idea of youthful death romantic and tempting, but denied having said he had discovered something so appalling he did not want to live. Dr Weston must have misheard or misunderstood.

My good young man, thought Antonia, I neither misheard nor misunderstood. And I don't think I'm misunderstanding that come-to-bed look you're giving me now, and if I'm right about it, we may have a problem ahead of us.

It was shortly after the fourth session that she became aware of the dark blue hatchback with the distinctive chipped number plate. It always seemed to be around, parked near her space at the hospital or driving behind her as she went to or from the clinic. It was not an especially remarkable occurrence, until she realized it was Don driving the car.

'He could be simply visiting someone in one of the wards and using the staff car park,' she said to Jonathan. 'But I think there's more to it.'

'Why?'

Antonia hesitated, and then said, 'Because during the last fortnight I've seen him too many times. In the supermarket and in the street near my home. Last week he was two rows behind me at the cinema.'

'Does he speak to you?' said Jonathan.

'Mostly he pretends he hasn't seen me. I know it could all be coincidence, but it's starting to spook me a bit.'

'Have you mentioned it to him? When he comes into the clinic?'

'No.'

'Hm. Is he becoming fixated on you?'

Antonia heard with gratitude the doctor speaking, the real Jonathan who cared very deeply about people and their tangled minds, rather than the frivolous flirt which was all most people saw. She said, 'I don't know. It happens sometimes.'

'Yes, it does. One of the occupational hazards. What treatment are you trying?'

'Mostly talking at the moment – you know how it goes. Winning confidence, implanting ideas, trying to get through the layers of protective armour to the real problem. I haven't prescribed anything, and I shan't unless things suddenly change. I've had him checked regularly for drugs, of course.'

'Good.'

'He's clean every time. He tested clean the night of the suicide bid, as well. So whatever triggered it wasn't drugs. He's covering up the real reason, and whatever it is, it's so deeply buried I'm nowhere near reaching it.'

'D'you want to switch him to me?'

'Not yet,' said Antonia, frowning. 'I'll see if I can get him to join a group session and you can sit in and make your own assessment.'

'All right.' He looked at her. 'Have you told Richard about this?'

'No, I haven't. I can't, can I?'

They looked at one another. 'No,' said Jonathan slowly. 'No, you can't, I can see that.'

'I don't think he's dangerous,' Jonathan said, after two of the group sessions. 'And at the moment I don't think he's *in* danger.'

Antonia had not thought so either, but she was glad to have it confirmed.

'But what I do think,' said Jonathan, thoughtfully, 'is that he's heading for a full-blown fantasy with you in the leading role, and that worries me. I have an idea he's visualizing the two of you in some close and rather emotional environment – maybe something like a humanitarian expedition to take medical aid to one of the third world countries, or something of that kind.'

Antonia supposed that as fantasies went, this might be just about credible.

'It is credible, and that's going to make it more difficult to dislodge. He's only a few steps away from imagining torrid nights of passion in deserts or mountains, or one of you dying heroically to save the other from a mercenary's bullet—'

'You're getting into the fantasy yourself now.'

'It's the black humour of the medical profession.' He smiled, and the familiar flippancy was back. 'I wouldn't entirely blame the boy for wondering about a torrid night of passion with you, though. I've wondered about it myself more than once.'

'Let's keep this professional,' said Antonia automatically.

'Well then, professionally speaking, on present evidence I don't think he wants to hurt you. He's more likely focusing on some visionary Utopia or Shangri-la – roses round a cottage door, or an island retreat. Like a 1940s film, with gauze over the camera for the final scene, and the strong rugged hero going hand in hand into the sunset with the grateful heroine.'

Shangri-la and torrid passion in the desert did not exactly fit with Antonia's work with the NHS which was infuriating and exhausting by turns, but which was a deep and integral part of her. They did not fit, either, with the modest social life she managed to have outside the hospital and they certainly did not fit with the presence of Richard in her life.

'I still think you should tell Richard,' said Jonathan, with his disconcerting trick of picking up a thought. 'But you're the judge of that. I don't think Don has any paranoia or any confusing of reality and fantasy. I don't think he believes any of his fantasies have actually happened, although I suspect he's writing the script for them.' He frowned. 'But there's no guarantee he won't turn psychotic, or that there won't be another suicide bid.'

'I do know that.' Antonia hesitated and then said, 'Jonathan, he knows where I live.'

'Are you sure?'

'Yes. I've seen him outside the bungalow.'

There was no need to tell Jonathan about the silent, motionless figure standing beneath the tree outside her home, sometimes well after midnight, watching the windows with such intensity that several times Antonia was aware of a compulsion to walk out of the bungalow towards him.

'In that case I'd better take over his treatment, hadn't I?' said Jonathan after a moment.

'I think so. Yes, please.'

'I do understand that it's a – a delicate situation with Richard,' he said. 'But if Don really is going to your home, oughtn't you to talk to the police? At least alert them in case something goes wrong.'

'If I tell the police Richard will find out. I can't risk it.'

'Would you like me to tell Richard?'

'No.' It came out more sharply than Antonia had intended, but Jonathan only said quite peaceably, 'All right. But what will you do if Robards breaks in?'

'I don't know.'

A week later she had had a drink with Jonathan after work and phoned Richard to say she would be a bit late. He had said he would have supper ready.

Antonia put the car in the garage at the side of the bungalow, locked it, and went along the path to the front door. She'd only had one glass of wine because of driving, but she was pleasurably relaxed. She had enjoyed parrying Jonathan's outrageous flirting, which he did not mean her to take seriously but which had still been fun. It was unusual not to see any lights on in the bungalow, but Richard was most likely in the kitchen at the rear, perhaps stirring a pan of risotto – he did a terrific seafood risotto.

She was hoping he had finally managed to master the difficult fingering of the Paganini *Caprice* – he had been working at one of the adaptations for piano over the last week and it had absorbed him almost to the exclusion of everything else. Antonia, whose tastes ran conventionally to Mozart and Beethoven, and who often played pop music from the seventies, especially during a house-cleaning blitz, knew the piece in a general way, mostly because it, or a version of it, introduced the *South Bank Show*. Still, since he had offered to cook tonight it probably meant the *Caprice* was finally sorted out and that he was rejoining the sentient world.

As she stepped into the porch, she heard and felt the crunch of splintered glass under her feet. Damn. Broken milk bottle, most likely. But a faint prickle of apprehension brushed against her. It looked as if the entire bungalow was in darkness, and unless Richard was absorbed in playing, when he was apt to forget everything, he hated the dark. He always said it became filled up with too many despairing memories. Antonia, who liked such things as firelight and moonlight, had always given way to Richard's need for light, because she understood only too well about his bouts of despair and his memories.

There was something wrong with the front door, something different. The glass panel, was it? Oh God, the glass panel had been smashed – that was why there was glass all over the ground – which could only mean someone had broken in. Her mind went instantly to the silent watcher, and there was a moment when she thought – Don? And then the thought was crowded out in the desperate concern for Richard.

She could never afterwards recall if she had shouted Richard's name as she stepped into the hall. She went straight to the music room – Richard's beloved sanctum sanctorum where he worked and planned and dreamed – and she knew she had not cared whether the burglars might still be in there.

There was a sliver of light in the room, because the street lamp outside shone in through the big uncurtained windows. It illuminated the overturned furniture, smashed ornaments and rucked-up Chinese rug near the fire. There was a puddle of red wine on the edge of the rug: Richard sometimes had a glass of wine around half past seven. He must have done so tonight.

Then she saw him. He was lying on the floor, near the glossily dark piano – the baby grand that had been lover and child and parent to him for as long as Antonia could remember – and it was not red wine on the carpet after all, it was blood . . .

Someone had stabbed him, using a kitchen knife, driving it into his neck – she could see the dreadful gaping wound. She could see where blood had sprayed onto the wall, and she could see the knife lying on the floor. Richard's hands were covered in blood, and Antonia had a swift, dreadful image of him struggling to pull the knife free, and trying to stop the spurting blood. But he would have been dead inside a couple of minutes. Even so she bent over the still form, feeling for a pulse, praying to find one. Nothing. Of course there was not. Even a cursory glance showed that his killer had stabbed straight into the carotid artery.

His killer. There was a movement from the deep bay window, and a dark figure stepped from the shadows. Antonia gasped and instinctively stepped back to the door, one hand going to her mouth. Whoever broke in, whoever killed Richard was still there. She sent a quick glance towards the half-open door. If she was quick, could she get down the hall and be out into the garden before he reached her?

The figure moved again, and Antonia saw who it was. Don Robards.

Fury rose up in her so overwhelmingly that she forgot about her own danger, forgot Don was a patient, a recovering suicide, and forgot Jonathan's belief that he was on the verge of delusional behaviour. She went across the room, grabbed his arms and shook him, tears streaming down her cheeks.

'You evil bastard!' shouted Antonia. 'You've killed him! You've killed Richard!'

'I didn't kill him,' said Don, but even in the dimness Antonia could see he was staring at Richard's body. 'I didn't,' he said again, more loudly this time. His hands curled around Antonia's wrists, frighteningly strong. 'I don't understand what happened – I came in here – I had to see you, Antonia. And then I realized he was lying on the floor—'

'You killed him!' cried Antonia. 'Of course you did. You're blacking it out.'

'I came to see you,' he said, and even in the dim room the vivid eyes were hurt and puzzled. 'I thought you had abandoned me. You stopped seeing me – I couldn't bear it. You made me go to that man at your clinic. Dr Saxon.'

He pulled her against him; Antonia fought like a wildcat, but his hands were like steel clamps. 'Let me go!' she said.

'I thought at first you'd done it deliberately,' he said, as if she had not spoken. 'So I wouldn't be your patient any longer. So we could be together.'

'We'd never have been together! You've been fantasizing about me – you've been following me—'

'But then I realized we couldn't be together while you lived with someone,' he said, as if she had not spoken. 'I thought you lived on your own, and then last week I saw that man. I was watching from the road. The lights were switched on because it was getting dark, and he was sitting at the piano. I watched him for ages – he was playing, but he kept breaking off to write something on the music. And then I saw you come into the room, and he smiled at you, and I saw he wasn't just a friend.' A note of almost childlike hurt came into his voice. 'How could you do that to me, Antonia?' he said, and began to drag her across the room. For a nightmare moment Antonia thought they were going to trip over Richard's body, lying in its own blood.

'But it's all right now,' Don was saying, 'because he's dead. He is dead, isn't he?' He stopped and looked down at Richard's sprawled body. 'I don't think,' he said, in a conversational tone, 'he put up much of a fight. Bit of a weakling, really. How could you be in love with a weakling, Antonia?'

Antonia, her mind still spinning with agony, cried, 'He's not a weakling! He's a cripple! For the love of God, that's his wheelchair lying on the ground! He hasn't been able to walk since he was eight years old!'

Tears were pouring down her face, but Don seemed unaware of it. He began to pull her from the room. His face was flushed and his eyes were brilliant with madness. Antonia fought him off furiously, kicking him and trying to claw his face with her nails.

Through the blazing hatred and the bitter anger that were almost overwhelming her, she was aware of falling back against the piano – Richard's piano – and then of being pushed onto the ground. Don's hands were tearing at her jacket, and pushing beneath the thin sweater she was wearing under it. He was breathing excitedly, and lying half on top of her – his breath smelt of whisky and Antonia felt the hot hardness of his excitement against her legs. Sick revulsion swept over her.

She thought he said, 'Whatever he was, Antonia, he's dead now – he can't come between us.'

'You stupid besotted child!' shouted Antonia. 'Richard was never between us! He couldn't have been! He was my brother!'

CHAPTER TWENTY-THREE

In the police interviews and then later at her trial, Antonia said, with complete honesty, that she had simply snatched up the nearest weapon to hand. Don had been trying to rape her, and she had been terrified. He had killed her brother, and she had been afraid he was going to kill her as well.

The prosecution made much of this. 'But you've just said, Dr Weston, that you thought Don Robards was going to rape you. In the same breath you're saying he was trying to kill you. Which was it?'

Antonia said coldly, 'When you're pinned down by a murderer, you're not in any condition to form precise conclusions. He was behaving violently, and as well as that his intentions were obviously sexual—'

'You're sure of that, are you?'

'Oh, for pity's sake, he had an erection like a gate post and his hands were inside my sweater!' said Antonia angrily, and was aware of the entire press bench frantically scribbling in their notebooks.

'So you stabbed him.'

'I grabbed the knife which was lying on the floor, but it might just as well have been the brass doorstop. I simply hit out with whatever came to hand.'

'And the thing that came to hand was the knife.'

'Yes. I can't even remember if I recognized it as a knife at that stage. But I can remember that the blade went straight in,' said Antonia tersely, not wanting any of them to see how sick it still made her to remember the feel of the knife puncturing Don's body, and to hear the harsh rasping of breath rushing from his lungs and the sudden warm wet gush of blood . . . But what none of them knew and what Antonia dare not let any of them guess, was that she had hated Don so deeply and so overwhelmingly for killing Richard, that for a short time she had not cared that he was dead. But this was so shameful a knowledge, she had resolutely ignored it.

'My client was acting solely in her own defence,' said Antonia's counsel, leaping to his feet at this point. 'And let's remember that the charge against her is manslaughter, not murder.'

'The knife,' said the prosecution, steam-rollering on, 'entered Don Robards' body through the left side and pierced his heart instantly and exactly. The jury should ask themselves whether this was a calculated action – an action committed by someone with medical knowledge.'

'Dr Weston is a psychiatrist, not a surgeon. While the jury are asking themselves your questions, they might do well to keep that fact in mind.'

'But she would have more knowledge of anatomy than a layman.'

'She was distraught at finding her brother dead, and frightened half to death by finding in her home the man who had been stalking her – and no, that isn't too strong a word,' said Antonia's defence, anticipating the next interruption but with one eye on the judge who looked about to intervene. 'What Dr Weston did was not calculated or deliberate. She was certainly in no frame of mind to judge where and how to penetrate a man's heart with a kitchen knife.'

'Mr Frazer, you will have your chance to argue your client's case presently,' said the judge. 'For the moment, we will proceed with the prosecution.'

The arguments had gone on and on – the parrying and thrusting, the time spent debating legal points and interpretations. Antonia had tried to follow carefully, but several times she lost the thread which panicked her because if she could lose the thread how much likelier was it that the jury would lose it?

Medical evidence was called, showing that there had been some minor abrasions on Antonia's hands. No, it could not be stated definitely that they were defence wounds, although they were consistent with a struggle. There had been nothing to suggest sexual assault or intention: no torn clothes, no bruises or lacerations to the defendant's thighs. It had been useless for Antonia's counsel to leap to his feet at that point, and say that the rape had not progressed to bruised thighs and torn clothes. Dr Weston had already described Don Robards' actions and explained about his obsession, and there was no reason to disbelieve her account. As for the sexual intent, he said caustically, these days any half-intelligent female outside a nunnery was perfectly capable of knowing if a man intended sexual intercourse.

The events leading up to Richard's death had been meticulously and methodically unfolded. Antonia and Richard's movements had been charted, and witnesses had been called to verify everything: a phone call Richard had made to a friend shortly after eight o'clock; colleagues who had seen Antonia in the hospital until half past six; the drink with Jonathan. In the hands of prosecuting counsel, the blameless glass of wine had sounded like a Bacchanalian orgy.

Jonathan Saxon described Don Robards' treatment at the clinic, and gave his own assessment of Don's mental frame of mind. Matters had been complicated when Don had developed an obssession with Dr Weston, said Jonathan. He had fantasized about her, and it was not putting it too strongly to say he had begun stalking Dr Weston. She had not called in the police because she had been afraid of the effect on her brother, of whom she was extremely protective, but also because she was aware of Don Robards' own precarious mental balance.

Yes, said Jonathan, he knew Don had told Antonia he had not killed Richard – that he had found Richard's body lying on the floor. Asked if the state of Don's mental health might have caused some kind of blackout or mental block, Jonathan said, yes, it was possible. A fugue might have intervened or some form of hysterical amnesia – to put it simply, the conscious mind may have refused to acknowledge the fact of the murder.

He gave his evidence clearly and firmly, and of his own volition he added that Antonia Weston was a very good doctor of psychiatry, concerned and committed to the care of all her patients, and that if this tragedy prevented her from continuing to practise, it would be an appalling loss to the hospital in general and his own clinic in particular. He glared at the prosecuting counsel as he said this, and Antonia was deeply grateful to him.

A neighbour of Antonia and Richard's, was called to explain that she had walked past their bungalow shortly before nine that night. She knew Antonia and Richard Weston slightly; they were on good-morning and good-evening terms, and Dr Weston had given her a lift into town a few times. Very nice people, very well thought-of, and it was a tragedy about Richard, such a marvellous pianist. He had been part of one or two charity events for Dr Weston's hospital. Concerts and things. She always bought tickets. And she always slowed down going past the bungalow in case Richard was playing – he had a music room overlooking the front garden. If the windows were open, such as they might be in summer, you could sometimes hear him, and it was lovely, as good as Classic FM.

No, she had not heard him playing on that last night. It had been dark and cold, and the windows had been closed. What she had heard was the sound of raised voices – people shouting – and she had been quite surprised at that. No, she had not been able to tell if they were men's or women's voices, just angry voices. No, she had not stopped to listen. Well, mostly because she was hurrying home for a TV programme, but also because you did not listen to other people's quarrels, especially if they were people you knew. So she had gone on to her own house, and had been in good time for her programme although if she had known what was happening to Richard Weston she would never have watched it, in fact she would never watch that particular series again. Thank you very much, my lord.

The second witness was a roughish-looking young man, who was wearing a suit, but who looked as if he would be more at home in biker's leathers. He had been in the pub on the corner, he said. Yes, it was the night the crippled bloke was killed. Yes he was sure. There was a pub quiz and he and a couple of his mates were on the home team. Nine o'clock it was due to start, so they had been keeping an eye on the time, like.

Anyway, this bloke had come in a bit after eight and ordered a large whisky – several large whiskies. No, of course he had not known it to be Don Robards then, said the witness, but the next day the Old Bill had shown a photograph round and he had identified him from the photograph. Yes, he was sure. He had noticed Robards particular, like, because he had been sat at the table they wanted for the pub quiz, and they had all wondered whether they could ask him to move. Tables took a bit of arranging for a quiz night. Robards had been a bit pissed. Not rat-arsed, but a bit pissed. All right, drunk. Anyway, a bit before nine he had gone, and they moved the table and had the quiz. The home team had won and the prize had been two bottles of wine, not that the witness was a great wine drinker, in fact he would never drink wine again because it would always remind him of the night that poor sod Richard Weston was topped.

The witness from the police forensic department confirmed that the kitchen knife that had killed both Richard and Don was part of a set of cooking knives belonging to the prisoner, normally kept in the kitchen. Not in a drawer, but on a rack just above a worktop – the jury would be familiar with such things from their own kitchens. As Richard Weston was permanently confined to a wheelchair, the kitchen was arranged so he could reach ordinary everyday implements. He had, it seemed, liked preparing the evening meal for his sister who was at the hospital all day; it was part of the pattern of their lives.

The knife was unquestionably the weapon that had killed Richard Weston and Don Robards. The shape and depth of the wound in each case, the angle of entry, the separate blood-stains on the blade— The details became technical and slightly over-long at this point, and Antonia, studying the jury, thought this was overdoing it. They looked intelligent enough, but this stuff about blood groups and angles of wounds was specialized knowledge.

When it came to the case for the defence, her counsel, pleading mitigating circumstances for all he was worth, made much of her distraught state at finding her brother's body.

'She wasn't so distraught she couldn't remove her own bloodied jacket and sweater before the police arrived,' said prosecuting counsel.

'I think,' said the defence dryly, 'we can accept Dr Weston's own explanation as a genuine one.' He flipped through a sheaf of notes, and then read, '"I was shaking and I felt sick. I managed to push him off me, and then I rushed to the cloakroom to be sick. It was only afterwards I realized I was soaked in Don's blood. I couldn't bear the smell of it or the wetness, so I took everything off and stuffed it in a plastic bin liner. Then I heard the police and the ambulance arriving, so I pulled on a tracksuit and let them in."' He lowered the notes and looked directly at the jury. 'I think most people will sympathize with Dr Weston's actions over that,' he said, and Antonia thought the women on the jury half nodded as if in agreement.

But she had known by then that a verdict of manslaughter was inescapable – the difference between manslaughter and murder had been explained to the court at the outset – but beneath the grinding pain at Richard's death, she had thought there might be a recommendation for clemency. Would it even result in a suspended sentence? Probation? But nagging at her conscience like an aching tooth was the memory of how she had felt when

Don died . . . Glad, strong, triumphant . . . You're dead, you bastard, and serve you right for killing Richard. It was absurd to think she should be punished for thinking and feeling that, and it was probably verging on clinical hysteria, but she did think it and she did feel it.

Summing up, the judge said the facts of Richard Weston's own murder seemed clear enough, and were not really in question. Don Robards had been seen in the area at the significant time, and he was known to have formed a violent passion for Dr Weston. It was reasonable to surmise that he had gone into the pub to bolster his courage with a few drinks before going along to confront her with his feelings for her.

They had the neighbour's evidence of raised voices from the bungalow, as of two people engaged in an argument, and although they could not know the state of Don Robards' mind that night, it was reasonable to assume he had taken Richard Weston to be Dr Weston's lover or husband, rather than her brother, and had attacked and killed him out of blind jealousy. Dr Weston had told the court this seemed to be Don Robards' belief in the last few minutes of his life, and there was no reason to disbelieve that. She had given a frank account of everything that had taken place, and there was no reason to doubt any of it.

And although the jury must take into account the fact that Antonia Weston had been distraught at her brother's death, and, if they were to believe her evidence, afraid for her own safety, they must not allow themselves to be unduly swayed by any false sentiment or sympathy. Now the court would rise, and the jury were to retire to the jury room and consider their verdict.

It took the jury the best part of eight hours to reach a verdict, but in the end it was that of guilty, as everyone had known it would be. Guilty of manslaughter.

Sentence was not passed until the following day, and Antonia spent a miserable night, watching the clock crawl through the hours. She tried to convince herself that she did not care what happened to her, but somewhere between midnight and four a.m. she knew she did care.

Caring what happened did not make any difference to the sentence. The judge told the court that the gaoling of a professional woman of considerable intelligence – a woman who had clearly been a dedicated and gifted psychiatrist – offended every sensibility, but that the facts could not be ignored. And those facts, quite simply, were that a doctor bound by the Hippocratic oath had killed a patient. There was a good deal more about the sanctity of the doctor–patient relationship and a fair amount about the judge's own reluctance to pass a custodial sentence.

But despite his reluctance, Antonia was sentenced to eight years in gaol.

Lying wakeful in Charity Cottage, reliving the trial and the dreary years in prison, Antonia felt again the ache of loss for Richard, and a wave of anger and bitterness that he had not lived to enjoy his music and his life. He had lost so much in the car crash that had killed their parents when he was eight and Antonia was eleven: he had lost the use of his legs because his spine had been irreparably damaged, and had lived the rest of his life in a wheelchair. One of the things Antonia had always found unbearably sad was that Richard would never know the closeness and the delight of being in bed with a lover. But he had clung tenaciously to optimism and had clung even more tenaciously to his music. He had worked hard, and so had Antonia, and after a few years – after she had qualified in psychiatric medicine and Richard had left the Royal College of Music – they had been able to buy the big comfortable bungalow. They liked living there, and they liked one another's company. Richard had acquired some pupils and was making a modest name as a music researcher. Life had not been perfect but it had been very good.

One of the many tragedies in this entire mess of tragedies, was that they had had such a few short years to enjoy it all.

CHAPTER TWENTY-FOUR

Each evening after dinner George Lincoln sat in the comfortable drawing room of Toft House. He derived a deep satisfaction from looking about him, and knowing that this house, this big well-appointed house, belonged to him. Who would have thought the young man from such modest roots – his father had been vicar of a small parish adjoining Amberwood – would have done so well for himself?

On a dank autumn night he was not expecting anyone to call, but shortly after half past eight there was a rather timid plying of the door knocker, and since Mrs Plumtree would have retired to her own sitting room upstairs, George went along to answer it himself. Standing on the doorstep was Mrs Minching, the housekeeper from Quire House, looking deeply anxious.

'Mr Lincoln, I'm that sorry to be knocking on your door, but I'm afraid there might be trouble up at Quire.'

'Trouble? What kind of— Is it Maud?' said George. 'Has something happened to Maud?' And then, belatedly aware of the chill night air, he said, 'You'd better come inside, Mrs Minching, and sit down. What's wrong?'

Mrs Minching, perched on the edge of the sofa, was inclined to be voluble. 'I'd been to evensong, Mr Lincoln. I always go along of a Tuesday evening. Miss Thomasina knows, of course, and I leave a cold supper out.'

George repressed a strong desire to tell her to get on with it, because if something had happened to Maud . . .

'Tonight it was getting on for eight o'clock when I got back, and that was when I found the kitchen door at Quire – the one I normally use – was locked. Not just locked, but bolted, Mr Lincoln. Well, I thought, that's not usual. So I went round to the other doors – the garden door, the front door, and the French windows of the music room – but at every one it was the same story. Locked and bolted.'

'Dear me,' said George, not seeing where this was leading.

'So then of course, I knocked. And without a word of a lie, I knocked until my hands were fair wore out, but no one came.'

'But,' said George, puzzled, 'aren't there two girls who work for you? Weren't they there?'

'One's in Chester seeing her sister who's just had a baby, and the other has the night off. I don't ask questions as to where she goes,' said Mrs Minching righteously.

'What about Miss Thomasina?'

'Miss Thomasina is away. And it's not my place to question where she goes.'

'No, but—'

'Miss Thomasina,' said Mrs Minching, compressing her lips, 'is in the way of sometimes going off by herself for a day or two.'

'Oh, I see,' said George, not seeing at all. 'But are you saying the house is empty? I'm sure Maud would have told me if she was going away with Miss Thomasina.'

'Oh, Miss Maud's in the house, Mr Lincoln. That's why I'm here now. My word, Miss Maud is there all right. She's seated at the piano, playing that belly-aching row. Beg pardon, sir, but I've been out in the cold knocking at the door of a house where I've worked for twenty years. Twenty years, I've been there, all the way up from scullery maid in old Mr Josiah's time – and reduced to shouting through the letterbox to be let in. It's enough to make a saint swear. I felt no better than a common fishwife, indeed I did.'

'I'd better come up to the house with you,' said George, still not overly worried. 'Maud may not have heard you. If she was practising her music she might have been lost to everything else. I'd better let Mrs Plumtree know I'm going out. Would you like a – some refreshment while you wait?' He made the offer hesitantly, because he had never really sorted out what was correct when it came to hospitality of this kind. Did you offer a drink to somebody else's housekeeper?

Mrs Minching took kindly to the idea of refreshment. She said she would not object to a little nip of gin, if Mr Lincoln had such a thing. 'It's a cold night, and a little nip of gin's wonderfully warming.'

The aura of the gin seemed to accompany them as they walked along Scraptoft Lane and approached Quire House. George rather wished he had had a nip of it himself, because it was a dismal kind of night. A thin, spiritless rain was falling, wreathing the trees in mist. The more he thought about it, the odder it became to think of Maud by herself in that great house, Miss Thomasina apparently absent, and all the doors locked against the world.

As they turned in at the gates George spotted a light shining through the trees from Charity Cottage, and it occurred to him that Cormac Sullivan might possibly have keys to Quire House.

'I suppose he might,' said Mrs Minching doubtfully. 'You could ask.'

'He's probably not at home,' said George. 'I believe I will try, though.'

But Cormac was at home, although did not have keys to Quire House. Thomasina Forrester, he said gravely, did not hand out keys in such a profligate fashion, and especially not to the tenantry.

George explained they needed to get into Quire, and why, and Sullivan said, 'Curiouser and curiouser. Will I come up there with you?' and it occurred to George this might be helpful.

'Wait while I get a coat, then,' said Cormac. 'And will we take a flask of something with us to keep out the cold?'

George, who was by this time starting to feel more concerned than puzzled, thought that between Mrs Minching's nip of gin, and Cormac Sullivan's flask, they would be lucky to get as far as Quire House by midnight.

Maud had spent all of last night and most of today trying to shut out the sounds of Thomasina and Simon tapping on Twygrist's walls, but in the end it had become impossible. *Tap-tap . . . Let-us-out . . . Tap-tap . . . We're-not-dead . . .* On and on it went, until she wanted to scream. All night she had lain in bed listening to it, and she had been grateful for the thin daylight that finally came into her bedroom because surely the tapping would not continue through the day. She felt sick and dizzy from not having slept.

By now those two must be dead. But what if they were not? What if they had found a way to get out – Twygrist's outer door was not locked – and had somehow crept back to this house? Maud would not put it past them to do that. Well then, they would have to be kept out. She thought about this, and remembered it was Mrs Minching's night for evensong, and that the two maids would also be out tonight. That was very good indeed; Maud waited until Mrs Minching was safely out of the house, then went round all the rooms, locking the doors and drawing the bolts. Aha, Madam Thomasina and Master Simon, you won't come sneaking in now! No one would come sneaking in – she had made sure of that.

She lit the lamp in the music room. It was warm and there was a comforting crackle from the logs in the hearth. The tapping seemed to have stopped for a while. Maud relaxed, and began to drift into a half sleep. It was nice to sit here and know she would not be forced to do 'It' with Thomasina or Simon ever again. Nice . . .

But it was not nice after all, because Thomasina and Simon

were waiting for her, just on the other side of sleep, reproachful and threatening. Their faces were already fading to a sick whiteness because of being shut away from the light. They had crawled across to the steel doors – it had taken them most of last night and all of today because they were getting weak with not having eaten, and because it was pitchy black in the kiln room – but they had managed it and now they were hammering against the doors. Simon said they would keep on hammering until someone heard. He lifted his hands up to show Maud how his fingers and knuckles were already starting to protrude through the skin. That was good, he said, because bones made effective hammers.

Maud managed to climb up out of the nightmare at this point, but even awake she could still hear the hammering of Simon's knucklebones against the kiln room doors. Dreadful dull knockings, over and over, like someone beating against a bruise in your mind . . .

That had been when she thought of blotting out the sounds with music, and had sat down at the piano and begun to play her beloved *Caprice* as loudly as she could. Part of Paganini's legend was supposed to be that he had sold his soul to the devil, and that this was a devil-inspired composition. Maud found this believable. She did not care if the music conjured up the composer's devils in this very room, if it meant they would keep her safe from Thomasina and Simon.

It was Cormac who banged the brass door knocker of Quire's main door. It echoed through the house like the crack of doom, and George could not believe it could not be heard inside. But even though Sullivan plied the heavy knocker several times, there was no response.

'Nothing,' he said, at last. 'We'll go around to the back and see what we can find there. Mrs Minching, you wait here, if you would.'

Without waiting for an answer he set off, and George followed, blundering into bushes in the dark, torn between annoyance at the way Sullivan seemed to have taken over, and relief at having decisions made for him.

'Nothing to be seen,' said Cormac, having peered in through all the windows. 'No sign of your girl anywhere. That's the music room, isn't it?'

'Yes.'

'Well, whatever she might have been doing earlier on, she isn't there now,' said Cormac, having peered through the partly open curtains. 'There's no one there. Nothing else for it, Lincoln, we'll have to break in.'

'Oh, we can't do that,' said George, shocked. 'Whatever will Miss Thomasina say?'

'Thomasina Forrester isn't here to say anything. If you want my opinion, she's sloped off to London on one of her jaunts. She has a liking for the ladies in Seven Dials, so it's said.' He glanced at George. 'You didn't know that?'

This was clearly nothing more than extremely distasteful gossip, but George could not think of a suitable answer so he mumbled something vague.

'But,' said Cormac, surveying the house, 'all things being equal, I think we'd be within our rights to smash a window. Will I do the deed, or will you? No? I didn't think you would.'

He found a heavy stone from the path, and smashed it against the windowpane. The glass splintered, and he reached inside to unlatch the frame.

'This house is empty,' he said, as soon as they had stepped through the French windows, avoiding the broken glass. 'It's odd, isn't it, how you can tell?'

George, who did not see how you could tell if a house was empty or full of people, said they should make a thorough search. Maud might be ill – she might have tripped and fallen and be lying helpless somewhere.

'So she might. Although if she was playing the piano half an hour ago . . . But we'll take a look.'

They let Mrs Minching in through the front door, and set off.

'It's a curious thing about Quire,' said Cormac as they went up the main staircase. 'There's all this orderly Georgian elegance' – he waved an expressive hand – 'all the smooth walls and pale ceilings – but there are pockets of deep unhappiness in some of the rooms.'

'I don't know what you mean,' said George. 'Unless you mean damp or dry rot. There's always a smell with that, of course.' There had been dry rot in the roof at Toft House a year or so ago; it had cost a shocking sum of money to get rid of it.

'I don't mean damp or dry rot,' said Cormac. 'I know all about those. This is like – it's like stepping without warning into a black icy puddle when you thought it was a warm summer afternoon. Like falling into a well. There's a bad one in the music room, did you not feel it? There's another in the bedroom that I think is your daughter's.' He glanced at George as he said this, but George had never heard such fanciful rubbish as pockets of unhappiness inside houses, and he set off up to the second floor without bothering to respond.

He had just paused on the upper landing to look out of a window – there was a clear view of Toft House's chimneys over to the east – when he caught a darting movement down on the ground. Leaning forward he saw a shadow detach itself from the darkness and go purposefully along the carriageway.

George screwed up his eyes, trying to see better. Could it be Maud? Yes, surely that was the cloak with the hood she sometimes wore. He went plunging back down the stairs, shouting to Sullivan.

'Are you sure it was Maud?' demanded Cormac when George had spluttered out what he had seen, and Mrs Minching had come puffing up from the kitchens. 'Mightn't it have been Thomasina?'

'Yes, I am sure it was Maud,' said George, annoyed at the implication that he could not recognize his own daughter. 'In any case, it wasn't tall enough for Miss Thomasina or for your daughter, Sullivan. And no one else is likely to be wandering around the grounds in the dark.'

'She must have been hiding outside while we were searching the house,' said Mrs Minching. 'But where she'd be going at such a time of night beats me.'

'It beats me as well, but we'll have to find out,' said George. He looked at Cormac, not wanting to ask for further help, but was relieved when Sullivan said, 'We'll go after her. You stay here, Mrs Minching. Ready, Lincoln?'

'Of course.'

George dared say Sullivan was used to slinking through the night in pursuit of game, either human or feathered, but he, George, was not. By the time they reached Quire's gates, he was considerably out of breath and Maud was some way ahead of them. But they had both seen her turn left onto the high road.

'Then she's not going towards the town,' said Cormac softly. 'Can you see her? In this rain she looks like a wraith.'

'Do you think she knows we're coming after her?'

'If I was by myself I'd say she wouldn't hear a thing, but you're clumping along like something with spurs or cloven hoofs and huffing like a grampus, so— God Almighty, will you look where she's going?'

But George had already seen. Maud was going towards Twygrist.

Twygrist was never a very prepossessing place at the best of times, and late at night with the rain sliding from the trees it was as gloomy as it could be. Even George, who had worked there from the days of being Josiah Forrester's under-manager, always found it forbidding after dark.

Despite Sullivan's earlier remark, he did not think Maud knew they were here. She walked straight up to the mill, pausing in its shadow to send a stealthy look over her shoulder.

'Will the door be locked?' said Cormac softly.

'It should be. But she won't go inside.'

'By the look of it, that's just what she's doing. We'll have to go after her.'

'Quietly, then. Don't alarm her.'

Twygrist's door was not locked after all. Maud pushed it open and was stepping into the yawning blackness as George and Cormac came up the grass-covered slope towards her. She turned, like a cornered animal, one hand going up, although whether in defence or to attack it was impossible to know.

Cormac reached her ahead of George. He took her arm and said, in a voice so gentle that for a moment George wondered who had spoken, 'Maud – this is a bad old night to be out. Come on home with us now.'

'You don't understand.' Maud sounded quite reasonable and sensible. 'Don't you hear it? The tapping on the walls? Listen.' She clutched at Cormac's arm, and for a dreadful moment George found himself thinking that there was a faint sound from somewhere inside Twygrist. As if something was tapping feebly against ancient bricks, trying to get out.

'That's what you'd do,' said Maud. 'You'd keep tapping on the walls until someone heard. Over and over. You'd wear away your flesh, wouldn't you, but you wouldn't care, because then you'd have your fingerbones, and bones make good hammers—'

'Maud, no one has any need to tap on the walls.'

Maud stared at the two men, and then said in a voice that caused an icy hand to clutch at George's vitals, 'But if you had been buried alive . . .'

For a dreadful moment the darkness seemed to swoop down on them, and a brush of wind stirred the shadows around Twygrist. George saw Cormac glance up at the crouching outline of the mill, then he said, 'Maud, my dear, no one's buried alive.'

'Oh yes,' said Maud. 'Oh yes, they're buried alive. They're both in there.' For a moment her face – the features George had always thought so pretty – sharpened, and became sly and furtive, and a deep memory stirred in him. He thought: that is exactly how her mother used to look sometimes.

To quench this image, he said, 'Maud, you're not well. I'm taking you home.'

'*No!*' It came out on a scream, splintering the night, and when George tried to take her arm, she pushed him away. 'I must stay here until the tapping stops,' said Maud. 'That's why I came out here, you see. To make sure. Because how long would you take to die – do you know? Hours? Days? Down there in the dark, hammering at the walls to get out.' She began to sob, and the sobs took on a shrillness, and then built up to dreadful piercing cries that splintered the night. Despite himself George glanced uneasily up and down the deserted road, because the hour was not so very late, and if anyone should come along . . .

It was Cormac who pulled out the silver flask, and said, in a sharp firm voice, 'Maud, your father is right and you're unwell. Drink this now for me – Oh yes, you will, there's to be no argument about it. And then we'll walk along to Toft House.'

That'll never work, thought George, but incredibly, it did. Maud drew in a deep shuddering breath. She stopped crying, and looked at Sullivan for a moment, then took the flask and tilted it to her lips. She gasped as the spirit – George supposed it was brandy – went down, but after a moment it seemed to kick her back to some form of sanity.

The fit, whatever it was, seemed to have passed. When they took her arms again, she walked between them with a docility that upset George far more than anything else that had happened tonight. To see his dearest Maud in this condition – crying and screaming, talking about macabre things – it was more than he could bear. It was more than any man should be expected to bear. And to think she had run here, to the very place where her mother . . .

But if he allowed himself to think about Maud's mother, George knew he would break down altogether. He turned his whole attention to the task of getting Maud back to Toft House.

If it had been an odd experience to steal along the dark lanes in company with Cormac Sullivan, it was even odder to sit with him in Toft House's drawing room.

Maud had been safely tucked into bed – George had roused Mrs Plumtree, telling her that Maud had succumbed to a sudden fever, and so in Miss Thomasina's absence they had brought her home. Mrs Plumtree had administered a tiny measure of laudanum, and that, probably along with the contents of Cormac Sullivan's flask, had sent Maud into a sound sleep. She's all right, thought George determinedly. A nerve storm, that's all it was.

He poured whisky into two glasses, handed one to Sullivan, and thanked him for what he had done. A great help. He did not know how he would have coped on his own.

'Oh, daughters are the very devil,' said Cormac. He was seated near the fireplace and he looked entirely at his ease, which was vaguely irritating of him. A man of Sullivan's morals and reputation ought not to be so at ease in a house of this kind.

He frowned, and said, 'Here's the thing, Lincoln. We need to take a look inside the mill.'

'Why?' said George at once. The word came out sharply, but beneath it he was aware of a churning panic.

'Because Thomasina and Simon Forrester are both absent without explanation,' said Cormac. 'And because Maud was talking about somebody – and it sounded like more than one somebody – being buried alive inside Twygrist.'

As George started to make a protest, Sullivan said, half to himself, 'It's remarkable, isn't it, that however much you think you're modern and without superstition, the primeval fears still grab you by the throat. Buried alive, that's what she kept saying. Down there in the dark, hammering on the walls to get out – Jesus God, I hope we're wrong about this, but we need to make sure, and we need to make sure tonight. If you're not up to it, Lincoln, say so, and I'll haul out Daniel Glass to come with me.'

'I'll come with you,' said George.

'We'll cut across the field,' said Cormac, when they reached Scraptoft Lane. 'It'll bring us out just below the reservoir and that'll save time. It's a short cut I often use,' he said offhandedly, and George glanced at him, and thought: I bet you do!

The underground rooms of Twygrist were dismal and dank and it was necessary to walk cautiously to avoid tripping over bits of broken or discarded machinery littering the floor. The oil lamp George had brought created grotesque shadows on the walls, and there was a faint drip of water from somewhere. Twygrist was probably leaking like a sieve; George had known that for years, though. It was one of the reasons the place had been closed down. As for the other reason – his mind shuddered away from that, and he concentrated on what they must now do.

Here was the kiln room, with the massive old doors firmly closed. George said, 'You know, I really don't think we need look in there.'

'I think we do,' said Cormac. 'And we'll get to it at once.' He grasped the edge of the left-hand door as he spoke. It moved reluctantly, and its hinges shrieked painfully in the enclosed space, but it slid slowly open.

'God Almighty, it's like the gates guarding the entrance to hell,' said Cormac 'But I think we've got it now. Give me something to wedge it in place, would you? That's better. Now hold up the lamp.'

As the light fell across the floor, Cormac swore softly and George felt as if he had been punched in the ribs.

Thomasina Forrester was huddled against the brick chimney at the far end of the room where once the fires had burned. Her face was turned towards them; it was hideously distorted and covered in livid crimson blotches – for a moment George was not even sure it was Thomasina. Her tongue, black and swollen, stuck out of her mouth. A few feet away, as if he had tried to crawl to the door, was her cousin Simon, his face, mercifully, turned away from them.

'Jesus God,' said Cormac softly, 'that would be a terrible way to die. Down here in the dark, all alone.' He bent over the dreadful thing that had been Simon Forrester, and then moved to

Thomasina, in case, George supposed, there might be a faint flicker of life left in either of them.

After a moment he straightened up. 'They're both dead. God knows how they became trapped down here, but it looks as if they tried to find the door to get out. It'd be pitch dark though, so they'd have no way of knowing where they were. Would they have suffocated, do you suppose?'

'I don't know. No, I don't think so. There ought to be some air down here – the drying floor's directly above.'

'I suppose they died from shock and exhaustion,' said Cormac. 'Daniel Glass will be able to tell us.'

George said, 'Thomasina must have thought she had reached the door, but it was the wrong door. It was the ovens.' He held the lamp up again, and they both saw the long scratches on the oven surface.

'You're right,' said Cormac. 'Look at her hands. The fingernails are all broken and bloodied. Lincoln, if you're going to be sick, go and do it somewhere else, because we don't want any more mess on the floor than we can help.'

For the second time that night, George and Cormac Sullivan sat together in the drawing room of Toft House.

George was still reeling from what they had found, and even Sullivan – who must presumably have seen a few strange things in his time – looked stunned. He had offered George his flask down there in Twygrist's darkness – it was brandy and George was grateful for it – but it was not until they were back at Toft House that Cormac spoke again.

'Lincoln, did Maud kill Thomasina and Simon Forrester?'

George said, as sharply as he could, 'No, of course not.'

'You do know it's a question that will be asked, though?'

'Will it? Why would anyone think Maud would do such a thing? A young girl – she's barely eighteen.'

'George, did it never occur to you to wonder why Thomasina Forrester invited Maud to Quire in the first place?'

'No,' said George. 'Miss Thomasina has always been very kind to the young ladies of the neighbourhood. Interested in them. I was pleased for Maud.'

'Jesus God,' said Cormac, making it sound like an invocation. 'All right then, we'll look at it in a different way. Why did Maud go out to Twygrist tonight? She knew they were in there, didn't she?'

'Yes, but— Does it have to become common knowledge?'

'Minching up at Quire knows at least half of it,' said Cormac. 'If you think she won't gossip about it, you don't know much about women. The story – or a version of it – will be halfway round Cheshire before the week's out.'

'Yes,' said George slowly. 'Yes, I see that.' He looked at the other man. 'What do I do?'

'To protect Maud from a police investigation? From a court hearing? Perhaps from a verdict of guilty, and a prison sentence or worse? For if they decide it was a double murder . . . I'm sorry to sound brutal,' said Cormac, 'but I think you have to face up to this.' He frowned, and then said, 'I know what I'd do. If it was Bryony, I wouldn't care a farthing's curse for the law. I'd get her out of Amberwood faster than a saint getting out of hell – probably back to Ireland.'

'Yes,' said George slowly. 'Yes, I see that. If there were somewhere Maud could go. Just for a while.' He stopped, and then said, 'Somewhere that would put her beyond the reach of the law.'

The two men stared at one another. Neither of them spoke, but a single word lay on the air between them.

Latchkill. *Latchkill* . . .

CHAPTER TWENTY-FIVE

After Cormac had gone, George passed a sleepless night.

Stamped on his mind was the image of Maud's face with the dreadful slyness coming down over it like a veil, and echoing in his ears were the words she had used, 'They're buried alive in there . . .' That was what she had said, and that had been when he had known, quite certainly, that Maud had deliberately shut Thomasina and Simon Forrester in Twygrist's kiln room. Had she intended to leave them there until they were dead? George did not know, and he did not want to know.

He had only the smallest knowledge of how the police worked, but he could not risk the truth getting out. If it became known what Maud had done – how oddly she had behaved, how she had gone out to Twygrist – she would be questioned. Somebody would be bound to tell the police the horrid gossip about Thomasina, and the result would be that Maud would be charged with murder. She would have to stand up in a courtroom and answer prying questions and cope with avid stares, and at the end of it, she might be found guilty, and hanged in the early morning, her body buried in some shameful squalid prison yard . . . And if that happened, George would have nothing left to live for.

Even if Maud were cleared of the charge, she would never be

free of it, even if they left Amberwood. There would be newspaper reports – perhaps with reproductions of the sketches made in court – and people would remember. Maud Lincoln? they would say. Oh yes, that's the woman who was tried for the double murder. The Forrester case, wasn't it? Two women together – oh yes, *I* see . . . The jury brought in a verdict of innocent, but you know the old saying about no smoke without fire . . . And the speculation and sniggers would follow Maud for the rest of her life.

Anything was better than that. Even Latchkill? said his mind. *Yes*.

It had been very late indeed when Cormac Sullivan had finally left, but before going, he had said, 'Lincoln, I'm an unconventional man and I believe in unconventional solutions, but I think what you have in mind is wrong. Listen now, we could get Maud over to Ireland quite easily. A ferry from Liverpool to Dún Laoghaire, and a journey across to the west coast. I have a house there, although it's tumbling into the Atlantic ocean with neglect . . .' He paused, and George glanced at him because for the first time he had heard a note of wistfulness in Sullivan's flippant tones.

A bit awkwardly, he said, 'Thank you, Sullivan. But I think my way is best.' Because she's mad, she's as mad as her poor mother was, and this is the only way she's going to be safe from the consequences of what she's done.

'Ah well, the offer's there,' said Sullivan. 'And we'll hope you've saved her from a – a bad future.'

'Yes. And I'll never forget how you helped tonight—'

'I'm a helpful sort of a man,' said Cormac offhandedly. 'But I'm not a man given to talking about what goes on in Amberwood, so you needn't be afraid of that. You won't be wanting to let them know Maud's real identity in Latchkill?'

'No.'

'Then how would it be if I deliver a note to Matron Prout some time tomorrow, asking her to call on you to discuss a – a private matter? I can do so without anyone seeing me, I believe. That would keep it fairly anonymous for you.'

'I'd be very grateful if you'd do that,' said George.

'You'd need to keep Maud from talking to Mrs Minching in the meantime.'

I'll need to stop her trying to get out as well, thought George, but did not say it.

'Could you give her a drop of laudanum? For God's sake don't overdo it though. Laudanum goes a devil of a long way.'

George belatedly remembered that Sullivan's daughter was a nurse in Latchkill.

'There's no need for Bryony to know any of this,' said Cormac, apparently following George's thoughts. 'In fact I'd rather she didn't know – that'll mean that if she's asked questions, she won't need to lie. In any case, she's mostly on duty in the public wards – the pauper wards they call them.' This was said with extreme distaste. 'She's not very likely to even know Maud's there. But if she did find out, or if I had to tell her, she wouldn't spread any gossip, you can trust me on that. There's your housekeeper, though. And Minching.'

But George had already worked this out. He would tell people that Maud had gone to stay with relatives of his wife for a few weeks. Mrs Minching might think Maud's behaviour tonight rather odd, but she had not known about the Twygrist visit, and there was no reason why she should. There was no reason why anyone should know. As for Mrs Plumtree, she was a loyal soul who had served his wife's family for years. She could be told a version of the truth – that Maud was displaying symptoms worryingly like those of her mother, and that George had arranged for a short rest in a place with proper medical care. Somewhere on the coast, he might say. Bracing sea air. That would be perfectly believable, and it would mean that Latchkill need not be mentioned at all.

'Good. That keeps it simple,' said Cormac, when George explained this. 'We'll have to report finding the bodies, of course, but we can do that tomorrow, and there's no need for either of us to mention Maud's part in it. We'll say we went searching for

Thomasina. You were concerned, what with your daughter staying at Quire. And it'd be natural for you to think of looking in Twygrist, wouldn't it?'

'Yes. Until my wife died, Twygrist was my whole life,' said George.

'Good man.' He dropped a light hand on George's shoulder that might have been a gesture of friendship or commiseration, and went out into the night.

When it came to it, the thing that upset George most was the subterfuge he had to employ to keep Maud's identity secret. It felt as if he was wiping away all traces of the child's very existence. But the alternative was too dreadful to contemplate, and so before Matron Prout was due at Toft House he got Mrs Minching out of the way by asking her to deliver a wholly unnecessary message to the rectory about hymn books and then went round the house putting all the photographs of Maud out of sight. Forgive me Maud, but I can't see any other solution.

Latchkill's matron was not a complete stranger; at one time George's wife had helped with some of Amberwood's charity events, and Freda Prout had been one of the other helpers. George remembered her as a raw-boned lady with ungainly hands and feet. When she came to Toft House in response to his note, he saw his memory had been accurate. She sat in the warm, comfortable drawing-room and George tried not to think there was a calculating glint in her rather small eyes.

'A very nice house, this,' said Freda, looking about her. 'Just as I remember it.'

George said he had not realized Mrs Prout had been to Toft House before. 'Oh yes. On two occasions, both times to discuss the organisation of charity events with your wife and some other ladies.'

Her voice was rather ugly; there was a discordance to it. George wondered if he could really shut Maud away in that terrible place with this hard-faced woman and her unmusical voice? Maud, who so loved music . . . ?

But he embarked determinedly on the little speech he had prepared for Mrs Prout. A young relative whom the family had reluctantly decided to commit to Latchkill for a time, he said. He hoped Matron could arranged that.

'Dear me, how very distressing for you.'

George said it was very distressing indeed. 'I'm afraid she is sadly disturbed, but we believe it to be purely temporary. I daresay you'll know how – how changeable young girls can be. Very excitable one moment, and deeply melancholic the next.'

'Indeed yes. And so often a young man is the cause of it.'

George wished it was as simple as that but did not say so. 'We thought – one of your private rooms. Just a few weeks. But proper medical supervision – sympathetic treatment – perhaps mild sedation . . .' Dammit, what were the right expressions! He should have asked Sullivan. 'And then after a little time she can return to her family,' he said.

'That may be possible, although I should have to see the young lady for myself.'

George had anticipated this. He said, 'She's in the large bedroom on the right of the landing upstairs.'

'A private room, you said?' asked Freda, back in the drawing room some little time later.

'Yes.' With the idea of establishing friendly relations, George suggested a glass of sherry might accompany their discussion. This was well received. Freda did not, it appeared, normally drink sherry – or any other alcoholic beverage – at this time of day, because of setting a good example to her nurses. But perhaps just this once.

'My word, what very nice sherry. Cheer-ho. Well now, Mr Lincoln, I can arrange a room for the young lady, although there will be a charge, you understand.'

'I had assumed that. I – the family – we are quite prepared to pay.'

Freda merely nodded, as if this was no more than she had

expected. She looked towards the desk in the window, where Louisa used to write her letters. George had hoped Maud might one day do the same, but she never had.

'I see you no longer have the photograph of your daughter on the secretaire,' said Freda, and George instantly felt as if something had smacked him across the eyes.

But he said, very firmly, 'Mrs Prout, my daughter is away visiting relatives at the moment.'

'You'll pardon me, Mr Lincoln, but your daughter is the young lady I have just seen in the bedroom upstairs.'

The small mean eyes met his. A flat denial, thought George. That's what I must do. 'I think you must be mistaken, Matron.'

'Oh no,' said Freda. 'Your wife showed us all the photograph the first time I was here. I remember it very clearly – a silver frame it was, and I thought at the time what a very pretty girl. You have put the photograph away since then.' She studied George for a moment, and then said, 'You mentioned a stay of a few weeks in Latchkill, Mr Lincoln. But matters are not always quite so straightforward. Latchkill is not an hotel for people to book in and out as the whim takes them. Or,' she added, 'as it takes their families. We have to comply with the requirements of the Lunacy Act.'

George, who had not expected this, asked for clarification.

'For a patient to be admitted, a justice must first make an order for lunacy, which must be signed by two separate doctors – neither of whom must be related to the patient or have any financial interest in him or her.' A pause. 'However, something might be arranged.'

'I don't—'

'Doctors – and the commissioners of the Lunacy Board – are sometimes open to persuasion, Mr Lincoln.'

'Oh, I see.' George thought he did see, and he did not much like it. It sounded a bit too glib. But another part of his mind felt grateful that there might be a way round the bewildering legal requirements. It can be done, he thought. I can put Maud into Latchkill, and once people have forgotten what happened to Thomasina and Simon, Maud can come home to Toft House, and life can go on just as before.

'But,' said Freda, 'I find it strange that you should wish to commit your only daughter to an asylum, Mr Lincoln. Especially when you must surely have enough money to care for her at home.' Again there was the appraising look round the room. 'Is it because you are ashamed? Or is there some other reason?'

There was a rather unpleasant silence, but at length George said, 'Before she died, Maud's mother was very disturbed. Maud is showing unmistakable signs of the same – disturbance. I want to keep it private.' This came out firmly and clearly.

'I daresay it's her delusions you want to keep private,' said Freda. 'Quite remarkable some of them. You had administered something to her, I think – laudanum most probably – but she was sufficiently awake to talk while I was with her.'

George felt as if something had a stranglehold on his throat, but he said, cautiously, 'Maud has a very dark imagination at times.'

'Indeed? Well, people whose minds are flawed exhibit the most extraordinary behaviour. You wouldn't believe the things some of my patients say. Confessions of all kinds of crimes. Even murder.' The little eyes were unreadable. 'For most of the time we keep an open mind, of course. And no one at Latchkill will hear if Miss – should we call her Miss Smith? – very well, no one will hear if Miss Smith talks about people being buried alive inside your mill. A curious coincidence, isn't it, that poor Miss Forrester and her cousin have been found shut in the underground room there. I heard some of my nurses talking about it before I left Latchkill. Quite a stir it's caused.'

George was not clear if the Prout woman thought Maud had killed Thomasina and Simon, or whether she thought Maud knew who had done it, or if she thought George himself was the killer. Whichever it was, he felt a sick panic in his vitals.

Freda was saying, 'But you know, Mr Lincoln – or may I be a

little forward and call you George? You know, George, I'm sure we can some to some arrangement. And – oh yes, perhaps just a small drop more sherry. Thank you so much.'

'Arrangement?' said George.

'I'm afraid it would mean extra work for my staff. And that would mean higher payments. Just to keep things in order. Not that there will be anything quesh – questesh – Pardon, *questionable* anywhere.'

A genteel blackmail, that was what this amounted to. George supposed he ought to have seen it coming. Was he prepared to submit to it? He remembered Maud's happiness – possibly even her life – was at stake, and thought he was. And, said an unpleasant little voice inside his mind, your own happiness? Isn't that at stake, as well? Isn't your pleasant comfortable life at Toft House at stake, as well? Toft House and the Rosen money, that you worked so hard to get? He said, 'I'm sure we can find an amicable agreement, Mrs Prout.'

'Freda, please. After all, we are friends. And – oh no, I really mustn't have any more sherry, my word, you'll be getting me tiddly. Well, perhaps just half a glass.'

'You do understand,' said George, refilling her glass and wishing he could stir in poison, 'you do understand, Freda, that everything I'm doing is entirely for Maud's sake.'

'Oh quite. Cheer-ho again, George.'

The news of Thomasina Forrester's death, and that of her cousin Simon, rocked Amberwood's little community to its roots.

Dreadful, said people, gathering outside St Michael's Church after Reverend Skandry had announced the tragedy from the pulpit. The most shocking thing. Trapped inside Twygrist's kiln room, seemingly, and unable to make anyone hear their cries for help. Oh dear, it did not bear thinking about. The mill had been closed down years ago, of course – that had been after George Lincoln gave up his work as manager – and the place had never really been made safe.

And what would happen to Quire House? If there were any other Forrester relatives, nobody in Amberwood had ever heard of them. It was possible they would turn up at the funeral, people did turn up at funerals: long-lost cousins and aunts whom no one had ever heard of. Anyway, whoever turned up or did not turn up, it would be quite an occasion. Reverend Skandry would give those two poor souls a good send-off, they could all be sure of that. Mrs Minching was going to put on a cold lunch up at Quire and everyone was invited to attend.

It was known that George Lincoln was very distressed by the news – he was looking quite ill, the poor man. This was hardly surprising, though, what with him actually having found poor Miss Thomasina and Mr Simon, and what with him having worked for the Forrester family for a good many years. And then Miss Thomasina had recently been taking one of her kindly interests in Maud Lincoln. This last was said without any conscious undercurrent; most people were sorry for George, poor old George, and genuinely concerned to learn that Maud had been unwell, and was presently recuperating with some family somewhere. Ah well, the best place for her, under the circumstances.

Bryony Sullivan went to the double funeral, although it had been difficult to get her duties changed to do so. A new patient had just been brought into the private section who seemed to be taking up a good deal of the Prout's time, which meant the general running of the main wards fell to the nurses. Poor little Dora Scullion was sent scuttling hither and yon like a demented rabbit, doing the work of three people – and probably getting less wages than one. Bryony would have preferred to stay and help Scullion and the nurses, but this was not a funeral that could be avoided.

'We're living on Thomasina Forrester's land,' said Bryony's father. 'And although neither of us cared for her much, attending the old girl's funeral is something we should do. There are decencies to be observed.'

He was so seldom bothered about the decencies, that Bryony

was quite surprised when he said this. She was even more surprised when he eschewed his usual shabby clothes and donned one of the few good outfits he still possessed.

'I can still shine myself up when the occasion requires it,' he said, coming down the stairs of Charity Cottage, and Bryony smiled, because if it was rare for him to bother about the decencies, it was even rarer for him to display any vanity.

A rather desultory wake was held at Quire House after the service. Mrs Minching had provided a buffet and sherry, confiding to Bryony as she handed round the food, that she would never get over the way Miss Thomasina and Mr Simon had died.

'What is the world coming to, Miss Bryony, tell me that?'

'It's so sad,' said Bryony.

'It's my belief,' said Mrs Minching, lowering her voice, 'that there's more to those two deaths than is being told. Accident, that's what they're saying, but to my mind, that's all so much eyewash, Miss Bryony, beg pardon for being so forward.'

'What do you mean?'

'It's my belief,' said Mrs Minching, 'that Maud Lincoln knows more than she should about what happened. Out for all she could get, that one, and very odd behaviour at times. And since she's gone off to be ill somewhere, I've found some very puzzling things in my household books.'

'What do you mean, puzzling?'

'What they call discrepancies, Miss Bryony.' The word was pronounced with care. 'Invoices and delivery notes for things never delivered to Quire, but not a one of them in my pantry inventory, and you can't argue against that, can you?'

Byrony supposed you could not, and did not say that at Charity Cottage food was bought as it was needed, and put in the meat safe or onto the cold slab, according to what it might be. The state of the larder was largely reliant on the state of the finances, although the larder's deficiencies were frequently augmented by Bryony's father. In the Irish house hospitality had been so casual but so lavish, that no one had ever seemed to mind if two people turned up for a meal or twenty. No one would have bothered about pantry invoices or discrepancies either, because it would not have occurred to anyone that such things needed to be written down.

'Very extravagant items of food they were, Miss Sullivan. Jars of preserved pears and peaches in brandy, and expensive foreign cheeses. Camembert and Brie, and the *best* water biscuits to go with them.'

She nodded several times, and Bryony looked round to see if there was any hope of being rescued from this, but the only person anywhere nearby was the Reverend Skandry. It would be better to stay with Mrs Minching who was saying that she would never believe Miss Thomasina and Mr Simon could have got themselves shut inside Twygrist, not if fifty crowners said so, and would Miss Bryony be so kind as to pass round the shrimp patties.

The idea of a memorial to Thomasina was being discussed in several corners of the room by this time. It appeared to have captured people's interest, although it sounded to Bryony as if opinions as to the form it could take differed wildly. It was perhaps as well that the suggestions being made by several gentlemen who had looked on the wine when it was red did not reach Reverend Skandry's hearing.

They had reached Dr Glass's hearing, though. Bryony saw his eyebrows go up at one point. He wandered over to where she was standing, and said had she ever noticed that funerals produced a remarkable degree of bawdiness in some people.

'It's simply the relief that they're still alive,' said Bryony. 'In Ireland they all get roaring drunk. In fact, I think there are still places where they prop the corpse up in a corner of the room.'

'Wouldn't the parish priest object to that?'

'He's usually roaring drunk with them,' said Bryony caustically.

Dr Glass grinned, and said, 'I've been to Ireland, but I've never seen your Ireland, Bryony, and I'd like to do so someday.' Before Bryony could think how to reply to this, he said, 'I was thinking though, that if Amberwood really wants a memorial to Thomasina, they could make it in the form of a bequest to one of the hospitals. A new ward, or, at the most, some new equipment. Do you think that's a good idea, Bryony?'

He had rather a nice way of saying her name. She said, 'I think that's a wonderful idea.'

'And if people want something permanent to look at and remember Thomasina Forrester, then I'll personally pay for something to be stuck on the side of Twygrist. A clock perhaps. It'd look hideous, but it's probably what people would like. What do you think?'

'I think it would look hideous too, but I think it would be very well received.'

At first Maud did not realize where she was, except that she was in a small room inside a rambling echoing place, with long soulless passages.

Awareness came gradually, like stagnant water trickling into her mind, and like sly throaty whispers inside her head.

Of cours-s-e you know where this is, Maud . . . Of course-s-s-e you do . . .

Latchkill. She was inside the place of nightmares, the place of huge heavy doors, the place where spider light lay thickly on all the rooms all the year round, so you could never be sure what might be crouching inside it, watching you. The place mamma used to stare at through the thick iron bars of the gates. But what mamma could not have known was that the inside of Latchkill was so full of pain and fear and despair that there seemed to be hardly any room for all the people who came and went.

People came and went in and out of Maud's own little room, which was quite bare, apart from the bed and a cupboard next to it. The woman everyone called Matron, who had a face like a slab of concrete and tiny mean eyes, came in quite a lot of times, and some nurses came in as well. At first Maud had hoped Bryony Sullivan might be one of these. She did not know Bryony very well, but she knew she was pretty and clever. She would be someone Maud might be able to talk to – she might explain why Maud had been brought here and what was going to happen next. But Bryony did not come.

Father came, although not very often. Maud was taken to a special room for his visits – a proper bedroom, it was, with a frilled bed-cover and cushions, a dressing-table with an embroidered runner, and a little table and chair in one corner. There was a marble washstand in the other corner, with a flowered jug and basin. Father liked the room. He looked round approvingly, and said, My word, very nice, very comfortable, and he was glad to see Maud was being properly looked after.

'I don't sleep here,' said Maud. 'I have another room. Not nearly as nice,' and father looked immediately worried, and said he would speak to matron about it. Maud did not really understand this, but she was more concerned with finding out if Thomasina and Simon had been found yet. She listened carefully, but father did not mention them at all. He just talked about ordinary things – about what was happening in the town – and he did not mention Twygrist or ask why Maud had been there that night.

Did this mean Thomasina and Simon were still in the mill? Surely it must. After a while Maud could not be bothered to listen to father's babbling any longer. She hated him because he had brought her to this place and was trying to pretend it was for her own good, and she did not think he believed her about the room. So she stared at a single point in the wall, which she had found was quite a good way to shut everything out – father's stupid talk, the nurses telling her to eat this, drink that, my word, you're a silent one, aren't you . . . One day she would have a very good revenge on all of these people.

But the one thing she could not shut out was the growing conviction that Thomasina and Simon must still be inside Twygrist. Were they both alive? Maud began to believe they might be – they were so sly and so clever, those two.

What if they were still there? They would not look very nice by this time. Their skin would be yellowing and dried out from being in the dark for so long, and the bones of their hands would be sticking through the flesh from where they hammered against the ancient bricks to get out.

Maud would not have thought she would be able to hear their fingerbones and knucklebones beating against Twygrist's walls from inside Latchkill, but she could. At first she thought the sounds came from outside, but presently she realized they were directly under the floor of her own room. This was surely impossible, but then Maud remembered again how very cunning they had been, and she counted up all the days and the nights they would have been down there, and she began to understand. They must be digging their way out – making a tunnel from beneath Twygrist all the way across the fields and lanes, until they reached Latchkill and Maud. And one night – it might be very soon – they would burst through the floor of her room.

But Maud was going to be ready for that. Thomasina and Simon might think that the spider light would hide them – they might even believe it would smother the sounds – but Maud was cleverer than those two by far! She began to lie down on the floor, pressing her ear closely against the floor boards so she could hear better, and so she would know exactly where they were, and how near to the surface they were. This was a very good idea indeed, and even though she was shut away in this terrible place, she began to feel safer.

CHAPTER TWENTY-SIX

The realization that Antonia Weston would have to be punished had grown gradually in Donna's mind. But before she could make a plan about this, she needed to know more about the bitch's life – where she lived, if she had any other besotted young men in tow. Donna took a few days' holiday from the restaurant. She was sorry to give such short notice of this, she said, but there were some family problems she had to sort out. No one questioned this and she thought it was an excuse that could be stretched to cover a fortnight if necessary.

It was easy to find out the times of Antonia's various clinics, then to wait for nights when Don was not around, and not using the car. Donna waited in the hospital car park and followed Antonia home. She was very discreet about it careful to keep at least two cars between them.

Weston lived in a bungalow a few miles from the hospital. It was not in the same class as the house where Donna and Don had grown up, but it was quite big and was a whole lot better than the poky flat which was all Donna could afford now. The sheer unfairness of the last few years rose up like bile in her throat.

The following day she went back there. It was four o'clock, a time when most people would be out at work. She drove slowly past, seeing that it looked comfortable and that there was a big garden at the back with a large lawn sloping down to some trees. Donna glimpsed a table and chairs beneath one of the trees. She imagined Antonia having meals there in the summer or inviting colleagues for evening drinks. Her parents used to do that. Her mother always ordered canapés from Harrods and her father always complained about the cost. It was only after their deaths Donna realized her father must have been on perilously thin financial ice for years.

She drove to the end of the tree-lined road, reversed, and came back. This time there was a definite movement in the large bay window; Donna pulled into the kerb, pretending to consult a map. For some reason she had assumed Antonia lived on her own, but she might be married or living with someone, or even have children. She parked in a side road, and walked back. At first she thought she had been mistaken: nothing moved inside the bungalow at all. Could she risk waiting, hoping to get a better look? Yes, she could. She needed to know as much as possible about Antonia Weston's life. Donna pulled a notebook from her handbag and pretended to consult it as if looking for a particular house number or name.

There was someone in the bungalow! Standing by the gate she had a clear sightline through the side pane of the bay, and she could see a man seated at a small grand piano. Baby grand, did they call it? Boudoir grand? Whatever it was called, it looked as if he was playing a few bars and then breaking off to make some kind of note. Donna was not near enough to see clearly but she had an impression of someone dark-haired and quite young. Late twenties or early thirties, maybe? She walked on, her mind seething.

So the bitch already had a husband or a live-in lover – a musician from the look of things. Perhaps he was a music teacher or attached to one of the big orchestras. They would have a good life together, living in this extremely nice part of North London, in this comfortable-looking bungalow with its big garden. They would have friends and money and interesting jobs, in fact, you could say that Antonia Weston had it all. The knowledge sent hatred searing through Donna. The bitch had so much, but she had still taken the one thing in the world that Donna wanted and needed above all else. She had taken Don.

Somehow she got back to her car and drove home. By the time she reached her flat, she knew exactly and precisely the form Antonia Weston's punishment would take.

These days, on most mornings Don said offhandedly not to bother about supper for him. If Donna asked where he was going, he always said, brusquely, 'Out.'

He treated the flat as if it was a dosshouse these days. His bedroom was a disgusting mess. Several times Donna had been late for work at the restaurant because Don had taken her car without telling her. But all this was Weston's fault, and so Donna put up with it. She cleaned Don's room, and bought a steering-wheel lock for her car and hid the key so Don could not use it without her knowing.

Antonia usually left the hospital at around half past six and each night Donna followed her.

Each evening Weston got home between seven and half past, put her car into the garage at the side of the bungalow, locked it, and then went in through the glass-panelled front door. She often had a briefcase with her, or a laptop. Donna imagined her having dinner with the dark-haired man, and then perhaps retiring to a study or a spare bedroom to work. Very cosy indeed. But not for much longer, Doctor Weston. There would surely come a night when Weston did not go straight home to the warm welcoming bungalow, and that was the night Donna was waiting for.

By the fifth night she no longer bothered with the hospital, she drove directly to the bungalow, parking in different places in the road each time, or using one of the side roads and walking back. At one end of the road was a small group of shops, with a pub. On one of the nights a man came out of the pub as she was passing it, and said, 'Hello darling, going my way?' Donna ignored him and walked quickly on, but the small encounter worried her and she was careful to park at the other end of the road afterwards. You never knew how much people might remember about even the most casual of meetings.

Every night Antonia came faithfully home and did not go out again. As the second week wore on, Donna began to panic because she could not extend her holiday much longer.

But two nights before she was due back at Jean-Pierre's, she sat in her car and watched the dashboard clock click its way from seven fifteen to seven thirty, and then to ten minutes to eight. Antonia had never been this late before. Might she have gone out straight from the hospital? Could Donna risk making her move? Supposing Weston had only called at a late-opening supermarket or was stuck in traffic?

Ten past eight. Surely the bitch was safely out of the way? Donna went over the plan one more time. There were one or two weak points, and the weakest of all was the necessity for the man being in the bungalow on his own. If he was not there, Donna would wait for another night when Weston was out. Fortune favours the bold, remember that, Donna, and the stars in their courses fight for the steadfast of heart. And it's a quarter past eight, so you'd better get on with things.

She put on thin cotton gloves and pulled on thick socks over the lightweight slip-on shoes she was wearing. She had picked up the idea about the socks from a crime book. If you put large-sized socks over your shoes, it gave you two advantages: it prevented telltale shoe prints being left anywhere, and if you trod in blood or glass all you had to do was step back out of it, slip the socks off, and walk away with them in your pocket and your shoes unmarked. Last of all, she pocketed the heavy glass paperweight, keeping it tied inside a clean handkerchief. Then she got out of the car, closed and locked the door, and walked along to the bungalow.

He was in! There was a light on in the room on the right. It was a fairly low light – it might be a table lamp – but the curtains were open and she could see Antonia's dark-haired musician clearly. He was seated at the piano as he had been before, and this time he was playing without breaking off.

She watched him for a few moments, her heart racing, and then, taking several deep breaths and glancing up and down the road to make sure no one was watching, she pushed open the gate. It swung inwards and she went in, careful to keep to the grass edges so her footsteps would not crunch on the gravel drive.

The man was playing the piano quite loudly; Donna could hear it now. Although she did not recognize what he was playing – she was not very knowledgeable about music – it sounded complicated and rather showy. Trickles and trills of notes cascading up and down.

The paperweight broke the glass panel in the front door as easily as if it had been Cellophane, and the glass fell inwards onto a carpet. Practically soundless. Donna replaced the paperweight in her coat pocket, and waited to see if there was any reaction from inside. If there was, she would be back down the drive and vanishing into the shadows within seconds. But nothing stirred, and the piano-playing continued. So far so good. Could she reach inside the door and release the catch? Yes, she could. The door opened, and she stepped inside.

The warmth and scents of Antonia's home folded around Donna, and her excitement spiralled upwards. This was it, the plan was gathering speed, and soon – perhaps in half an hour's time – this bitch would get what she deserved.

The piano music was still going on so the man really had not heard her. She vaguely recognized the music now – it was used for the opening of one of those late-night arty-type programmes. The *South Bank Show*, was it? Standing in the darkened hall, Donna began to dislike the music very much; she began to feel that something inside it was watching her, and it was conjuring up jeering demons, red-eyed and sly.

We know what you're going to do, said these slant-eyed demons. *We know about the plan, and we approve, Donna . . . But if you get into trouble, don't expect us to help you . . . We like murder but we're the last people to ask for help if something goes wrong, in fact we're more likely to grass on you to save our own skin.*

This was utterly ridiculous. There were no voices inside the music, and this was stupid nerves, nothing more. Donna stood very still. The bungalow was in darkness, except for the soft low light spilling through the half-open door of the music room. She would have to do something about that light.

Listening intently to the piano-playing, every nerve tensed in case it suddenly stopped, Donna went cautiously along the hall. Would the kitchen be at the back of the bungalow? Yes, here it was, a big room, dim and cool. There was a tiled floor and modern fittings, and someone had partly prepared a meal: on a work surface were diced peppers, and chicken and tiger prawns defrosting in a shallow dish. A crusty French loaf was on a chopping board. It looked as if Weston was coming home to eat, which meant she could be home at any minute, which meant that Donna had better buck up her ideas.

Next to the chopping board was a long sharp-bladed knife and the next piece of the puzzle slid neatly into place. She had intended to use the paperweight for the next stage of the plan but the knife would be far, far better. In three paces she was across the tiled floor and had picked it up. Even through the cotton gloves the thin blade felt strong and as if it was sizzling with its own energy.

She went stealthily back to the hall. Had the musician heard anything? No, he was still playing. Very good; now for the light. It was necessary to switch that light off. She dare not risk being seen in case things went wrong and the man was able to identify her later on.

Nothing would go wrong, but Donna preferred complete darkness, which meant either switching the light off in the room itself – which was clearly impossible – or finding the mains switch.

There was often a cupboard under the stairs for electric meters and switches, or even a cellar, but there were no stairs here, and the bungalow looked a bit modern for a cellar. How about a pantry in the kitchen? Or a cloakroom out here in the hall? As the thought formed, she saw the door midway along the hall, on the other side to the music room, and saw that it was the kind that had slats in it – louvres, weren't they called? A cloakroom? A meter cupboard?

She moved silently forward, and inched the door open, every nerve stretched in case it made a noise. But it did not, and she breathed more freely. Inside, were several coats hanging up – the kind of semi-battered jackets most people kept handy for dashing out to post a letter in the rain or collecting the Sunday papers – together with a couple of umbrellas and wellingtons. It was all a bit higgledly-piggedly. Bit of a slut when it comes to housework, are you, Doctor Weston? I suppose you'd say you hadn't time for housework, what with your patients, what with your musician, what with your toy boys . . .

But there, behind the door, was a row of switches with modern trip-switches, and if the cupboard itself was a bit untidy, the switches were all marked. Heating. Lighting. Cooker. Power. Mains. *Mains.* A smile curved Donna's lips and, keeping a firm hold of the knife with her right hand, with her left she reached up to the mains switch and depressed it.

There was a soft click, and the bungalow fell into thick cloying darkness.

But it did not fall into silence. The piano-playing – the jeering prancing music that had whispered its jibes into Donna's mind – continued.

For a moment this almost completely unnerved her. For several panic-filled moments she had absolutely no idea what to do. She had no idea why the man was continuing to play. Surely anyone, suddenly plunged into what would appear to be a power cut, would display some form of exasperation, break off whatever he or she had been doing, and go in search of candles and matches?

But the pianist did none of these things; he simply went on playing, and the more she listened, the more Donna could hear a frightening madness within the music. Things jeering, things mocking . . . *We know what you're going to do, Donna . . .*

There was a moment when it suddenly occurred to her that the man might be blind – you often heard about blind people being musicians. Then she remembered the first time she had seen him he had broken off his playing to scribble notes. Not blind then. But there's a madness in here – I can feel there is, and I can feel that it's very close to me indeed.

Had the man heard her break in after all? Was he ignoring her in the hope that she would go away? Was he so arrogant he had assumed she was just a common house-breaker who would go away if ignored, or was he simply a coward?

It did not much matter what he was, because he was about to die. He was about to die so that Antonia Weston should suffer. Her hatred of Antonia enveloped Donna's whole being, sending her courage and resolve sky high. She was ten feet high, she was a giant – a giantess! – she was unstoppable and invincible and she could do this and walk away scot-free, exactly as she had done at Twygrist that day.

As she pushed the door wide, no longer worried about being heard, the voices of the music demons were all around her, laughing and jabbing into her mind, urging her on, saying, *Go on, Donna, go on . . . Let's do it, Donna, let's do it . . .*

The man reacted at last. As the door crashed back against the wall, he stopped playing and turned his head. Donna could see him outlined against the uncurtained bay window. Incredibly he was still seated at the piano, not even bothering to stand up: simply sitting there, waiting and watching her.

He said, quite coolly, 'I suppose you're after money. The desk's by the window, and there's plenty of cash in the drawer. Take it and get out.'

The sound of that cool, unafraid voice in the dark room sent bitter fury boiling up. Out of the scalding waves of pain and anger, came a voice that screamed at this smooth-voiced pianist, that it was not money she was here for, it was justice and punishment.

The sound of this shrill voice filled the room. The man stared at her uncomprehendingly for a moment and then said, 'Oh God, you're high on drugs or something, aren't you?' and the pity in his voice slammed into Donna's mind like a blow. The voice screamed again, shouting that she was not high, she was not some squalid drug addict. But somewhere under the screaming was another voice, saying don't lose your cool, Donna, stay with the plan.

The plan. Donna snatched at the word and held onto it like a talisman, and the out-of-control voice shut off. In two bounds she was across the room, the knife lifted high above her head. It came down in a sizzling arc, printing a razor-line of brilliance on the dark room, and it came down on the man's neck exactly as she had planned. He half fell back against the piano with a cry of pain and shock. Aha! you weren't expecting that! Blood spurted from his neck, coming at Donna like a fountain warm and thick. Disgusting! You hadn't allowed for the blood, had you, Donna? You forgot it would shoot out like that. You'll have to burn every stitch of clothing you're wearing, and bath and wash your hair a dozen times tonight to get rid of the smell and the feel— Stop that! Never mind about the blood, you need to find out if he's dead, that's what you need to find out now.

He was not dead. Dear God, he'd had a six-inch blade driven into his neck, and he was still alive! He had fallen to the floor, clutching at the piano as he went, bringing some of the furniture down with him, but he was still moving, flailing at the air, grabbing at a small side table and overturning it, clutching at the edges of the piano. Nothing for it, then, better stab him again. She bent over him, and brought the knife down a second time and this time it went in deeper. Donna felt the scrape of bone. Collarbone? Breastbone? Oh, who cared what it was, and who cared that the knife, Antonia Weston's own knife, had embedded itself so deeply in bone and flesh.

'This is Antonia's punishment,' said Donna, staring down at the blood-soaked figure on the floor. 'She's taken Don away from me, so I'm taking you away from her. She'll find you dead, and she'll go through agony, and it'll serve her right.'

He struggled again, but it was a poor weak struggle now. Why wouldn't he die! The knife was still sticking out of his neck but he had managed to grasp the handle, his fingers were curling around it. Donna backed away at once, because supposing by some faint chance he managed to get sufficient purchase on the knife to pull it free and managed to struggle upright and attack her? She remembered the paperweight, still in her pocket, and began to reach for it. If he really did start fighting her she would bring it smashing down on his skull and that would finish him off. It would make it even more shattering for Antonia Weston when she found him.

The knife came free with a wet sucking sound, and dropped harmlessly to the floor. The man's head fell back, there was a rush of exhaled air from the torn windpipe, then he was dead.

It was an extraordinary moment. Seconds earlier he had been alive, the blood pumping out everywhere – oh God, yes, she was covered in it – and then quite suddenly he was nothing. Empty.

Donna could not stop looking at him. It was remarkable to realize you had taken the life of someone without knowing anything about him. He was dark and thin-faced and quite slightly built. His skin had the translucent pallor of someone who spends a good deal of time indoors.

Had he and Antonia been married? How long had they been together? Donna straightened up, for the first time looking around the room which was not entirely dark due to a street lamp outside. She had a sudden deep need to know more about this man, about the kind of life he and Antonia had had. She stared about her: at the furnishings and the things on the high narrow mantelshelf over the fire.

Then she saw one of the pieces of furniture that had been overturned was the chair the man had been sitting in. She saw it was not a conventional piano stool, or even an ordinary dining chair. It was a wheelchair. The man she had just killed had not been a coward or disdainfully contemptuous of a house-breaker. He had been a cripple. Probably he had heard her from the moment she had broken the glass of the door, and had gone on playing in the hope that she would take whatever valuables she wanted, and go away leaving him unharmed. You heard of people doing that: you even heard of them pretending to be asleep when burglars got into their bedrooms, because they were afraid of confronting the burglar.

Well, I'm sorry, Mister Whoever-you-were, said Donna to the dead remote features, but it's too late for regrets. I'd probably have done all this even if I had known – although I might have done it a bit differently.

She stepped carefully back from the mess of blood, removing the thick socks when she got clear – she was pleased she had remembered about those – and went into the hall. It was then that she heard the crunch of footsteps on the gravel drive outside, and she stopped, her heart skipping several beats. Was it Weston coming back? Donna had not heard a car or the garage being opened or closed. She was momentarily angry with herself for not being more aware.

She glanced at her watch. Nine o'clock. It could only be Weston, coming home for that meal the musician had been going to cook for her, but that Weston would not now eat. Donna hesitated, looking towards the oblong of pale light that was the bungalow's front door. Half of her wanted to stay and hide somewhere so she could witness Weston's agony, but the other half knew she must not risk it.

A shadow moved just beyond the door, and Donna darted back to the kitchen. Back door? What do I do if there isn't one? But there was a half-glazed door that opened onto a paved area beyond the kitchen. Locked? Yes, but the key was in the lock. She turned it, and stepped out into the cool night air, and as she did so, she heard someone tread on the broken glass and push open the shattered front door.

Donna went around the far side of the bungalow, skirted the edge of the lawn, hopped over the low wall, and was back out on the street and walking towards her car.

She made herself an enormous greasy fry-up when she got back to the flat, and drank most of a bottle of wine. After this she went to bed, and slept until the alarm woke her at half past seven. The radio came on with the alarm, and the seven thirty news contained an item about the violent murder of Richard Weston, the wheelchair-bound brother of a doctor of psychiatry at a big North London hospital.

Donna stared at the radio. The musician had not been Weston's husband or boyfriend at all. He had been her brother. From out of the confused tumble of her thoughts, she heard the newsreader say that the body of a second man – believed to have been the murderer – had been found next to the body, and that Dr Antonia Weston, was being held for questioning in connection with this second death.

It was only then that Donna realized Don had not come home last night.

CHAPTER TWENTY-SEVEN

Antonia was grateful when a thin morning sunlight eventually filtered in through the cottage's windows, because the night had seemed endless. She got up and went into the kitchen, discovering Raffles composedly seated on the windowsill outside. Invited in, he padded round the kitchen a couple of times, paused rather dubiously at the corner Antonia thought of as the haunted corner, then came back to accept a saucer of milk.

'So you know about the ghost, do you?' said Antonia to him. 'But it certainly wasn't a ghost who left that grisly hangman's noose here for me to find yesterday.'

She waited until nine o'clock and then phoned Jonathan Saxon, who had better be told that she had used his name and department to the local police yesterday. It was annoying to find that she ended in telling him more than she had intended.

'So there's some weird character playing sick jokes,' he said, thoughtfully.

'Yes, and I don't know if I need a psychic investigator or a psychiatrist, or even a private detective. I don't even know if I simply need a smack in the face.'

'I don't know about the psychic investigator or the private

detective,' he said. 'But the psychiatrist we can manage. Shall I come up there to hold your hand?'

For a perilous moment, Antonia thought she might burst into tears. So she said, very sharply, 'Certainly not. I don't need anyone to hold my hand.'

'Antonia,' he said, with extreme patience, 'my clinic finishes early tomorrow – I could drive up then and stay until the following day. You can pour it all out and have a beautiful psychotic crisis.'

'It really isn't—'

'And I'll behave like a maiden aunt,' said Jonathan. 'I'll come to the cottage, and we'll go out to dinner somewhere. But I don't need to stay at the cottage; if there's a pub in the village I'll book in there for the night. Does that persuade you?'

'There is a pub in the village,' said Antonia slowly.

'Ah. Oh well, I was afraid there would be. But you're calling the tune, so the pub it shall be, although I will continue to hope, like a languishing nineteenth-century swain. You can give me a lock of your hair to wear next to my heart. But before giving me that, give me the directions to your haunted cottage – Yes, I have got a pen, I'm in my office, what do you expect?'

Antonia gave suitable directions.

'OK, I've got all that. And I'll be with you tomorrow evening as soon after six as I can manage. All right?'

'All right,' said Antonia and rang off. An apology to Dr Toy and Professor Remus for yesterday's melodrama had better be part of today's agenda – she would walk across to Quire and do that now, before she got cold feet.

Godfrey Toy had been exceedingly busy since breakfast, on the track of a seventeenth- or eighteenth-century cookery book. Somebody from the BBC – actually the BBC! – had written to Quire House to ask about availability and cost of authentic recipe books. It seemed a television programme of eating habits down the ages was being envisaged, and they wanted bona fide recipes for it. There was no guarantee the programme would actually be made, they explained politely; this was just preliminary and very tentative research.

But Godfrey, reading this letter, had instantly renounced his plan for a scholarly best-seller about Bernard Shaw, and thought he might instead make his mark on television. ('And now here is our resident specialist, Dr Godfrey Toy, who is going to tell us how people lived and ate in the eighteenth century . . .')

He abandoned the tedious task he had assigned to the morning (cataloguing some early editions of Byron's poetry which he himself had bought because he had liked the binding, but which Oliver said would never sell), and scuttled hither and yon to see what Quire's current stock had in the way of cookery books. It was not something they would normally deal in, but Godfrey had a feeling there was just the thing somewhere, and it turned out he was right. There, neatly reposing on a back shelf, was the *exact* book, published in 1725 and beautifully divided into different dishes for the seasons of the year, according to your standing in life.

There was a recipe for Lenten Pottage which Godfrey thought sounded shockingly dreary, but then there was a really lavish one for lobster, although it was unnecessarily explicit, telling how to prevent the live lobster from trying to climb out of the vat of boiling water while you were cooking it. Godfrey, who normally enjoyed lobster, shuddered, and turned the page to an entry for Sod Eggs, which would probably cause some ribaldry if it were to be included in the programme. But on closer inspection Sod was a corruption of the word seethed or boiled, and the dish itself was a tarted-up version of boiled eggs.

It was at this point that Antonia Weston arrived, apparently to apologize for the fracas of yesterday. This threw Godfrey completely, partly because he had not expected to see her, but also because it was a touch difficult to know what to say to someone who seemed to have suffered such a bizarre hallucination. It was even more difficult to adhere to Oliver's edict about not letting Miss Weston get her hands on any more of Quire's archive material. Godfrey thought he would not actually mention this, in fact he thought he would give her the cardboard folder of stuff on Latchkill, and be blowed to Oliver.

It was worth risking Oliver's annoyance, because when he handed the folder to her, she smiled and it was the genuine smile that Godfrey had hoped to see. Because he loved seeing her smile like that, he told her about the TV request for the cookbook, and read out a recipe for Mumbled Rabbit, which explained that in order to properly mumble your rabbit, you had first to chop it very finely, and then stir in a bundle of sweet herbs.

She enjoyed the recipe; she said he had cheered up her morning, and promised to let him know how the Latchkill papers turned out. After she left, Godfrey happily wrote to the BBC about the cookbook, describing it in sufficient detail to whet their appetites, but not actually giving away any of the recipes. This done, he felt that he could tackle Lord Byron after all, so he summoned Greg Foster to help him, because he could never remember how you found files on the computer.

Carrying the folder back to Charity Cottage, Antonia was aware that she was smiling inwardly at the prospect of entering Daniel Glass's world again. It was like travelling to the comfortable house of an old and dear friend, and realizing you were almost there.

But spread out on the gateleg table, the papers Godfrey Toy had found did not look as informative as the first batch; they looked to be mostly elderly account books.

A real historian would have said this was primary source stuff and the basis of good research, but Antonia could not get much of a buzz from household bills and the buying of oatmeal (Freda Prout and her seven a.m. porridge again), or scrag-end of mutton and haricot beans.

She paused over what appeared to be a household inventory, clipped to a note in rather laboured writing, that said, 'Dear Miss Bryony, here is the listing for the things I told you of. Peaches in brandy, preserved pears, goose-liver pâté, Camembert cheese and Brie.' This last had been originally spelled Bree, and then crossed out.

'Also there were some pickled walnuts and a bottle of French brandy, so you will see what I mean when I say that young madam was playing fast and loose with my stores,' finished the note, and signed itself, 'Respectfully yours, C. Minching (Mrs)'.

The note was brittle and faded, and it gave Antonia a feeling of reaching out to touch a fragment of the past. She wondered who among Amberwood's cast of characters might have been having illicit orgies on preserved peaches and pickled walnuts, and passed on to a list of medical supplies. From the look of this, Freda Prout had held to her belief in hyoscine as a sedative, but there was also a fragment of what looked like some case notes, recording several doses of chloroform administered to a patient resident in one of the private rooms.

> . . . was confused and only semi-conscious. Placed in Room 22.
> 5.00 a.m.
> Patient became aware of surroundings, and displayed extreme agitation. Bromide administered.
>
> *Thursday 2nd October*
>
> 2.00 p.m.
> Patient alternating between highly excitable state verging on hysteria and a deep melancholy.
>
> 4.00 p.m.
> Bromide again administered – patient threw it across the room. (Dora Scullion summoned to sweep up broken glass and mop floor with carbolic and baking soda.)
>
> *Memorandum to Night Staff*
> Apomorphine mixed with hyoscine to be administered to

this patient if necessary. All questions relating to treatment are to be referred to Matron *not* to Dr Glass, who will not, for the moment, have the care of this patient.
Signed: *F. Prout* (Matron)

Monday 6th October
Patient in Room 22 melancholic and withdrawn. When nurses or visitors present, she crouches in corner of the room, with her eyes shut. Later observed lying on her left side on the floor, pressing her head against the ground, and scrabbling at the floor with her hands.

Conclusion is that the patient is afraid of the light above the ground. To be treated with this in mind.

And that, infuriatingly, was all there was. Antonia read it several times, as if doing so might cause the rest of the notes to materialize.

Afraid of the light above the ground. Or – afraid of the vast and threatening open spaces that exist above the ground? Agoraphobia? Was that what had afflicted this unknown patient? Was there a connection to Charity Cottage – had it been an acute level of agoraphobia that had left that frightened imprint there? The same person? If so, it was no wonder Antonia was so deeply affected by it.

She replaced the photocopied sheets in the folder. What next? Oliver Remus had probably put her on the banned list as far as Quire's intriguing cellars went, but there was no reason why she could not see what the local libraries had in the way of archived material.

Antonia had to make a conscious effort to leave the cottage for the journey into Amberwood Magna and the library. In the end, she took Daniel with her, and got through the short drive by imagining how he would have reacted to the volume of traffic on today's roads. Would he have found it exhilarating or merely noisy? At least he would not have known what a terrible driver she was.

The library was a nice old Victorian building in a corner of the little market town's square, and once inside Antonia felt safer. The first floor had been made into a small coffee shop. She thought she would make notes until lunchtime, and then study them over coffee and a sandwich.

This part of Cheshire seemed to have quite a lot of interesting snippets of history. Antonia went carefully through all the indexes, but the only thing vaguely connected to Quire House or Latchkill was a listing for some church records of St Michael's Church, spanning the period between 1883 and 1899. Worth a look? Yes, 1899 had been the date on Daniel's angry letters to Latchkill's matron. Antonia asked for the records at the librarian's desk.

'I think there's restricted access to those particular books,' said the librarian, who was a youngish boy with a face that for some reason reminded Antonia vaguely of Raffles. 'I'm sorry about that.'

Restricted access. It sounded more like something you would encounter in a traffic system. Antonia said, 'I don't want to take anything away. Just to look at it and make some notes. If they're the original records, I'll be careful with them.'

'I'm really sorry,' said the boy, sounding genuinely so. 'But you'd need what we call a private research card.'

'Well, could I get one?'

'I can give you an application form, and you can fill it in now, but then we'd have to send it to our County headquarters. And they're inclined to be long-winded. It could take at least a fortnight for it to come through.'

Antonia said, 'Oh, but—' when a man's voice broke in.

'Put Miss Weston's request on my research card, would you, Kit?'

Antonia looked round sharply.

'Have this one on me, Miss Weston,' said Oliver Remus.

The annoying thing was that the professor merely scribbled a signature, nodded an acknowledgement, and appeared to consider the matter closed. Antonia managed an awkward, 'Thank you very much,' to which he responded with a brusque nod, and then went to sit at a distant table, appearing to become instantly immersed in some research of his own.

Well, bother him and his cool disapproval.

But the records from St Michael's Church, when they were brought, were disappointing. There were columns of births and marriages and baptisms, all recorded in a clear, graceful hand, which Antonia found rather depressing. When it came to the reckoning, was this the sum total of a life? Neat lists of names and dates? Daniel, thought Antonia, if you're somewhere in here, I'm not finding you, and I'm not finding Latchkill either.

There were several references to the Forrester Benevolent Trust being administered, but on closer inspection these were little more than lists of payments made, or dates of meetings. These entries were in a thin spidery hand, with a signature at the foot of each page – the Reverend Arthur Skandry, who had, it seemed, been the incumbent of St Michael's Church from 1896.

Arthur Skandry, had visited Latchkill Asylum quite frequently. He had recorded these visits diligently – so diligently that Antonia, who half an hour earlier would have traded, Faust-like, with the devil for anything about the place, found her attention wandering, until an entry for September 1899 snapped her concentration back into place. Skandry had spent time in something called Reaper Wing, ministering 'to the poor unfortunates incarcerated there, bringing a little calm to their agitation after a recent thunderstorm, to which most of them had assigned the old pagan beliefs . . .'

But other that this, there was nothing of much interest. Antonia was closing her notebook, when a shadow fell across the table and Oliver Remus said, 'I'm sorry to interrupt your work, Miss Weston, but the library closes for lunch and they'll need to lock everything away.'

'Yes, of course. I've finished anyway. Thank you again for the ticket thing.'

'My pleasure,' he said formally, and glanced at the leather-bound folios with their tarnished metal clasps. 'Remarkable how soulless those old records can be, isn't it? Do you have a particular interest in church history, Miss Weston?'

'Not a particular one. It's Latchkill Asylum I'm trying to trace.' She caught a flicker of something behind his eyes. 'Just a research project. Or were you wondering if it was a case of poacher turned gamekeeper?'

'Not in the least. You clearly saw something yesterday that frightened you. I shouldn't think you were normally an hysterical type.'

'I'm not,' said Antonia shortly, and then, 'Could I buy you a cup of coffee by way of peace-offering for the hysterics?' It came out awkwardly, because she had got out of the way of this kind of thing, and she fully expected a polite refusal.

But he said, 'If you'd rather have something stronger than coffee we could walk across the square to the Rose and Crown.'

They ended up having cider and cheese rolls in the Rose and Crown – the boy from the library came in after them, and nodded politely, before seating himself near the bar, and becoming absorbed in a book and a plate of sandwiches.

Oliver Remus talked – a bit guardedly at first, and then more easily – about Quire House and Amberwood and the villages around it. Antonia was interested, but had to remind herself not to relax too much in case an awkward question was suddenly put to her. Are you here on holiday, Miss Weston? Where are you from? Do you have a job, or do you just make a career out of bizarre hallucinations?

But Oliver Remus did not ask any questions, and he did not volunteer anything about himself. Antonia, who had built her own barriers, was aware that he was deeply reserved, but by the time he had ordered two cups of coffee to round off their modest meal, she thought it was probably all right to ask how long he and Godfrey Toy had been at Quire.

'Six years,' he said, readily enough. 'It was very neglected. After Thomasina Forrester – you've come across the lady, have you? – well, after she died there was no heir, and it got passed around various local authorities, none of whom were really responsible for its maintenance. Rather bizarrely the First World War saved it – it was requisitioned for a military nursing home and the army spruced it up quite well. We're just starting to get it on the tourist map now. Along with the antiquarian books set-up.'

'That must be rewarding.'

'Yes, it is, but there's not a great deal of money in it. Or were you cherishing a romantic view of antiquarian book dealers? Tracking down lost Shakespearean first folios or unpublished sonnets of Keats? Ransacking forgotten libraries and archives in remote corners of ancient cities, with sunlight picking out the tooled leather of calf-bound books—'

'Trekking out to ancient houses whose owners have died, and haggling with greedy relatives,' said Antonia caustically. 'And flogging the results to collectors with money but no discernment or museums with discernment but no money.'

He smiled, and Antonia saw that he was younger than he had first seemed – perhaps early forties – and also that he was no longer so hostile. He said, 'Godfrey is always expecting all kinds of priceless gems to turn up, but they rarely do.'

It was said with a kind of affectionate exasperation, but there was still an air of distance about him, as if he disliked the world and preferred to keep it at arm's length. Antonia had the sudden impression that he had buried his real self so deeply that a kind of brittle ghost-façade had developed and was called into service for public occasions. There had been a time when this would have attracted her professional curiosity and when she would have wanted to get behind the carapace and find out what had created it. But she only said, 'Will your Trust buy up any of the other old buildings?'

'We'd like to, but it's down to funds.

'There're some marvellous old places in this area; I'm loving seeing them all. I want to take a look at Twygrist Mill.'

'You'd probably do better to avoid Twygrist,' he said at once, and if the reserve had been melting, it was instantly and firmly back.

'Is it so derelict?'

'It's not a place for tourists,' he said. 'It has a rather distressing atmosphere.'

So that was it. He had remembered he was talking to a flaky female, and he was warning her away from potential triggers. Antonia said, 'It looked interesting.'

'Not so very interesting.' He hesitated, and then said, 'Miss Weston—'

'You could drop the formality and call me Antonia. Especially since we've been on hysteria-exchanging terms.'

'Antonia. May I ask a small favour?'

'Yes, of course.'

This time the hesitation was more marked, then he said, 'Don't mention Twygrist to Godfrey Toy.'

Antonia looked at him in surprise.

'Some years ago there was a – a tragedy there,' said Oliver. 'It affected Godfrey very deeply. I don't think he ever really got over it. He's a sensitive man for all his comic ways.'

'I'd already realized that. Of course I won't mention the place to him.'

'Thank you.' He set down his cup, and glanced up as the boy from the library came over to their table.

'Professor Remus, they're bringing that archive stuff up for you at two.'

'Thank you, Kit. I'm on my way back.' Oliver Remus hesitated, and then said, 'Antonia, Kit is a bit of Amberwood's history in a way.'

'You don't look like history,' said Antonia smiling, liking the boy's narrow green eyes and mop of tow-coloured hair.

'I'm afraid he is. He's the present holder of the Clock-Winder appointment – the memorial clock on the side of the mill.'

'The wretched job was wished on me when I was too young to resist,' said Kit promptly. 'They're a sneaky lot around here, Miss Weston. And it's kind of a hereditary thing. Father to son or nephew, all the way back to the Flood.'

'I read about the Clock-Winder tradition,' said Antonia. 'I rather liked it: it's so very English.'

'It's so very tedious,' said Kit. He gave her a sudden blinding smile, and went out.

'His family's lived here for generations,' said the professor. 'Kit pretends that the clock's just a joke, but he does the job faithfully, and I think he's actually quite proud of it.' He stood up. 'And now Miss Weston – Antonia – if you've finished, I'd better get back. I enjoyed our lunch.'

Donna could not believe it. She simply could not believe that the bitch had picked up not just one man, but two. Two! One of them was the donnish-looking Professor Remus from Quire, but the other was a young man! At it again, you slut? Not five minutes out of prison, and already you're getting your claws into another young boy!

If Donna had not been parked in the concealment of trees outside Quire's main gates, and if she had not followed Weston's car to Amberwood Magna, she might never have known about this. And she needed to know everything – knowledge was power. She must overlook nothing about Weston's life.

She had followed Weston and Oliver Remus into the Rose and Crown, and had bought a drink and some sandwiches, taking them into one of the chintzy alcoves along with a newspaper. She read the paper, checked her watch rather pointedly a few times, and then pretended to make a call on her mobile phone. Anyone particularly watching would assume she was here to meet a friend and that the friend had been delayed.

Weston and the professor seemed very in tune with one another; it was odd how you could sometimes sense that. But it had not stopped the trollop from sending out her lures to the golden-haired boy who went over to their table to talk to them. It had not stopped her from looking at him with the harpy-greed in her eyes.

Weston and Oliver Remus went out together, and Donna, glancing through one of the pub's narrow little windows, saw Antonia walk across to her own car and Remus go back across the square. Weston was blithely swinging her shoulder bag as if she had just passed a pleasant hour, and was finding life enjoyable.

She should not be enjoying anything at all. She should have been disintegrating with fear and nervousness, but here she was carousing with a pair of attentive men, apparently not turning a hair. If Donna was not careful, Antonia would end up being happy – more to the point, she would end up unpunished.

Donna had intended to make several more moves before the final one – she had thought out a number of ploys – but she saw that she would have to bring the finale forward. Her heart began to beat faster at the prospect. Could she do it? She remembered Don's beloved face, and knew she could indeed do it.

Tonight? *Yes . . .*

CHAPTER TWENTY-EIGHT

Godfrey had been delighted to hear about Oliver's encounter with Antonia Weston in the library, and the lunch they had had. Oliver had been offhand about it – saying he had merely lent Miss Weston his research ticket and then it had seemed courteous to accept her offer of a lunchtime drink – but Godfrey was pleased to think of Oliver having some female companionship for an hour or two. He did not socialize much, these days, poor Oliver, not unless you counted the sales and the occasional trips to London for the Reading Room or Oxford for the Bodleian, which Godfrey did not.

It was entirely understandable that after what had happened five years ago, Oliver had put up barriers against the world. Godfrey often wished he could put up a few barriers himself, because no matter what the professor might nowadays feel, he, Godfrey, could never see that grisly watermill without a sick shudder. He would prefer it if the place were closed down, but just as Quire House had not seemed to belong to anybody after Thomasina Forrester's death, neither had Twygrist, and none of the local authorities wanted to admit responsibility. Oliver said it ought to be possible to trace the mill's ownership through land registration and Ordnance Survey maps, but they had never got round to it, and it continued in its owner-less state.

Godfrey hated Twygrist, just as he hated autumn, although once it had been his favourite season. But the memory of one November night was printed indelibly on his mind and he would never forget it, not if he lived to be a hundred and twenty.

Oliver had returned from a buying trip and had got back to Quire just after lunch. He had managed to buy some really beautifully bound early editions of Shelley's poems quite reasonably, and a box of excellently preserved early copies of *Punch* and the *Strand* magazine, which would command very good prices among enthusiasts. There was a remarkable market for that kind of thing. There had been some nice lithographs as well.

Oliver and Amy had been going to the theatre in Chester on that November night. Godfrey could have gone with them, but he had a sniffly cold and was going to tuck himself up with some hot milk and whisky. Quire was not open to the public in November anyway so he could lock up early, and Amy had promised to brew up her grandmother's marvellous honey posset for him before she went out. She liked making a fuss of Godfrey; Godfrey liked it as well. He thought Amy beautiful and intelligent and good company, and he liked the way she kept Oliver from becoming too serious and too deeply absorbed in his work and made him laugh.

He had been hunting for aspirin when Oliver had come into his flat to ask if he knew where Amy was. But Godfrey had not seen her since the morning, although he had heard her car drive off before lunch. It was a Mini with a distinctive growly note because the exhaust was blowing, and Amy could not be bothered to get it fixed. She found mechanical things boring and usually forgot to get them dealt with. Oliver found mechanical things boring as well. He and Amy had almost exactly the same way of looking at life, which was probably why they had such a happy marriage.

By four o'clock Amy had still not returned which was slightly worrying. It was to be hoped she had not had a prang, although they would surely have heard. Most likely she had met a friend for lunch and her car had broken down miles from a phone. This had been before mobile phones were as common as they were today. Still, it was not like her to be out so long, and it was nearly an hour's drive to Chester which meant they would have to leave about six.

At half past four Oliver had rather diffidently phoned the police, just to make sure no accidents had been reported. Godfrey, perched on the edge of the sofa in Oliver's flat, worriedly sucking throat lozenges, had heard the disinterest at the other end of the phone, and Oliver had heard it as well. He had slammed down the phone, and walked out. Minutes later Godfrey heard his car roar away down Quire's main drive. He had wasted at least ten minutes wondering whether to follow but, in the end, he had put on his quilted jacket and a woollen muffler and gone outside to his own little car. St Michael's church clock had just been striking the hour as he set off, five o'clock it had been, he remembered hearing the chimes very clearly indeed.

At five o'clock on an early November day, it was not completely dark, but it was already the vaguely eerie half light that Godfrey disliked. You could never be quite sure what might be hiding inside that kind of blurry dusk.

Driving through the deceiving light, his cold expanding to include a pounding headache, Godfrey turned left instead of right, and the car he had thought was Oliver's turned out to be driven by a stranger. It was not until they went past the brooding outline of Twygrist that he realized this and slowed down, thinking he had lost Oliver anyway and it might be better to head back to Quire to await events. Amy was probably long since back and wondering where everyone was.

If he had not reversed into a farm gate, he probably would not have seen the car parked off the road, under some trees at the side of the mill. But he did see it, and saw at once it was Amy Remus's scarlet Mini.

There would be some very ordinary explanation for Amy's car being here, Godfrey thought. Perhaps it had broken down and she had pushed it off the road and gone in search of a lift or a phonebox. Yes, but she went out shortly before twelve and it's now well after five. How long does it take to walk into Amberwood or even back to Quire House? An hour? Certainly no more than that.

Godfrey had never actually been inside Twygrist – it was the kind of place you drove past, and said, vaguely, that one day you really must explore it. Spooky-looking old place, you said comfortably, and drove on and forgot about it. But clearly he could not do that now, clearly he must investigate, and so he took a torch from the glove compartment, locked his car, and went up the slope.

The eerie dusk-light was lying over Twygrist like a shroud. When Godfrey pushed the door open the stench of dirt and decay met him head on. Dreadful. Like a solid wall of black sourness. There was a smell of damp as well – that massive volume of water in the reservoir, held back by the sluice gates! – and there was a dull rhythmic beating of something overhead. It was several moments before Godfrey realized it was the horrible old memorial clock, ticking away to itself, reverberating inside the mill's emptiness. It was rather a macabre sound: like a monstrous heart beating somewhere deep in Twygrist's bones. Godfrey found himself remembering the classic Gothic tale about the murdered heart that went on beating after death. Edgar Allen Poe, was it? Yes, it was, and it was not a story you would want to remember in these circumstances. Still, he would take a quick look round to see if there were any clues that might indicate Amy's whereabouts, and then he would go back to Quire.

He shone his torch, trying not to squeak in surprise when the light fell on the massive silent machinery. Everything had long since fallen into disuse, but you could see how it would once have operated. There were the millstones that once had ground the corn, and the culvert where the water would have rushed in from the reservoir, and a chute for tipping the sacks of grain down from the mezzanine floor above. There were the huge mute waterwheels enclosed in their vast, rotting tanks, their teeth festooned with dripping cobwebs.

There was something extremely menacing about the waterwheels. Godfrey thought that even though it must be dozens of years since they had moved, there was still a latent energy about them, as if it would not take much to call them into clanking, ponderous life. If the sluice gates were opened – or if they gave way with age – and the water came pouring into the mill once more, would the force of it smash the half-rotting tanks? It seemed strange to have wooden tanks, but perhaps they had been more durable than metal. Metal rusted and corroded; wood, if you treated it carefully, lasted well.

The lower tank had not lasted very well, though. Even from where he stood, Godfrey could see how the wood had crumbled to an unpleasant sponginess; he could see long pallid streaks near the bottom. Some sort of timber infestation, most likely. There had been a small patch of dry rot in Quire's attics – like a network of thin strands of spun cotton, it had been, and the surveyor had said the spores would multiply and spread at an alarming rate, and they must have it treated absolutely at once. Godfrey remembered it had cost a great deal of money to get rid of it.

It would cost an even greater amount of money to get rid of the dry rot in here because it looked as if it had spread over most of the tank's side. In the light from the torch it almost looked like long pale strands of hair growing out of the split corner, wetly plastered to the old wood.

Pale strands of hair . . . It was curious how this half-light could play tricks with your vision. Godfrey could almost imagine there was a hand within the hair – a thin hand with long tapering fingers, reaching out in supplication . . .

At this point he realized he was shaking so badly that the torchlight was shivering, lending a horrid semblance of life to the machinery. He made himself grip the torch more firmly and the eerie illusion vanished. Godfrey remembered that light and shadows were notorious for twisting quite ordinary things into something sinister-looking. Still, he would reassure himself before he went away.

Still gripping the torch, he went forward. The floor sagged as he walked across it, and the worn joists creaked like giant's bones. The nearer he got to the rotting tank the more it looked as if human hair really was spilling out through the rotting wood, and as if a human hand really was reaching out . . . And the beating of the horrible clock no longer sounded like the minutes ticking away, it really did sound like a human heart.

'The hellish tattoo of a terrified human heart in the minutes before death?'

Oh for pity's sake! He was standing in the middle of a medieval watermill with a smeary twilight all round him and Twygrist's hideous clock pounding the seconds away, and all he could do was quote Edgar Allen Poe! He reached the waterwheel in its decaying tank and, taking a deep breath, shone the light.

Oh God, it really was a human hand reaching out through the rotted wood, and it really was human hair spilling out. Godfrey felt as if his temperature had soared to at least a hundred, but an icy hand seemed to be clutching at the base of his stomach. There *was* somebody inside that grim tank. Somebody had fallen inside it – all the way down – and was lying under the monstrous teeth of the waterwheel. The force of the fall had caused the decaying wood to rupture so that whoever it was had half fallen through.

Amy? Please don't let it be Amy. But if it does have to be Amy – and I know it won't be – please let her be just injured, nothing worse than that. A bit bruised – a broken arm or leg. Repairable. And let her just be knocked out, because you come round from being knocked out . . .

Godfrey began to shake so violently that he thought he might fall down. He took several deep breaths, and set the torch on the ground so it created a little pool of light against the water tank. It showed up the burst-open sides, and the small pool of black brackish water that had spilled out. It showed up the reaching hand, and made a square-set amber ring in an old-fashioned setting glint. Godfrey recognized the ring at once. Amy always wore it; she liked Victorian jewellery. He knelt down and reached for the hand.

Dreadful. Oh God, it was the most dreadful thing he had ever known. The nails were broken and bloodied, and the hand itself was appallingly bruised and torn. But the skin was cold and flaccid, and it was Amy, just as he had known it was, and she was quite certainly dead. Oliver's bright lovely wife was dead.

The post-mortem showed that Amy Remus had suffered multiple injuries, and had been badly torn by the jutting cogs and pinions of the ancient waterwheel. Her injuries were too many and too severe to draw any safe conclusion, but her death had been caused by massive trauma to the skull, almost certainly from where she had fallen against the inside of the tank. She had died sometime between midday and two p.m. on the day Godfrey found her.

The inquest, held two days later, concluded that Amy had fallen into the tank, although there was no telling how it had happened. It was not the kind of place into which someone would fall by accident, just as Twygrist was not a place anyone would enter without a definite purpose.

Godfrey, there to give evidence of finding the body, in agony for Oliver all the way through it, had seen the shuttered look come down over the professor's face at this part of the proceedings, because the implication was unpleasantly clear. The coroner and the police believed Amy had gone to Twygrist to meet a lover, although nobody actually came out and said so. But Godfrey could feel them thinking it, and he wished he had the courage to stand up and denounce this unsaid accusation. Amy would not have had a lover in a million years: she and Oliver had been deeply happy.

The final twist of the knife had come from the police pathologist. From the position of the body when it was found, he said unhappily, and from the condition of her hands, they were forced to the conclusion that Amy Remus had not died instantly from the fall. The splits in the ancient wood were not from the force of her falling. They were from where she had tried to batter her way out.

They had never talked about it. After the inquest and the funeral were over, Godfrey had tried several times to discuss it with Oliver, but the the professor had retreated behind barriers so impenetrable that it would have taken a braver person than Godfrey to force through them.

The local newspaper had made the most of reporting the tragedy, of course, and some bright journalist had dug out an article about how two people had died at Twygrist several years earlier, and used words like deathtrap and eyesore. The paper had mounted a campaign, saying Twygrist should either be properly renovated or demolished, and people had sent in letters saying it was a disgrace to let such an historic place fall into decay and that somebody should do something about it. There had been talk of setting up a Save the Mill Society, but in the end people had been too engrossed in their own lives, and in any case, the various communities around Twygrist were too small and too widely spread. Godfrey was aware of the irony of it all, because once he and Oliver would have suggested the Quire Trust spearhead such a society. But in the end, the responsibility for Twygrist had again been shunted from local authority to county authority, and all the way back again, and in the end nothing had been done at all.

Godfrey and Oliver had continued to work amicably together – although Oliver had become more distant, and less patient when Godfrey got into a muddle, which he sometimes did. The workings of the Quire House Trust was one of the things that muddled Godfrey most of all, because balance sheets sent him into a panic, but he did know that after a couple of years the Trust started to show a small but acceptable profit.

And presently, little by little, it began to seem as if life was not quite so anguished.

But since Amy's death, Oliver had never, so far as Godfrey knew, spent any time alone with a lady, or even met one for so much as a cup of coffee.

Until Antonia Weston came to Charity Cottage.

CHAPTER TWENTY-NINE

Antonia spent what was left of the afternoon piecing together the notes she had made on Latchkill. It was infuriating that there was no exact date on the notes about the woman who had shut her eyes against the world and crouched in a corner. Antonia would have liked to tie them into Daniel's letters but it could not be done.

Eventually she set the notes aside, put some chicken in the oven to cook, and went upstairs to wash her hair. This last was nothing to do with Jonathan's arrival tomorrow; it was simply that it was a long time since she had been taken out to dinner, and she might as well look halfway decent. She would wear the autumn-leaf outfit she had bought on that first day of freedom in London; the fabric was silky and expensive-looking, and it would look terrific.

Her hair was dry by this time and pleasantly scented with shampoo, and she sat down at the kitchen table to eat the chicken. She was still enjoying the novelty of being able to eat what she wanted when she wanted. It was raining quite heavily outside, but the cottage was warm and snug. Or – was it? What about that shadowy corner of the kitchen? It was still there, that patch of fear and despair, and it would not take very much for it to rear up into a solid wall of suffocating panic. Once upon a time, someone had crouched in that corner.

'... *pressing against the ground, and scrabbling at the floor ... afraid of the light above the ground.*'

Antonia frowned, and carried the dishes over to the sink. While she washed up, she half listened to the seven o'clock news headlines on the radio, and she was just drying her hands when she caught a sound from beyond the kitchen window. Probably it was only the rain splashing down the gutters or her own imagination.

No, there it went again, and it was not imagination at all; it was a definite sound. A footstep. And then the brush of someone pressed up against the window. If I opened the curtains now, thought Antonia, her heart thudding, what would I see? Don Robards, his eyes dead and staring as they had on the night I killed him?

The sounds would be from the radio, though. She switched it off, and silence closed down. For a few minutes nothing stirred. It must have been the radio after all. She reached for the kettle to fill it for a cup of coffee.

From somewhere inside the dark night beyond the cottage, unmistakeably and clearly, came the sound of a too-familiar piece of music. Paganini's *Caprice*.

Somewhere very close, someone was playing Richard's death music.

Antonia was so furious she did not stop to weigh the danger. Anger swept over her in a scalding flood – how dared this madman taunt her with Richard's music.

She wrenched the kitchen door open and the cold night air rushed straight at her. The music stopped, and there was nothing except the sound of the rain falling, but Antonia stayed in the doorway, scanning the darkness, beyond caring if the prowler could see her. After a moment the music came again, and this time she could hear that it was thin and tinnily mechanical. A battery-operated CD player? A Walkman? At least that proves it isn't a ghost, she thought.

The rain was quite heavy and it was difficult to see anything except the shape of the trees fringing the cottage and the thick hedge separating it from Quire Park. But the music was very close, and it filled the night with its prancing beckoning cadences. Richard used to say this particular piece might even be regarded as a skewed salute to the sinister legends threading through musical history. The faceless demons and devils who had danced jeeringly through the Middle Ages. The Hamlin Piper charming the rats away from the town, or the Black Man of Saxony beckoning children into his master's lair. Antonia had liked listening to Richard in this mood, but she had always maintained a pragmatic outlook.

She glanced round the room, and then pulled on the jacket which had been lying over a chair. Was the mobile phone in the pocket? Yes, it was. She reached for a pewter jug from the dresser – it was small but very solid and it would make a reasonable defence weapon if necessary.

She started to go out and it was only then, when the darkness came up to meet her like a thick wall, that fear came scudding in, so that she paused, and cast a longing glance behind her at the warm safety of the cottage's kitchen. Wouldn't it be better to lock all the doors, and dial 999? But that doesn't mean you'd be safe, said a horrid little voice inside her mind. Because he gets in when he wants, remember? Even a locked door doesn't keep him out. So hold on to that burst of anger, Antonia, and let's try to get some concrete evidence this time, something that will stop Sergeant Blackburn *and* Oliver Remus thinking you're delusional. And if this twisted creature pounces, smash that chunk of pewter down on his head, and *then* you can dial 999.

On the crest of this thought she stepped determinedly outside, making sure to close and lock the door, and drop the key into her pocket. Several layers down she knew this to be pointless; the intruder must certainly have a key, but she did it anyway.

As the lock clicked home, there was a darting movement and the impression of a dark-clad figure going towards the trees, taking the music with it. Towards Quire House, was it? Yes. And there were lights on in the upstairs rooms, which meant Godfrey and the professor were within yelling distance. This made Antonia feel so much safer that she took a deep breath, and then went out into the rain-drenched night after the music.

Beneath her resolve she was still very frightened, but this entire thing was starting to take on a dream-like quality. Antonia found herself wondering if any of it was actually happening, or if she was asleep and dreaming it all.

The dark figure ahead of her looked real enough. He was going swiftly along the footpath with the high hedges on each side. The tinny music was tangling eerily with the night and Antonia remembered Richard's theory again. Out here, pragmatism was not so easy, the rain itself was starting to turn into the dancing feet of the demons who had pranced through the legends.

But this was a flesh and blood man, and there was nothing other-worldly about any of this. As he vanished around the curve in the path, the music momentarily fainter, Antonia stopped, and reached into her pocket for the pewter jug, because if he had some idea of hiding and leaping out at her . . .

No, it was all right. The music was moving away, towards Quire House, and she went on again. As she came out onto the main driveway, she saw him ahead of her. He stopped and glanced back as if to be sure she was still following, and then he ran towards Quire's main entrance, vanishing inside.

Antonia took a deep breath, and went across the lawn in pursuit.

Quire's main door was partly open, which was unexpected. What now? thought Antonia, glancing uneasily about her. Is this a trap, and do I walk into it, like one of those wimpish horror-film heroines going artlessly into the dark spooky old house?

Quire was not especially spooky but the ground floor seemed to be in near-darkness, and the person Antonia had been following might very well turn out to be the chief villain in this particular scene. And if there was not the throbbing organ notes of Bach's Toccata and Fugue for atmospheric background, there was a piece of music composed by a man whose contemporaries had believed him to practise devil-worship.

What if this madman belonged to Quire itself? How possible was that? Nice little Godfrey Toy with his white-rabbit scurryings and his eager, elderly-cherub face? Oliver Remus, with that impenetrable reserve but sudden disarming smile? But Antonia thought that although she could believe a great many things, she could not believe that.

The music was still faintly discernible, and she stood very still, trying to sense exactly where it was coming from. The hall was in shadow, but there was a faint spill of light from the two narrow windows on each side of the main door. There must be a security light on somewhere, because it was not as dark as she had expected. But as her eyes adjusted, she saw the light, whatever it was, came from a room at the far end of the hall.

The music room. Of course it would be the music room. Then this is certainly where I go bounding up the stairs to hammer on Godfrey Toy's door, to tell him there's an intruder and please call the police at once.

She began to move cautiously across the hall, and she was almost at the foot of the stair when the *Caprice* suite faded and then cut off altogether. There was the faint scrape of something – a window opening? – and then nothing. Antonia hesitated, and looked towards the music room. The door was wide open and from here she could see that the narrow French windows were wide open as well.

It might be another trick, but Antonia did not think it was. She thought the man had got her out here, and then slipped out into the night. But was he hiding somewhere outside, waiting for her to retrace her steps? She sent a hesitant glance to the stair, wondering if she could still go up there and tell Godfrey or Oliver Remus what had happened. Would they believe her? It was unlikely they had heard the music – Quire was a solidly built house. Would it be better to simply beat a discreet retreat? But the prospect of walking back to the cottage through the dark was a bad one. Antonia did not think she could do it; the scalding anger that had driven her earlier had drained away, and she was too frightened of what the darkness might hold.

It was then that she saw that something was lying on the floor of the music room, half under the spinet. It was a coat, lying on the silky Indian rug, but Antonia stared at it, because there was something wrong about it – something that was starting to send unpleasant flurries of nervousness through her stomach. In another minute she would make sense of this, she would understand what it was she was seeing, although surely it was only a coat that had slipped off a chair back or been forgotten by its owner. But it was odd that the careful Godfrey Toy had not tidied it away before going up to his own flat for the night. It was even odder that he had apparently left the main door open.

The arms of the coat were flung out at right angles, and there was a smudgy blur of paleness just above the collar. That's the part that's wrong, thought Antonia, and a sick coldness began to steal over her. She already knew what was wrong, and somewhere near her a small scared voice was whispering over, and over, 'Oh no, oh no . . .'

The coat had not been flung down or forgotten by its owner at all. Its owner was still wearing it; there on the floor of the lovely room. There was blood on the front of the coat, and some of it had seeped out onto the silky rug – Godfrey Toy was going to hate that, because he loved Quire and its beautiful things and he would hate having the Indian rug ruined by bloodstains.

Antonia fought incipient hysteria, and glanced towards the open windows, and then back to the shadowy hall. Was the music-maker still in here after all, watching from some dark corner, gloating? No, she had no sense of anyone's presence. She forced herself to go nearer to the dreadful thing lying by the spinet. There was a bad moment when her mind rebelled, and when she thought – but I'm a psychiatrist, I can't do anything about this! I need to call for help – paramedics, hospital . . . But what if a spark of life still struggled to keep going, and what if it was a question of a few minutes pressure on a wound making the difference between life and death? Instinct kicked in, and she bent down to feel for a pulse.

The pale smudge resolved itself into a set of features and she knew, even with the dreadful glazed eyes, even with the fallen-open jaw, who this was. Quire's sullen, eighteen-year-old work-experience boy. Greg Foster. There was no pulse beating at his neck, but Antonia forced herself to open the blood-soaked coat to feel for a heartbeat.

He was dead and beyond all help, and whoever had killed him had stabbed him in the heart with a long-bladed kitchen knife. Exactly as Richard had been stabbed in the heart five years earlier.

The sheet music for Paganini's *Caprice* was lying next to him, spattered in his blood.

Godfrey Toy had written and posted a careful description of the cookbook for the BBC, had quoted a sale price that might be thought reasonable but not greedy (although there was no knowing what the BBC's yardstick might be), and had diligently locked up all the rooms.

After this, he had taken the cookbook to his flat because although it had been lying innocuously in the stock cupboard for quite some time, it would be just the way of things for it to be filched in the way the jewellery and snuff-boxes had been filched, or for a fire to break out, or even for Raffles to choose it as a dinner plate for a newly captured or messily half-eaten vole. The possibilities were disastrous and numerous.

He thought it not improbable that the BBC would want to know if the recipes were still viable, so he was going to spend the evening in a modest culinary experiment. He took a quick survey of his pantry, and chose something called Friggise of Chicken. Friggise sounded a bit aggressive and slightly Anglo-Saxon – the kind of word you might hear pugnacious twelve year olds shouting at one another – but of course it was a derivative of fricassee.

He had most of the ingredients in his larder, and with it he was going to have something called a Drunken Loaf: a concoction involving butter, cream and cheese, all of which might admittedly be a touch high on calories and cholesterol. Still, there was red wine in the chicken, which was supposed to be good for the arteries. There was actually also a drop or two of red wine in the loaf as well, in fact not to put too fine a point on it, there was half a bottle. Godfrey thought he might be a bit potted when he had eaten all this. Just a bit.

He was in the process of slicing mushrooms when somewhere downstairs in one of Quire's rooms, somebody screamed.

Godfrey dropped the mushrooms, and in a dither of panic, took up the poker and went scurrying down the stairs. The scream had come from the back of the house, and most likely there was a perfectly mundane explanation for it, but you could never tell.

On the half-landing he collided with Oliver, coming down from the second floor.

'What in God's name . . .?'

'No idea,' said Godfrey. 'But it's inside the house.'

'It's inside the music room,' said Oliver.

They crossed the hall, rather erratically switching on lights as they went. The door of the music room was flung open, and Antonia Weston, her face sheet white, the pupils of her eyes shrunk to pinpoints with terror, came running out to meet them.

She half fell into Oliver's arms, and she was shaking so badly that for a moment she could not speak.

Then she managed to say, 'Could you get the police at once – and an ambulance. Oh God, yes, you'd better get an ambulance as well, because he's certainly dead, but we'd better be absolutely sure.'

'Who's dead? Antonia, tell me who's dead?' said Oliver. And then, 'Godfrey get some brandy.'

With a superhuman effort, Antonia managed to stop shaking, and discovered she was clutching Oliver as if he was a liferaft. She stepped back, and said, 'It's Greg Foster. Somebody's stabbed him – he's in the music room – I'm perfectly all right, but I will have that brandy, if you don't mind.'

Detective Inspector Curran was a tall thin gentleman with alert eyes and close-cropped, grey hair. The stolid Sergeant Blackburn was in attendance. Antonia, who had hoped not to have to deal with the sergeant again, retreated into a deep armchair in the corner of Oliver Remus's sitting room.

Even two floors up, it was possible to hear sounds of activity downstairs, and it was impossible not to be jolted back to the sick confusion of Richard's and Don Robards' death. Scene-of-crime officers, thought Antonia. People in disposable paper suits scraping at the carpet and the skirting boards, and sealing the grisly harvestings in minuscule sterile phials. The flashing of police cameras on the body. Richard's and Don's bodies had not been moved for what had felt like hours, while the forensic experts assessed how and when they had fallen, at what angle the knife had gone in, the trajectory of the blood . . .

Greg Foster had been moved, though. They had heard a heavy engined police ambulance drive up a little while ago. There had been the sounds of shuffling feet and solemn voices, then the slamming of car doors. Antonia had known they were taking the body away. (And the *Caprice* music? Had they taken that?)

Godfrey Toy was perched worriedly on the edge of a chair. After he had called the police and an ambulance, he had been given a large brandy by Oliver, but he had been shaking so badly he had spilled half of it. Antonia was not shaking, but it was only by dint of extreme concentration that she was not.

By contrast, the professor, standing by the mantelpiece, appeared to be as cool as a cat and about as uncaring. As if to emphasize this, Raffles wandered into the room in the wake of the two police officers, and sat by the fire, looking like a bored Egyptian cat-god.

D. I. Curran courteously asked Antonia to explain precisely what had happened tonight, from around six o'clock up to the time she had found Greg Foster's body. In her own words, if she would be so good. Sergeant Blackburn would make notes, and they would prepare a statement for her to sign.

Antonia had to grip her hands very tightly together in case they began to shake again. Even to her own ears the account of tonight's incident sounded like the wildest flight of fantasy. When she reached the part about following the prowler through the park and finding the body, she broke off to say defensively, 'I do know how ridiculous this must seem, but truly inspector, I've been the victim of several macabre tricks since I came to Amberwood.'

'We meet stranger things in our working day, Miss Weston. Is it Miss, by the way?'

'I believe it's Doctor if you want to be precise,' said a voice from the fireplace. Antonia felt as if someone had picked her up and dropped her into a pit filled with ice-cold water. 'I don't see why Doctor Weston shouldn't be given that courtesy, at least, do you?' said Oliver, looking at the inspector. 'I expect she worked extremely hard to acquire it.'

Antonia supposed that as nightmares went, this was about as bad as it could get. She stared miserably at the floor, but was still aware of Sergeant Blackburn impassively making a note. She thought Godfrey Toy turned to stare at her. She wondered if Oliver Remus was watching her with that cool dispassionate regard, so to counteract this, she said angrily, 'You'd better all stay with Miss. I'm not entitled to the Doctor part any longer.'

Curran studied her thoughtfully, and then said, 'Presumably you're going back to Charity Cottage tonight?'

'Yes, of course.'

'In that case, I'll walk across the park with you. Blackburn, see if they're still searching the grounds, will you? And check whether they've nearly finished downstairs while you're about it. Dr Toy – Professor Remus – stay here for the moment, will you?'

'Do we have a choice about that?' said Oliver.

'No, but you asked me to be courteous. I'm doing my best.'

'Are you?'

'I'll be back shortly,' said Curran, ignoring the sarcasm in the professor's voice. 'Miss Weston, shall we go?'

After they had gone, Godfrey demanded of Oliver what on earth that had been about.

'You mean why was I rude to D. I. Curran?'

'I don't care if you insult the whole of Cheshire,' said Godfrey, who would have been torn apart before he would have committed any kind of discourtesy himself. 'I mean Antonia Weston. *Is* she a doctor?'

'She was,' said Oliver, refilling his brandy glass. 'But she was struck off. Did you really not recognize her?'

'I really did not. Will you stop being so melodramatic and mysterious, and tell me what's going on.'

'I can't recall the details,' said Oliver. 'But I'm fairly sure Antonia Weston was convicted of murdering one of her patients.'

'How? An overdose or something?'

'No. She was a psychiatrist and there was a young man she was treating. He killed her brother, and she went for him with a knife or something like that. I told you, I don't remember it all. I think there was a plea for self-defence and mitigating circumstances, but they still found her guilty.'

'She was sent to gaol?'

'Yes, I'm sure she was. The boy was her patient – that was what really damned her.'

Godfrey, still trying to absorb this bombshell, asked how long ago this had all taken place.

'About five years.' Oliver said it in a remote voice, and nothing in his tone so much as hinted that anything that had happened in that year was memorable because of Amy's death. He said, 'And if I was rude to the inspector, it was because I didn't like some of the questions he was asking her.'

'If there's a murderer on the loose they're bound to question everyone.'

'Certainly they are. With particular attention to lone females who take holiday cottages in the middle of nowhere in November. But too many policemen suffer from extreme tunnel vision. They go hotfoot for the likeliest prime suspect.'

'You think Antonia Weston would be their prime suspect?'

'Don't you?'

'But look here, she wouldn't kill Greg Foster,' said Godfrey. He was so incensed he very nearly forgot about feeling ill at the memory of that poor young man's body sprawled on the music-room floor. 'She hardly knew him.'

'I don't think she killed him. But you can see why Curran might?'

'Yes,' said Godfrey unhappily. 'Yes, I can.'

It was hard to believe Oliver's story, but Godfrey knew he would not have made up such a tale. Antonia had been convicted of murdering a young man who had killed her brother, and had been sent to prison. Prison. Locked doors, barred windows and exercise yards.

Godfrey, hunting out his best silk pyjamas to wear tonight in case there was some new crisis that hauled them all out of bed, could not stop thinking about Antonia. He kept seeing the sudden smile that lit up her eyes, and remembered her quick bright intelligence and sensitive hands and voice. He found it impossible to believe she had actually killed someone. Doctors did not kill people – at least not intentionally.

But Godfrey knew it was not the possibility that Antonia really had committed a murder that would keep him awake tonight. It was the nightmare images about how life might have been for her in prison.

'Sleep as well as you can, Miss Weston,' said Inspector Curran standing outside the cottage. 'I'll just come inside with you to take a look around if that's all right.'

He made a quick tour of the house, going into each room.

Antonia, standing at the foot of the stairs, heard him opening the wardrobes, and she thought he drew back all the curtains.

He came down the stairs and smiled at her. 'All serene,' he said. 'We'll be around for a few hours yet.'

'Then you do believe what I've told you?' said Antonia. 'About someone getting in? And the music and the hanging rope and all the rest of it?'

'I don't precisely disbelieve you,' he said slowly. 'Not yet, at any rate.' He paused, and then said, 'It was obvious that finding that boy's body gave you a massive shock.'

'Yes. The music was – it was the music my brother was playing when he died. The music was next to his body. And the method was the same . . . the stabbing . . .' She sent him a covert look, unsure how much he knew about her.

But Curran merely said, 'You've got a phone, have you?'

'A mobile.'

'I'd better have the number. Has anyone else got it?'

'Only my ex-boss. That's Dr Saxon – I gave him as a sort of reference to your sergeant.'

'So you did.' He wrote the mobile number in a pocketbook, and then scribbled another number, and gave it to her on a torn-off page. 'That's my direct number. Just in case you need it tonight.'

'To confess or to call for help?' said Antonia angrily.

'You never know. Make sure to lock all the doors after I've gone, won't you.'

'That won't do much good if he's got a key, which clearly he has.'

'We'll be within call for most of the night,' said Curran non-committally. 'Shall you be able to sleep? Have you got any pills you could take?'

'No.'

'The police surgeon's still around somewhere. I could ask him for a sedative.'

'Thanks,' said Antonia. 'But if the prowler does come back . . .'

'Revisiting the scene of the crime, were you thinking? That's very unlikely – tonight at any rate.'

'I suppose you're thinking I should know that anyway?'

'Because you're a psychiatrist, or because you've been convicted of murder?'

Antonia was glad he had stopped avoiding the issue. She said, 'Either of those things, Inspector. Or maybe both of them.'

'I'm just being concerned for you, Dr Weston. Is there anyone you could call to come up to stay with you?'

'A friend's coming up tomorrow as a matter of fact.'

'Good. But for tonight, won't you take even a couple of paracetamol?'

'No, I won't,' said Antonia again. 'If this sewer rat comes back I don't want to be too zonked by pills to deal with him.'

CHAPTER THIRTY

George Lincoln had not taken laudanum to help him sleep for years – not, in fact, since Maud's mother had died. He did not like doing so, but since the dreadful night when he had decided to put Maud into Latchkill he had used it several times. It made him feel dull and frowsty the next morning, but it was the only way to avoid lying awake thinking of Maud in that bleak little room with the narrow bed and the squalid, lidded-bucket contraption in one corner.

He had visited her, of course, but he had not dared visit too often, in case people wondered why he was spending so much time at Latchkill visiting a young lady. George could easily imagine them sniggering behind their hands, speculating as to whether the lady in question could be an illegitimate daughter or a mistress. One would be as bad as the other, but neither would be as bad as people knowing that Maud was inside Latchkill to keep her out of the law's reach in case she had murdered Thomasina Forrester.

He was a little concerned about this question of Maud's room, though, and he had a word about that with Matron Prout. Maud had told him she did not spend her days in the room with the flowered bed-cover and the nice chairs, he said. What had she meant? He hoped his instructions had been clear; Maud was to have every comfort possible while she was in Latchkill. He was paying quite highly for that as Mrs Prout very well knew.

Mrs Prout was reassuring. Of course Maud spent her days in that room, she said, and it was one of their very nicest rooms. She had chosen it herself for the child. Dear goodness, what on earth was being suggested? The truth was that Maud became confused at times – most likely because of the sedation they were giving her. Mr Lincoln must not worry; Freda could promise him that the money he was paying was being properly spent on Maud's comfort.

George felt a little better after this; he felt he had indicated to the Prout woman that he was not a man to be duped, although it would not hurt to keep watch on things.

But behind all these worries, was the memory of how Maud had crouched in Twygrist's shadow that night, the dreadful sly look on her face like a mask, whispering about people being buried alive . . . Saying that fingerbones made good hammers – and saying it in such an ordinary conversational tone that George's skin prickled to remember it. Maud had stared at Twygrist, in exactly the same way her mother used to stare at Latchkill. Louisa had hated and feared Latchkill, but she had been unable to resist going back to it, over and over again.

'Because once you have seen what crouches inside the spider light, you can never afterwards forget . . .'

George had always tried to tell himself that Louisa had been entirely normal in the early years. He held on to the conviction that there had been ordinary, happy times. The birth of Maud had been as normal as anyone could wish, and George had loved Maud from the very first; he had thought he would do anything for this dear exquisite child. But hadn't Louisa been a little – well, a little odd, even then? What about those afternoon walks? Nothing should be more normal than a mother taking her small daughter for an afternoon walk, but Louisa had always taken Maud to Latchkill, and Maud had been frightened.

'I don't like that place,' she once said. 'We have to look through horrid black gates – for hours and hours we have to do that. And mamma looks all funny, and she talks about spider light and how things hide inside it.'

George had attempted to reassure Maud; he said there was nothing in the world she need be frightened of, and there was no such thing as spider light, it was only one of mamma's stories. (Is it, though? his mind had said. Because you know, perfectly well, what once happened in the spider light, all those years ago . . .)

He had tried to put a stop to the walks. Why not go in a different direction? he had said – but he suspected Louisa continued to walk along Scraptoft Lane to Latchkill. It had only been later – when Maud was growing up – that Louisa had stopped going out altogether, staying in her room with the curtains closed. It was safer like that, she had said; the curtains kept the spider light at bay. George had not known how to coax her outside.

If he had known it would turn out like that, would he have married Louisa all those years ago? But he thought he would, because Louisa had been a way of achieving a dream he had always cherished – a dream that centred on his living in a big house with servants and large grounds. In the dream people referred to him as Mr Lincoln of Something-or-Other House, and treated him with that particular respect you saw given to the rich and the aristocrat. Pipe dreams he had thought them in those days; castles in the air. Or were they? Mr Forrester was pleased with his work at Twygrist, and if George continued to prove himself and work hard, who knew what might lie ahead? Mr Lincoln of Something-House. It might happen.

Most of it had happened, and considerably sooner than he could have expected. He had become Mr Lincoln of Toft House (Toft House, that beautiful mellow red-brick house he had always admired so much!), known and respected. And when old man Rosen died, there had been the Rosen money as well. He had got almost everything he wanted, but he also got Louisa, and it could not be denied that at the end, Louisa, poor soul, had unquestionably been mad.

George managed to hush up Louisa's dreadful death, as much for Maud's sake as for all the other reasons, but when he looked back over the last eighteen years, it seemed to him almost everything he had done and every decision he had made had been for Maud's sake. Everything – all the way back to that night in Twygrist . . .

He had been walking home from a church meeting in Amberwood Magna – his uncle had been vicar at St Michael's for several years, and encouraged the young George to be part of the various church activities. George had gone to the meeting in his uncle's place because his uncle had been unwell.

It was late October, and just starting to grow dark – that time of the day which was not quite evening but which was no longer really day. George walked part of the way home with several people who had been at the meeting – it was barely two miles, and he thought he would enjoy the exercise. He bade farewell to the others at the crossroads on Amberwood's outskirts and prepared to walk the rest of the way by himself.

This last part of the journey took him along what he thought of as the Twygrist Road. The mill stood by itself, fringed by trees and surrounded by pasturelands, with the reservoir a little way up the hillside behind it. George had a deep affection for the mill. He liked his work, and loved the way the place hummed with life when the farmers came to have their corn ground. He enjoyed overseeing the raising of the sluice gates, and feeling the mill shiver as the water came rushing down into the culverts and the immense waterwheels clanked into life. People sometimes said it would shake itself to pieces one day, old Twygrist, but George knew it would not; it was rooted too firmly and too deeply in the ground.

Here was the curve in the road, and a little way ahead was the crouching outline of the mill itself. It was strange to see it like this, silent and wreathed in the thickening shadows, its doors shut against the world.

Except that Twygrist's doors were not shut against the world at all. They were standing open.

George slowed his footsteps, and then stopped, uncertain whether he needed to do anything about this. It might be that Mr Josiah was in there, attending to some unexpected task, although there were no lights showing anywhere. The door's lock was not a very strong one – Mr Josiah was always intending to have it replaced, but no one was very likely to break into the place because there was nothing that could be removed. But it was unusual to see the door standing open like this, and George thought he had better look inside to make sure nothing was wrong. At least he could close the door to stop animals getting in.

He reached the threshhold, but then paused; it was rather forbiddingly dark inside, and perhaps after all this was not such a good idea. It was then that the sounds reached him, and he glanced uneasily over his shoulder. The wind in the trees, was it? But there was hardly any wind, and whatever he was hearing came from inside the mill itself. He waited, and presently it came again: a thin keening sound, it was, rising and falling, as if the bones of the mill were moaning in pain. George felt the hairs on the back of his neck prickle. There had always been rumours about Twygrist, just as there were rumours about any really old building. In Twygrist's case they hinted that the women who came to sort and husk the corn – most of them local farmers' wives or daughters – dabbled in witchcraft. It was absurd, but understandable: the women always wore black because of the constant dust, and were not allowed lighted candles or oil lamps in the husking room. It could not be denied that as they sat bent over their work, at the long wooden table, they had the uncanny look of a group of witches mumbling and mowing over incantations.

Supposing the sounds he could hear were something to do with that – supposing those women really were witches? That was ridiculous! It was an animal – an injured animal. Holding resolutely onto this notion, George went inside. As he walked across the wooden floor, the old joists creaked under his weight, and something moved in one of the corners near to the bottom of the wheels – something that had been huddled into the darkness, and something that was too large to be an animal.

George did not quite cry out, but his heart came up into his throat. Then the darkness shifted, and he saw the shape was human and female: a youngish girl with fair fluffy hair. Relief washed over him, and he was able to say, 'Who is it? Is something wrong?'

At first she shrank back into the shadows, both hands thrust out as if to ward off an attack, but George had already recognized her. Miss Rosen, Louisa Rosen, from Toft House – the mellow old house that had formed part of that wild pipe dream.

He said again, 'Is something wrong? It's Miss Rosen, isn't it? You know me, surely? George Lincoln from the rectory.'

Now he was nearer he saw her face was streaked and swollen with tears, and her gown was ripped. He was not very used to young ladies, but he took off his jacket and put it around her shoulders, then knelt down on the wooden floor and took one of the small hands, trying to warm it between his own. He asked if she was ill. He was not sure what family she had, so he just asked if he should go along to Toft House and fetch someone for her.

'No!' cried Miss Rosen. 'No, you mustn't do that. I shall be all right presently. There's only my grandfather, and he mustn't be distressed. He has a – something wrong with his heart.'

George said, 'You came to live at Toft House last year, I think?' At least she had stopped crying.

'Yes. My grandfather wanted new surroundings after my parents died in a carriage accident. We like Amberwood. But he mustn't know what's happened to me – he hasn't got over my mother's death. And if he found out about the man this afternoon—'

'What man? Miss Rosen, has someone hurt you?'

'He was from – that place,' said Louisa, shuddering and starting to cry again.

'What place?'

'You know. The asylum.'

'Latchkill?' said George in surprise, and another shudder went through her. But he persisted. 'D'you mean someone who works there or a – a patient?'

'A patient. One of the mad people.'

George did not know a great deal about Latchkill's occupants, but he knew, as everyone in the area knew, that the asylum's gates were kept firmly locked and bolted at all times, and that patients were not permitted to roam around unchecked.

So he said, 'But you can't have been attacked by one of the patients, not unless you were actually inside Latchkill's grounds, that is. Were you visiting someone, or— No, I'm sorry, of course you weren't. Please don't start crying again, I'm sure it's not good for you.'

But more of the story tumbled out, as if Louisa wanted to get rid of the words as quickly as possible.

She had, it seemed, been intending to pick wildflowers to press and use for making birthday cards to send to friends throughout the year; it was something she had done ever since she was a child, she said, and George nodded, and thought it a very nice, very lady-like occupation. He imagined Louisa bent over a table, the flowers and the tissue paper scattered around, her fair curls tumbling free of a ribbon.

But, said Louisa, she had stayed out longer than she had intended and had not noticed how dark it was getting. Mr Lincoln would know that early autumn twilight that seemed to creep in from nowhere and catch one unawares? Quite frightening it could be.

'So I was going to walk very quickly past Latchkill, and go home along Scraptoft Lane.'

She had been almost level with Latchkill's gates, walking along the grassy bank that fringed the road.

'I didn't much like it, but I thought I'd soon be past the gates, and I was going to be firm about not looking in through them. Only then, a – a figure stepped out from behind a tree, and barred my way.' The tears began to flow again. 'I ran off at once, but he came after me – I could hear him running along behind me – like a giant pounding on the ground. And I didn't really look where I was going – I just wanted to get away – or hide somewhere safe . . . That was when I saw the mill, and I thought I might be able to hide there. The door was locked, but it was only a thin sort of lock, and when I pushed hard it snapped off. I didn't think Mr Forrester would mind, and I thought I could explain to him – I do know him; we've been to luncheon at Quire House, and for sherry after church on Sunday.'

George knew a ridiculous stab of envy at the casual way she said this, as if it was an ordinary thing to do. But for her, it would be an ordinary thing. Louisa and her grandfather would be invited to Quire House as guests, as a matter of course – they were neighbours, equals. It would not occur to old Josiah to invite an employee, a hireling, and it ought not to occur to the hireling, either. But one day, thought George, *one day* . . .

'I didn't think the man would follow me in here,' said Louisa, 'but he did. So I tried to hide over there' – she indicated the huge silent waterwheel – 'and I huddled right down behind it, and it smelt horrid – there's some water in the bottom of the tank-thing. I prayed he wouldn't find me – I prayed so hard, Mr Lincoln.'

'Of course you did. It's all right. You're safe now.'

'But he did find me. He came right up to the mill, and stood in the doorway for a moment. He was *huge*. He was the hugest man I've ever seen, and I was so terrified I couldn't even scream.'

She broke off again, sobbing.

'Miss Rosen, do try to be calm. I'm sure we can—'

'He shut the door,' said Louisa, as if George had not spoken. 'So I couldn't get out. And he saw me at once: he pulled me out from behind the waterwheel, and pushed me down on the floor over there. He was laughing – a horrid throaty sort of laughing

– and then he lay on top of me— His hands felt like iron bars – he was so strong. I can't tell you how strong he was.'

'But look here,' said George, not really wanting to know what had happened next. 'None of this actually proves it was someone from Latchkill.'

'He *was* from Latchkill,' sobbed Louisa. 'I know he was. He was mad – anyone could have seen that. He had great grinning teeth – like a giant's teeth in a fairy story – and immense clutching hands. He slobbered over me – all over my neck, I thought I was going to be sick when he did that. And he lay on top of me for what felt like ages – he was so heavy I thought he would crush me to death, and I couldn't cry out because he put one of his hands over my mouth. But he used his other hand to unfasten . . . And then he – he kept on hurting me, over and over, only I don't quite understand what he did—'

'You don't have to tell me that part,' said George hastily, recognizing this for extreme naivety, but nevertheless deeply embarrassed. 'What did the man do afterwards? When he had stopped – uh – hurting you?'

'He stood up and laughed again, as if he thought he had done something very good indeed. And then he went out,' said Louisa. 'I didn't see where he went because I was crying and I was trying not to be sick – I didn't dare go outside in case he was still there, and I thought I might have to stay here for hours and hours. It was awful, because my grandfather wouldn't know where I was – nobody would know. And then you came in.'

'Miss Rosen, I'm afraid we'll have to tell someone about this. Because if you mean you were raped—'

She flinched at the word and began crying again, and this time it ended in what sounded, even to George's inexperienced ears, dangerously like hysteria. He had a vague idea you smacked people's faces if they were hysterical, but clearly this was unthinkable in the present situation so he said that Miss Rosen must calm down, and he would take her home. Did she feel well enough to walk along to Toft House if he helped her?

'You don't need to tell your grandfather any of this if you think it would make him ill. Perhaps you could say you fell over somewhere? That wouldn't upset him, would it?'

'I don't know. But I feel a bit better now. And I don't think I was really – what you said – do you?'

'Raped?' said George, and her cheeks burned with embarrassment.

'I can't possibly have been,' she said. 'It's a very shameful thing, isn't it? People talk about you in whispers, and you never get a husband. So I really don't want it to have been that. Only . . .'

Oh God, what now? 'Yes?' said George, warily.

'I don't know how to explain it to you.' Even in the dimness he saw the hot colour come to her cheeks. 'There's blood,' she said in a rush, not looking at him. 'It's – I mean it's where he hurt me.'

George, struggling with his own embarrassment, managed to ask whether a doctor should be fetched.

'No, please don't. I'd be too ashamed,' said Louisa at once. 'I don't know, really, why I told you, only you were so kind and I was so upset.'

'The – the bleeding is part of being raped,' said George after a moment.

'Is it his blood or mine? If it's his, I don't care, but if it's mine I don't know what to do – Will I die from it?'

In as down to earth a tone as he could manage, George said, 'It will be yours, but I don't think it will go on for very long.' He hoped this was right. 'Could you walk home if I came with you? It's not very far to Toft House, is it?' He knew exactly where it was, of course: it was one of the houses that formed part of that absurd private dream. How many times had he walked past it, and stared longingly through its gates, and thought – if only . . . He glanced at Louisa Rosen, and the speck of an idea dropped into his mind.

As he took her arm, ideas were tumbling through his mind. Once at Toft House, Mr Rosen would surely invite him in –

the nice, well-mannered young man who had been so kind to his granddaughter. He might offer George a glass of sherry, which was what the people in those houses did, George knew all about that. If so, he would accept the sherry and make polite conversation.

Aloud, he said, 'I think we might tell your grandfather that you tripped and turned your ankle in a rabbit hole. And that you lay stunned and helpless for a little while. I know it's an outright lie, but—'

'I'll have to lie, won't I?' said Louisa. 'I shan't like it, but if grandfather thinks I was – attacked, he'd probably be ill again. And even if he wasn't, he'd want the man found and brought to justice, so the truth would come out, and everyone would know what had happened.'

'Dreadful for you,' agreed George. 'Shall we set off?'

At Toft House, he was indeed invited in, and old Mr Rosen, who had the fragile, papery look of ill health, was very grateful indeed to the unknown young man who had brought his granddaughter home after she had taken a fall. It was not sherry that was offered, but Madeira, and sipping it, George looked about him, and felt a surge of what the Bible called covetousness. This is what I want. I want to live in a house like this.

A second glass of wine was offered, but George declined, and said he must be leaving. But perhaps he might call in a few days' time, to see if Miss Rosen had recovered? What else could Mr Rosen say to that, other than yes?

The news of Latchkill's escaped patient got out of course, in the way things did in any small community. Apparently the man had been caught almost at once, and taken back to whatever room or dormitory or cell he had inhabited. Latchkill's new matron, a hard-faced female only a little older than George himself, was believed to have said that escapes from properly run institutions were very rare indeed, and this had been an isolated incident.

George felt matters could be allowed to rest for a brief time. He would watch for his opportunity carefully, but he would allow

Louisa a little time to recover from her ordeal before he made the promised call to Toft House.

But although he did call, and although he was made welcome, Louisa seemed withdrawn. It's not going to work, thought George, despairingly. But perhaps she just needs a little longer to recover and forget.

Three months later he learned there was to be a consequence of that day which would ensure Louisa Rosen would never forget. Learning the truth had caused old Mr Rosen to suffer one final, fatal, heart attack.

If it had not been for the sudden death of her grandfather, the solution to Louisa's dilemma might not have been so easy. A marriage between Miss Rosen of Toft House and the virtually penniless George Lincoln would probably not have been permitted. Or, if it had been permitted, it certainly would not have happened with such unseemly haste.

As it was, eyebrows were raised slightly. A burial and a wedding so close together? said people. Not what you would expect. Had anyone actually known of the attachment between Miss Rosen and Mr Lincoln? Ah, no one had. A secret romance, perhaps? Well, whatever it was, it was all very mysterious, although fair was fair, and nobody who knew George Lincoln could possibly suspect him of anything improper. Dear goodness, he was the vicar's nephew, and one of old Josiah Forrester's under-managers up at Twygrist. Josiah Forrester did not employ people who were not entirely respectable. But it could not be denied that George had done very well for himself. Louisa Rosen would have inherited Toft House and the Rosen money, which, put in plain terms, meant George Lincoln would be the owner of Toft House.

CHAPTER THIRTY-ONE

After she had been in Latchkill for a little while, Maud found all kinds of ways to avoid the things they tried to do to her. They gave her pills and horrid-tasting draughts; some made her sick and others made her crouch over the lidded-bucket-arrangement in a corner of the room, her stomach clenching in agonising spasms. She became skilled at pretending to drink the draughts, and then pouring them away afterwards. She folded the pills in a corner of her handkerchief and hid them, because you never knew what you might need.

But the thing she did not manage to avoid was the stone trough in the bath-house. The first time they took her there, Maud thought she was being taken to bathe in the ordinary way, and she was pleased because she had not washed properly for several days. She hated the smell of her own unwashed body, and of clothes she had worn for too long. Father had said he had left some of her clothes with matron – he had packed some of her nicest gowns himself, he said – but when Maud asked about these, the nurses said they did not know what she was talking about. She must be dreaming, they said.

Most of the nurses did not call Maud by name. Even the ones who brought her food called her 'girl'; Maud was not even sure if they knew her name. But the two nurses who took her to the bath-house knew it. They called her Maudie, and they said they knew all about her being one of Thomasina Forrester's little girls, and she was unnatural and a monster. Maud hated them, but she was quite afraid of them and so when they told her to undress, she did so. They made her put on a canvas robe, which was a bit like a bathing costume. It did not smell very nice but Maud did not say anything because of being frightened of them, and also because of wanting a proper bath.

The bath-house was a dreadful place. The walls and the floor were of rough harsh granite, and when Maud walked across the floor there were little gritty bits on it, which might have been flaking fragments of granite, but which might as easily be nail cuttings from people's toenails that nobody had swept up.

The baths were like the stone troughs you saw on farms, and Maud was made to sit on the edge of one. The two nurses piled her hair onto the top of her head, and before she understood what was happening, they cut it off – scissoring it away in great ragged clumps that fell down around her shoulders. Maud struggled and tried to get away, but they grabbed her arms and pinned them to her sides.

'Restraints, I'm afraid,' said the elder one. She had a hatchet profile and mean little eyes. 'Matron's orders. Thought we'd have to use them on this one, didn't you, Higgins?'

'Vain,' said Higgins, nodding. 'All the same these vain ones. Don't struggle, girl, you'll only make it worse for yourself.'

Her arms were twisted behind her back, and then leather straps were put around her wrists. A buckle pulled too tight bit into her flesh. More straps were fastened around her ankles.

'And you'll have the gag as well if you don't shut up,' said hatchet-face, and they went on shearing her hair.

'We shan't mind if we have to gag you,' said Higgins. 'Quite enjoy it, in fact.'

'We quite like punishing unnatural creatures who get into bed with other women,' said hatchet-face, and they both laughed in a horrid jeering way.

Maud sobbed with despair and frustration, but neither of them took any notice.

'If we take off the restraints for the bath, will you behave properly?' said hatchet-face at length.

'Or have we got to drop you in with the straps still on?' said Higgins.

'Take them off, please,' said Maud, hating herself for pleading but hating the straps even more. 'I won't struggle again.'

'That's better,' said hatchet-face. 'But keep the gown on. We don't want to see all you've got.'

'We aren't Thomasina Forrester,' said Higgins. 'Nor one of her pretty little sluts from Seven Dials.' Both women laughed coarsely.

Maud clambered over the high sides of the bath. The granite scraped her skin through the canvas gown, and there was a scummy line where it had not been properly scrubbed out. The nurses brought two tall cans of water and poured it in a quick splashy torrent. Maud gasped because it was much too hot, and her skin had turned bright pink where it touched her. But when she tried to climb out, they held her down.

'Stay where you are,' said Higgins, and hatchet-face fetched something that had been lying ready in an enamel bowl. At first Maud thought it was a bathing cap, fashioned from the same scratchy canvas as the gown, and wondered if they were protecting her shorn head from the hot water. They clamped the cap tightly down over her head, and Maud screamed, the sound echoing in the enclosed space. The cap was icily cold, and sent spears of pain slicing through her entire head.

'Pounded ice,' said Higgins. 'You're having the cold treatment, see. Hot to the body and cold to the head. Very effective.'

'Only quarter of an hour, though,' said hatchet-face. 'Don't want to . . . What is it we don't want to do, Higgins?'

'Inflame the membranes of the brain,' said Higgins, reciting this parrot fashion. 'And we replace the ice every five minutes.'

Maud had no idea whether the two women followed this

regime, because by the time they put the second application of ice on her head, she had already entered a world where there was no room for anything but the spiking pain in her temples. When finally they carried her back to her own room, she was dizzy with the contrast between the fiery heat in her limbs and the icy agony of her head. Thomasina and Simon were there, of course, still hammering their way out of Twygrist as they were on most days, but for once Maud could not pay them any attention.

As the day stretched out and the light began to fade, she had the beginnings of an idea for escaping from this place. There was an irony about this, because it was almost as if the ice-cap had made her brain work again. Ways and means for escaping wreathed in and out of her mind: half-remembered snippets of things that had happened in Quire House; fragments of gossip and conversations and things found and heard. Little by little Maud began to see a way of getting out of Latchkill. And, what was even more important, she began to see a way of ensuring that she stayed out.

As soon as Maud was sure she had the details clear in her mind, she set about putting her plan into action. She waited until the evening spider light lay thickly across Latchkill, and then tidied herself as well as she could without a mirror, combing her hair as neatly as possible. It would eventually grow to a decent length of course, but that might take months or years. In the meantime it felt dreadful. Like an urchin's hair, or a beggar's. Or a lunatic's? But I'm not a lunatic, thought Maud angrily. How dare they treat me as if I am?

She waited until she heard the clatter of the supper trays being brought round, and then sat in her usual corner, apparently staring at the wall. Her heart beat furiously but her hands were perfectly steady.

Here came the footsteps along the passage, together with the rattle of the metal dishes. From the tread it sounded as if Nurse Higgins was on tray-duty tonight, which pleased Maud very much.

She stayed absolutely still, listening as the door was unlocked and opened. It was Higgins. She brought with her the unappetizing smell of mutton stew.

'Here's your supper,' she said, and stepped into the room to put down the tray. That was when Maud moved, springing forward and smashing the tray upwards so it slammed into the woman's face. Hot glutinous gravy splashed across her eyes, and she cried out, and flung her hands to her face.

Maud laughed triumphantly and snatched up the lidded enamel bucket which she had placed nearby, and brought it crashing down on Higgins' head. There was the sound of a crunching blow and Higgins slid to the floor. A huge delight swept over Maud: this was the woman who had cut off all her hair and jeered, and who had exulted over those agonizing ice-cap treatments. Was she genuinely unconscious? Maud bent over to make sure. Yes, she was breathing in an unpleasant snorting way and a line of white showed under her eyes. *Good.*

She half-carried, half-dragged the woman onto the bed, and arranged her so she was lying with her back to the door. Anyone looking in would think it was Maud herself, hunched up in one of her silent sulks, staring at the wall. Maud already knew it was quite usual for the nurses to ignore a patient who was withdrawn. 'In a sulk again,' they would say if they looked into the room. 'Leave her alone for a few hours – she'll soon be hungry enough to behave.' But she had no idea how long it might be before Higgins was found, so it was important to move as quickly as possible. Once Higgins came round, she would raise the alarm anyway. That might be several hours, but it might be much less than that.

Maud stared down at the woman, and saw she was wearing a cotton petticoat under her uniform. Within minutes she had torn three wide strips from it. One strip tied Higgins' hands behind her back, a second tied her ankles together and the third formed a gag over the woman's mouth. With the sheet pulled up, the gag and tied hands and feet could not be seen from the door. Now, even if Higgins came round quickly from the blow she would not be able to yell for help. Maud was very pleased with the way everything was working out. She looked down at Higgins again, wondering if she should put on the drab gown and apron, but thinking it might take too long. There was the cap, though: she could take that. She unpinned it from the woman's head, and pulled it over her own short hair. She made sure the stored-away pills she had pretended to take were safely tied in her handkerchief, and tucked the handkerchief in the pocket of her gown.

Then she wrapped her own cloak around her – the cloak she had been wearing the night they brought her here – and holding her head high as if she had nothing to fear, she walked into the dim passage, shutting the door of her room and drawing the bolt across.

As she stole down the passage, she had the feeling that her mother was quite close to her, warning her to be careful. There were things inside spider light that you did not know existed – things that could suddenly pounce out on you.

She found her way to the ground floor by a narrow staircase. Probably it had been a servants stairs in the days when Latchkill had been a privately owned house. It was difficult to imagine a family ever living here – children and parents and ordinary life.

There was no-one around, and Maud thought she had chosen the time well. The nurses would still be serving the suppers or having their own meal – there was a big kitchen at the back where they all ate. But she still could not see any doors leading to the outside world. She hesitated at the foot of a wide, shallow staircase. Beneath the stairs, fixed to the wall, was a big notice and, although she was aware that anyone might come out and catch her at any minute, Maud paused for long enough to read what the notice said.

The orders for the governing of the hospital, Latchkill, in the environs of Cheshire County, are exceeding good, and a remarkable instance of the good disposition of the governing Trust, especially the rules laid down, viz to wit:

1. That no person, except the proper officers who tend them, be allowed to see the lunaticks of a Sunday.
2. That no person be allowed to give the lunaticks strong drink, wine, tobacco or spirits, or to sell any such thing in the hospital.
3. That no servant of the house shall take any money given to any of the lunaticks for their own use; but that it shall be carefully kept for them till they are recovered, or laid out for them in such things as the committee approves.
4. That no officer or servant shall beat, abuse or offer any force to any lunatick, save on absolute necessity.

It was the most terrible thing Maud had ever read in her life. It was as if whoever had written it thought people would come to Latchkill to view the patients just as they might go on a day-trip to a fairground to view the freaks in the sideshows. And worst of all, it gave sly permission for the nurses to ill-treat any of the patients.

She could hear a faint clattering of crockery nearby, that must mean she was near the kitchens and therefore surely at the back of the house. There was the sound of a door being opened, and a cheerful voice calling out something about only another hour before going off duty, followed by the sound of quick footsteps on the stone floor. Maud glanced frantically about her. Several doors opened off, and one of them looked like a broom cupboard. Dare she risk opening it? Yes.

It was a broom cupboard – there were pails and mops, but better still, two nurses' cloaks hung on a peg. Maud discarded her own cloak, and donned the Latchkill one. With the cap, she could surely pass as one of the staff.

The sounds of voices had faded, and she stepped out into the passageway again. There, a little further along, was surely the door to the outside world she had sought. A huge heavy door it was – too heavy and huge to be an ordinary inside door. There were massive hinges and black iron bands across it – was that to keep people out, or to keep them in? No matter. Maud reached for the latch, praying it would not be locked and it was not: the handle turned easily, and the door opened.

It was not the door leading outside! She was in another of the soulless passages and there was a stale, too-warm smell, like rotting vegetation. Maud beat down a wave of panic, because there was something dreadfully familiar about this.

Something remembered or heard, or even dreamed.

Dreamed . . . her old childhood nightmare of the black iron door that began to swing slowly open, and that you knew must be slammed back into place, because it was there to shut in something terrible.

Maud pushed these thoughts away, and went determinedly on. But it was as if something that crouched at Latchkill's heart had stirred into life, and the nightmare was closing around her again, like a huge knuckled hand gripping her throat so she could not breathe. I'm inside the nightmare again, she thought. Only this time I'm awake, and I shan't be able to escape.

She turned a corner of the passageway, and there it was: the black iron door. It was *real*; it was in front of her, massively hinged, and with a thick bolt drawn across.

Maud was not going to open the door; of course she was not. But a little silvery voice deep inside her mind whispered that it would be better to know what the frightening thing was. Wouldn't it be better to confront it once and for all, to stare it in the face and banish this nightmare for ever?

No! It would be the worst thing in the world! But she saw with horror that her hand had developed a life of its own; it reached out to the immense bolt and drew it back. It moved smoothly and almost soundlessly, and the door was open. It swung slightly inwards.

The first thing Maud was aware of was that the spider light was far thicker beyond the door than anywhere else in Latchkill.

At first she was aware of a huge relief, because there was nothing so very terrible in here: a long table with plates and mugs on it, and a window high up in one wall. Maud frowned, waiting for her eyes to adjust to the light trickling through.

When they did she thrust a fist into her mouth to stop herself screaming, because what she saw was impossible and terrifying and must be a nightmare after all. Such things did not exist!

Drawn up to the long table were six or seven chairs, and seated on each of the chairs was a grotesque figure, bulky, repulsive, *immense*. Giant bodies and giant faces. Giant hands resting on giant knees, all sitting round their supper.

They had heard the door open, because the huge huge heads with the overhanging brows turned to look at her.

'A new little girl,' said one of them in a clogged kind of voice.

'A little girl-nurse to see us,' said another. 'Isn't that nice?' It got up from the chair and came lumbering towards her, massive hands outstretched.

Of course this was what was beyond the black iron door, this was what had always been behind it, this was what mamma had warned her against.

' . . . the dangerous thing about spider light, Maud, is that it hides things – things you never knew existed in the world. But once you have seen those things, you can never afterwards forget them . . .'

The spider light room tilted and spun. Maud gasped and tumbled dizzily back into the dark corridor, slamming the door and drawing the bolt back with a hand that shook violently. Then she ran, without looking back, through the passageways until at last – oh merciful God, oh thank you, Jesus! – she saw a door half open, and beyond it Latchkill's grounds.

The nightmare of the black iron door went with her as she ran. It's real, thought Maud, going through the thick shrubbery and the leafless trees, gasping when a low branch caught her cloak and half dragged it off. It exists, that door and that room – they're both there, at Latchkill's heart. But how could they be in my dreams all those years ago? Don't think about it yet, though; just think about getting safely outside.

The gates were ahead of her at last: they were like black jutting teeth in the darkness. They would be locked and guarded by the lodge keeper, but people must come and go through those gates: delivery carts with provisions, the nurses going on or off duty. In the dim light, with the dark blue Latchkill cloak around her shoulders Maud might pass as one of the nurses. But supposing the lodge keeper knew them all? He would certainly know the times they came and went. Maud thought about this, and then remembered the cheerful voice that had called out about only another hour before going off-duty. St Michael's church clock was just chiming nine, so it was a reasonably safe guess that the changeover to the night staff would happen at ten. Very well, she would wait until ten. It was quite a cold night, but not icily so, and the ground was perfectly dry. She would trust to luck that her escape would not be discovered in the next hour, and she could slip out with the nurses going off-duty. She wrapped the cloak around her, and sat down in the thickest part of the shrubbery.

Memories came flooding in, all the way back to that last morning with mamma. The morning that was the tangled bloodied part of memory – the long-ago morning when the spider light had lain thickly over Amberwood.

It had been her eighth birthday, and Maud had understood by then that mamma lived in her own room, and did not go out. It did not seem odd; it was just what mammas did. She was taken to see her each evening by Mrs Plumtree, after she had had her milk and biscuits, and sometimes mamma said quite ordinary, quite happy things, like, 'Oh, there's my dearest girl,' and, 'What have you been doing today, my precious one?' But sometimes she said things Maud did not understand, and that were quite scary. 'Child of fear,' she said. 'That's what you are, my dear.' And as Maud's birthday got nearer, she said, 'They think I forget the date, but I don't.' Maud thought this must mean her birthday, and that mamma was not going to forget it, but later she heard mamma say to papa, 'It's the anniversary. One day *he* should know what he did. *He* should be made to pay.' Maud did not know who *he* was, but in reply, papa only coughed in the nervous way he had when he did not know what to say. But the next morning, he had said to Mrs Plumtree that the mistress was restless again. He dared say it would pass, but in the meantime, perhaps Mrs Plumtree would keep a close watch. Mrs Plumtree had said she would, trust her for that, sir, and was Miss Maud to be taken in as usual?

'Oh yes,' papa had said, after a moment. 'I think that's perfectly safe.'

And then, early on the very morning of her eighth birthday, mamma had come into Maud's bedroom, and had said Maud was to be very quiet and to do exactly as she was told, because there was a secret. The secret meant that Maud had to get up at once, get dressed and go with mamma. They had to be mouse-quiet, said mamma, because it was important not to wake papa or Mrs Plumtree.

It was a bit strange for mamma to be out of her room, but Maud had thought it might be something to do with her birthday – it might be that they were going to see a puppy or a kitten. But wherever they were going, Maud almost had to run to keep up with mamma, and mamma kept looking back over her shoulder as if she was worried about somebody seeing them. Once she stopped and tightened her hold on Maud's hand, and peered into the hedges on the side of the road. Now that Maud was a bit more awake she saw that mamma looked strange: her hair was not coiled up into a neat bun as usual; it was wispy and straggly, and the buttons of her gown were not properly done up – her chemise showed through. Maud hoped they would not meet anyone, because it would be embarrassing for people to see mamma like this. She tried to ask where they were going, but mamma said, 'I told you, it's a secret.'

Maud had not exactly been frightened, but she was no longer

used to being with mamma like this – it was a long time since they had taken their afternoon walks together. She started to feel cold and shivery inside, and wondered if mamma would be angry if she let go of her hand and ran back home.

When they came to Latchkill's gates, mamma had stopped, and said, 'That's where we're going.' Maud looked up in astonishment, because it was still spider light time – there had been a huge scuttly spider on the marble washstand in her bedroom yesterday morning – and mamma had always said you must never be caught near to Latchkill at that time. Spider light was when the bad things happened.

But the spider light did not seem to matter today because mamma was tugging on an iron rope. A bell jangled and a man ran out of the little house at the side of the gates, and said, 'Good morning madam, and little miss, and what can I do for you?'

Mamma said in her haughtiest voice, 'I wish to come inside, if you please' and the man looked at her for a moment, and then nodded. The gates opened, and they stepped through.

Latchkill was as frightening as Maud had always known it would be. It had high-up windows with jutting-out bits of stone so they looked like eyes under too thick eyebrows staring down at the people on the ground. It was a dirty-grey colour, and it had a crooked look as if the people who had built it had not measured it properly, so it had ended up twisted. If it had been a person, it would have been a hunchback, or a man limping.

Mamma seemed to know the way they must go. Holding Maud's hand very tightly, she led the way around the side of the house. 'This is the door we'll use to go inside, Maud.'

'Are we going to see somebody?'

'Yes. Yes, we are. We're going to see somebody we should have seen a long time ago.'

Mamma's eyes were glittery, and although her face was pale, there were two spots of red on her cheeks as if she had painted them on.

As well as being dark, the inside of Latchkill smelt horrid as if somebody had boiled cabbage for too long, or as if the people who lived here did not wash often enough. Maud hated it, but mamma was striding along a passage, still holding firmly to Maud's hand. If they met anyone, they must say they had been sent for because a relative was ill. Did Maud understand that?

'Yes,' said Maud in a very small voice.

They did not meet anyone. They went into a passageway where it was quite difficult to see the way because there were no windows, and mamma said, 'Yes, I think this is it.' She pointed to a notice fixed to the wall. It was in big black letters, and Maud read it carefully.

Reaper Wing.

There was no reason why she should start to feel even more frightened by these words, but she did. In a small scared voice, she said, 'What's Reaper Wing?'

For a moment she thought mamma was not going to answer, but then she said, 'Reaper Wing is the place where your father lives.'

CHAPTER THIRTY-TWO

The place where your father lives.

The eight-year-old Maud had not understood. Her father was at home, and on most days he went to Twygrist Mill to work. He was not here in Latchkill: he was at Toft House where they all lived.

Then mamma said, in a different voice – a voice that brought all the shivery fear back, 'This is the place, Maud. They thought I didn't know where he lives – George thought I didn't know – but I do know because I listened to people talking. I've known for a very long time. We have to go through the black iron doors and we have to do so today because it's your birthday. That's the right day to do this.'

Maud saw they were standing in front of huge black doors – like the doors people put in books about giants. She wanted to shout to mamma not to open the doors because there might be something terrible beyond them – something that they must not see. But she had been too frightened to speak, and mamma had drawn back the bolt.

Maud, curled into the shrubbery of Latchkill's grounds, waiting to slip out, could see the ghost of her eight-year-old self clearly. She could see mamma's hands – thin, white hands because mamma had not gone out into the sun for all those years – drawing back the bolt.

The grown-up Maud half understood that there was something wrong with the people in the shadowy room: the people who had been there that morning, and who had still been there tonight when she opened the black door. She thought that some deformity, some tragic freak of nature had made them like that. But the eight-year-old Maud had not understood at all. She had thought the people were giants, ogres, who gobbled up human children or carried them off to their castles. She had stared at them in horror, and thought that if one of them were to snatch her up, he would go striding across the countryside in his seven-league boots, carrying her with him, and nobody would catch him, no matter how hard they ran.

She had started to step back into the safe darkness of the passage, thinking mamma would surely come with her now they had seen what was in here. But mamma did not move. She said, 'Which of you is the one who attacked me one night nearly nine years ago?' She appeared to be waiting for an answer, which Maud thought silly of mamma, because giants did not answer ordinary people's questions.

Mamma said, 'It's taken me all these years to understand what happened. I didn't know about Reaper Wing and about you. But now I do know – I've met the matron here and she's talked about you, so I understand.' She made an odd, half-ashamed, half-proud gesture at Maud. 'But I wanted you to see the result of that night,' she said. 'Your daughter.'

Maud had known that there was something wrong with mamma ever since she had come into her bedroom. But now she could hear that her voice was too high, there was a cracked sound to it as if something deep inside her had splintered like when you broke a glass.

The giants were listening. Several of them had tilted their heads to one side, as if they were trying to understand. One of them, sitting at one end of the table, got up and came towards them.

Maud stifled a cry because he was so tall and had shaggy hair like a thatched roof, and his hands were clenching and unclenching. Huge hands, with massive knuckles and thick nails.

There was a dreadful moment when she thought mamma was going to stay where she was, facing the man who was coming towards her. Maud glanced fearfully up and saw mamma staring at him with a look of such fear she thought mamma might be about to swoon. Maud tugged on mamma's hand to make her come away. She thought mamma said, 'Yes. It was you. Then this is your daughter,' but she was never afterwards sure if she had only imagined this.

After a moment mamma seemed to realize the danger, and turned and ran hard down the passage, half dragging Maud with her. Twice Maud stumbled and almost fell but each time mamma jerked her up and they ran on.

He was following them. Maud did not need to hear the thudding footsteps; she knew *he* was coming after them. When they reached the little door where they had come in she glanced back, and he was still there, the thick hair flopping over his face, grinning and reaching out his hands to them.

Mamma scooped Maud up in her arms, and carried her outside. Then she began to run towards the gates.

Whether the man meant them any harm, or whether he was simply seizing the chance of freedom – whether his mind was, in fact, as distorted as his body – Maud, at eight, had not known. Thinking back, she still did not know.

The lodge-keeper must have seen them coming along the carriage-way because he came out to them. Maud had no idea if he meant to stop them, but her mother suddenly slowed to an ordinary walk and when they were near enough to be heard, she called out, 'Could you let us out again, please? We have delivered our message.' Her voice sounded normal and the lodge-keeper tipped his cap and went over to the massive bolts, drawing them back. It seemed to take ages; Maud willed him to hurry, but he was fumbling and the minutes stretched out and out. Maud's mother glanced over her shoulder, and Maud did the same. Supposing the man had followed them? But nothing moved anywhere and in another minute they would be through the gates and they would be on the way home.

The gates finally opened. The lodge-keeper smiled at Maud as they walked through and Maud smiled back a bit uncertainly. They were outside, and they were safe. When she glanced back the lodge-keeper was standing there waving to them so she waved back.

Mamma did not speak as they went along, but she held Maud's hand very tightly, and her hand was cold and trembly. Maud wondered if she dared ask about the man, but she was afraid mamma's voice might take on the dreadful mad sound again so she said nothing. They were just over the little crossroads, and nearing the turning to Scraptoft Lane when a figure stepped out from behind a tree. The man was in front of them, barring their way.

There was no time to wonder what had happened or how he had got out. Mamma gasped, and then keeping tight hold of Maud's hand began to run back the way they had come. The lane was bumpy and rutted; Maud stumbled several times and struggled to keep up. She thought the man was following them, but surely at any minute they would be bound to meet someone who would help them – a carter or a farmer about an early-morning task.

But there was no one. There were not even any cottages where they might have knocked on the door and asked to be taken inside. Her mother hesitated, and then took the road that led past Twygrist. 'We'll have to go this way,' she said, gasping with the effort of running. 'We can't go home because he's behind us. Blocking the way. So we'll go towards Amberwood Magna – there are houses just beyond the bridge. We'll ask for help at one of them.'

'I can't run any more – mamma, I can't—'

'Then I must carry you.' But they had only gone a very short way before mamma had to set Maud down and double over, gasping for breath. The bridge was still some way ahead of them and clearly they were not going to reach it before the man caught them. There was only one building along this stretch of the road where they might hide. Twygrist.

Mamma, still struggling to get her breath, stared at it, and when Maud said, 'In there? Can we hide in there?' she shuddered. But then she said, 'Yes. Yes,' there's nowhere else.'

They had gone up the slope together and in through the door – Maud could not remember now if it had been open or if her mother had broken the lock to get them in – and then they had been in the safe dark silence of the mill. Mamma pushed the door nearly closed, and they stood behind it.

'We'll stay here, Maud. He won't see us and even if he does, he won't dare come inside. He must have slipped through the gates while the lodge-keeper was waving to us, that's what must have happened.'

Her voice was strained and frightened and Maud saw she was listening very hard for the sound of footsteps. Maud was listening for them as well, but everywhere was quiet.

Her mother peered through the chink in the nearly closed door, and said suddenly, 'He's coming. Oh God, he's coming. We'll have to hide – but where? Where?'

'Up there?' said Maud, pointing.

'Yes, clever girl. Quickly then. We can crouch down and even if he does come in, he'll never see us. Don't make a sound.'

So they had gone up a little flight of flimsy wooden stairs, and had hidden in the corner behind the stone grinding wheels. Maud, whose teeth were chattering with terror, thought they should not really hide from a giant behind grinding wheels: giants liked things like that, they sang a song about grinding men's bones to make their bread. If the giant knew there were grinding stones in here, he would be sure to come inside. She glanced nervously behind her at the waterwheels towering into the shadows.

Here he came now. The door was pushed open, and the dull morning light came in. There was the sound of heavy footsteps, and of the floor creaking under them. It was an old floor and it creaked a lot.

She could not see what the man was doing, not without peering around the edges of the stones, and she was not going to do that, not even for a tiny moment. But she could hear the screech and scrape of machinery a bit further down and she frowned, because this was not what she had expected. She had expected the giant to come stomping over the floor, bellowing to know where they were.

But he did not, and after a moment Maud realized that something was happening, something huge and frightening like the first dull rumble of thunder before a great crashing storm. There was a heavy scraping – something going groaningly up and up, and then a great roaring and splashing.

She looked questioningly up at mamma. Her mother started to speak, but in that moment Twygrist began to shudder to its bones. Behind them, in the dimness, something began to move, and Maud looked round in terror.

Slowly, with the agonized groaning of a struggling monster, the great waterwheels began to turn, and Maud understood that the sound had been the sluice gates opening. Water was pouring into Twygrist, and the mill's huge machinery was starting to move.

It ought not to have been so fearsome – Maud had often heard and seen the waterwheels turn – and probably it would not have been fearsome at all if they had not been there on their own with a giant on the floor below hunting for them.

Her mother said they must move away from the machinery, and she thought the man had gone, although it was quite difficult to hear her properly, because the water was rushing down and down and the waterwheels were swishing round much faster. Maud glanced up at them. Huge oak and iron wheels, they were, and if you went on looking at them for too long, you began to see them as gobbling teeth, chomping down and down.

As mamma stood up and began to move forward, Maud saw two things both at the same time.

One was that it was not the giant who had opened Twygrist's sluice gates, it was papa. Her father must have come into Twygrist early as he sometimes did. Maud could see him clearly; he was bending over a wheel near the ground, frowning as if there might be something not quite right with it. Did he know they were there? No, he could not know or he would have called out to them.

The other thing she saw was the man from Latchkill – the giant-man with the reaching hands – who must have come into Twygrist while the machinery was groaning and clattering. He was coming up the stairs towards them.

Mamma gave a cry of fear, and her father looked up and saw them for the first time. As the giant-man reached the top of the steps, the waterwheels spun faster and there was a hard flinty sound as the grinding stones directly in front of them began to turn. Her mother screamed. The giant-man lunged forward, his hands outstretched to her, knocking her off her feet, knocking her onto the grinding stones.

There was a hard crunching noise that sent a terrible pain through Maud's whole body – like having your teeth torn out, or having all your fingernails ripped off. Then her father wrapped his arms tightly around her, and carried her outside, saying over and over that she must not look, everything would be all right, so long as Maud forgot everything she had seen and heard. Would she promise that? From a long way away, Maud heard her own voice obediently promising.

Papa had nodded, and said something about never forgiving himself, but how was he to know Louisa would be here, he had come in early because there was a lot to be done today. Maud must stay out here, just for a very little while, because papa must go back inside the mill. There was a thing he had to do.

So Maud had stayed outside. It had been very cold outside the mill and she could hear the waterwheels still gobbling and clanking. But she would do what papa had told her, and keep the promise she had made to forget everything that had just happened.

She had kept her promise, and she had forgotten. Or so it had seemed.

After mamma's funeral she had been sent to stay with some cousins of mamma's, then she had gone to school, and she had forgotten the morning when mamma had fallen between the grinding millstones inside Twygrist.

But she could see now that she had not really forgotten. She could remember how, after a few minutes, the waterwheels had slowed down and then stopped, so she knew papa had closed the gates to stop the water pouring in. It was quite a long time before he came out – far longer than the very little time he had said – but when he did come out, Maud saw there was a frown between his eyes that had not been there before. It had frightened her, but then papa had smiled and they had gone home, and talked about Maud visiting mamma's cousins for a while.

Throughout all these years, the memory of what had happened that morning had remained so deeply buried Maud had not known it was there. All that had remained were nightmares of the black iron doors that opened onto Reaper Wing.

St Michael's clock was chiming ten when two nurses, both unknown to Maud, came along the path. They were talking animatedly, and one of them called cheerfully to the lodge keeper to let them out, Albie, and be sharp about it because it was freezing enough to turn you to ice out here.

It was too dark for the lodge keeper to make out the individual features of people who went in and out. Maud waited a moment, and then ran out onto the path, as if she had been trying to catch the nurses up. The gate keeper saw her, sketched a good-night salute, and let her through.

She was outside the gates. Free. She would do anything to avoid being taken back to Latchkill. She would kill someone, if necessary. With a jolt of surprise she remembered her plan, and that she would have to kill. It would have to be tonight, and she knew who the someone would be.

CHAPTER THIRTY-THREE

Donna had spent five years working out her plan; she had polished it until it was foolproof, and now, when it was almost time for the final blow to be administered, she could see all her careful work was going to pay off.

The catalyst for the final chain of events was to be the murder of someone within Quire House. The identity of the victim had never mattered – Donna had known she must go for whoever was around at the right moment, but she had always hoped there would be a young boy, and so there had been. She had seen Greg Foster on her careful forays to Quire House – she had visited the place a few times over the years at deliberately-spaced intervals, deliberately choosing term-times when there might be school parties working on projects, or when there would be enough visitors for her to pass unnoticed. She changed her appearance each time; no one must connect her with the seldom-seen lady who rented Charity Cottage, but she needed to keep a close check on the component parts of her plan and Quire House was one of those parts.

So on one occasion she was an earnest collector of architectural information, wearing an indeterminate-coloured jacket and skirt with a felt hat crammed over her hair, and on the next she was an untidy student in jeans and a t-shirt. Another time she wore a flowing Indian-print cotton skirt with wooden beads and earrings. She kept a low profile during these visits but she kept her eyes open for anything that might be incorporated into her plan. For a long time there was nothing and Donna became anxious, but the week after it was announced that Antonia was to be shortly freed, she saw something that would fit into her plan with beautiful precision.

She saw the sulky-faced boy who had worked at Quire for the past few months take two pieces of Victorian jewellery from a display table and slide them furtively into his pocket.

From then everything unrolled immaculately. The boy was a work experience student or something like that, and Donna had waited for him when he left Quire for the day.

He had been suspicious at first, disinclined to trust this unknown female, but when Donna confronted him with what she had seen, he turned truculent. Yes, he had taken stuff, he said. So what? They had enough, didn't they? All those things, just for people to come in and stare at. They wouldn't miss one or two.

'Or three or four,' said Donna very deliberately.

They looked at one another. Donna said, 'We're in the same game. And here's the deal. You let me into Quire, we'll take the stuff, and I'll get rid of it. We split fifty-fifty.'

'How do I know you won't rip me off?'

'You don't.'

'How do I know you aren't a copper?'

'You don't know that either. But suit yourself,' said Donna, and turned to walk away. She had taken four steps before he said, 'How would you get rid of it?'

'I'd take it to one of the jewellers in London who deals in secondhand stuff.'

'Wouldn't he guess it's nicked?'

He was so small-time, so naïve, Donna wanted to laugh. She

said, 'For God's sake, look at me! I'm the ultimate in respectability.' And so she was that day, wearing a plain suit, with her hair combed back behind her ears. 'I simply say it was my grandmother's jewellery or china – no, I'll make that great-grandmother – and that I need the money. And believe it or not, that's perfectly true. I'm flat broke. That's why I went to Quire House today.'

'To see what you could nick?'

'Yes. It's a good scam,' said Donna, mentally reading from the script she had prepared for herself. 'I go round museums and smaller stately homes – places like Quire. But I only take small things – things that I can pocket. No one ever suspects me, because I don't look like a thief. Then I sell what I've picked up. I use a different jeweller each time, of course.'

The suspicious eyes assessed her for a moment. Donna's heart thumped. Had she sounded convincing? Most of her expressions had come from crime books and might be wildly off the mark, but she did not think Greg Foster was likely to know the real jargon.

'All right,' he said at last.

'You'll do it?'

'Yeah, why not? Nothing to lose, is there? If you grass on me, I can deny it. Or say you approached me and I told you to sod off. I'll get the stuff and meet you here.'

'No,' said Donna. 'I've already seen that you haven't the least idea of what's valuable and what isn't. So I'll be the one deciding what we take and what we leave.' She frowned, as if thinking hard. 'Quire House doesn't have any electronic alarms or anything like that, does it?'

'No. Dr Toy locks the doors when we've all gone and that's it.'

'Good.' Very good indeed; this had been one of her real worries. She reviewed the time-scale of her plan, and said, 'We'll make it the day after tomorrow. You let me in after the place has closed. I don't suppose you've got a key, have you? No, I thought you wouldn't have. In that case you'd better pretend to go home at the usual time and sneak back to hide somewhere. A loo or a cupboard or something like that. At a quarter to seven I'll come to the main door and you'll let me in. Be there on time, Greg, or I really will grass you up.'

'I'll be there.'

'We'll choose what we take, and be gone by seven – quarter past at the latest.'

Donna thought he had been half over-awed and half-afraid, but whichever it was he had played his part. He had let her into Quire shortly before seven and they had gone like two shadows into the music room. Once there Donna swung the sandbag at his head. It had been child's play fashioning that; a stocking filled with actual sand and she had worn a jacket with deep pockets so that it was quickly accessible.

Greg Foster had gone down like a pole-axed bull, and Donna bent over him and took the knife from her other pocket, and thrust it into his heart. Straight in between the fourth and fifth ribs. You did not need to be a surgeon to find out the required information to stab someone, and you did not need very much strength behind the thrust, either. Killing Richard Weston had already taught Donna that.

She waited just long enough to be sure he was definitely dead, arranged the *Caprice* sheet music on the floor nearby, then slipped out and went through the park to Charity Cottage. The portable CD-player with the Paganini disc was slung around her neck, Donna had not risked leaving it hidden in the grounds for anyone to find.

She had been slightly out of breath as she went through the bushes towards the cottage, but not unduly so because killing Greg had not been especially exciting. There had not been much emotion involved; it had simply been a matter of needing a newly killed body for Weston to find, that was all, and of arranging it to reflect those two other deaths – Richard Weston's and Don's.

She thought she had done that well: the scene was almost an exact mirror-image of that other night, right down to the music and the glossy piano nearby.

And once again Weston had reacted almost exactly as Donna had predicted. She followed the music, of course, and went into Quire House and found the boy's body. Donna had been careful to leave the door ajar; she did not think Dr Toy or Professor Remus would be likely to come downstairs once they had gone up to their respective flats, and so it proved.

Antonia had screamed – oh really, Dr Weston, how boringly predictable of you! – and then had run into the main hall to call for help. By that time Donna had slipped through the French windows, and was watching through a chink with Paganini's music switched off, so that Weston should think her enemy was out of range.

But once Weston yelled for help, Donna left. The next part of the plan was not especially tricky, but if she was not very careful this was the part where she might be caught. It would be necessary to keep her wits about her for the next few hours.

She sprinted around the side of the house going as quietly as she could. The police would be called at once, and they would spend some time interviewing Weston and Dr Toy and Professor Remus. They would search the grounds, of course, and the place would be crawling with scene-of-crime officers for most of the night. But would they search Charity Cottage? Donna thought it highly unlikely, but as she went across the parkland, careful to remain in the shadows, she was keeping the possibility in mind.

The cottage was in darkness as she let herself in, and she made a quick check of all the rooms. They were all empty because Weston was at Quire House, and unlikely to be back for some time, but Donna was taking no chances. She locked the door again, pocketed the keys, and then carried a bathroom stool onto the landing, positioning it directly beneath the attic trapdoor. Under her anorak was the rope ladder she had bought months earlier. It had taken a great deal of searching before she finally found a suitable one in a marine supply shop. The ladder was the kind people used on the sides of boats; it had steel hooks at one end, which allowed it to be secured almost anywhere. Donna had tried it out a number of times while she was living here, and it hooked very firmly and very satisfactorily onto the rim of the attic trapdoor opening and hung almost to the ground.

She stood on the stool, reached up to dislodge the trapdoor, sliding it to one side, and then hooked the ladder in place. The hooks bit into the timber, and the rope unravelled. So far so good. She took the stool back because nothing must seem out of place when Weston returned making sure she had left no footprints anywhere.

It was quite difficult to actually ascend the rope ladder; it was very light and swung back and forth. It was made harder by the close-fitting balaclava helmet and the long gloves, but Donna was still being painstaking about leaving any DNA. In the end she managed it, and clambered over the edge of the trapdoor into the attic. She peered down at the stairs and the landing, shining the large torch which she had slung around her neck. Had she left any telltale signs anywhere? Any flurries of dust on the floor? No, there was nothing. She knelt on the edge of the attic opening, pulled the rope up, and then pushed the trapdoor back into position. She was as sure as she could be that it would seem undisturbed from below.

The attic was cramped and hot and it was going to be uncomfortable up here for several hours, but Donna did not care. It was fairly dusty but it was not as dusty as it might have been, because she had cleaned it out herself while she was staying here. Before she gave up the tenancy she had been careful to leave a couple of old travelling rugs up here, some cushions, and a couple of old packing cases. Even if the attic were later to be searched, it was not very likely that these things would strike anyone as suspicious. She spread the rug out behind a packing case, switched off the torch to save the battery, and settled down to wait.

It gave her a deep pleasure to think of the agonies Antonia

would be enduring – of how finding Greg's body with the knife sticking out of his chest and the *Caprice* music lying alongside it, would have taken her another step nearer to the mental disintegration that Donna was aiming for. Might she even now be questioning her own sanity? At the very least, she would know that the peace of Amberwood and the anonymity she had sought had been destroyed, and that would be agony in itself.

It was all working out exactly as Donna had intended. For the next few hours she would have to be very alert indeed in case the police searched the cottage, but there would be no signs that anyone had got up through the trapdoor, and even if they did get up here, they would probably only take a cursory look. In that situation Donna would have plenty of warning and she would huddle under the travelling rug. She was fairly confident she would not be seen.

It would be all right. Every detail was worked out; she had covered every eventuality, and she was prepared for the unexpected.

She had not been prepared for the unexpected on the day, five years ago, when she had first driven out to Twygrist. Weston had just started her prison sentence and Donna's plan had still been in its early, tentative stage.

Her mind had already focused on the dark squat silhouette of the old Amberwood mill where her parents had died. Twygrist. There would be a certain justice if Twygrist could play a part in Antonia Weston's final downfall. Donna thought she could at least drive up and take a look round. There was no one to wonder where she was going, or ask questions, not any longer.

Twygrist, seen by a dull autumn light, was as forbidding and as secret as she remembered. She parked her car at a distance so as not to draw attention to her presence, and walked up the slope to the derelict oak door. It creaked as she pushed it inwards. The stench of the place hit her like a solid wall, but Donna knew at once that this was where Antonia Weston must eventually die.

The kiln room again? There were at least eight years to wait before Weston was freed, and Maria and Jim Robards' death would surely be forgotten by then. In any case, everyone had believed their deaths to have been a tragic accident. She would see if the steel doors were still in place; she had brought a torch with her.

But first she walked round the main floor, liking the way the machinery seemed to watch her, liking the feeling of its latent energy. Into her mind slid a new thought, like a questing serpent, How easy would it be to open the sluice gates, and to force Twygrist into life again?

An immense stillness seemed to fall over everything, as if the dark core of the old mill had heard and was listening. It's alive, thought Donna. It's been decaying and idle for years – decades – but there's still something here that's living. And that something has heard my thoughts, and it's waiting to see what I'll do.

How did the sluice gates work? Donna had a distant memory of her father saying something about a pivot wheel that would have to be turned with a splined key. The same principle you used when you opened a tin of sardines or corned beef, he said, and Donna's mother had instantly said that if he was going to use analogies, please would he use ones they could understand, because she had never opened a tin of corned beef in her life. Donna's father had laughed, and said, all right, then, a horizontal wheel, with a grooved shaft at the centre; you slotted the key down into that shaft, and then turned the key.

Donna saw the wheel almost at once. It had black spokes and jutted up about a foot from the floor. It was quite near the door leading underground. What looked like the spline key was lying nearby.

She walked slowly forwards, her eyes fixed on it. It would not work, of course: the mechanism would long since have seized up. And even if, by some slight chance, it did work, the culvert would have rotted away years ago. She glanced overhead. Yes, there was the culvert, just as she remembered from that last summer here.

The clay had broken away from most of it, but it might be still be watertight.

She picked up the spline. It felt cold against her fingers and the surface was pitted with age. Presumably you slotted it down into the wheel's centre, as her father had said, and then turned it using the t-shaped handle. The splines would force the wheel's mechanism to rotate. It really did look as if it worked on the corned-beef-tin principle.

The wheel was about two feet across. Donna leaned down and tried the key in the centre. It slid home obediently, and she grasped the t-handle. Just a tiny pressure, just to see if the wheel was still capable of rotating. She turned it slightly to the right, encountered resistance, and then tried it the other way. This time the whole shaft of the key seemed to engage, and the wheel moved to the left. Only a little – barely the distance of one of the spokes – but Donna instantly felt an answering tremor. Like thunder growling far away. And had the oak floor shivered briefly at the same time, or had that been her imagination?

Her hand was still on the key. She was not going to take this much further, but if she could just know how workable the mechanism was . . .

The wheel turned a little further, and this time there was no doubt about it; an unmistakeable tremor went through the floor, like the accounts you read of the start of an earthquake. At the same time a breath of something stagnant and cold seemed to brush against Donna's skin.

If the sluice gates were raised, hundreds of tons of water would tumble down into Twygrist from the reservoir, and the water-wheels would begin to turn.

The light shifted suddenly, and there was a new sound behind her – a sound that had nothing to do with the struggling old mechanism. Donna spun round, and in the centre of the floor, watching her with puzzled eyes, was a woman of thirty or so, with shoulder-length fair hair.

After a moment the woman said, 'I didn't realize anyone was

here.' But her eyes were on Donna's hands, still grasping the sluice wheel. 'That's awfully old machinery,' she said after a moment. 'It's probably a bit dangerous to be too close to it.'

'Yes,' said Donna straightening up. 'Yes, it is dangerous.' She removed the spline key from the sluice wheel, and held it between her hands thoughtfully.

There are moments in life when your body thinks ahead of your mind, and when sheer instinct takes over. Donna knew this woman had seen her rotate the sluice wheel, and she also knew that the woman was not going to forget it. She would talk about it, telling people about seeing Donna here. Not necessarily accusingly, but mentioning it as a curious incident. And people would remember, they would *remember* . . .

On the crest of this thought, Donna moved towards the woman, slowly, keeping the heavy iron shaft of the key in her hands.

As if trying to smooth over an awkward moment, the woman said, 'It's a macabre old place, isn't it? I haven't lived here very long – my husband's come up here to work – he's one of the curators at Quire House, and they're thinking of taking on some of the other old buildings in the area. So I thought I'd take a look at Twygrist for him. I didn't expect to find anyone in here, though.'

'Neither did I,' said Donna, and bounded forward.

The old mill worked with her again, exactly as it had done years before, and the woman fell backwards in a surprised tumble. Donna felt a shiver go through the oak floor and saw the woman fling up a defensive hand across her eyes. Too late, of course. The sluice-wheel key was heavy and powerful; it swung up over Donna's head and then came smashing down. There was a crunch of bone, and the woman fell forward. Dead? Oh, who cared, she would be dead very soon. Donna dragged her across to the half-rotted tank enclosing the lower waterwheel, and by dint of pushing and lifting, finally tipped her over.

She fell down inside the tank, hitting the giant cogs of the waterwheel as she did so. There was a faint menacing thrum from the old iron and oak, and then a shallow muddy splash. The stench of the sour water rose up, and the old rotting timbers groaned, and splintered slightly at the bottom. Donna, one hand over her mouth to shut out the sour breath of the splashing water, waited to see what happened next, but the only sound was from the wheel, still vibrating slightly from the impact. The sound stayed on the air for what seemed to be a very long time, but eventually it died away, and Twygrist sank back into its brooding silence.

Donna stood on tiptoe to peer down into the tank, to make sure that even if the woman was not dead, she would not be able to get out. She was reassured. Nobody – and certainly nobody who had been given such a crunching blow to the head – could possibly get out of there.

Later that night, reviewing what she had done, she was glad to know she had been able to deal quickly and efficiently with getting rid of the unknown woman who might have spoiled the whole beautiful plan. Also – and this was the important thing – she had done it without getting caught.

She had not been caught when she killed Greg Foster earlier tonight, either.

Curled into the dark attic, Donna speculated on what would be happening at Quire House. It was not likely that Weston would be actually suspected of the boy's death – she would have no connection with him, and the police would find that out very quickly. It was probable that the killing would be put down to a burglar; it was a safe bet that Dr Toy and Professor Remus would have reported the missing items which Greg had taken. It was also possible that some drug connection might be found; so many teenagers were into drugs these days, and Greg had looked just the sulky ill-mannered type who would think it was cool to be part of a drugs-ring. But Donna did not really care what conclusion they reached.

If by some outside chance Weston was suspected – if she was found guilty and sent to prison again – it would not be disastrous;

it would simply delay the reckoning. Time meant nothing in all this. Donna would wait for twenty years if she had to.

She flicked on the torch to check her watch. Nine o'clock. She settled down to wait for Antonia to return to the cottage, and for night to fall.

CHAPTER THIRTY-FOUR

After Inspector Curran had left, Charity Cottage felt oddly unfriendly. Antonia stood in the doorway for a moment, watching him walk across the park, then closed and locked the door. He had not seemed to think the murderer would return tonight but she had not needed his final reminder to lock the doors. After she had done this she went systematically round the house, placing chairs and stools directly in front of the doors and the downstairs windows. If Greg Foster's killer – who was presumably the same person as Antonia's intruder – did try to get in, he would trip over the chairs and the noise would alert her. If that happened she could shut herself into the bathroom with the mobile phone and summon help; Curran and his officers were only across the park at Quire. And if the killer sustained a viciously painful injury trying to get in – a pulled hamstring or a chair-leg jabbed into the groin – it would be no less than the bastard deserved.

This reasoning made her feel better, and she made a cup of tea and then switched on the television for the late-night news. She did not take in very much of it, but it gave her the feeling of being still a part of the ordinary world. There was probably not much point in trying to sleep tonight, and to go to bed was unthinkable: she would lie awake listening for the sounds of someone trying to get in. It was annoying to find that she was counting how many hours there were before Jonathan reached Amberwood. This was purely because he was a good friend, and would continue to be a good friend no matter what she was thought to have done. He would come in to bat on her side – he always had done.

After thought, she decided to spend the night on the sitting-room sofa with a book. There might even be a late-night TV film she could watch. She could keep the sound turned down very low so as to hear any stealthy footsteps outside, or the sounds of doors being tried or locks being tampered with. With any luck she might even manage to stop seeing Greg Foster's body with the knife sticking out of his chest where someone had stabbed him in exactly the same way Don Robards had been stabbed when he had attacked her that night. And exactly as Richard had been stabbed. The music was there as well: don't forget that Richard's music was lying next to Greg Foster's body. Whoever he is, this madman, he knows all about me. He knows all the vulnerable spots. Antonia spent several fruitless moments wondering about the identity of the man but could not come up with any useful possibilities. If Don Robards had had family she might have speculated whether this could be some warped revenge-plot, but all through his clinic sessions he had been definite about not having anyone and certainly no relatives had been called at the trial.

But it would be better not to think about Don tonight. She went upstairs to pull on a tracksuit which would be comfortable if she did fall asleep but practical if the killer came back. The bedroom was cold, and glancing out of the window Antonia was aware again of the dark isolation that surrounded Charity Cottage. The Inspector had said his men would be around for some time, but Antonia thought it would not hurt to check the barricades again. She went round the rooms, making sure that everywhere was locked and bolted and that the stools and chairs – in one case a clothes-airer – were all firmly in position. If Sergeant Blackburn could see her, he would file her under N for Neurotic, or even M for Mad, and Oliver Remus would probably agree. Antonia did not care what the professor thought. She did not care what any of them thought.

The sitting-room was warm, and the mobile phone was comfortingly within reach. The only sound in the room was the steady ticking of the clock on the mantel. It ought to have been a soothing sound, that rhythmic ticking, but somehow it was not. Antonia was dizzy with exhaustion but she was too frightened to give in to the need for sleep. Every creak of the cottage's timbers sounded like a furtive footstep, and twice she sat bolt upright, the first time thinking she had heard a door being stealthily pushed open, the second time that someone had walked across the bedroom floor overhead.

She lay down on the sofa again, and finally began to relax. Sleep was starting to drag her eyelids down – dare she give in to it? The table lamp was on, so anyone prowling around would assume she was awake and think twice about breaking in. In any case, he'd fall over the clothes airer, thought Antonia, and aware how absurd this sounded finally allowed herself to sink into a sleep.

It was not a very peaceful sleep. It pulled her down into a disturbing world of bleak asylums with harsh treatments and venal matrons in charge, where an unknown, un-named patient pressed down into a cold stone floor, as if trying to escape the light. And from there into a world where a madman played music that trickled menacingly through the night, and where a hangman's noose swung slowly back and forth, ready to strangle a murderer. Where the ticking of clocks somehow changed pace and became soft footsteps that sounded exactly like the stealthy sounds of someone creeping down a darkened staircase . . . At this point Antonia woke with a gasp, abruptly aware that the sounds were not in her dream: there really was someone coming down the stairs.

There was no chance to snatch up any kind of weapon or to reach for the phone or even to make a dash for the front door. The intruder was here, he was inside the cottage – I locked him in with me, thought Antonia in horror. He's been in here all the time.

The door opened and the figure was there – dark, quite slenderly-built, wearing some kind of mask over its face. Antonia leapt up, but before she could do anything the intruder was upon her. Eyes, glittering and filled with hatred, framed by blackness, glared down at her.

A voice – an unmistakably female voice, said, 'This is all for Don, you bitch. It's to punish you for killing Don.'

Before Antonia could even cry out an arm was lifted and something came crashing down on the top of her head. There was an explosion of pain and a brief blinding flash of light behind her eyes. She spun straight down into a black gaping void where there was nothing at all.

From the dark attic Donna had heard Antonia return around eleven, and she had heard the murmur of a man's voice. Then the police had come back with her! She lay down under the travelling rug at once, willing herself not to move, hearing the sounds of doors opening and closing and then of footsteps on the stairs. Oh God, oh God, the man was searching the cottage. Looking in the bedrooms – checking cupboards and wardrobes. Would he come up here? Would he even see the trapdoor over the landing? It seemed to Donna that hours crawled by while she waited, and that the whole world shrank to this dark stuffy attic where she crouched.

But it was all right. The footsteps had gone back down the stairs, and there was the murmur of voices again, and then the sound of the front door opening and then closing. After that came the unmistakable rushing of water from the plumbing as the tap downstairs was turned on. Donna dared to sit up, and risked a quick flick of the torch to see the time. Half past eleven. She visualized Antonia making herself a last cup of tea or coffee before going to bed. A pity the creature could not be tricked into drinking arsenic along with it.

Several times in the hours that followed she had to cautiously stretch her limbs to ward off the beginnings of cramp. Once she risked standing up, but the old floor timbers creaked so loudly that she froze and did not dare move again.

The hands of her watch crawled around to two, and Donna cautiously pushed the rug aside, sat up, and checked that she had everything she would need. She had fixed on two as the best time to make her move. The police were unlikely to be around at that hour – they had had five or six hours to pursue their investigations and they would hardly be searching the grounds in the pitch dark. The only real risk facing Donna was getting Antonia out of the cottage and into her car, but the car was parked close to the front door and she did not think the risk was so very great. It would mean driving down the narrow access road and onto Quire's main carriageway but she thought she could do that without switching on the car's lights and the cottage was far enough from the main house for the engine not to be heard.

She half-crawled, half-slid across to the trapdoor, and working with infinite patience, lifted it out and set it down on one side of the opening. It made the barest scrape of sound – nothing that could possibly be heard below. She secured the hooks of the rope-ladder to the edges of the opening, and climbed down. This was not an entirely silent manoeuvre but she prayed Weston would be asleep. Once on the stairs she took the sandbag from her anorak pocket. Now for it, you murderous bitch!

It was briefly disconcerting to discover the bedroom was empty. Donna stared at the unoccupied bed. Had Weston gone back to Quire House to sleep, and Donna had not heard her go? No, she was still here, Donna had heard her making tea and moving around. And she could feel her presence in the cottage now. She began to steal down the stairs.

As soon as she saw the spill of light from the sitting-room she understood that the creature had remained downstairs for the night in case of a break in. Very clever, Dr Weston, but not quite clever enough. This is it, Donna. This is what you've waited five years to do. Her heart racing with a mixture of nervous tension and pulsating excitement, Donna pushed the door wide and went into the room.

There was a deep satisfaction in seeing Weston's terror as she started up from the sofa, and there was an even deeper one in bringing the sandbag smashing down on Weston's skull.

She went down as easily as Greg Foster had done, and an emotion so overwhelming and so vast gripped Donna that for a moment she was quite unable to move. She stared down at the unconscious figure. She had never seen Antonia Weston close to; she was smaller than Donna remembered from the trial, and she was thinner. *Older.* But even though Donna knew she must move quickly, she could not stop looking at the woman who had killed Don. She had not known she would feel like this – exalted and excited – and she had not known that she would hiss those last words to Weston. 'All this is for Don,' she had said, because it suddenly seemed vital that Weston understood why she was being punished. Had that been a touch foolhardy? Not really. Antonia would not be able to tell anyone; she would not speak to anyone ever again.

Donna sprinted back up to the landing, and climbing onto the bathroom stool again, dislodged the rope-ladder and slid the trap-door back into place. She returned the stool to its rightful place, and coiled the rope ladder around her waist; it could easily be burned or flung into the Amber River later on.

She opened the front door, and glancing round to make sure no one was about, unlocked the door of Antonia's car. Then she hooked her hands under Antonia's arms, and dragged her out, tumbling her onto the back seat. She fell in a twisted huddle that looked painfully uncomfortable. Good. Donna went back into the cottage and looked round. Had she left anything that might provide a clue? No. She closed the cottage door, hearing the lock click home.

Her own car was parked about half a mile from Quire, well off the road and hidden by trees. She would have preferred to be driving it now for this difficult, risky journey, but it might be seen and recognized, or traced afterwards. It did not matter very much if Antonia's car was seen although it must not be seen before she was clear of Quire's gates. Hardly daring to breathe, Donna fired the ignition and steered slowly through the darkness onto Quire's main carriageway. Nothing stirred anywhere and she went through the gates without mishap. Then she switched on the headlights and drove towards the road that led to Twygrist.

At first Antonia was not sure where she was.

She thought, to begin with, that she had fallen asleep on the sofa of Charity Cottage. There had been a clock ticking. Then she thought she was back in prison, huddled onto the thin bed in her cell, dreading the morning.

But as consciousness returned, she realized she was in neither of these places. She seemed to be lying not on a bed or a couch, but on a hard cold surface. The smells were all wrong for prison or the cottage, wherever this was, it was filled with a stifling sourness, like the soot from a very old chimney.

She opened her eyes to nothing. The pitchest of pitch blacks. Panic swept in instantly. I'm blind, she thought. No, I can't be. But surely nowhere could be as thickly dark as this. She brought her hand up in front of her eyes, and could not see it. Panic clutched her all over again. I *am* blind. I've been ill or I've been in an accident – a road smash – and my head must have been injured because it's aching dreadfully. I don't know where I am, but I don't think there's anyone here with me.

Her mouth felt dry, but she called out, 'Hello? Is someone here?' and heard her words whispered eerily back to her. *Someone here . . . S-s-someone here . . . here . . . HERE . . .* And then they died away, and there was only a feeling of emptiness. Then I really am on my own. Oh God, where is this?

Some semblance of reasoning was starting to come back. She thought she could not be blind because the blackness was too absolute; blind people almost always had at least a slight perception of light and shade.

She sat up cautiously, but when she tried to stand a fresh jab of pain skewered through her skull. An injury then. But no bandages from the feel of it. She put up a careful hand to explore and found a lump on one side under her hair.

Memory was starting to return with agonizing slowness, and in snatches, like a jerky, badly cranked old film. Being in the cottage after that boy's death. Locking all the doors against the murderer. Only the murderer had already been in there – hiding, waiting to creep out. Antonia remembered those hate-filled words: 'This is for Don, you bitch. All this is to punish you for killing Don.'

A woman's voice. 'This is for Don.' And then that crunching blow on her head. Had it been a girlfriend of Don's? Family that he had not admitted to? Whoever it was, was she going to come back?

Antonia was not going to sit here meekly, hands folded, waiting for her captor to come back. She made another attempt to stand up and, although it made her head throb, this time she managed it. It was horribly disorienting to stand in absolute darkness like this, but it would have to be endured. She would find a wall so she could feel her way along it. It would be something definite to do, and concentrating on it might help her to ignore the darkness and the silence.

But with this thought came the realization that it was not absolutely silent. Antonia had half consciously been aware of a pounding against her mind, which she had ascribed to the blow to her head. But it was not inside her head at all. It was outside it: a slow regular sound that made her think of machinery. Something beating along a prescribed course. Something thudding against metal or wood . . . Maddening, inexorable.

Something beating, over and over, like a distant sledgehammer in a far-off forge – No! Not beating. *Ticking.* The ticking of a huge, unseen clock.

Memory clicked into place, and Antonia saw the road that led down to Quire House and the building that skulked at its side.

A building whose wheels and sluices and grinding stones had long since ceased to work, but a building that had, set into one of its walls, an immense clock.

She was inside Twygrist. And from the feel of it, she was somewhere below ground. The stifling sense of darkness, the sour stale air . . . But let's not think about how much air there might be down here.

Had Twygrist underground rooms? Yes, it had: there was that display in Quire House, complete with the sketches of the machinery and the layout – Antonia remembered studying it on her first visit. There had been a room well below ground level – something to do with drying the grain, she thought. A furnace room with a brick oven, and what had been some sort of perforated floor directly above. Did that get her any nearer to escaping? She could not see that it did, and on balance she would have preferred not to know about the crouching bulk of the old mill directly over her head.

She inched her way to the right, both hands outstretched, and without warning came smack up against a wall. Its surface felt dry and harsh, but Antonia began to feel her way along it, praying not to encounter anything that moved or scuttled. Or had a thin boneless tail and tiny sharp teeth, because goodness knew what lurking creatures might have their homes down here. She shut this thought off, and concentrated on the image of a doorway, because doorway there must certainly be.

And here it was! Oh thank you, thank you. Quite a big door as well, not timber, some kind of metal, and possibly steel. Well, of course it would have to be metal; if there were ovens down here it had presumably been necessary to seal the place off when the fires were lit. Antonia felt all round the door's outline. It was fairly solid and there were scratches on the surface. Pitted with age? She could feel the marks quite plainly, but what she could not feel was a handle or a latch, or any means of opening the door.

This was not acceptable. This simply could not be happening.

She felt all round the door again. Be careful not to panic, Antonia, because panic's the very last thing you can allow yourself. The door was as smooth as an egg. It was very nearly seamless.

She was shut into the underground room of the old mill, and somewhere above her was a clock banging the minutes away, and beyond all this, perhaps getting ready to stalk Antonia through this sour-smelling darkness, was a murderer.

CHAPTER THIRTY-FIVE

During the comfortable years spent in Toft House, George Lincoln had got into set habits. There was nothing wrong with that; it was what people did.

At ten o'clock each evening, Mrs Plumtree always brought in a tray of tea and sandwiches for his supper, and then went off to bed. George drank his tea, ate his sandwiches, and by eleven o'clock, almost to the tick, he was on his way upstairs to bed.

It was a routine that suited him very nicely, although since Maud had been in Latchkill it was no longer a comfortable one. Every time he thought about Maud, George could still scarcely believe what he had done, but in the days following the discovery of the two bodies in the mill, he was aware of a certain relief. The police had questioned everyone about Thomasina and Simon Forrester's deaths – who had seen them, and when and where, and why they might have been in Twygrist in the first place – and George was thankful that Maud was safely out of their reach. He thought the sergeant asking the various questions had barely even realized that George had a daughter.

George himself told the sergeant that Miss Thomasina had mentioned to him the possibility of starting Twygrist up again. He had been careful to say this as if it was something he had only just remembered, and he thought this had helped tip the balance to the verdict of accidental death. Clearly, said the coroner presiding over the inquest which was held at the nearby Rose and Crown, these two unfortunate people had gone out to the mill to take a look at its condition, and become trapped in the kiln room. He was not a local man, and appeared to have thought up for himself a happy little picture of two cousins – he made no doubt they had been good friends and childhood companions – going off on their little expedition to see if their family's business might be revived. On a sterner note, he added a little homily about the proper securing of old and potentially unsafe buildings, although, as a number of people said afterwards, Twygrist had belonged to Miss Thomasina anyway, and she of all people ought to have known the dangers of the kiln room.

Now the funeral was over, the shock and speculation were dying down. No one had given Maud a thought, other than to commiserate with George about the child's illness. One or two ladies had even pressed little gifts for her onto George, which had made him feel dreadful at deceiving them all. He had put the embroidered handkerchiefs and the lavender water into a drawer in Maud's bedroom for when she came home, and had thought, guiltily, how kind people could be. Cormac Sullivan had been kindest of them all, of course: when George remembered how Sullivan had behaved that night, he thought he owed the man a debt of gratitude that he might never be able to repay. It was amazing how you could misjudge someone.

But the small gifts for Maud might have to remain in the drawer for a very long time. George was only just now admitting to himself how very disturbed Maud really was. How much of that might be due to her parentage, he did not know. Louisa had unquestionably been unbalanced – those bouts of melancholy, those later years when she had cowered in her room. Had she actually been mad? And what about the man who had been her real father? George loved Maud dearly, and he thought of her as his own daughter, but he had never forgotten Louisa's description of

Maud's real father – the man who had broken out of Latchkill, and who had laughed as he raped her. What was in the meat came out in the gravy, as the saying went, and George was already wondering if Maud's stay in Latchkill might have to be a longer one than he had originally thought.

He had also never forgotten what had happened on the morning Louisa died – the morning when he had sent Maud to wait for him, and how he had set about dealing with what was inside Twygrist . . .

It had still been very early – no one had been about, and mist had been lying thickly on the Twygrist's reservoir like a shroud. George rather liked autumn, with crunchy leaves underfoot and the scents of bonfires and chrysanthemums, but that morning the scents inside the mill had been those of the spilled blood on Twygrist's millstone. Dreadful.

Louisa's body had lain broken and bloodied on the ground, and the millstones themselves had been spattered in blood. George had stared, horrified, and there had been a moment when he thought he might be sick. But then he remembered Maud. He scooped her up in his arms, took her outside, and told her to wait there, to be a good girl for papa.

He went back into the mill, and flung his coat over Louisa's body. Only when he had done that, had he turned to look at the other occupant of the mill.

He was huge, Louisa had said, all those years ago. He had great grinning teeth – like a giant's teeth – and immense clutching hands.

The rotating millstones had caught the man a glancing blow that sent him reeling back against the wall. He was lying in an ungainly sprawl, and there was blood on the side of his head. He was breathing with an ugly harsh sound and a rim of white showed under his eyelids.

Trying not to look at what lay beneath the millstones, George went unsteadily across to the sluicewheel, and wrenched it around until he heard the groaning sound of the gates descending. The waterwheels slowed and shuddered to a stop,and the water drained away leaving silence. Except that Twygrist was never wholly silent; it was always filled with rustlings and creakings, and with its own strange murmuring voices just out of human hearing.

George stared down at the unconscious man. He was a great hulk of a creature: even in the dimness it was easy to see that standing up he would be much taller than even the tallest of men – quite frighteningly so. It was almost as if his bones had gone on growing after he reached adulthood, but had done so in a haphazard way. His jaw was massive and lumpen – as if a slab of clay had been slapped onto the lower half of his face and left there without being shaped, and his hands were gross and hugely disproportionate to his body. It was chillingly easy to imagine those hands reaching avidly out to a victim, and to visualize that great jaw grinning with evil intent. Against his will, George remembered the old biblical words: There were giants in the world in those days, and a shiver of atavistic fear trickled icily down his spine.

I don't know what you are, he said, silently addressing the unconscious figure. I don't know if you're sick or only misshapen, or if you're plain bad. I don't know how you come to be here, either. But I'm as sure as I can be that you're the man who attacked Louisa all those years ago, and if that's so, I can see she didn't exaggerate about you.

As if this last thought had penetrated the man's mind, he opened his eyes and looked straight at George. With a dreadful grunting cry, half of pain, half of fury, he lurched upwards and came lumbering forward.

George did not stop to think. He snatched up an old cast-iron handle that had broken off a pulley, and as the massive hands lunged at his throat he brought the heavy lump of iron smashing against the side of the man's head.

He fell back at once, and as he did so Twygrist's greedy darkness picked up the sound of the blow and magnified it a hundred times over so that the terrible crunch of iron on bone echoed around and around the mill. George dropped the iron handle and forced himself to thrust one hand inside the man's jacket, to feel for a heartbeat. Nothing. Absolute stillness. I've killed him. Don't think about that though – not yet. Think about what's ahead: there'll be an inquiry into all this – Louisa's death, and the man's. Think what that inquiry might turn up.

It was unlikely that George would be suspected of killing Louisa, but it was not impossible that he would be suspected of killing the man. The earlier escape might be dredged up, and it might be realized what had happened all those years ago – eight years and nine months ago to be precise. Although George had acted in self-defence today, the police could argue that he had a long-standing grudge against the man, and the result might be that he would have to stand trial.

But if the man's body was never found: if only Louisa's body was found, it would be a different story. George might be considered guilty of neglecting his responsibilities at Twygrist – unsafe machinery, people might say – but nothing worse than that.

If the man's body were never found . . .

The thought slid like a serpent into his mind, and in that moment it was as if something that was no longer George Lincoln, the respectable, law-abiding citizen, took over.

He saw at once what he would do, and he also saw he would have to do it very quickly. He glanced towards the half-open door, but Maud, dear good child, was still seated patiently and obediently where he had left her. She could not be left outside for much longer though, and other people would soon be around.

Moving as swiftly as he could, he lit one of the oil lamps from the garner room, and used it to prop open the door behind the waterwheel – the door that led down to the underground stone rooms. After this, he dragged the dead man across the floor and through the little door; it did not take very long, but the man was heavy and by the time George reached the stone steps, he was drenched in sweat. He straightened up, wiping his face and neck with the back of his hand, and then exerted all his strength to tumble the man's body down the stone steps.

He went down after him, and half-lifted, half-dragged the body into one of the little handcarts they used for moving the charcoal into the kiln room, hooking the oil lamp onto the handle. The cart's wheels shrieked like a thousand souls in torment, and the flickering lamplight lent a dreadful semblance of movement to the man's dead features, so that the short walk through the narrow underground rooms was a nightmare. But George set his teeth and went on until he reached the kiln room.

The ovens were set into the wall facing the steel doors; they were about three feet up from the ground and had thick iron doors of their own. George propped the handcart as near to them as possible, and set the lamp on the ground. It cast a sickly yellow light over the dead man, but it was important not to look at him. It was better to remember that this was the creature who had raped Louisa all those years ago, and that if it had not been for him, Louisa might have remained sane and ordinary. (But then you might not have married her and got Toft House, said a hissing little voice in his mind.)

He ignored the voice, and opened the doors of the ovens, pushing them flat against the wall on each side. He hooked his hands under the man's arms, and after an initial struggle, finally succeeded in cramming him head first into the kiln. The ovens were deeper than they looked from outside, and he pushed the body as far back as he could. After this he shovelled in all the available charcoal, until he was satisfied the man was unlikely to be seen by anyone opening the doors. He slammed them firmly shut, dusted himself down, and went back upstairs, being careful to position the handcart exactly where he had found it, and to take the oil lamp back.

He made one last search to reassure himself that there was nothing suspicious anywhere, and only then did he go out to find Maud. He was working out what he would say to people: a shocking accident to his dear wife, he would say, and would then allow himself the luxury of giving way to grief. Twygrist would have to be closed down until his poor Louisa's body could be properly removed.

He would do all he could to see that Twygrist, and what lay at its heart, stayed closed. If it did not, then George would simply make sure he was there to oversee the next firing of the kilns.

But Twygrist, once closed, stayed closed. Miss Thomasina said there was really no question about it. George told her he really did not think he could ever bring himself to go inside the place again, and she said she entirely understood. In fact, she had been thinking that the old place was no longer a practical or a profitable concern. The Corn Laws had long since been repealed, and cheap corn was being imported, so there was very little call for a mill of Twygrist's calibre. That being so, it only remained for her to thank George for his years of devoted service to her father, and to hope he would accept this small sum of money – not a pension, of course, but a token of her gratitude.

George had accepted the money because Toft House did not run itself on nothing, and a man had to live. The amount was nicely judged; Miss Thomasina had not been miserly about it, but she had not been embarrassingly lavish. Everyone in Amberwood had been very kind to George, saying what a shocking thing for Louisa Lincoln to die in such a way, and poor George there to see it, and the child just outside, dear innocent mite.

He had not missed Twygrist, although he had missed the companionship of the farmers, and all the daily bustle of the place, but he had become involved in one or two little charitable works, and there were always things to do at St Michael's Church.

And in the end, life had gone along much as before, except that there had not been that darkened bedroom in Toft House, with Louisa's mournful figure in it.

Miss Thomasina kept saying she would do something about

Twygrist – although what she would do, she was not quite sure, and neither was anyone else.

And what lay at its heart, shut inside the disused ovens, rotted quietly away, without anyone knowing it was there.

These were not good memories to have on any night, but sitting by himself in Toft House with Maud inside Latchkill (entirely for her own safety, George said to himself firmly), they were bleak thoughts indeed. But at least the discovery of Thomasina and Simon's bodies had not necessitated opening up the kiln. George had had some very bad moments indeed worrying about that, but it had not happened.

At a quarter to eleven he made his usual rounds of the house, checking locks and windows, and at eleven o'clock he was in bed. He was just sliding down into sleep, when something jerked him awake, and he half sat up. A sound downstairs, had it been? There ought not to have been any sound in the house at all: Mrs Plumtree was long since in bed, and the only other servant was a girl who came in twice a week for the cleaning.

It came again, and this time George identified it. A creak on the landing outside his room. And then another. Someone was walking stealthily across the landing. Towards this room? He had no idea what to do. There was no lock on the bedroom door, and there was no other door in or out of the room. The bathroom was on the other side of the landing on this floor, and it might, of course, be Mrs Plumtree, coming to use it. George did not, naturally, concern himself with Mrs Plumtree's bathroom routines, but she had never, so far as he knew, made use of the bathroom at this hour. Perhaps she was ill.

He lay down again. It had been Mrs Plumtree after all, because he could hear the creak of the second set of stairs. She must be going back up to her room. George listened, and caught a muffled thud, and then the sound of bedsprings creaking a bit. It seemed that all was well. He rearranged himself for sleep, and this time it was a proper deep sleep. It was so deep that he did not hear the creaking of the stairs again, or the soft footfall outside his room. Nor did he wake when his bedroom door was pushed slowly open, and a figure peered round the door.

Maud had waited until the hour when her father would be in bed, then gone quietly in using the back-door key George had given her before she went to stay with Thomasina. The key had been in her bag which they had not taken away from her in Latchkill, although they had searched it and she thought the hateful Higgins had taken some money.

The familiar scents of Toft House closed round her as she went in through the scullery. She waited long enough to be sure no one was about, then went softly up the main stairs. There was a moment when the floorboards outside her father's room creaked loudly – she had forgotten those particular creaking boards – and she froze, her heart pounding. There was a faint sound from his bedroom, but nothing happened and she went up the second flight of stairs.

Mrs Plumtree's bedroom was at the back of the house; Maud slipped inside, carrying the pillow she had taken from the airing cupboard, and stole across to the bed. She was quite sad about having to kill Mrs Plumtree, but it was a necessary part of the plan and it had better be done as quickly as possible. She pushed the pillow down onto Mrs Plumtree's face; the woman gave a muffled gasp and struggled. Maud had to use quite a bit of force to keep the pillow in place. It was not really difficult, although the struggles went on for longer than she had expected. She watched the little clock on the bedside cabinet ticking the minutes away, because it would be helpful to know the length of time it took to smother someone. After ten minutes it seemed to be over, and Maud removed the pillow. Yes, it was all right. Goodbye, Mabel Plumtree. Now for the next part.

She had no qualms about killing her father, who was the one person who might spoil her escape and ruin her plan. He had betrayed her by taking her to Latchkill, and Maud was not going to feel in the least conscience-stricken about this. But it was important his death remained undiscovered for as long as possible, which was why Mrs Plumtree had had to die as well – she would certainly have raised the alarm if she had found her employer dead in the morning. With both of them dead it would be at least two days – maybe three or four – before anyone realized what had happened, and by then Maud would be miles away. Safe. Free.

Her father slept in the big front bedroom on the first floor. Maud, the pillow held firmly in her hands, eased the door slowly open. Careful now, he mustn't wake up. But it was all right: she could hear him snoring. It was a horrid ugly noise. He was sound asleep, lying on his back with his mouth open. Maud was grateful to him for sleeping on his back because it would make her task much easier. She crept over to the bed, every muscle tensed in case he woke up.

He did not wake; he went on snoring. When Maud put the pillow over his face, he spluttered and gurgled, and fought the air with his hands, trying to beat her off. But Maud was ready for that – she had known he would fight harder than Plumtree – and she knelt on the bed and brought all her weight down on the pillow. The clock said fifteen minutes to midnight, and she watched the hands tick round. Three minutes – five. He was still struggling, but not quite so frenziedly. Seven minutes. Surely he was almost dead. It had only taken Plumtree ten. But he was still twitching a bit, and his limbs were still jerking and really, you would have thought he would be dead by this time. Twelve minutes – thirteen . . . Ah, he had stopped struggling. Better not to take any chances, though. Maud remained kneeling on the bed, her hands pressed flat down on the pillow. Two more minutes? Yes, better be sure.

In the end, it was seventeen minutes before she dared lift the pillow, and her wrists were starting to ache quite badly with the pressure. But it was all right. He was definitely dead: his lips were swollen, and blue-looking, and his eyes were wide and staring. Maud steeled herself to feel for a heartbeat just to be sure, but there was nothing.

She left the pillow on the bed, went along to her old bedroom and put several things into a small valise. Night things, a change of linen. Hairbrush, toothbrush, soap. Carrying the valise, she went back down the stairs. Her father had always kept a reasonable amount of money in his desk, and Maud needed money for what lay ahead. She had a little jewellery, some of it her mother's, but most of it was at Quire House and she did not dare go back there.

There was almost £200 in the desk, which was very gratifying. Maud tucked it into her pocket, and went out through the back door.

CHAPTER THIRTY-SIX

Maud knew she needed a good deal of resolve for what now lay ahead. She would have to do several things she had not done before, but she thought she could manage it. The main thing to remember was the address she had found that day in Thomasina's desk – the address that had been tucked into a drawer, rather than being in Thomasina's proper address book. Number 17, Paradise Yard, Seven Dials, London. And a name: Catherine Kendal.

Maud could see now that Thomasina meant Catherine Kendal to be kept secret, partly because the address was not in her proper address book, but also because of what Higgins had said in the bath-house at Latchkill about Thomasina: 'One of her pretty little sluts from Seven Dials.' Maud had instantly remembered Catherine Kendal and the Seven Dials address, and what Thomasina had said that day: 'There's a girl who lives in a poor part of London. She's had to do some dreadful things to avoid starving, and she has a sick sister. She'd do anything in the world for that sister . . .'

Maud set off along the lanes. It was a quarter past midnight – a lonely time to be out, but she was unlikely to meet anyone. She needed to get to Chester where she could get a train to London.

If she could walk as far as one of the small market towns – Barrow or Tarporley – there were little country trains. Milk trains usually ran around four a.m. and Maud did not mind travelling into Chester on a milk train.

It would be a very long walk to Barrow but she did not mind that either. She knew the way because she had quite often been there for shopping, and there were signposts and milestones. She would have little rests on the grass at the side of the road as she went.

If she had to, she was going to say she was a parlourmaid, dismissed because the son of the house had forced his way into her bedroom. Or was that a bit too much like a penny novelette? Perhaps she could say she was going to see her mother who had been taken ill. Yes, that would be better; it would get people's sympathy. And if she had to give her name to anyone on her journey, she was going to say it was Catherine Kendal and that she lived in London.

Catherine Kendal, with that Seven Dials address. Catherine Kendal was one of Thomasina's pretty little sluts, who would do anything to avoid starving. And who, Thomasina had said, was exactly Maud's own age, *exactly Maud's own age* . . .

It was easier than she had dared hope. There was indeed a milk train from Barrow, and the incurious train driver had said, Oh, yes, he was going to Chester all right, so hop in miss, and help yourself to a drink of milk from that churn while you're about it. And she had hopped in and once at Chester had managed to get on a train bound for London.

It was a long journey, and as the train bumped and jolted along, Maud slipped in and out of sleep. Sometimes the tapping of the train wheels got mixed up with Thomasina and Simon relentlessly tapping on the walls of Twygrist – those sounds were fainter by this time, but Maud could still hear them. But sometimes the wheels sounded like the running feet of the man who had chased her and mamma through that long-ago autumn morning. Heavy menacing footsteps they had been, and when

Maud looked fearfully back over her shoulder, she saw the man clearly. She had seen his face, which had been huge and misshapen, and she had seen that he was grinning with delight because he had been sure he would catch them.

Maud still did not entirely understand about that last morning with mamma. 'We're going to the place where your father lives,' mamma had said, and the place they had gone to had been Latchkill. Had the man who followed them really been Maud's father? Maud thought she had forgotten about him, but drowsing in the stuffy train, with the rhythmic hum of the wheels going on and on in her ears, she found she remembered him very clearly indeed. She could hear him pounding after them through the misty half-light, and she could feel the heaviness of his tread. Exactly like a giant running after a poor little human. Was that why she had thought of Thomasina as a giant on the night she had hidden in Charity Cottage when Thomasina had come striding across the park to catch her?

London, when she reached it in the early afternoon, was bewildering. Maud had been there twice, but once had been a school trip when they had all been taken to the Tower of London, and the other had been with the cousins she had stayed with after her mother died. One of the older cousins had been getting married and they had all gone to Debenham & Freebody to buy bridesmaids' clothes. Still, it meant she knew about the ladies' room at the station, where she had a wash and brush-up, and about the buffet, where she had hot coffee and fresh rolls. She knew, as well, about hailing a cab when she got out of the station.

'Seven Dials, miss? You sure?'

'Quite sure.' Maud wondered whether to proffer the story of her sick mother again, or switch to the one about the housemaid ravished by the son of the house, but she remembered in time that people in London are too busy to be much interested, so she said nothing, and the cabman, clicking his horse, said, 'Least it's the daytime. You wouldn't want to go there at night, miss.'

When finally they reached Seven Dials, Maud thought she

would rather not have come here in the day either. She paid the cabman, who doffed his cap, and by way of friendly departure pointed out Paradise Yard.

'Would you wait for me, please?'

'Here? No bloomin' fear, miss.'

'Then,' said Maud, 'would you return for me? In – in half an hour's time?' She fished out a half-sovereign. Was it enough? Too much? She had no idea of the value of money in this situation, but it was several times' the amount of the fare from the railway station. 'I'll pay you this if you return and take me – and a friend – back to the railway station.'

It seemed the half-sovereign was more than enough. 'Half an hour,' said the cabbie, doffing his cap. 'I'll be here.'

The cab clattered away over the cobblestones. Maud did not entirely trust him to return and she did not know if half an hour would be long enough for what she had to do, but she had done her best.

The noise, smells and sights of Seven Dials were like a series of violent blows. All round her was a jumble of streets and a seething mass of people. Some were scurrying along with anxious faces, some were propped against doorposts, staring at the world with despairing eyes, some were calling their wares from horrid mean little shops. Children ran along the streets, ragged and thin, with sharp, wise, little faces. The smaller ones played tip-cat and battledore and shuttlecock, but the older ones had an air of purpose.

Once the houses in some of these streets had been quite prosperous, lived in by merchants and city men, rather like George Lincoln. But by whatever curious alchemy governs such things, the houses and the streets had ceased to be prosperous and well cared for. They had slid grubbily down into extreme poverty, and the once imposing houses had been divided and sub-divided. Basements that had been intended for sculleries and servants' quarters had turned into old clothes' shops and shoe-menders and wig-makers. Despite the poverty, alehouses and gin shops of all kinds were everywhere. Maud thought it must be the most appalling place in the world.

Paradise Yard was an enclosed area just off one of the streets, and Number 17 was in one corner. Maud hesitated, looking up at it. It was as mean and as neglected as all the others, although tattered curtains hung at one or two windows as if someone had tried to make it slightly comfortable.

Stepping around the piles of squalid rubbish that strewed the cobblestones, Maud went towards the door of Number 17. She was nervous, but not actually frightened, and although she had no idea if this part of her plan was going to work, she knew what she was going to say.

She had thought she would knock on the door, which was what people in her world did, but this door was already open. Beyond it was a dank hallway, with doors opening off it. Were the rooms behind them all occupied by different people? If so, how would she find Catherine Kendal? Would she recognize her?

But Maud thought she would recognize her; firmly in her mind was that odd little conversation with Thomasina.

'A girl who lives in a poor part of London,' Thomasina had said. 'She's exactly your age, Maud.' She had added, 'There's a sick sister – I think she'd do anything in the world for that sister.'

A girl who was exactly Maud's age. A girl who had accepted Thomasina's charity. And there was a sister who was sick, and for whom Catherine Kendal was prepared to do all kinds of things . . .

She had no idea which door to try first, but as she was trying to decide, there were sounds from overhead, a door slammed and quick light footsteps came along the landing and down the wide, once-beautiful staircase. The girl stopped halfway down and stared at Maud from suspicious, wide-apart eyes.

'Catherine Kendal?' Maud knew it was. ('She resembles you a bit,' Thomasina had said, that day. 'If it wasn't for the chance of birth, you might be in her shoes and she might be in yours.')

And although this girl was not exactly a mirror image of Maud, she was very similar. She resembles you . . . She might be in your shoes . . . And if only the sister looked the same . . .

Maud scarcely waited for the girl's nod of wary assent to her question. She said, in a firm voice, that she came from Miss Forrester, and that Miss Forrester wanted to offer medical help for Miss Kendal's sister. No, she herself did not know the exact details, said Maud. Her tone suggested she was an employee of Thomasina's: perhaps a companion or amanuensis, and that the medical details were not her concern. The thing was, the girl would have to come up to Amberwood. Well, yes, right away. She believed it was a matter of a specialist being in the area for a few days, and it was thought he might be able to help. Naturally Miss Forrester would pay for all the travelling and so on.

The girl listened to all this, not speaking. She put her head on one side, as if considering Maud in a way Maud did not much like. When Maud finished speaking, she said, 'How do I know it ain't a con?' It was the accent of this dreadful world: this place of street urchins and poverty and evil smells.

Maud said, 'A con . . . ? Oh, I see. It's perfectly genuine, I assure you. Your sister will be at Quire House with Miss Forrester.'

'Not me as well?'

Maud had been ready for this. She said, 'Miss Forrester only seemed prepared to pay for one. Of course, if you wanted to buy your own train ticket, you could come. Or you could follow in a few days' time.'

'Have to think about that,' said Catherine Kendal. 'Leaving London an' all. I got my ladies to consider.'

'Are you a sempstress?' said Maud, and Catherine Kendal laughed.

'You been working for Thomasina and you think that! Bit of an innocent, aincha? No, it ain't sewing I do for my ladies. Nor for the gentlemen who come here, neither.' She went on studying Maud, and Maud began to feel uncomfortable. She did not dare risk looking at her watch to see if the half hour was up yet, but she thought it could not be far off, and she had not yet seen the sister. Supposing the sister did not exist – that it had simply been a – what had she called it? A con. Supposing it had been a con to get money out of Thomasina.

Then Catherine said slowly, 'She'd be at Quire House,' as if the name was a charm that might open doors.

'Yes.'

'A proper doctor who might help her?'

'Yes, certainly.'

'Wait here,' said Catherine. 'I'll see what she thinks.'

She was only gone a few minutes, but to Maud, who was in an agony of suspense, it felt like several hours. At last Catherine reappeared.

'She'll come.'

'I'm so glad,' said Maud, managing to sound as if it was a matter of complete disinterest to her. 'Can she be ready at once? I've arranged for a cab to collect us in about ten minutes.'

'Hardly time to pack winter furs, is there?' There was a sudden grin, oddly reminiscent of a cat's purring smile, and then Cat Kendal whisked back up the stairs and into the room overhead. In less than the ten minutes she was back, carrying a pitifully small bundle of things, a thin girl with translucent skin and tow-coloured hair at her side.

'Nell,' she said, by way of introduction. 'Ellen if you want to be posh about it.'

Maud stared at the girl. It's all right, she thought. The resemblance is strong enough. It's going to work. But there's one more thing, and I have to be sure.

Catherine said, 'She don't speak,' and Maud, who had not until now trusted Thomasina's other words that day, knew it was going to be all right. She knew that the last and most crucial piece of her plan had dropped silkily into place. ('A sick sister,' Thomasina had said, that day. 'A mute. Fair-haired – pretty little thing. Great tragedy, though – she's quite unable to speak.')

'She understands everything you say,' Catherine was saying. 'But she don't never speak. She can't.'

In a brisk voice, Maud said, 'Oh, I see. Well now, Ellen – Nell – we're going to take the train to Chester, and from there we'll hire a conveyance of some kind to take us to Amberwood – that's quite a short journey.'

It all came out as casually and as confidently as if she was accustomed to travelling up and down the countryside every day, ordering cabs and making complicated journeys. It had to be complicated, of course, this journey: the nearer they got to Amberwood, the more unobtrusive they would have to be.

So Maud made sure they got an afternoon train, which would mean they would not reach Chester until after dark, and not reach Amberwood until late in the evening. She bought lunch in the station buffet, relieved to see that although Nell Kendal ate hungrily, her table manners were acceptable. She wondered briefly about the two girls' parentage, but since it was clearly impossible to question the girl, she concentrated on getting her back to Toft House.

As the train jolted its way out of London, she tried not to stare too greedily at this girl who might have changed places with her, and who could not speak . . .

CHAPTER THIRTY-SEVEN

Godfrey Toy had been preparing for a quiet evening, which he thought was owed to him after the horrors of the last twenty-four hours. He was still very upset indeed. He told Oliver this, and Oliver said they were all very upset, and had recommended Godfrey to go to bed early with a hot drink, a good book and a couple of aspirin. He could put the phone by his bed if he was nervous, or even take the dinner bell to ring out of the window to summon help.

Godfrey thought this was unnecessarily flippant of Oliver, but he did think he would follow the first part of the suggestion. He would make himself a nice hot toddy to drink in bed. He might take one of the *Barchester* novels to read, so he could make the old joke about going to bed with a Trollope, but actually he would probably end up with Dorothy L. Sayers. He had always admired Harriet Vane's angry independence, and he loved Sayers' depictions of 1930s Oxford colleges.

He was just washing-up his supper things when there was a peremptory hammering at Quire's main door. His heart skittered into a panic-stricken pattern, because although it was only seven p.m., what with murdered bodies in the music room and hangman's ropes and convicted killers in Charity Cottage, you could no longer be sure who might turn up on the doorstep.

He waited until he heard Oliver's second-floor door open, since, if there was some murderous maniac outside Godfrey was not going to confront him by himself, and then pattered down the stairs in the professor's wake. Faint but pursuing, that was the keynote, although if he really had had a dinner bell he would have taken it with him, and if the caller had looked at all suspicious he would have swung it with vigour.

The caller did not look particularly suspicious; he looked impatient. He was a dark-haired man in his late thirties and he introduced himself as Jonathan Saxon and wanted to know if they could throw any light on the fact that Antonia Weston, whom he had come to see by prior arrangement, was missing. And that Charity Cottage was in darkness, its doors locked, and Dr Weston's car was nowhere to be seen.

Godfrey was thrown into such a dither by this that he was grateful to Oliver for saying, quite coolly, 'How do you do. Is it Doctor Saxon, by the way?'

'It is.'

'I thought it must be. You were Miss Weston's boss at her hospital?'

'I was. Where is she?'

'I'm afraid I haven't the remotest idea. I'm Oliver Remus, by the way. This is my colleague, Dr Toy. Has Miss Weston been in touch with you in the last twenty-four hours, Dr Saxon? I mean, to tell you what happened here last night?'

'I haven't spoken to Antonia since the day before yesterday, but I know she's been the victim of some appallingly cruel tricks since she got here. I haven't come to fight any battles for her, because she's perfectly capable of fighting her own battles – I'm here because it sounded as if she needed a friend.'

Clearly he did not think Antonia was likely to have many friends in Amberwood, and equally clearly he did not know what had happened last night. Godfrey could not even begin to think how they would explain, and he was extremely relieved when Oliver said, 'I think, Dr Saxon, that you'd better come in.'

They sat in Oliver's big comfortable sitting room, and Oliver explained, briefly and succinctly, about Greg Foster's death.

'I'm extremely sorry about that,' said Jonathan Saxon. 'But it doesn't explain Antonia's disappearance.'

'No, it doesn't. That's why I'm about to phone Inspector Curran,' said Oliver, already dialling the number.

Inspector Curran arrived within ten minutes, and listened carefully to the story of Antonia's call to Dr Saxon.

'I suggested I drove up here for a day or so,' said Jonathan. 'And Antonia booked me in somewhere – the Rose and Crown I think she said. That's in case any of you were thinking a different arrangement might apply.'

'Oh no,' said Oliver politely, and Godfrey glanced at him uneasily.

'I don't care who sleeps in whose bed,' said the inspector, 'but I do care about finding Miss Weston. We've tried her phone, but it's switched off – although that might not mean anything. Her car's gone and, as Dr Saxon says, the cottage is in darkness.' He frowned. 'Normally we wouldn't concern ourselves with a lady who ducked out of a dinner date, but given the circumstances we'd better search the cottage. Have any of you got a key.'

'No,' said Godfrey.

'Your sergeant asked that when Miss Weston reported that business of the rope,' said Oliver. 'We didn't have one then, and we haven't got one now.'

'Dr Saxon?'

'No, I haven't got a key. Dr Weston isn't, so far as I know, in the habit of giving people her door key. But if you're going into the cottage, I'll come with you.'

'So will I,' said Oliver at once.

'I'd like to have someone from the Quire Trust anyway,' said Curran equably. 'We'll do it now, shall we? Best not to waste any time.'

'Then you do think something's happened to her?'

'I'm reserving judgement, Professor Remus. But we've had a

violent death here and we don't know who's responsible for it. We're putting out calls to the nearby railway stations – Chester's the main one, of course – but if Miss Weston's gone anywhere of her own free will, she's gone in her own car. And on that basis, we've also notified motorway service stations.'

'You've got the car's registration, have you?' This was Oliver.

'Oh yes,' said the inspector. 'We've had that all along. It'll be quicker if we drive to the cottage, I think, and my car's just outside. Dr Toy, will you stay here?'

Godfrey, appalled at the thought of remaining in the house on his own, said, 'Well, I thought—'

'It's mostly in case Miss Weston turns up here. Or telephones.'

'Yes, of course I'll stay,' said Godfrey, and sat down to plan how they would welcome Antonia back when she was found. Because of course she would be found, perfectly safe and well. Anything else was too dreadful to contemplate.

Inspector Curran broke the kitchen window of the cottage, and Jonathan climbed through and unlatched the rear door. But the cottage yielded no clues at all. There were no signs of a struggle, and no notes left.

'Would either of you know if any of her clothes have gone?' said Inspector Curran, surveying the wardrobe in the bedroom.

'I wouldn't. I remember she was wearing that jacket when I happened to meet her in the library a few days ago,' said Oliver. 'But other than that, I can't help.'

'Dr Saxon?'

'I can't help either.'

'Her phone doesn't seem to be around, which is a nuisance,' said Curran. 'I'll get Blackburn to make a proper search, though, and we'll get on to the main cell-phone networks and try to find out what calls she made or received in the last twenty-four hours. That might give us something to work on. Oh, and there's a laptop downstairs – did she have an email account?'

'I don't think so,' said Jonathan.

'I'll switch on in a minute and take a look.'

'Isn't that a bit of an invasion?'

'Professor, if Miss Weston has been carted off by this killer, nothing's an invasion. And if she's the killer herself, it's not an invasion, it's necessary evidence.'

There was a brief silence, and then Oliver said, 'You don't really think she's the killer, though?'

'He might do,' said Jonathan. 'He's probably thinking that she's killed once, and – how old did you say that boy was last night?'

'Nineteen or twenty.'

'Don Robards was twenty-two,' said Jonathan. 'On that basis, I should think Antonia's your prime suspect for this, isn't she, inspector?'

'I wouldn't say that, sir. What I would say is that if those incidents she reported really happened, then there's a very twisted, very sick mind in all this.'

'And,' said Jonathan, angrily, 'if Antonia made the incidents up – or even set them up herself – then she's the one with the twisted mind, that's what you're thinking, isn't it?'

'She struck me as perfectly sane,' said Oliver and for the first time Jonathan sent him a quick glance of approval.

'She is perfectly sane,' he said. 'She was a very good, very hard-working doctor of psychiatry, and it's our loss that she was struck off. She admitted to killing Don Robards because he attacked her, but she shouldn't have been given a prison sentence. If Robards hadn't been her patient at the time, it probably wouldn't have been prison at all.'

'The law always was an ass,' said Oliver. 'D'you want any help with the search for the phone, inspector?'

Antonia was aware that she was starting to tread a very fine line between keeping hold of sanity and tipping over into something that would not be sanity at all.

At times she was afraid she had already stepped over the boundaries. She thought she heard the *Caprice* suite being played somewhere nearby and for a moment she believed Twygrist's monstrous clock had wound itself backwards, and she was with Richard again and the nightmare of his death had never happened. She listened, to see if Twygrist picked up the music and spun it echoingly around her head, but it did not, and she thought after all she had imagined it. It faded after a time, but she heard her own voice, and realized with a shock that she was talking to Daniel Glass.

'You helped me through the agoraphobia thing once or twice, Daniel, you seemed almost to be with me when I went out, so how about helping me again now? I don't quite know how you could do it, but there must be something . . .'

It was at this point she discovered she was speaking aloud, and her words were swooping above her head in the darkness.

Drag me through the worst, Daniel . . . The worst, the wor-s-s-t . . . There must be something, s-s-something, there must, there MUST . . .

Antonia clapped her hands over her ears to shut out Twygrist's evil echoing voice, but that made the silence and the darkness so absolute she could not bear it. Even the inexorable ticking of the clock above her was preferable.

She sat down with her back against the wall and tried to think logically. If she could not get out she would die from hunger or thirst. Dying from thirst was a particularly unpleasant death – didn't you go mad at the end? How did I end up here, in this dreadful place, entirely on my own, facing madness and death? But I won't believe I'm on my own: I'll believe Daniel's here. No, stop that, Antonia. Keep a grip. But what if that woman who knocked me out means to come back? That's a nasty possibility. But I ought to be able to match her if it comes to a fight. Except that she's clearly mad, and she'll have the strength that sometimes goes with it . . . No, I'd better not think about that. I'd better focus on the practicalities of the situation. How long have I been down here, I wonder? It feels like quite a long time but for all I know I've lost all sense of time. The air's reasonably fresh – does that mean it's getting in from outside? How? From where? *Think*, Antonia. It's not coming from those doors – I've felt every millimetre of them and they're as tight-fitting as they could be. Then where else?

For a moment there was only the thick darkness and the thudding of the clock, but she forced herself to think back, to that day in Quire House when she had looked at the sketches and diagrams of Twygrist's interior. All the levels had been neatly depicted, all the way down to the underground rooms: the garner floor, the chute for the grain, the kiln room where they used to light fires to dry grain spread out at the top of the chimney vent . . .

The chimney vent. Hope surged upwards, because if this really was the old furnace room – and Antonia thought it must be – then the air could be coming in through the chimney vent. Did that mean part of it had fallen in? And if so, might it be possible to get out by climbing up the chimney itself? Sanity teetered again, because it sounded like something out of a farce. Escaping up the flue. I don't care how farcical it is if it gets me out, thought Antonia. And what a tale it would make – the kind of tale I could have told around a table with Richard and the friends we had all those years ago. For a moment an image of the big comfortable bungalow swam in front of her eyes, and the ache for Richard was as painful as it had ever been. She pushed it away angrily, got up, and began to feel her way along the wall again. After a few feet she stumbled over something lying on the ground, grazing her ankles, and making her head throb all over again with the impact. When she explored with her hands, she discovered she had fallen over a jumble of old bricks, and the thin curl of hope strengthened slightly. Had the bricks fallen out of the chimney wall? If so, it ought to be possible to knock more out; she could use one of her shoes as a hammer.

The surface of the wall suddenly changed under her hands: from being stone it became brick. The start of the chimney wall? Yes, surely it was; it jutted into the room exactly as most chimney walls did, and here, about three feet up from the ground, was an unmistakable oblong of metal – steel or iron? Antonia felt all round it; as far as she could make out it was an oblong door, about four feet wide and about three feet high.

Showers of rust broke away away as she pulled on the handle, but despite her efforts it refused to move. Despair gripped her. She took a firmer hold of it and this time something in the door's mechanism yielded slightly. Antonia threw her entire weight onto the handle and, with a sound like human bones crunching, it turned and the door came partly open.

Light came in: a dull clogged kind of light which might have been daylight or evening, it was impossible to know. But to Antonia it was the most wonderful sight in the world.

She grasped the door's edge and forced it back, and there was a slithering movement from within that made her jump backwards as if she had been burnt.

Clouds of evil-smelling dust billowed outwards, and with them came something that had been huddled against the oven door – something that was pale and brittle and infinitely sad. It tumbled onto the floor, and Antonia backed away, gasping and shuddering. A human skeleton. Stupid to mind about such a long-dead body, such a dried-out remnant of humanity, but she did mind. The skull was turned slightly towards her, so the empty eye-sockets stared beseechingly at her, and the finger bones seemed to be reaching towards her.

She finally managed to stop shaking, and when the clouds of dust began to settle, in the uncertain light, she could see it was the skeleton of a man. Her anatomy was rusty, but the human frame, once taught and understood, stayed with you. Yes, it had been a man, of quite large build, as well. Even in this light she could see that the femur bones were long, and the jawbone was unusually pronounced. Fragments of clothing adhered to the bones – the remains of leather shoes or boots were around the metatarsi, and there were wisps of hair on the skull.

Whoever you were, I hope to God you were dead when somebody crammed you in there, thought Antonia. Or were you trying to escape? Whatever you were doing, I don't like that split-second image I had of you pressed up against the oven door, as if you had hammered against it to get out . . .

Summoning all her resolve, she sat on the edge of the open oven, and swung both her legs into it. Easy enough. Like levering yourself onto a low window ledge. The light was definitely coming from above. Antonia crawled deeper in, hating the grittiness under her hands, like little piles of instant coffee granules. But they were only the dried-out cinders of decades.

She stood up, very cautiously. The chimney shaft was deeper than it had looked, although it seemed to narrow quite a lot as it went up. But cool air was brushing her face, and if she could get up to where the light was, she could yell for help. It looked as if it was daytime – although which day it might be, Antonia had no idea. But with reasonable luck there would be people within earshot.

Now for the real test. Was there any way of climbing up towards that light. Rungs embedded in the wall? Surely the chimney must have needed cleaning from time to time, in the way of all chimneys? What about those poor little Victorian chimney-sweep boys? She began to examine the surrounding wall, inch by painstaking inch, scraping at the encrusted soot and dirt, trying to dodge the worst of the clouds of soot she dislodged.

After what felt like a very long time, but was most likely only about half an hour, she forced herself to accept the fact that there was no means of getting up the chimney shaft.

Donna had not been able to resist that last jibe at Antonia Weston with the music. She crept onto the old ceramic floor over the kiln-room ovens, and played the *Caprice* suite on the battery-operated CD-player. The floor was covered with a thick layer of concrete but there was a reasonable chance that Weston would hear. If so, she would do so through a nightmare of uncertainty and fear.

It had been quite difficult to drag the inert body down into Twygrist's bowels, but Donna found a discarded trolley, rather like a wheelbarrow, and managed to tip Antonia into it. She was wearing gloves and a tracksuit and the same balaclava she had worn in Antonia's car, with the hood of her anorak tightly pulled over it. When Weston's body was eventually found – as, of course, it would be – these tunnels would be combed for DNA evidence. And among the fragments from tramps and winos, somebody might just match up a single stray hair, or a thread of skin, and see that it was from the daughter of Jim and Maria Robards, both killed here, and the sister of Don Robards, murdered by Antonia.

So she was very careful indeed, and only when she had got Antonia into the kiln room, and shone her torch around to make sure there was no way of escape, did she begin to relax.

It was almost over. She had achieved what she had set herself to do all those years ago, and perhaps now there would be some peace.

She went back to Antonia's car, which she had parked well off the road, and drove it away from Twygrist. Her own car was just a mile further along. She was simply going to leave Antonia's car parked on the roadside, and drive her own car away. Antonia's car would be found, of course, but there would be nothing to link it to Twygrist.

After today there would be nothing to link Donna with Twygrist, either. She had got away with it.

CHAPTER THIRTY-EIGHT

Maud had been worried about the actual arrival at Toft House because there was a sign on the gateposts proclaiming the name, and Nell Kendal was expecting to be brought to Quire House. But her most pressing concern was that the bodies of George and Mrs Plumtree might have been found. It was barely twenty-four hours since she had gone into their bedrooms and smothered them, and discovery was not very likely, but Maud was keeping the possibility in mind.

It was a relief, therefore, when the pony trap she hired at Chester railway station jolted its way up the lane, and she saw that Toft House was completely in darkness. And the gatepost sign was easy: she simply drew attention away from it by pointing to the house, and saying that Miss Forrester was at the infirmary, making the arrangements for Nell's treatment. She had hoped Miss Forrester would be back by now, said Maud, but clearly she was not.

Once inside, it was clear Nell did not like the house. Her eyes were huge and scared, and she kept glancing over her shoulder every few minutes.

Maud said, briskly, that Nell could wash and tidy herself in the bathroom, and there was a bedroom at the back of the house where she would sleep. The bathroom was at the far end of the upstairs passage, beyond George's bedroom, and as they went past it, Nell Kendal seemed to shiver. This was ridiculous: she could not possibly know what lay beyond that door, but Maud had a sudden disturbing vision of George (whom she no longer thought of as 'father'), twisted and contorted on the bed, his eyes staring sightlessly upwards. Didn't people's bodies stiffen like wooden boards when they were dead?

She pushed this from her mind, and sat down to wait in the deep window at the half-turn of the stairs. Once it had been the place where flower-like girls sat out dances in the days when Toft House had hummed with life, but Maud could only remember it being used for the cleaning women to put their polishing rags and beeswax when they cleaned the stairs. Tonight it would be where she would put one of the oil lamps, because it looked out over the high road, and a light up here would be seen for miles, and Maud wanted people to see lights here tonight. Some time during the next few hours, her escape from Latchkill would be discovered, and as soon as that happened, they would come out to Toft House to talk to George Lincoln. That they had not done so yet was apparent from its dark silence. Even so, she had better work swiftly.

She took Nell back downstairs, saying it would soon be time to set off. A carriage would come, she said. It felt quite strange to be talking into the silence like this, and receiving no response. But Catherine – Cat – had said her sister could hear and understand, even though she could not speak. Even so, it was disconcerting to be with someone who knew what you were saying but never replied.

She brought Nell a glass of milk and a plate of biscuits. The pills, squirrelled away in her handkerchief while she was in Latchkill, went into the glass – Maud was pleased to see that they dissolved almost at once. Within ten minutes of drinking the milk, Nell was dazed and sleepy, and submitted to being led back to the drawing room, and to the window seat. She could wait there, said Maud. She would be able to see the carriage when it came.

By this time Nell was too dazed to argue; her eyelids were already closing, and within minutes she was asleep. There was no time to be lost. Her sewing basket was in the desk where it always was, and Maud took the pinking shears from it. Working quickly, she sheared off the long light-coloured hair so that it resembled her own ragged crop. She was careful to sweep up the hair and put it all in the kitchen range. What else? Ought she to dress the girl in one of her own gowns? Yes, of course she ought. She did so, disliking the flaccid feel of the thin body, but doggedly pulling Nell Kendal's own worn garments off, and putting them in the kitchen range along with the sheared hair. There should be time later to light the range and burn everything.

Everything was working exactly to plan. The only thing she had not been able to plan for was whether the people who came for her would be people who knew her. Apart from Matron, she had only ever seen two nurses while she was in Latchkill – Higgins and the hatchet-faced one whose name she had never heard. Matron was unlikely to come and Higgins would probably be nursing her sore head after Maud had knocked her out. But hatchet-face might come, and Byrony Sullivan might come. Even Dr Glass. If that happened, the plan would fail.

But it was a very small risk, and every risk she had taken so far had worked. This would work now. When people came to Toft House – as they certainly would – they would be expecting to find Maud Lincoln, and they would find a creature they would assume was Maud – a creature who was bewildered to the point of being beyond speech.

They would find other things in Toft House, as well. Two dead bodies. They would assume Maud had killed them and they would know she was helplessly mad. By the time the truth was discovered, the real Maud would have slipped out of Amberwood and be miles away. Safe and free.

* * *

Bryony had not expected to be summoned to the Prout's office halfway through her ordinary spell of night duty on Latchkill's main ward, but Dora Scullion had breathlessly delivered the message shortly after ten o'clock. Please to report to Matron's office at once, Scullion had said.

It was unusual to be summoned to Prout's sanctum at any time of the day, and it was usually to receive a reprimand for some trifling misdemeanour. But ten o'clock at night was not generally one of Prout's times for dealing with miscreants, nor was it customary for Dr Glass to be present on those occasions. But he was there, standing by the window. He gave Bryony a quick smile and then looked impatiently at Prout.

'Well, Matron? What's this all about?'

'There has been,' said Freda firmly, 'an unfortunate incident.'

'Incident?' said Dr Glass sharply.

'A patient has – somehow managed to get out,' said Freda, and Bryony saw Daniel's black brows snap down in a frown.

'Someone from Reaper Wing?' he said.

'No, it is not someone from Reaper Wing,' said Freda. She spoke sharply, but her eyes shifted. 'It's a patient from one of the private rooms. We have her listed as Miss Smith.'

Chancery lunatic, thought Bryony, remembering what her father had once said. Or at the very least, something a bit underhand.

Daniel Glass appeared to be thinking on the same lines, because he said, 'Ah. An anonymous lady. From the sound of things, another of the poor creatures who get shuffled into an asylum under cover of darkness, surrounded by so much secrecy you'd think it was a crowned head. Not that the royal families of Europe are strangers to the odd whiff of madness. Well, Matron? Who and what is Miss Smith?'

Prout hesitated for longer this time, but just as Bryony thought she had decided not to reply, she said, 'It's Maud Lincoln.'

Bryony and Daniel both stared at her. Bryony said, 'But – what was Maud Lincoln doing in Latchkill?'

'And,' said Daniel, 'more to the point, when did she escape, and where is she likely to be now?'

'What she was doing here is not a matter for your concern, Nurse Sullivan. But I can say that Miss Lincoln had become a little disturbed of late, and so her father thought . . . a private room, of course, and I promised that the child's identity would remain secret.'

Daniel did not say anything, but Bryony saw that he was thinking the promise would have involved money changing hands. The Prout was as venal as a Shakespearean money-lender. Bryony thought the private room was more likely to have been one of the bleak cell-like places on the second floor.

Maud Lincoln, said Freda, resolutely, had apparently lain in wait for Nurse Higgins the previous evening, and had thrown a plateful of stew into Higgins' face the instant the woman went into the room. After that, she had hit her smartly over the head, and bound and gagged her so that Higgins could not raise the alarm when she came round. After which, Maud had made off into the night, wearing Nurse Mordant's cloak which had been hanging in a broom cupboard.

'When did this happen?' said Daniel.

'Last night. Supper time.'

'But that's an entire day! Did no one go into the girl's room today?'

'My nurses have a great deal to do,' said Freda. 'They looked into the room of course, but thought Miss Lincoln to be asleep.' This was said with studied casualness, and Bryony guessed that whoever had been on duty had simply glanced into the room, decided the patient was sulking, and taken the food away again.

Dr Glass had clearly come to the same conclusion, but he said impatiently, 'Has the child gone back to Toft House?'

'I don't know. But it is a strong possibility,' said Freda. 'I must, of course, go along there now to search the house and talk to George Lincoln.' She hesitated, and then said, 'I should like you both to come with me.'

'Why?' said Daniel. 'I mean why us?'

'Maud was violent last night and she may be violent when we bring her back to Latchkill. For that reason I need to have someone with me. But I am trying to preserve the secrecy George Lincoln requested. Anyone coming with me to Toft House will instantly guess who Miss Smith is. But you both know Maud already.'

She paused again and Daniel said, 'And that being so, you think you might as well trust us with the whole thing.'

'Exactly.'

Toft House, when they got to it, was lit only by a single lamp in one of the downstairs windows. The curtains of the window were not drawn, and Bryony found this oddly sinister, although she could not think why. For all she knew, George Lincoln left his windows uncurtained every night of the year.

Daniel said, 'That's a bit odd, isn't it?' and Bryony was relieved that she had not been alone in finding the uncurtained window disturbing.

It was Prout who said, 'I see nothing odd, Dr Glass,' and Daniel said, 'Yes, look.'

'What? Where?'

'There's someone sitting in the window.'

'I don't see that that's particularly odd—'

'I do. Whoever it is, is either asleep or . . .' He did not bother to finish the sentence. He ran the rest of the way along the path, and hammered on the door.

Bryony went with him, beyond reason or logic, but knowing instinctively that there was something dreadfully wrong.

They had to get into the house through a door at the back; Bryony thought that if she had been on her own she might have simply given up, but Daniel Glass had taken one look at the figure slumped in the lamplit window, and had gone doggedly around the outside until he had found what seemed to be a scullery door with a lock flimsy enough to snap under pressure.

There was only the thin soft light coming from the room at the front. Bryony, who had never been in Toft House before, looked uneasily about her. It was a big old place; there was a large hall at its centre, and narrow stairs winding upwards to the bedrooms. Everywhere was silent, which surely was strange, because they had made a good deal of noise getting in, and they were making even more noise now. Daniel bounded across the hall to the front of the house, and his footsteps rang out loudly on the polished oak floor. Bryony glanced rather nervously at the darkened stair, and then went after him.

He was bending over the figure seated in the window when she caught him up, and he was feeling for a heartbeat when Freda arrived, out of breath and flushed from the exertion.

'Oh, thank goodness she's here. Dr Glass—'

'She isn't here,' said Daniel shortly, not bothering to look round. 'This isn't Maud Lincoln. Bryony, would you help me, please? Whoever this girl is, she's been heavily drugged.'

'There'll probably be mustard and salt in the kitchen,' said Bryony. 'I can make an emetic.'

'No need, I've got apomorphine in my bag,' said Daniel. 'I dislike using it, but she's clearly taken some kind of opiate – her pupils are massively dilated – and apomorphine will be quicker than mustard. I'll inject it, but I'll need to do it in the scullery or the bathroom, because she'll start vomiting almost at once.'

'The kitchen will be easier,' said Bryony. 'Nearer.'

'So it will. Good girl. Can you give me a hand?'

'Nurse Sullivan is better placed for that,' said Freda at once. 'I cannot undertake to lift any patient—'

'Then perhaps you'd help by lighting the kitchen range,' said Daniel, 'and setting a kettle to boil and a hot brick or a stone water bottle to heat up.'

He did not bother to see if these orders were carried out, and in fact Bryony never discovered if they were. She and Daniel carried the unknown girl into the kitchen, and propped her against the big square sink. The injection had been given, and they had been working on her for an unpleasant quarter of an hour, when Daniel suddenly said, 'This house is far too quiet. Where on earth is George Lincoln?'

'I'll go upstairs and take a look round,' offered Bryony.

'Would you? This one's on the way back to us, I think. Matron, is that kettle boiling yet? We'll see if we can get some hot tea into her now.'

Bryony took the lamp from the big drawing room, and went cautiously up the stairs.

It was ridiculous to feel so uncomfortable about this; there would be some perfectly ordinary explanation for George Lincoln's apparent absence and for the drugged girl downstairs. But the stillness of Toft House was starting to rasp against her nerves. As she reached the head of the stairs, and looked along the passageway with its narrow strip of carpet along the centre, she was aware of her heart starting to race, and she was very thankful indeed to know that Daniel was within calling distance.

This must be the main bedroom, just off to the right. It would look out over the front – there must be quite a nice view of the lanes and fields. Would this be George Lincoln's room? Bryony thought it would, and when she cautiously turned the handle and pushed the door open, a faint scent of bay rum met her.

The bed was behind the door – a massive rather old-fashioned bed, with a mahogany bedhead and posts. A washstand stood against one wall, and there was a big deep wardrobe in the corner. Bryony glanced at it, and then shone the lamp onto the bed.

George Lincoln, his face contorted and frozen in the last agony of death, glared sightlessly at her.

Bryony cried out, and began to back away from the bed, still clutching the lamp, her free hand thrust out in front of her as if to ward off the sight of the terrible thing lying on the bed. Stupid, he's dead – he's been dead for hours by the look of him . . . he can't possibly hurt you, poor old George.

She was halfway along the landing, heading for the stairs, to summon Daniel Glass and Prout, when above her head – which presumably was Toft House's attic floor – came a series of soft creakings exactly as if someone was walking stealthily across a floor.

CHAPTER THIRTY-NINE

At the last minute Maud had decided to stay hidden in the house to watch the final unfolding of her plan. It was so beautiful a plan, so neat and smooth, she could not bear to just go away and not know its culmination.

And something else kept her here – something she hardly dared admit to, but which had been gradually nagging. Where was she to go? She tried to ignore this nagging thought, but it got a claw-hold on her mind, squeezing almost everything else out. Where will you go, Maud? It's all very well to have made that frantic journey to Seven Dials, and you did that very well indeed. But you had a purpose, an aim, and once this is over, you won't have any purpose at all.

Maud could not think what she could do or where she would go. She had almost all of the £200 from the desk, and that would last quite a long time, but what would she do when it was all used up? Would she have to find work? She had no knowledge of how you went about finding work. All she could do was paint and play the piano. She might get a position as a governess, but she thought you needed references for that, and she did not have any.

But first things first. She would make absolutely sure what

happened here tonight. She would lie in wait and watch. She decided to hide in the attics, at the head of a narrow little flight of stairs through a small door. If she left that door ajar, she would be able to hear most of what went on. She would not be able to see any of it, which was a pity, but you could not have everything.

The attics were silent and dark, and there was a thick layer of dust everywhere. Maud's eyes adjusted to the dimness fairly quickly, and she made out the shapes of discarded household items. Pieces of furniture that no one had a use for any longer or that needed mending; bundles of old newspapers; two or three deep old tea chests which would contain clothes or curtains. She thought her mamma's clothes were up here. It was quite comforting to know that, as if a little part of mamma was still in the house, looking after her.

At one end of the attics was a massive water tank, with a pipe opening into the roof to catch the rainwater. The tank took up the entire space between the floor and the sloping ceiling on that corner of the house, and Maud found its squat blackness somehow sinister. But there was no need to sit anywhere near it; she could curl up by the door, with her back to the tank.

She found some old brocade curtains in the smallest of the chests, and made herself comfortable. She had no idea how long she might have to wait, but it did not matter.

Bryony had half fallen down the stairs, and was across the hall and into the safe warm scullery almost without realizing it.

She gabbled out what she had found, and halfway through the story discovered she was clinging to Daniel as if he was a life raft in a tempest. She blushed, and tried to withdraw her hands, but he held on to her.

When Bryony said, 'I may have imagined the sounds, but I didn't imagine George Lincoln's body,' he said, grimly, 'I don't think you imagined the sounds at all.'

'Who . . .' But Bryony already knew the answer to that.

'At a guess,' said Daniel, 'it's Maud Lincoln.' He looked across at Freda, who was staring at them both, her mouth a round O of surprise, and said, 'Matron, do you feel up to walking down to Amberwood and bringing the police sergeant back here? You'll be perfectly safe – our quarry's in this house. But I think we're going to need some help with what's ahead of us.'

Really, thought Bryony, Prout was a cold-hearted, self-serving creature, and she would not have wagered tuppence on her honesty, but you had to hand it to the old girl – when it came to a situation of this kind, she was no coward.

She said, 'I'll go at once, Dr Glass. I'll be as swift as I can.'

'Bryony, you stay here. I'll go upstairs.'

'Armed with only a hypodermic needle?' Bryony was glad this came out firmly and very nearly ironically.

'Chloroform,' he said, reaching into his bag. 'It'll be effective and fast.'

'I'll come with you. She may not be there, though. I may have imagined it.'

'I don't think you did,' said Daniel.

Maud had heard them all come in, and her heart leapt. She edged cautiously to the door and listened. With a shiver of fear and anger, she recognized the three voices. Matron Prout, Bryony Sullivan and Dr Glass. The very three people she prayed would not come! The very ones who would recognize her!

She frowned, thinking hard. Even though her beautiful plan for putting Nell Kendal into Latchkill was going to fail, there was nothing to prevent Maud herself from getting away. Was there?

It sounded as if someone was in George's room now – was it Bryony? Yes, that was surely her voice crying out in shock. Then there was the sound of running footsteps, going back down the stairs. Within a couple of minutes the footsteps returned, and this time Maud definitely heard Bryony's voice and also Dr Glass's. Might they come up here after all? This was getting a little dangerous – she ought not to have stayed in the house after all.

Maud glanced back into the attics. If anyone did come up here it should be possible to hide somewhere. In one of the corners? Behind the water tank? She still did not like the tank much, but if it was a choice between that or being dragged back to Latchkill . . .

She began to move warily across the floor, trying not to make the old timbers creak under her feet because if Bryony or Dr Glass heard that they would know she was here. She moved round the piles of household jumble, testing each floorboard before putting any weight on it. Back and back . . . almost there. They're about to find Plumtree's body.

Maud's heart was hammering against her ribs – or was it her heart? She frowned, listening. Wasn't it Thomasina and Simon again? Tap-tap . . . Tap-tap . . .

Anger mixed with despair flooded over her. She thought those two had gone. Surely they must be dead by this time? But they were not dead; they were still hammering to get out of Twygrist . . . Tap-tap . . . Maud put her hands over her ears to shut the sounds out. In Latchkill that had blotted them out very well indeed, but it did not do so tonight. Was that because Toft House was nearer to Twygrist than Latchkill? Was it because Thomasina and Simon were getting nearer to the surface? She closed her eyes, but that was worse because they were both there in the darkness behind her eyelids – their hands were worn right down to the wrists now. Thomasina turned her dreadful, hollow-eyed face to Maud, and said it did not matter at all: the bones of their arms were making much better hammers. They would soon be out, and then they would come to find Maud . . .

She was pressed up against the water tank by this time; she could feel the surface against her arm, cold and faintly damp. When she knocked against it with her hand there was the faint slop of water inside. Horrid.

Footsteps were coming up the attic stair now; if she did not hide properly she would be caught. She shrank right down onto the floor, folding her arms tightly over her head. If only

Thomasina and Simon would be quiet for a while she could concentrate on remaining hidden, and on what she would do when she escaped.

But Thomasina and Simon would not be quiet; they banged harder and harder, and the banging became mixed up with the too-fast beating of Maud's heart, and with the faint sinister lapping of the dark cold water inside the tank. Maud suddenly saw she might never be free of those two, it might take years and years for them to batter their way out of the kiln room. Years and years, during which Maud would know they were getting nearer and nearer . . .

She huddled into the tiniest space she could, and was trying so hard to shut out the sounds she did not hear Daniel and Bryony open the door and cross the dusty attic floor to where she crouched.

She hardly felt the sting of the needle, but as the chloroform spun her down into oblivion, she was blessedly aware that the hammering from Twygrist's bowels had finally ceased.

'She's gone far away from us,' said Daniel Glass, seated in Charity Cottage with Bryony and her father. 'I shall keep trying to reach her, but I think she might be beyond reach. She won't talk about anything that happened – her father's death, the astonishing switch she made with the strange bright-eyed little creature called Nell Kendal.'

'Did she really think that would work?' asked Cormac.

'Oh yes. We've managed to get most of the story out of Nell – she can't speak, but she's an intelligent little thing, and she's written most of it down. We're going to see if we can find somewhere here for her to live, and some kind of work. There's a sister in London, we've talked to her, but' – a grin curved his lips – 'the sister's a different pair of shoes altogether. She's set on coming up here to live with Nell, but I'm not sure if she will. She's one of those tough defiant little creatures and wherever she ends up, she'll survive.'

'So Maud brought Nell Kendal to Amberwood deliberately?'

'It seems like it. It seems she found the two sisters in London – God alone knows how or why – and tricked them into letting Nell come to Amberwood for some sort of medical treatment.'

'And,' said Bryony incredulously, 'Maud thought she could put Nell Kendal into Latchkill in her place, and that people wouldn't know?'

'Yes. It might even have worked, you know; hardly anyone at Latchkill saw Maud. George Lincoln put her there under a false name, only Maud didn't know that. She assumed Matron would quite openly send someone out to Toft House. The substitution would have been picked up eventually, of course, but Nell might have spent months there. And since Nell can't speak . . .'

'Could she have written down the truth?'

'Yes, but you know as well as I do that asylums are full to the rafters with people who insist they're sane.'

'Yes, I see that. Everyone would have been fooled,' said Bryony. 'Except for—'

'Except for Maud's own father. That's why he had to die – and Mrs Plumtree with him.' He glanced at Bryony, and in a much gentler voice, said, 'Maud is quite beyond sanity, you know. I'm assuming George Lincoln realized that, and that's why he put her there. But I don't suppose we'll ever know the exact details.'

Cormac said, 'I don't suppose we will. Will she ever live outside an institution?'

'I don't think so. I'll give her what treatment I can, but she really has gone very far away indeed. At times it's as if she's listening to something, and whatever it is that she's hearing, it terrifies her. We saw that when we found her, didn't we?'

'She was pressed against the wall,' said Bryony, trying not to shudder at the memory. 'With her hands over her ears and her eyes tightly shut. Like a child.'

'Yes. But there might be ways of helping her,' said Daniel. 'I'm hoping to try mesmerism – that's quite a new idea for the mentally sick, but there's a lot of interesting research being done into it. In any case, now that Prout's leaving, Latchkill will be far better for the patients.'

'I'm glad she's leaving,' said Bryony. 'I'm glad you came to explain it all to us, as well.' She glanced at her father, who promptly said, 'Dr Glass, by way of gratitude for that, will you stay to supper? There's a game pie, and more than enough for three.'

'Game pie,' said Daniel expressionlessly.

Cormac grinned, and said, 'Bryony made it. The best ingredients went into it, but if you're a gentleman, you won't ask where the pheasants came from.'

'I don't care where they came from. I'd love to have supper with you.'

As they sat round the table, Bryony had the absurd feeling that something was happening between the three of them – something very good and very strong, and something that might remain in the atmosphere of Charity Cottage for a very long time. It was probably ridiculously fanciful to think that somewhere in the future, someone would sit here and feel this good strong emotion, but she did think it.

There was a wheel of Stilton and a dish of crisp ripe apples to follow the game pie, and then some of Cormac's whiskey to round it off. It was not until the glasses had been filled a second time that Daniel said, 'There's something more that I have to tell you.'

'Ha,' said Cormac. 'I thought there was.'

'When they went through the things inside Toft House,' said Daniel, 'they found a will. George Lincoln made it very recently indeed, and it's simply drawn up, but apparently perfectly legal.' He was looking at Cormac very directly now. 'It seems, Sullivan, that at some time in the past you did George Lincoln a – a service that he never forgot.'

'A man helps another man where he can,' said Cormac offhandedly.

'Well, whatever help you gave him must have been quite

considerable,' said Daniel, 'because he's left the Rosen money in a trust fund for Maud, but he's left Toft House to you.'

There was a long silence. Bryony tried to think of something to say, and failed utterly.

'Well now,' said Cormac at last. 'Isn't that a fine thing for a man to be told,' and Bryony heard that the Irish which to some extent he had lost since living in England, was strongly back in his voice.

'Isn't it just?' said Daniel.

'Yes, it's a very fine thing, in fact – In fact, tell me now, Glass. Would you think a place like Toft House could be sold?'

'Yes, certainly.'

'And – I have no knowledge of property prices in England – but would you think it would fetch a fairly good sum of money?'

'Yes,' said Daniel. 'I would think it would fetch a very good sum indeed.'

'That's very interesting,' said Cormac softly. He looked across at Bryony and although he did not say anything, Bryony knew with incredulous delight they were sharing the same thought.

The tumbledown house in Ireland.

CHAPTER FORTY

Antonia had left the kiln door open, because she could not bear to lose the thin light that came down from above. She had no idea what she would do when the light started to dim, but for the moment at least she could see where she was. She managed not to look at the sad huddle of bones near the oven door, and was convincing herself that even when the light began to fade, there would be moonlight. She was not sure how she would manage to sit in the pitch dark with human remains so close, because she was afraid she would start to hear them creeping towards her . . . Stop it, Antonia!

She was not especially conscious of hunger, but she was by now very conscious of thirst which was what she had dreaded. Her watch said it was three o'clock. At this time of year that meant about two more hours of daylight, or maybe a bit less. Would anyone miss her? What about the police? And Jonathan – what about him? Had he arrived as promised, and was he instigating a search? Surely he would not just drive away when he found the cottage empty? But would a search come out here? Mightn't they assume she had killed Greg Foster, and then run away? In which case, Amberwood was the last place they would search.

She had reached this point in her reasoning when she became aware of a shift in the rhythm of the clock's beating. Had it slowed down? It had not stopped, that was for sure. Antonia could still hear it and she could still feel it, hammering relentlessly along its mechanism, like the beating of a fleshless fist on the inside of a kiln door . . . She glanced at the thing on the ground.

The clock's rhythm had definitely changed. It was quickening – so much so that it almost sounded as if someone was winding it forwards.

Winding it . . . Someone was winding it!

Antonia dived for the kiln and scrambled inside, tearing her hands and legs in the process, but hardly noticing. She straightened up inside the shaft again, and turning her head up to the light, shouted at top of her voice. 'Help! I'm trapped down here!'

Her words echoed sickeningly in the enclosed space, and showers of soot fell onto her. She shouted again. 'Is someone there? Please – can you hear me? I'm shut in down here!'

Another moment for the echoes to die away, and then the light overhead shifted slightly, as if something might be blocking it out. A voice – a voice that Antonia dimly recognized, called, 'I'm here. I'll get you out. Are you all right?'

'Never better. For God's sake come down to the kiln room and get the doors open!'

'I'm on my way,' said Kit, and this time Antonia heard the clang of ladder rungs. There was a long silence during which she had time to imagine half a dozen disasters, and then came the sound of the steel doors being pulled open.

As Kit appeared in the doorway, Antonia said, 'Thank God for memorial clocks,' and to her fury, began to cry.

Godfrey Toy was almost beside himself with delight. Antonia was safe and sound – all thanks to that nice Kit from the library – and although Godfrey had not got all the details yet, it had been all to do with winding the old Twygrist clock. Kit, it seemed, had been amazingly good, dragging Antonia out of the grisly kiln room, and phoning police and ambulances and whatnot. He had phoned Quire House as well – they had all been there when the call came, and Godfrey thought he had never seen anyone move as fast as Oliver and Jonathan Saxon. Out of the house and into the car inside minutes: Oliver had not even paused to put on a coat, and Kit told Godfrey it had been Oliver who got to Twygrist ahead of anyone else. Godfrey was still considering this, not daring to hope that it meant anything, but hoping all the same that it might.

After the phone call, he had scurried round Quire, putting a large pot of coffee to filter in Oliver's kitchen, and then dashing down to his own flat to gather up a few snacks for them all to eat while they talked. Antonia could not have eaten for at least twenty-four hours, and there would be all kinds of things to hear about. It sounded as if quite a lot of people would be converging on Quire. Godfrey himself and Oliver and Antonia, of course. Dr Saxon and Kit Kendal. Inspector Curran, and perhaps Sergeant Blackburn as well. He counted up the numbers in his head, and made a few more sandwiches.

'Dear God,' Oliver said when Godfrey eventually staggered up the stairs with his tray, 'are you feeding the starving tribes of the world?' but Godfrey said breezily it had been a long and worrying twenty-four hours, and Antonia had better be fed after her ordeal. Oliver merely said, 'Smoked salmon sandwiches and chicken vol-au-vents. Oh, and vichysoisse. I see.' Godfrey explained that the soup was for Antonia and the salmon needed eating up anyway.

Antonia devoured the soup and the sandwiches, and thanked Godfrey. Even like this, white-faced, and exhausted-looking, there was still a light in her eyes. She had, it seemed, already made a full statement to Inspector Curran, who was seated at the table with Sergeant Blackburn, but there were still a lot of questions and answers.

'She was hiding in the cottage's attic, of course,' said Antonia. 'I locked all the doors but she was already inside.'

'I should have thought you could have made a better search,' said Jonathan to Inspector Curran. 'Or were you treating Dr Weston as the tethered gazelle for the hungry tiger?'

'Jonathan, I've been called many things in my time, but—'

'Actually, it's usually a goat they tether, I think.'

'Well, at least you substituted gazelle for goat.'

They grinned at one another, and Godfrey saw that they had the ease of long and familiar friendship, and felt exceedingly glum. He risked a quick glance at Oliver, but the professor's expression was unreadable.

'You weren't the tethered anything,' said Inspector Curran. 'We simply didn't expect the killer to still be around.'

The killer. Antonia shivered, and then said, 'Do you know who she is? I thought all the time it was a man, but just before she knocked me out, she spoke to me.'

'If you could remember the exact words, Miss Weston.'

Antonia said, 'She said that what she was doing was for Don – to punish me for killing Don.' She looked round the room. 'I did kill Don,' she said, defiantly. 'The charge was perfectly justified and the verdict was right. But he had just killed my brother and I thought he was going to kill me as well.'

Jonathan started to say something, but it was Oliver who said, 'Self-defence. And if you've just seen someone you love very much brutally killed—'

'I didn't actually see it happen,' began Antonia.

'Don't be so incurably honest. Inspector, you were about to tell us if you know who this woman is. Presumably she killed Greg Foster, as well?'

'We're working on that assumption,' said Curran in answer to Oliver. 'We aren't absolutely sure who she is yet, but we do know Don had a sister.'

'A sister? Are you sure? He said he had no family at all,' said Antonia. 'I thought – we all thought – he was completely on his own.'

'I'm sure,' said Curran. 'There's a sister. Donna.'

'Will you be able to find her?' asked Antonia. 'To – to question her?'

'We've found her already. We haven't questioned her yet, but we will.' Curran looked at Antonia. 'We don't always get things right, Miss Weston, and we didn't with this. Your attacker talked about punishing you for Don Robards' death, but to my mind you were punished very heavily for that. An eight-year sentence, wasn't it?'

'Yes, but I only served five.'

'Whatever you served, I'm very sorry indeed that you had to go through this second ordeal in Amberwood.'

'It allowed Kit to play knight errant,' said Antonia, and Kit, curled into a corner of the window seat, Raffles next to him, both of them eating sandwiches with industrious pleasure, smiled.

'Did the woman think Antonia would suffocate down there?' asked Oliver. 'Did she know the old drying floor was concreted over?'

'No idea yet,' said Curran. 'I'd guess that she did think Miss Weston would suffocate, though. It was only because of Twygrist's tumbledown state that you didn't actually do so, Miss Weston.'

'The chimney shaft,' said Antonia, remembering. 'Part of the brickwork had fallen away. I tripped over some of the bricks while I was down there.'

'Yes. We've still to examine the place more closely, but it's a fair bet that the collapse of the bricks allowed air down into the room.'

'Well, thank God for a collapsed chimney,' said Jonathan.

'How about the body Antonia found in Twygrist?' said Oliver. 'Is it ever likely to be identified?'

'I shouldn't think so. It's a very old skeleton. Eighty to a hundred years old, forensics think. A man in his late thirties or early forties. There's a slight depression to the skull, and that's the only clue to what might have killed him. They think, though, that he was a sufferer from . . .' He frowned and reached for his notebook.

'He suffered from acromegaly,' said Antonia.

'Yes, that was the word. I'd never heard it before.'

'It's quite rare,' said Antonia. 'But it's a chronic condition that causes enlargement of the bones of the hands and feet – quite often the head and face as well. Sufferers used to become grotesquely misshapen, and often unnaturally tall. I don't know a great deal about it, but I think they can deal with it very early on nowadays so you hardly ever see it any more. It comes from an excessive secretion of something within the pituitary gland – I've got that right, haven't I, Jonathan?'

'Near enough. The reverse side of its coin is dwarfism, of course. But in the good old, bad old days, people ascribed all kinds of menace to the poor sods who had it. They thought of them as unnatural – creatures to be feared. Sometimes the condition brought about swelling of the soft tissues as well, including the tongue, which made speech difficult. That would add to the sinister air of it all. If the skeleton was a hundred years old, that means he lived in a time when he could have suffered one of two fates. He could have been exhibited as a freak, or – more probably – been shut away somewhere.'

'Latchkill,' said Oliver softly.

'Yes, that's more than likely. It's not so long since it was known as giantism.'

'Blunderbore or Pantagruel, and seven-league boots, or the blood-sniffing lament of Child Rowland approaching the Dark Tower,' murmured Godfrey, and then turned fiery red, and apologized.

'Well, whatever he was or wasn't, and wherever he came from,' said Curran, 'we'll make sure he has suitable burial in the church-yard.' He stood up. 'Miss Weston, I'll let you know what happens with Miss Robards.'

'I'd have to give evidence, wouldn't I?'

'I'm afraid so. Is that all right?'

'Yes,' said Antonia. 'But whoever it was – Donna Robards or someone else altogether – I think you'll find she isn't fit to stand trial.'

* * *

'Will you come back to the hospital?' said Jonathan to Antonia, as they left Quire House. 'To work, I mean.'

'I don't know. Would it be possible?'

'I think so. The board's talking about expanding my department – making a full-time drug rehabilitation unit. They'll need someone to head that – maybe undertake some research as well. I could probably swing it your way.'

'I don't want anything swung my way. I'd rather get things by my own efforts.'

'You would get this by your own efforts. You'd be a good person for the job. Are you going to try for reinstatement?'

'I don't know.' Antonia did not say she was afraid of doing this, because a refusal would be too much of a blow.

'You could start getting back into things with the new unit,' said Jonathan.

'Prove myself all over again, and then go cap in hand to the GM? "Please let me be a doctor again."'

'Don't be so spiky. I'm trying to help you.'

'I know you are. I'm sorry. Can I think about it?'

'Yes, of course. You aren't going to stay here though, are you?'

'I'll have to stay for a bit longer.'

'Why? The police investigation's wound up. What is there to stay for?'

'Oh,' said Antonia vaguely, 'loose ends to tidy up.'

CHAPTER FORTY-ONE

Dear Daniel

Your letter reached me earlier today – I was in the gardens here, and although I wasn't wearing a shady hat like my grandmother apparently used to, I was cutting sheaves of lilac for the rooms as she once did. It's not to scent the rooms, you understand – it's to drive away the smell of the paint. My grandmother probably had only the sounds of rooks cawing or doves cooing or something equally idyllic: I have the sound of hammering and sawing from within the house, although at least the bailiffs have gone, which my father says is God's mercy. I should think they were very glad to go – they must have had a thin time of it here, what with the rain coming in through the roof in about forty different places, and death-watch beetle feasting off the timbers.

So it isn't quite the Irish idyll you said you visualized, but to me it's still the most beautiful place in the world, and – will you understand this, I wonder? – it's *my* place in the world, just as it's my father's place. I won't wax absurdly lyrical about soul places, but I think he and I both knew that one day we would come back here. My father says he thanks whatever saints are appropriate that there were entails thicker than leaves on the ground in autumn, and that he was still the owner – he smiles when he says this, and tries to pretend he doesn't care one way or the other, but he does care, of course, and he'll be eternally grateful to George Lincoln for that astonishing legacy. He's sent quite a large sum of money to help the endowment of the new wing for Latchkill – he's done that anonymously, so I'm trusting you not to tell anyone.

Thank you for telling me about Maud. She was so confused and unhappy, wasn't she? But the piano is a wonderful idea – perhaps she will find some kind of peace in her music.

I'm glad the memorial clock to Thomasina Forrester is in its place at last, but I'm not surprised that your prediction about it was right, and that it's the most appalling monstrosity imaginable but it's very generous of you to pay for its installing, and to set up the little fund for someone to wind it every week. I think I do understand what you said about liking to know it will be there in the future. You always have felt deeply about things, and there's no accounting for these feelings, is there?

I'm working in a hospital just outside Connemara for two days in each week, and I love that. When you get here next week, I'll take you to see it.

And yes, of course, you can stay here just as long as you want to.

Bryony

Antonia finished reading the faded writing, and felt the past brush against her mind all over again. For several moments she was unable to speak. So, after all, Daniel, you were with me, and after all, you did save me. You had a part in arranging for that dreadful, blessed, old clock to be installed and looked after, and it sounds as if you also created the Clock-Winder position. Did you have a feeling it would be needed one day? It's a pity you can't know how very much it was needed, Daniel, or that in a future you couldn't possibly have envisaged, it meant I escaped from Twygrist and from Donna Robards.

Daniel was becoming shadowy now – Antonia recognized this without sadness, but she rested her hand on the letter for a moment. Trying to keep hold of the past, Antonia? No, I'm letting it go. But I'm glad that I touched that past once or twice. Thank you, Daniel. I hope you went to Ireland and to Bryony who lived there. I think you probably did, somehow.

She withdrew her hand from the letter and smiled at the man seated across the table. 'Oliver, you're brilliant to have found this.'

'I am, aren't I?' He did not exactly smile back, but somehow a smile seemed to be between them.

'Kit Kendal thinks the first Clock-Winder was a several-times great-aunt – he thinks her name was Ellen, but he isn't absolutely sure,' said Oliver. 'I told you the Clock-Winder appointment was virtually hereditary, didn't I? I didn't know the first incumbent was female, though. Nice that, isn't it? Women's equality as far back as the beginning of the nineteenth century.'

'I wouldn't have thought you were a particular supporter of feminism.'

'You'd be surprised,' he said. 'I haven't been able to find out anything about Ellen Kendal yet, but I think the Maud mentioned in Bryony's letter could have been Maud Lincoln.'

'The miller's daughter,' said Antonia. 'Was she?'

'The records do show that George Lincoln had a daughter named Maud.'

Maud. Had she been the withdrawn creature in Latchkill, about whom the day book had recorded that she pressed into the ground as if afraid of the light?

'How about Bryony?'

'I shouldn't think we'd ever trace her,' said Oliver. 'There's no surname or address to start from.'

'No, of course not,' said Antonia, but to herself she thought she might see if there had ever been any record of a Bryony Glass who had lived somewhere near to Connemara.

'If I can find out anything more, I'll let you know,' said Oliver.

'Would you? I'd like to know about them.'

'I'd like to know as well. More wine?'

'Please.'

They were facing one another across the table at the cottage's comfortable heart. Antonia had lit an old oil lamp she had found in the back of a cupboard, and the curtains were drawn against the night. Raffles, who had wandered in with Oliver, had found his favourite place by the radiator.

Antonia was not quite sure how this evening had come about. Oliver had phoned earlier in the afternoon to say he had found Bryony's letter tucked in a box. He had been looking for something else at the time, he said, but as was so often the way . . .

Anyway, would it be all right if he walked down to the cottage later that evening so she could see it? Antonia had said, yes, of course, and managed not to ask if he could bring it down there and then.

He had somehow ended in staying to dinner. Antonia had put together a halfway reasonable meal from odds and ends in the fridge, at which point it had turned out that Oliver had brought some wine, a wedge of beautifully creamy Brie, and a box of luxuriously out-of-season strawberries and raspberries.

'Peace offering,' he said.

'Thank you very much. But it truly wasn't necessary.'

'I thought I'd like to do it anyway.' He set the box on the kitchen table. 'I'm behaving a bit like Godfrey, aren't I?'

'Bringing extravagant food? Yes.' Antonia smiled. 'Is Godfrey all right? He was dreadfully upset by it all, wasn't he?'

'He's recovering. I think he was secretly planning a crusade to prove your innocence,' said Oliver. 'But if so, you spiked his guns by telling us all that you were guilty as charged. Are you always so defensive?'

('Don't be spiky,' Jonathan had said.)

'I thought I'd better clear the air,' said Antonia.

'Saxon offered you a job at your old hospital, didn't he?' he said abruptly.

'Yes. Heading a project to expand the department – they'd like a proper rehab centre for drug users. How did you know?'

'He told me he was going to.' Oliver's tone was devoid of expression. 'He said it in a rather challenging way. Shall you accept the offer?'

'I don't know.'

'Can struck-off doctors be reinstated? I'm sorry if that sounds a bit . . .'

'It doesn't sound a bit anything,' said Antonia. 'It's nice and direct. Doctors can be reinstated, but it really comes down to whether it's thought to be in the public interest to let them loose on patients again. I don't think they'd let me loose,' she said. 'Whatever the rights or wrongs, I really did kill Don. I was beside myself with grief for my brother, and I was frightened to death of Don on my own account. A lot of high-minded stuff was talked at the trial – the sanctity of human life, and the trust that patients have to have in doctors – but it's all perfectly true.' She paused. 'I'd like to go back to psychiatric medicine but I don't think I could bear it if they refused to reverse the original decision.' It was odd she had not been able to say this to Jonathan, but could say it to Oliver.

'What will you do?'

'I like the idea of being involved in drug rehabilitation,' said Antonia. 'There are all kinds of areas I could work in without needing to have my licence restored. And I could still be involved with the victims. It would be a compromise, but I think I could be quite useful.'

'Does the compromise have to be London again?'

They looked at one another. 'No,' said Antonia at last. 'It doesn't have to be. There are several very good hospitals around here.'

'Good.' He refilled the wine glasses. 'You do know you could have this cottage for as long as you want?'

'Could I? Along with the ghosts?' Antonia had no idea why she had said this.

'Everyone has ghosts, Antonia. But after a while they can be lived with.'

'I know that. And there aren't precisely ghosts in this cottage,' said Antonia. 'But—'

'But there are pockets of something a bit odd, aren't there?' he said. 'Especially the part where the kitchen goes through into the old outhouses.'

'Yes.' Antonia looked up at him. 'You know about it?'

'Of course I know. Why wouldn't I?'

'I didn't think anyone else would understand.'

Oliver seemed about to reach for her hand, and then thought better of it. But he said, 'I understand all about ghosts. And there's the same feeling of – of oddness in parts of Quire House. Unhappiness – something stronger than unhappiness, even. But I don't know any more than that.' He looked at her very intently. 'Do the ghosts matter? Or can they be lived with?'

The ghosts. Richard and Don. Oliver's wife who had died at Twygrist. Daniel Glass, and Bryony who had written that letter to him from her raggle-taggle Irish idyll. The body of the man in the kiln room. And poor sad Maud inside Latchkill . . .

Antonia said, very carefully, 'Yes. Yes, I believe the ghosts can be lived with,' and saw with delight he was reaching for her hand, and this time he was not going to think better of it . . .

They said there was always one thing you forgot when you killed someone. Always one mistake you made.

Donna had not thought she had made any mistakes – she had had five years to make sure that mistakes would not happen, but . . . The Clock-Winder. The one thing she had not thought about – had hardly even known about. But if it had not been for that young man – another young man for Weston to get her claws into! – Antonia would have died in Twygrist. She ought to have died: Donna had wanted her to die alone and in the dark.

Instead the bitch was free, the police had discovered Donna's existence, and she was being questioned. They had turned up at her flat, hammering on the door, giving her no chance to escape, or even to think.

Now she was locked up in this appalling interview room, with everything she said being recorded on a machine, and with serious-faced men and women asking her questions. Why and when and how? Then breaking off to give her a rest, not because they wanted to, but because it was the law, and then beginning it all over again.

And then, quite suddenly, Donna saw something she had not seen before. If she told these people the truth – everything – she would clear Don's name. Everyone thought Don had killed Richard Weston that night, and only Donna had known he had not. But she could put that right. She could exonerate her beloved boy. A huge wave of delight surged up inside her. She would do it. She would make this sacrifice for Don's memory.

Most likely it would mean prison, but she would bear it. Once she had vowed to wait as long as it took in order to be revenged on Antonia Weston: she would wait twenty years if she had to, she had said. That still held good. Because even if she did have to wait twenty years, one day she would be free, and on that day . . .

On that day she would begin a whole new plan for Antonia Weston's punishment.

As Godfrey pottered around his flat, he saw, from his windows, the lights shining in the cottage's sitting room. He was pleased that Oliver seemed to have stayed with Antonia for the whole evening. She might have cooked a meal, perhaps, and they would have enjoyed eating it together. Oliver had taken a bottle of wine, and fruit and cheese.

He went into his bedroom to get ready for bed, and he saw the lights of the cottage's sitting room dim to a soft amber glow, as if the two people in there had thought it might be rather nice to sit together in the firelight. Godfrey, who had a strong sense of propriety, drew his curtains very firmly at this point. He would not have dreamed of doing anything so intrusive or impolite as staring at the cottage, to see if a bedroom light went on.

But he could not help hoping very strenuously that a bedroom light did go on and, as he got into his own bed, he was smiling at the thought of Oliver and Antonia together in the firelight.